Where the Line Bleeds
Jesmyn Ward

A Bolden Book

AGATE

CHICAGO

This novel is a work of fiction. Names, characters, incidents, and dialogue, except for incidental references to public figures, products, or services, are imaginary and are not intended to refer to any living persons or to disparage any company's products or services.

Printed in Canada.

Library of Congress Cataloging-in-Publication Data

Ward, Jesmyn.

Where the line bleeds / by Jesmyn Ward.

    p. cm.

Summary: "Twin brothers struggle with the responsibilities of adulthood and family in the post-Katrina Mississippi Gulf coast"--Provided by publisher.

ISBN 978-1-932841-38-1 (alk. paper)

1. Twins--Fiction. 2. Brothers--Fiction. 3. Gulf Coast (Miss.)--Fiction. I. Title.

PS3623.A7323W47 2008

813'.6--dc22

                           2008021651

9 8 7 6 5 4 3 2 1

Bolden Books is an imprint of Agate Publishing. Agate books are available in bulk at discount prices. Single copies are available prepaid direct from the publisher.

Agatepublishing.com

Dedication

For Joshua Adam Dedeaux,
who leads while I follow.

"And Isaac entreated the Lord for his wife, because she was barren: and the Lord was entreated of him, and Rebekah his wife conceived. And the children struggled together within her; and she said, If it be so, why am I thus? And she went to inquire of the Lord. And the Lord said unto her...two manner of people shall be separated from thy bowels...."

— Genesis 25

"Why Jesus equipped with angels and devils equipped with Pac?
For God so loved the world that he blessed the thug with rock.
Won't stop until they feel me.
Protect me devil, I think the Lord is trying to kill me."

— Pastor Troy, "Vice Versa"

Prologue

THE RIVER WAS YOUNG AND SMALL. AT ITS START IT SEEPED FROM THE red clay earth in the piney woods of southern Mississippi, and then wound its way, brown and slow, over a bed of tiny gray and ochre pebbles through the pines, shallow as a hand, deep as three men standing, to the sandy, green lowlands of the gulf of Mexico. It slithered along, wide and narrow, crossed by small wood and concrete bridges, lined by thin slivers of white beach, in and out of the trees, before it divided itself into the bayou and emptied itself into the bay. Near the river's end, at one such bridge, two teenage boys, twins, stood at the apex. Legs over the side, they gripped the warm, sweaty steel at their backs. Underneath them, the water of the Wolf River lay dark and deep, feathered by the current. They were preparing to jump.

The sun had only risen a few hours ago, but it was hot even for late May. Christophe, thinner of the two, let his arms loosen and leaned out, testing the height. His muscles showed ropy and long over his shoulders and down his back. Christophe wondered how cold the water would be. Joshua, taller, and softer on account of the thin layer of fat across his stomach and chest and bigger in the arms, rested his rear lightly on the steel of the railing, shying from its heat. Christophe looked at his brother, and thought the air around him seemed to waver. Joshua kicked, spewing sand and gravel from the edge. He laughed. Christophe felt his hands slip and grabbed at the rail. He looked over at his brother and smiled, the side of his mouth curving into a fishhook. Christophe knew he was sweating more than normal in the heat, and it was making his hands slippery. He and his twin were still drunk from the night before. They were graduating from high school in three hours.

"What the hell y'all doing?"

Dunny, their cousin, stood below them on the sand at the edge of the water with a beer in his hand. He'd parked the car and walked to the bank while they'd taken off their shirts and shoes. His T-shirt hung long and loose on him except where it pulled tight over his beer belly, and his jean shorts sagged low. This was one of the tallest bridges on the coast. When they were younger, all the kids from Bois Sauvage would ride their bikes there and spend all day in a circuit: plummeting from the bridge, swimming to the shore, and then running on their toes over the scalding concrete to fall to the water again. Now, the twins were almost too old to jump. Christophe thought he and Joshua had jumped once the previous summer, but he was not sure. While Dunny had egged Christophe on when he thought of the bridge at 4 a.m. after he and Joshua finished off a case, Dunny had refused to jump. He was twenty-five, he had said, and while the twins could still balance on the iron railing like squirrels on a power line, he couldn't.

"Y'all niggas gonna jump or what?" Dunny asked.

Christophe squinted at Joshua, at the face that was his own, but not, full lips, a jutting round nose, and skin the color of the shallows of the water below that named them twins. If he leaned in closer, he could see that which was different: freckles over Joshua's cheeks and ears where Christophe's skin was clear, Joshua's eyes that turned hazel when the sun hit them while Christophe's eyes remained so dark brown they looked black, and Joshua's hair that was so fine at the neck, it was hard to braid. Christophe moved closer to his brother, and when his arm slid along the length of Joshua's forearm, for a second it was as if Christophe had touched himself, crossed his own forearms, toucher and touched. Christophe was ready to leap. His stomach roiled with a combination of beer and anxiety, but he'd wait. Christophe knew Joshua. Christophe knew that while he liked to do things quickly, Joshua was slower about some things. His brother was looking across the water, eyeing the river winding away into the distance, the houses like small toys along the shoreline that were half hidden by the oak, pine, and underbrush rustling at the water's edge.

"That one up there on the right—that white one. Looks like the one Ma-mee used to work at, huh?"

What Christophe could see of the house through the trees was large and white and glazed with windows. He nodded, feeling his balance.

"Yeah," Christophe said.

"I always wanted to have a house like that one day. Big like that. Nice."

Christophe loved to look at those houses, but hated it, too. They made him feel poor. They made him think of Ma-mee, his grandmother, back when she was healthy and could still see, scrubbing the dirt out of white people's floors for forty years. He knew she was waiting for them now at the house, regardless of her blindness and her diabetes, with their gowns laid out on the sofa, pressed. He swallowed, tasting warm beer. Those stupid houses were ruining the jump.

"Well, the house going to rot into the ground before we can buy it, Jay." Christophe laughed and spit a white glob out over the river. It arced and fell quickly. "Can we jump so we can graduate and make some money?"

Sweat stung Christophe's eyes. Joshua was staring at the water, blinking hard. Christophe saw Joshua swallow; his brother was nervous about the drop. His own throat was clenching with the idea of the fall. It was so early in the summer that Christophe knew the water would be cold.

"Come on then, Chris."

Joshua grabbed Christophe by the arm and pulled. He threw his other arm into the air, and leaned out into space. Christophe let go and leaped into Joshua, hugging him around his chest, and felt him burning and sweaty in his arms, squirming like a caught fish. They seemed to hang in the air for a moment, held in place by the heavy, humid blue sky, the surrounding green, the brown water below. In the distance, a car sounded as it approached on the road. Christophe heard Joshua exhale deeply, and he clenched his fingers around Joshua's arms. Then the moment passed, and they began to fall. They dropped and hit the water and an eruption of tepid water burned up their noses. Their mouths opening by instinct; the water was silty on their tongues and tasted like unsweetened tea. In the middle of the surging murky river, both brothers felt for the bottom with their feet even as they let go of each other and struggled to swim upward. They surfaced. The day exploded in color and light and sound around them. They blew snot and water out their nostrils; Christophe tossed his head and grinned while Joshua screwed a pinky finger into one ear.

On the bank, Dunny was rolling a blunt from his selling sack, laughing. He licked the cigar shut, blew on the paper, and lit it. White smoke drifted from his mouth in tufts. He stood at the edge of the water, the river lapping at the tips of his basketball shoes. Squinting, Christophe could see the tips of the crimson leather turning dark red. Dunny hopped away from the water and held the blunt towards them. Christophe's lungs burned and his stomach fluttered with nausea.

"Y'all want to smoke?"

Joshua immediately shook his head no, and spit water in a sparkling brown stream. Christophe thrust himself toward his brother and grabbed him around his shoulders, trying to shove him below the surface. Joshua squirmed and kicked, flipping them over. Christophe slid below the water, the current gripping him, sure as his brother's fingers. He could hear Joshua laughing above him, muted and deep beyond the bronze wash of the river. Everything was dim and soft. Christophe exhaled crystal bubbles of air, grabbed his brother's soft, squirming sides, and pulled him to the quiet below.

1

I N THE CAR, JOSHUA PLUCKED A WATERLOGGED TWIG, LIMP AS A shoestring, from Christophe's wet hair. Dunny drove slowly on the pebbled gray asphalt back roads to Bois Sauvage, encountering a house, a trailer, another car once every mile in the wilderness of woods, red dirt ditches, and stretches of swampy undergrowth. Joshua watched Dunny blow smoke from his mouth and attempt to pass the blunt he'd rolled on the river beach to Christophe. Christophe shook his head no. Shrugging and sucking on the blunt, Dunny turned the music up so Pastor Troy's voice rasped from the speakers, calling God and the Devil, conjuring angels and demons, and blasting them out. Christophe had taken off his shirt and lumped it into a wet ball in his lap. His bare feet, like Joshua's, were caked with sand.

Joshua stretched across the backseat, shirtless also, and tossed the twig on the carpet. He lay with his cheek on the upholstery of the door, his head halfway out the window. Joshua loved the country; he loved the undulating land they moved through, the trees that overhung the back roads to create green tunnels that fractured sunlight. He and Christophe had played basketball through junior high and high school, and after traveling on basketball trips to Jackson, to Hattiesburg, to Greenwood, and to New Orleans for tournaments, he knew that most of the south looked like this: pines and dirt interrupted by small towns. He knew that there shouldn't be anything special about Bois Sauvage, but there was: he knew every copse of trees, every stray dog, every bend of every half-paved road, every uneven plane of each warped, dilapidated house, every hidden swimming hole. While the other towns of the coast shared boundaries and melted into each other so that he could only tell he was leaving one and arriving in the other by some landmark, like a Circle K or a Catholic church, Bois Sauvage dug in small on the back of the Bay, isolated. Natural boundaries surrounded it on three sides. To the south, east, and west, a bayou bordered it, the same bayou that the Wolf River emptied into before it pooled into the Bay of Angels and then out to the Gulf of Mexico. There were only two roads that crossed the bayou and led out of Bois Sauvage to St. Catherine, the next town over. To the north, the interstate capped the small town like a ruler, beyond which a thick bristle of pine forest stretched off and away into the horizon. It was beautiful.

Joshua could understand why Ma-mee's and Papa's families had migrated here from New Orleans, had struggled to domesticate the low-lying, sandy earth that reeked of rotten eggs in a dry summer and washed away easily in a wet one. Land had been cheaper along the Mississippi gulf, and black Creoles had spread along the coastline. They'd bargained in broken English and French to buy tens of acres of land. Still, they and their poor white neighbors were dependent on the rich for their livelihood, just as they had been in New Orleans: they built weekend mansions along the beach for wealthy New Orleans expatriates, cleaned them, did their yardwork, and fished, shrimped, and harvested oysters. Yet here, they had space and earth.

They developed their own small, self-contained communities: they intermarried with others like themselves, raised small, uneven houses from the red mud. They planted and harvested small crops. They kept horses and chickens and pigs. They built tiny stills in the wood behind their houses that were renowned for the clarity of the liquor, the strong oily consistency of it, the way it bore a hole down the throat raw. They parceled out their acres to their children, to their passels of seven and twelve. They taught their children to shoot and to drive young, and sent them to one-room schoolhouses that only advanced to the seventh grade. Their children built small, uneven houses, married at seventeen and fourteen, and started families. They called Bois Sauvage God's country.

Their children's children grew, the government desegregated the schools, and they sent them to the public schools in St. Catherine to sit for the first time next to white people. Their children's children could walk along the beaches, could walk through the park in St. Catherine without the caretakers chasing them away, hollering nigger. Their children's children graduated from high school and got jobs at the docks, at convenience stores, at restaurants, as maids and carpenters and landscapers like their mothers and fathers, and they stayed. Like the oyster shell foundation upon which the county workers packed sand to pave the roads, the communities of Bois Sauvage, both black and white, embedded themselves in the red clay and remained. Every time Joshua returned from a school trip and the bus crossed the bayou or took the exit for Bois Sauvage from the highway, he felt that he could breathe again. Even seeing the small, green metal exit sign made something ease in his chest. Joshua rubbed his feet together and the sand slid away from his skin in small, wet clumps that reminded him of lukewarm grits.

When Joshua and Christophe talked about what they wanted to do with their lives, it never included leaving Bois Sauvage, even though they could have joined their mother, Cille, who lived in Atlanta. She sent Ma-mee money by Western Union once a month to help with groceries and clothing. Cille had still been living with Ma-mee when she had the twins, and when she decided to go to Atlanta to make something of herself when the boys were five, she left them. She told Ma-mee she was tired of accompanying her on jobs, of cleaning messes she didn't make, of dusting the underside of tabletops, of mopping wooden living room floors that stretched the entire length of Ma-mee's house, of feeling invisible when she was in the same room with women who always smelled of refined roses. She told Ma-mee she'd send for the twins once she found an apartment and a job, but she didn't. Ma-mee said that one day after Cille had been gone for eleven months, she stood in the doorway of their room and watched them sleep in their twin beds. She gazed at their curly, rough red-brown hair, their small bunched limbs, their skin the color of amber, and she decided to never ask Cille if she was ready to take them again. That was the summer their hair had turned deep red, the same color as Cille's, before it turned to brown, like a flame fading to ash, Ma-mee said.

Three weeks after that morning, Cille visited. She didn't broach the subject of them coming back to Atlanta with her. She and Ma-mee had sat on the porch, and Ma-mee told her to send $200 a month: the boys would remain in Bois Sauvage, with her. Cille had assented as the sound of the twins chasing Ma-mee's chickens, whooping and squealing, drifted onto the screened porch from the yard. Ma-mee said it was common to apportion the raising of children to different family members in Bois Sauvage. It was the rule when she was a little girl; in the 1940s, medicine and food had been scarce, and it was normal for those with eleven or twelve children to give one or two away to childless couples, and even more normal for children to be shuffled around within the family, she said. Joshua knew plenty of people at school that had been raised by grandparents or an aunt or a cousin. Even so, he wished he hadn't been torturing the chickens; he wished that he'd been able to see them talking, to see Cille's face, to see if it hurt her to leave them.

Now Cille was working as a manager at a beauty supply store. She had green eyes she'd inherited from Papa and long, kinky hair, and Joshua didn't know how he felt about her. He thought he had the kind of feelings for her that he had for her sisters, his aunts, but sometimes he thought he loved her most, and other times not at all. When she visited them twice a year, she went out to nightclubs and restaurants, and shopped with her friends. Joshua and Christophe talked about it, and Joshua thought they shared a distanced affection for her, but he wasn't sure. Christophe never stayed on the phone with Cille longer than five minutes, while Joshua would drag the conversation out, ask her questions until she would beg off the phone.

But once when she'd come home during the summer of their sophomore year, a kid named Rook from St. Catherine's had said something dirty about her at the basketball court down at the park while they were playing a game, something about how fine her ass was. Christophe had told Joshua later the particulars of what Rook had said, how the words had come out of Rook's mouth all breathy and hot because he was panting, and to Christophe, it had sounded so dirty. Joshua hadn't heard it because he was under the net, digging his elbow into Dunny's ribs, because he was the bigger man of the two. Christophe was at the edge of the court with the ball, trying to shake Rook, because he was smaller and faster, when Rook said it. Christophe had turned red in the face, pushed Rook away, brought the ball up, and with the sudden violence of a piston had fired the ball straight at Rook's face. It hit him squarely in the nose. There was blood everywhere and Christophe was yelling and calling Rook a bitch and Rook had his hand under his eyes and there was blood seeping through the cracks of his fingers, and Dunny was running to stand between them and laughing, telling Rook if he wouldn't have said shit about his aunt Cille, then maybe he wouldn't have gotten fucked up. Joshua was surprised because he felt his face burn and his hands twitch into fists and he realized he wanted to whip the shit out of dark little Rook, Rook with the nose that all the girls liked because it was fine and sharp as a crow's beak but that now was swollen fat and gorged with blood. Even now Joshua swallowed at the thought, and realized he was digging his fingers into his sides. Rook, little bitch.

Joshua felt the wind flatten his eyelids and wondered if Cille would be at the school. He knew she knew they were graduating: he'd addressed the graduation invitations himself, and hers was the first he'd done. He thought of her last visit. She'd come down for a week at Christmas, had given him and Christophe money and two gold rope chains. He and Christophe had drunk moonshine and ate fried turkey with the uncles on Christmas night in Uncle Paul's yard, and he'd listened as his uncles talked about Cille as she left the house after midnight. She'd sparkled in the dark when the light caught her jewelry and lit it like a cool, clean metal chain.

"Where you going, girl?" Uncle Paul had yelled at her outline.

"None of your damn business!" she'd yelled back.

"That's Cille," Paul had said. "Never could stay still."

"That's cause she spoiled." Uncle Julian, short and dark with baby-fine black hair, had said over the mouth of his bottle. "She the baby girl: Papa's favorite. Plus, she look just like Mama."

"Stop hogging the bottle, Jule," Uncle Paul had said.

Joshua and Christophe had come in later that night to find Cille back in the house. She was asleep at the kitchen table with her head on her arms, breathing softly into the tablecloth. When they carried her to bed, she smelled sweetly, of alcohol and perfume. The last Joshua remembered seeing of her was on New Year's morning; she'd been bleary and puffy eyed from driving an hour and a half to New Orleans the night before and partying on Bourbon Street in the French Quarter. He and Christophe had walked into the kitchen in the same clothes from the previous day, fresh from the party up on the Hill at Remy's house that had ended when the sun rose, to see Cille eating greens and cornbread and black-eyed peas with Ma-mee. Ma-mee had wished them a Happy New Year and told them they stank and needed to take a bath. They had stopped to kiss and hug her, and after he embraced Ma-mee, Joshua had moved to hug Cille. She stopped him with a raised arm, and spoke words he could still hear.

"What a way to start off the New Year."

He had known she was talking about his smell, his hangover, his dirt. He had given her a small, thin smile and backed away. Christophe left the room without trying to hug her, and Joshua followed. After they both took showers, Cille came to their room and embraced them both. Joshua had followed her back to the kitchen, wistfully, and saw her hand a small bank envelope filled with money to Ma-mee. She left. Joshua thought that on average now, she talked to them less and gave them more.

He couldn't help it, but a small part of him wished she would be there when they got home, that she had come in late last night while he and Christophe were out celebrating with Dunny at a pre-graduation party in the middle of a field up further in the country in a smattering of cars and music under the full stars. Wrapped in the somnolent thump of the bass, Joshua closed his eyes, the sun through the leaves of the trees hot on his face, and fell asleep. When he woke up, they were pulling into the yard, Dunny was turning down the music, and there was no rental car in the dirt driveway of the small gray house surrounded by azalea bushes and old reaching oaks. Something dropped in his chest, and he decided not to think about it.

Ma-mee heard the car pull into the yard: a loud, rough motor and the whine of an old steel body. Rap music: muffled men yelling and thumping bass. That was Dunny's car. The twins were home, and judging by the warmth of the air on her skin that made her housedress stick, the rising drone of the crickets, and the absence of what little traffic there was along the road in front of her house, they were late. She'd pressed their gowns and hung them with wire hangers over the front door. She thought to fuss, but didn't. They were boys, and they were grown; they took her to her doctor's appointments, cooked for her, spoke to her with respect. They kept her company sometimes in the evenings, and over the wooing of the cicadas coming through the open windows in the summer or the buzzing of the electric space heater in the winter in the living room, described the action on TV shows for her: *Oprah* and reruns of *The Cosby Show* and nature shows about crocodiles and snakes, which she loved. They called her ma'am, like they were children still, and never talked back. They were good boys.

The front screen door squealed open and she heard them walk across the porch. She heard Dunny step heavily behind them and the sound of wet jeans pant legs rubbing together. The twins' light tread advanced from the front porch and through the door. The smell of outside: sun-baked skin and sweat and freshwater and the juice of green growing things bloomed in her nose. From her recliner seat, she saw their shadows dimly against the walls she'd had them paint blue, after she found out she was blind: the old whitewash that had coated the walls and the low, white ceiling had made her feel like she was lost in an indefinite space. She liked the idea of the blue mirroring the air outside, and the white ceiling like the clouds. When she walked down the narrow, dim hallway, she'd run her fingers over the pine paneling there and imagined she was in her own private grove of young pines, as most of Bois Sauvage had been when she was younger.. She'd breath in the hot piney smell and imagine herself slim-hipped and fierce, before she'd married and born her children, before she started cleaning for rich white folks, when she filled as many sacks as her brothers did with sweet potatoes, melons, and corn. She spoke over the tiny sound of the old radio in the window of the kitchen that was playing midday blues: Clarence Carter.

"Y'all been swimming, huh?"

Christophe bent to kiss her.

"And drinking, huh? You smell like a still."

Joshua laughed and brushed her other cheek.

"You, too!" She swatted him with her hand. "Y'all stink like all outside! We going to be late. Go take a shower. Laila came over here to braid y'all's hair, but left cause y'all wasn't here, your Uncle Paul coming in an hour to take us to the ceremony, and y'all know y'all worse than women—take forever to take a bath. Go on!" Under the smell of the worn sofa upholstery, mothballs, pine sol, and potpourri, she smelled something harsh and heavy. Something that caressed the back of her throat. "That Dunny on the porch smoking?"

"Hey, Grandma Ma-mee," Dunny said.

"Don't 'hey Grandma Ma-mee' me. You dressed for the service?"

"I ain't going." His voice echoed from the porch. The sweet, warm smell of his cigarillo grew stronger.

"Yeah, right, you ain't going. You better get off my porch smoking..."

"Aaaw, Ma-mee."

"And take your ass down the street and get cleaned up. You going to watch my boys graduate. And tell your Mama that I told Marianne and Lilly and them to be over at her house at around six for the cookout, so I hope she got everything ready." His feet hit the grass with a wet crunch. "And don't you throw that butt in my yard. Them boys'll have to clean it up."

"Yes, Ma-mee."

"Hurry up, Dunny."

"Yes, Ma-mee."

From a bedroom deep in the house, she heard Joshua laughing, high and full, more soprano for a boy than she expected, and as usual, it reminded her vaguely of the cartoon with the singing chipmunks in it. It made her smile.

"I don't know what you laughing for," she yelled.

Joshua's laugh was joined by his brother's muffled guffawing from the shower. One couldn't laugh without the other. She pulled her dress away from her front so as to cool some of the sweat there: she wanted to be fresh and cool for the service. She'd bought a dress from Sears for Cille's graduation; where this one was shapeless, the other had fit tighter, and had itched. It was polyester. Ma-mee had given Cille a bougainvillea flower to wear. She closed her eyes and leaned her head back into the sofa cushion, and she could see Cille at eighteen, her skin lovely and glowing as a ripe scopanine as she walked to collect her diploma. She had just fallen in love with the twins' father then, and it showed. Cille bore the twins two years later, and by then her face had changed; it looked as if it had been glazed with a hard candy.

Joshua replied; it sounded as if he was speaking through clothing. Probably pulling a shirt over his head, she thought.

"Yes, Ma-mee."

In the shower, Christophe soaped the rag, stood with the slimy, shimmering cloth in his hand and let the water, so cold it made his nipples pebble, hit him across the face. In the bottom of the tub, he saw sand, tiny brown grains, traced in thin rivulets on the porcelain. He washed his stomach first, as he had done since he was small: it was the way Ma-mee had taught him when they'd first started bathing themselves when they were seven. That was when she had first learned that she had diabetes.

It wasn't until Christophe was fifteen that her vision really started going: that he noticed that she was reaching for pots and pillows and papers without turning her face to look for them, and that sometimes when he was talking to her and she looked at him, she wouldn't focus on his face. She scaled back on the housekeeping jobs she'd been doing. She said that some of her clients had started complaining that she was missing spots, which she'd denied: she said the richer they got, the lazier and pickier they became. She hated going to the doctor, and so she had hidden it from them until he'd noticed these things. Late one night after they'd come back from riding with Dunny, he lay in the twin bed across the room from Joshua, and told him what he suspected. He'd heard of people with diabetes going blind, but he never thought it would happen to Ma-mee.

After Joshua had fallen asleep, Christophe had turned to the wall and cried: breathing through his mouth, swallowing the mucus brought up by the tears, his heart burned bitter and pulled small at the thought of her not being able to see them ever again, at the thought of her stumbling around the house. He'd talked to his Aunt Rita, Dunny's mother, and she'd forced Ma-mee to go to the doctor. He'd confirmed she was legally blind. While Rita sat in a chair next to Ma-mee holding her hand, Christophe and Joshua stood behind them, half leaning against the wall, their heads empty with air and disbelief, as the doctor told them that if they had caught it earlier, they could have done laser surgery on her eyes to stop the blindness from progressing. So then, too late, she'd had the operation. Afterwards, she sat pale and quiet in the living room that she'd had them empty of most of the porcelain knick-knacks and small, cheap plastic vases and shelves so she'd have less to clean and worry about breaking or banging into. The bandages were a blankness on her face. When the doctor took them off and proclaimed her healed, she said she could see blobs of color, nothing else, but Christophe felt a little better in knowing that at least she wouldn't be closed in total darkness, that at least she could still see the color of his skin, the circle of his head.

He dried himself off, wiped the mirror clear, and tried not to, but thought of his father. Their father: the one that gave them these noses and these bodies quick to muscle. Before their mother left them, he was someone the twins saw twice or three times a month. They were happiest when he would stay over for days at Ma-mee's house: the twins would stay awake and listen to him and Cille talk in the kitchen, and later the muffled laughter that came from Cille's room. Inevitably, he and Cille would fight, and he would leave, only to come back a week or two later. Ma-mee had told them that their father refused to go to Atlanta with Cille, and that he liked living in Bois Sauvage just fine; that had caused the final break between them.

After Cille went to Atlanta, he became scarce. His visits tapered off until a day came when Christophe saw him from the school bus on the way home and realized his father hadn't visited them in months. His father was filling the tank of his car with gas at a corner store, and Christophe jumped. Christophe had nudged his brother, and Joshua had joined him in looking out the window, in watching their father shrink until he was small and unreal-looking as a plastic toy soldier stuck in one position: right hand on the roof of the car, the left on the hose, his head down. Suddenly trees obscured their view, and Christophe had turned around in his seat to face the front of the bus, and Joshua, who had been leaning over him in his seat, straightened up and faced forward. Both of them stared at the sweating green plastic upholstery of the seat before them: they were so short they could not see over it.

Christophe wiped a rag over his face and bore down on his nose. Over the years, Christophe and Joshua would see their father around Bois Sauvage when they were riding their bikes and doing wheelies in and out of the ditches, or when they were stealing pears from Mudda Ma'am's pear tree and carting them down the road in their red wagon, and later when they were older, walking with their friends and sneaking blunts. His name was Samuel, and while the boys grew up calling Cille by her name instead of calling her mother, they didn't call Samuel by his name because he didn't talk to them, and because they felt more abandoned by him than by their mother, who at least had the excuse of being "far away." Whenever they saw Samuel, he was always with his friends, and had a red and white Budweiser can in his hands. When they talked about him, they called him "Him" and "He," and any questions or comments about him from others they ignored, or stared hard at the asker, silently, until the question evaporated in the air. As they grew older, when he came up in conversation with others, they called him what everyone in the neighborhood called him: Sandman. When they were thirteen, they began to hear rumors filtered from the neighborhood drug dealers, who had just discovered crack cocaine, and were learning how to cook it from cousins who were visiting from New Orleans, from Chicago, from Florida: these rumors explained why he seemed to be skinnier each time they saw him, why he never drove a better car than his old beat-up, rust-laced Ford pickup, and why he hung out in his friends' yards so much.

Sandman was an addict. Fresh told it to Christophe one day down at the park. While Christophe sat on the picnic table bench and watched Fresh count his money into neat piles of hundreds and twenties and re-bag his crumbs of crack and stash them according to size and price in different pockets on his carpenter's pants, Fresh had said to him, "Boy, except for your nose, you look just like your mama." He'd paused while he folded his wad of bills, had looked up and stared at Christophe, weighing him like a pit he was thinking about buying, and then said, "You knew he on this shit, right?" And in that moment, Christophe knew by Fresh's look who he was talking about. Everything had clicked into order in his head like a stack of dominoes falling in a line. "All of them older ones that used to snort powder when they was young for fun, all of them doing it now. This take them to that other level." Fresh had glared at Christophe. "Don't never do that shit. I keep my shit clean, still got all the hair in my nose." Christophe had looked away from Fresh's diamond-studded gold tooth gleaming in his mouth and had shrugged his small thirteen-year old shoulders, bony and broad under his too big jersey top, and looked away across the park to the basketball court, the baseball diamond, the trees bristling green and rising on all sides. Christophe watched a crow circle and land at the top of a pine and join about a dozen more so that they looked like dark flowers blooming in the blowsy needles, and thought of the last time he'd seen him. He hadn't even so much as nodded at Christophe: Sandman was sitting on the tail of his pickup in Mr. Joe's yard and was so drunk he hadn't even known Christophe was the pre-teen walking past him.

Now, Christophe swiped his hand through his hair and curled it backwards. According to what Fresh had told him about six months ago, Sandman was in Alabama, where he'd gone to stay with his brother and enter rehab. Christophe put on lotion, and walked in a towel to the bedroom. He passed Joshua and punched him in his shoulder as Joshua brushed against him in the narrow hall on the way to the bathroom.

"Hope you left some cold water for me."

"Ha."

Christophe shut the door and began to dress, pulling on jeans, a Polo shirt, his new Reeboks, and greased his hair with pink oil moisturizer so that it curled close to his scalp. He'd be clean, look nice for his aunt and uncles so they could watch him cross the stage, grab his diploma, and throw his tassel across the cap. He wanted to hug Ma-mee with his diploma in his hand and smell good for her, smell clean with soap and cologne. He sprayed a little on himself from the bottle he shared with Joshua, and then went out to the living room to sit next to Ma-mee on the sofa, to move as little as possible to guard himself from sweating unduly, to talk to her about the day, about the cookout at his Aunt Rita's, about whether she cared if he had a beer once they were there even though he knew he'd probably drink regardless of what she said: he'd just hide it. Christophe fleetingly thought that Sandman might show up, but then he told himself that he didn't give a damn if he showed up or not.

Crackheads were known for taking credit where none was due. Most of them were a little crazy. Christophe would rather that he didn't show up. Christophe decided that if he did appear out of some misplaced sense of pride or because he was trying to fulfill some stupid rehab self-help shit, Joshua would have to stop him from punching Sandman in his face.

On the way to the graduation, Ma-mee sat in the front seat with one arm out the window. While her fingers felt at the seam of the glass, her unseeing eyes turned to blink watery and half-closed at the bayou as the wind pushed thick and heavy as a hand at her throat. Paul drove, his blue short-sleeved button-down shirt fastened to his neck, his hands careful on the steering wheel as he slowly followed the curves; his fists were positioned at ten and two. Already, he was sweating dark rings under his arms. Christophe and Joshua sat awkwardly in the backseat of the Oldsmobile with their legs open at the same angles as their uncle's forearms and their arms akimbo at their sides. They leaned away from each other and watched the bright green marsh grass lining the side of the road, the water, interrupted by islands thick with pelicans and white cranes and brush, slide by. The bayou splayed out away from the gray asphalt on both sides, eclipsed the horizon, and sizzled with cicadas and crickets. The twins' windows were rolled down as well.

Ma-mee hated air conditioning. She never wanted it on in the car, and she refused to install an air-conditioning unit in the house. She said the cold air made her feel like she couldn't breathe, and that it made her short of breath. So in the summer months, they sweated. The boys grew up accustomed to the wet heat, the droning indoor fans, the doors that swelled and stuck with the rise in temperature. In their shared room, they slept on top of their twin beds' coverlets with their mouths open, their spindly limbs and knobby knees and elbows exposed, and wore only white briefs. As they grew older, they stripped their beds to the fitted and flat sheets, and took to sleeping in old gym shorts, or boxers.

Joshua propped one arm on the door, and rested his hand on his chin. He didn't lean back because he didn't want to crush his curls flat against the headrest. Outside, the edge of the road shimmered, and ahead the road wavered so that it looked as if snakes, tens of them, were crossing the road in the distance. When he was little he'd always been amazed when they disappeared the closer he got: but then again, back then he'd twisted around in his seat facing the rear window because he'd thought the moon and the sun followed the car, and he liked to watch them sail through the sky and chase him. He looked over to Christophe, who had arranged his head and arm similarly, and was looking intently out the other window. As they were walking to the car, Christophe whispered his warning about the possibility of seeing Sandman there. Joshua had started to laugh at the impossibility of it. Then Joshua had looked at Christophe's mouth, and he'd stopped laughing and nodded: yes, he'd watch out for Sandman. The set of Christophe's shoulders as they got in the car made him think of Cille: he wondered if Christophe was wondering if she was coming, if perhaps Ma-mee knew she was coming and was trying to keep it a secret so it would be a surprise. He let his hand fall out the window and drag in the current of the wind: she would wear red, her favorite color, he knew.

They arrived at the school ten minutes before the start of the program. With their gowns held gingerly in their hands, they climbed out of the car and walked across the small parking lot, past the sprawling red brick buildings couched among the moss strewn oaks and the football field stretching away to the left, to the gym directly behind the cluster of classrooms. The family entered the gym together and stood still for a moment; they were a small group in a milling confusion of parents and students and relatives.

Every other person led neon balloons that read "Congratulations Class of 2005" in yellow and sported tails of sparkling, curly streamers, and carried cards stuffed fat with money. The smell of perfume and cologne was thick in the air. The basketball court had been remade into an auditorium: folding metal chairs were lined in precise rows down the length of the floor. The more punctual family members claimed choice seats in the metal rows while the less punctual consigned themselves to the bleachers. While Uncle Paul led Ma-mee by the elbow to her seat next to Aunt Rita and the rest of the extended family at the front of the gym near the long dais that served as the stage, Joshua and Christophe skirted the crowd and found their way to the rows of graduating students. The graduating class had nearly two hundred students, but still, they filled only around ten rows: St. Catherine High was a small high school, even with all the students from the town of St. Catherine and its country neighbor, Bois Sauvage. About half the students were white, half were black, and there was a smattering of Vietnamese. While most of the Vietnamese kids' parents had immigrated to the area after the Vietnam War to work in the shrimping and fishing industries, most of the black and white families had been living in the two towns since their foundings, and some of them even shared last names with each other, which was the result of little-acknowledged intermarriage. Their seating in the gym belied their social interactions: the two groups lived mostly segregated lives.

Joshua peered into the crowd and saw Laila; he waved. She had eyes that turned to slits when she laughed, a curvy waist, and lips he thought about kissing every time he saw her, but he'd never told her that. He and Christophe had lost their virginity to two sisters from St. Catherine when they were fifteen. Dunny had taken them along when he'd gone to their house to visit the oldest sister. While Dunny disappeared in the bedroom with his girl, Christophe and Joshua had sat sweating on the sofa. Lisa, the middle sister, had just walked over and sat on Christophe's lap and flirted with him. She laughed at his jokes. Within minutes, they'd disappeared down the hallway. Nina, the youngest, had sat next to Joshua and told him she had seen him around school—and did he think she was cute for a ninth grader? When he'd told her yes, she'd kissed him. The next thing he knew, she was partly naked and on top of him and the remote control was digging into his back and the TV went black and he didn't care.

Afterwards, Christophe had laughed when Dunny asked him about it, but Joshua had been quiet in the backseat. Since then, every time he had sex seemed a lucky accident, while Christophe grew more and more confident. He had just broken up with his latest girlfriend, he said, for being too clingy. Christophe tugged him toward their seats. Joshua and Christophe found their assigned chairs in the "D" row; Christy Desiree sat on their right, and Fabian Daniels on their left. Christy was busy pulling at her blond hair and reapplying lip-gloss. Fabian curved into his seat with his arms crossed over his chest: he looked as if he were sinking. Joshua ignored Christy and perched at the edge of his chair, scanning the program.

"So what y'all going to be doing after this?"

Christophe turned to Fabian and adjusted his robe where it had bunched beneath his legs. He could hardly move. He knew it was going to be wrinkled when he walked across the stage, but he didn't want it to be too wrinkled. He knew Aunt Rita would talk.

"Look for a job, I guess. You don't know anybody trying to get rid of a old car for cheap, do you?"

"Naw." Fabian pushed his cap up and back on his head since it had begun to slip down over his dark, broad forehead. "If I hear something, I'll let you know. I probably won't hear nothing before I leave—I'm going offshore. My uncle already got my application in. I start in two weeks."

"I couldn't be out there on that water all the time, cooped up. I'd go crazy." Christophe shifted his robe again, resettling it flatly beneath him. "Who knows, though. They make good money. Maybe when I get older, I'd go offshore for that kind of money." The only way he could ever consider leaving Bois Sauvage to work was if he was older, and only if Ma-mee was gone. She'd spent her entire life working for one rich white household or another to earn money to feed them, dressing them when they were younger in clothes her employers had given her to take to the Salvation Army, providing for them the best she could. Now it was their turn.

The hum of conversation in the gym was almost deafening, and already Christophe was growing tired of the rustling of programs, the shrieking of small children, the loud boasting of men, and the sense of interminable wait. He hated official shit like this. He just wanted to get his diploma and hear his name over the loudspeaker, the light patter of applause, and then get to the cookout, to the rest of the summer, to the rest of his life. He was ready to be done with school; he was tired of watching his principal, sweating at the neck, now barking orders at the first five rows, his teachers, dressed in long, loose dresses replete with maiden collars, darting around nervously, the secretaries, bored and severe, picking at the microphone and the fake flowers next to the podium. The gym was cold, and he felt the sweat dry on him and goose pimples rise on his arms under his gown as the satin, now cool like water, slid over them. The principal, Mr. Farbege, leaned into the row and barked, "Remember your cues!" and Christophe barely resisted the urge to flip him off. Joshua leaned over to Christophe, the program in his hand.

"Look at this," he said.

Joshua thought she might do something like this. The only reason he was looking at the program was to look at the family advertisements in the back: he knew that he'd find at least a couple of choice photographs of his classmates in embarrassing ads that said things like, "You're a star! Follow your dreams" and "From Maw-maw and Paw-paw. We love you." There, on the last page, was a small ad, measuring around three by five inches. In it was a small picture of he and Christophe; it had been taken when they were five. Cille had asked Aunt Rita to take it, a picture of all three of them, on the day she left for Atlanta. She was kneeling on the ground between them with her arms over both of their shoulders: her smile was wide, and she had sunglasses on, large dark ovals, because as Christophe remembered it, she had been crying. At her sides, the twins looked like small, young-faced old men: their T-shirts hung on them, their heads were cocked to the side, and neither of them was looking toward the camera. Joshua was looking off into the distance, his fists clutching the bottom of his shirt as he pulled it away from his small round stomach. Christophe's eyes were squinted nearly shut, and the set of his mouth was curved downward and puckered: he looked as if he had just eaten something bitter, like he looked on the day they snuck the small, bitter grapes from Papa's old grapevine that grew curled on crude posts behind the house and ate them.

Under the picture was printed in small, bold-faced print: *Congratulations to Joshua and Christophe. Love, Cille.* That was it. Joshua knew as soon as he saw the small picture, the miniscule line, that she wasn't coming. He knew that she wasn't already sitting in the audience with Aunt Rita, that she wasn't just running late, that she wouldn't appear at their cook-out with the rest of the family, that she wasn't just going to walk casually out of the kitchen with a pot in her arms to set on the long wax-covered table beneath the trees while the outdoor fans buzzed in the background and blew her dress away from her legs. Joshua let Christophe take the paper as he leaned further back and down in his chair. He purposefully spread his legs to take up more space so that Christy squeaked as she had to smash her knees together to make room for him; he hated her lip-gloss and her prissiness and for a second he felt a strong urge to press his hand across her face, to smudge her makeup. He didn't turn and say he was sorry.

Christophe read the program and folded it in fourths and placed it in his back pocket along with his own program. Who knows, he thought, one day Joshua might actually want it. He heard Mr. Farbege giving the opening remarks, and he tuned out as he began to make a list in his head of where he and Joshua could go to look for jobs: Wal-Mart, the grocery store in St. Catherine, the McDonald's.

Joshua ignored the valedictorian and salutatorian's speeches, the cheesy slide show (he and Christophe were in one picture: their hands in their pockets, they stood outside on the benches used for break—he thought that Christophe looked like he was high). When the principal began calling graduates' names, Joshua waited patiently as he watched the other students cross the dais: some of them danced and played the crowd for laughs when they got their diplomas, some pumped their fists in the air, while others walked across quickly, heads down, nervous, and seemed to shy away from the applause that clattered from the stands.

"Christophe DeLisle."

Christophe rose, walked to the podium, and smoothed his gown. Once there, he shook Mr. Farbege's hand with his left and grabbed his diploma with his right. The leather casing was cool in his hand, and it slipped slightly, and he realized he was sweating. The lights were so bright and hot that he didn't attempt to look out into the crowd or find Ma-mee: instead, he turned and put on his cockiest smile, hoping Aunt Rita was relating everything to her, and walked off the stage.

Joshua stood when he saw his brother exit.

"Joshua DeLisle."

Joshua ascended to greet the principal. He couldn't focus on Mr. Farbege's sweating, red face or the secretary fumbling with the diplomas. He turned to the audience, the lights blaring, squinted, and tried to smile. He knew he wouldn't be able to make them out against the glare of the spotlight, but he looked in the direction Ma-mee and Uncle Paul had gone anyway, and tried to see if he could see her. He saw nothing but a mess of faces and bright, bold outfits, so he raised his hand and waved a little in their direction in time to the applause, and hoped that they knew he was waving for them. He walked to his seat, shuffled past the rows of the students, sat, and realized that he'd been nervous, that the tiny, golden hairs at the back of his neck and on his arms and legs were standing on end. He shivered, feeling as he had when he was little and he'd run into the river just after the sun rose. They'd camped with Aunt Rita and Uncle Paul and the rest of the family on a Friday night, and he'd awoken the next day before everyone else, jarred awake by the sand pressing into his stomach through the sleeping bag where he'd slept on the floor of the tent. He'd run out to the water, wanting to be the first one in, expecting it to be languid and warm, but instead was shocked by the cold of it, the bite of it on his legs up to his knees, how his skin seemed to tighten and retreat across his muscles from the chill. He grimaced and gripped his diploma. He couldn't believe that he and Christophe had graduated. He leaned closer to his brother, sideways, in his chair, until he could feel their shoulders touching. The litany of names was a buzzing drone in his head, and he waited for it to end.

The sun was turning the tops of the trees red, and from the woods surrounding Aunt Rita's trailer, the night insects began calling to one another, heralding the approach of the cooler night. Under the young, spindly oaks dotting the yard, Christophe, Joshua, and Dunny sat at one of several folding wooden tables in creaking metal and plastic chairs, plates of food before them. Ma-mee ate slowly, feeling her way around the food on her plate: tiny barbecued drumsticks, meatballs, and potato salad. Children darted back and forth across the yard like small animals, chasing and teasing each other in packs. Most of the twins' uncles, Cille's brothers, sat in a circle away from the steel drum barbecue grill, passing what Joshua suspected to be a bottle of homemade wine around and smoking.

There were four of them: Paul, Julian, Maxwell, and David. Aunt Rita, Cille's only sister, was sweating over the grill: her hair was pulled back in a loose ponytail, frizzed and messed by the humidity, and she cooked with one hand on her hip while the other basted the chicken and ribs with sauce. Myriad gold earrings shone at her ears. She swatted a mosquito away from her head, and lifting one foot to scratch her leg, continued the cooking, mumbling to herself. She was a shorter, rounder version of her sister: Joshua thought there was something different about her movements, something more settled than Cille, as if her lower center of gravity made her more solid, more dependable, less susceptible to disappear from a place. Friends and neighbors filled the chairs around the twins, drinking and smoking, talking and laughing. Joshua waved a fly away from his food and took a sip of his Budweiser; the can was pleasantly cool in the palm of his hand. Christophe was busy fielding questions from Uncle Eze, Rita's husband. Eze had moved his chair close and ate with both elbows on the table; his arms dark and thick with muscle as he licked his fingers. Once every few minutes, he'd pause to reach over and snake his hand around Aunt Rita's waist. Then he'd grab his napkin and dab at his face where beads of sweat bloomed large as pearls.

"So, what y'all going to do now? Y'all thought about going to school?"

Joshua snorted and half-smiled, then picked up a boiled shrimp from his plate and began to peel it.

"You better be glad we graduated!" Christophe laughed.

They'd barely passed senior English, and the only reason they hadn't been in more detention was because they were a team. After smoking blunts with Dunny a few mornings when he gave them rides to school or when they checked themselves out early and skipped class, they watched out for each other: they juggled each other's excuses, finished one another's lies, and generally kept one another out of trouble. Joshua placed the naked, pink shrimp on Ma-mee's plate, and she smiled and reached for his hand before he could remove it and squeezed; the pads of her fingers, even after all those years of scrubbing and washing, were still soft and full on his wrist. He squeezed in return and then began peeling another shrimp.

"Well, then, what y'all going to do?"

Christophe scooped potato salad onto a piece of white bread in spoonfuls so big they threatened to break the plastic spoon in half. He folded the bread and then took a large bite of his potato salad sandwich before chasing it with a swallow of his own beer: the rim of the can was flecked with bits of barbecue sauce and meat, and smeared with grease.

"We going to get a job. We got a whole bunch of places we can go put applications in at. We going to make some money."

Eze paused to wipe his hands on his napkin, and leaned back in his own chair. He'd sucked the bones on his plate clean. His voice was lower when he spoke.

"Y'all thought about what y'all going to do about a car?"

Christophe took another bite of his sandwich and frowned.

"We was gonna borrow Dunny's car while he was at work to fill out applications until we could save up enough money to buy one. Somebody got to be selling one for cheap sometime soon. People always trying to get rid of old Cutlasses; it shouldn't take too much money to buy one and get it running good."

Joshua noticed Aunt Rita had closed the top of the grill and was standing behind Eze. Her arms were folded across her chest, and her head was cocked to the side. He realized she was looking at him, that she was blinking at him solemnly. Her eyes were large and dark in her face and the liquid eyeliner she'd worn at the graduation was smudged below her eyes; it made them appear bruised. Dunny picked up a beer and paused with the rim of the can to his mouth and found Joshua watching him. Dunny winked, grinned around the can, and tipped the beer back so that it hid his face.

Eze tapped his finger on the table once, twice, and then stood. He dropped his napkin so that it fell as slowly as snow to the paper tablecloth. Christophe looked at Ma-mee. She was chewing thoughtfully on the shrimp and had a small grin on her face. Shrimp were her favorite food. Away from the citronella candles and electric bulbs illuminating the trees into the surrounding darkness, Eze walked into the ascending crescendo of the raucous night, calling back over his shoulder, "Well, come on, I got something to show you."

Christophe glanced at Joshua and widened his eyes. Joshua shrugged and stood to follow Eze. Christophe stabbed a hot link with a fork and took it with him when he pushed away from the table. Joshua waited for him to catch up. Eze disappeared around the side of the trailer where he and Aunt Rita parked their cars. Once Christophe rounded the corner, he stopped alongside his brother, who stood at the tailgate of Eze's Ford pickup. Joshua was still. He stared past Eze's trunk and Aunt Rita's small red Toyota and noticed that there was another car in the hard-packed dirt driveway, a four-door, gray-blue Caprice. Eze was leaning against the hood. Joshua heard Dunny's dog, chained to a post in the woods at the side of the house, growl and bark once, high and sharp.

"What do y'all think?" Eze placed one hand on the body and patted it twice, softly. "Your mama Cille sent me the money for it, told me to find something for y'all so that y'all could have something to drive once y'all got out of school. Bookie from over in St. Cats was selling the body for five hundred: I got a motor for six hundred, and then parts came to a little less than four. Used up all the money she sent. She said she'd been saving up for a little bit and she wanted y'all to have something dependable. I got it running pretty good, and it should get y'all to work and back." He smiled, a glimpse of his teeth in the dark, then walked towards them and held out a key ring with four bright metal keys on it before them. "It's a good car."

Joshua stared at the ring that gleamed from the faint reach of the porch light. Christophe was the first to react: he plucked the key ring from Eze's hand. Neither twin spoke until Eze cleared his throat, nodded to them almost awkwardly, and then walked away and around the trailer.

"Well," Christophe said low, out of the side of his mouth, "I guess we know why she didn't come." He tossed the keys in the air; they glittered in the dim light and fell with a dull metal crush into Christophe's palm.

"Why show up when you give us a car? Guess she's really done, now."

"Yeah, I guess she is."

Joshua blinked, felt his eyelids slide heavily down, then open. He let the feeling of her absence sink to his throat, skirt his collarbone to settle in his chest, to throb stronger than it had when he had seen her dedication to them in the program. He looked away from the car. He was glad that Christophe had grabbed the keys; he would let his brother do all the driving. He knew that if he reached out to touch the metal of the hood, it would be warm as the night, insect-ridden air, warm as skin, but not so soft. Joshua spoke in a voice lower than his brother's.

Christophe slid the key ring into his pocket. He moved to nudge Joshua with his other hand, but then seemed to remember the sausage on the fork.

"Shit." He plucked the sausage away from the metal and then wound his arm back and threw it in the direction of the dog in the woods. It flew through the air, a dark blur, and hit the leaves of the trees with a falling rustle. The dog barked again, sharply, once. Christophe sucked the sauce from his thumb and forefinger and bumped his brother with his shoulder. He was still hungry, and while there was nothing but them and the silence and this car here, there was more potato salad and hot, spicy meat in the front, and Ma-mee was waiting for them. So, Cille hadn't shown up, and she'd gotten them this car instead. It felt like a bribe. From the front, Christophe heard Dunny shout at one of the little kids, and an answering giggle. Christophe gnawed at a piece of jagged skin on his thumb, and thought of Ma-mee, smiling and expectant in her pressed dress waiting for them out front. This would make it easier for them. He would be grateful. "Well, we did need a car. Come on."

Christophe turned, and Joshua followed him into the dark brush at the side of the trailer. Joshua was an inverse shadow: full where Christophe was thin. Christophe seemed more of the darkness. The dog was quiet, and Christophe hoped he had been able to find and reach the food. Under the night sounds, Christophe heard the links of its chain clink.

2

THE FLUORESCENT LIGHTS IN THE CEILING POPPED AND SIZZLED: Christophe flinched and stabbed the tip of his pin into the McDonald's application. Joshua frowned, and looked over to find the ink bled black in a smudge that vaguely resembled a tiny heart. Through the window, the dawn washed the water and the sky of the beach a pale, milky blue: the sun was a small, bright light on the horizon. Joshua loved the coastline in the morning: a small part of him always thought that God had just dipped his hand in the water and cleansed it. Ma-mee had woken them while it was still dark outside: she woke them to the tepid morning, to grits and bacon on the stove. Christophe scrawled his name across the paper in a nearly illegible sweep: Joshua knew he hated the smell of fried fat and antiseptic that suffused the air in places like this. Christophe told him that he didn't really want to work there, but they needed something. They'd done yard-work sometimes with Uncle Paul when they were in high school, but they couldn't depend on it: the work was too sporadic. Christophe covered his mouth and nose with his left hand and scribbled with his right.

Across the table, Joshua squinted inches above the application and printed his name, their telephone number, and their address in careful, even cursive. Christophe always told him he wrote like a girl. As for work history, he placed a terse line through each open space. They had pooled the money their mother sent Ma-mee every month with what they earned doing yard-work with Uncle Paul and it had satisfied them; they grew up tailoring their needs to fit the amount of expendable cash they had available. They'd coped in different ways: while Joshua would forego Nikes and buy Reebok so he could have shoes and a new shirt, Christophe would wait and hoard his money so he could spend his portion on the latest Jordans—damn clothes.

The night before, they'd lain on their beds in their rooms and discussed their options. Both twins lay on their backs, clothed only in boxer shorts, and stared at the ceiling fan slowly revolving in circles above their heads. The night insects had poured their insistent calling and wailing into the open screen of the window, but still the boys pitched their voices low. Their list was a dull litany of choices: McDonald's, Burger King, Sonic, Dairy Queen, Piggly Wiggly, Circle K, Chevron, Wal-Mart, K-Mart, the Dockyard and the Shipyard. None of their options were in Bois Sauvage. There wasn't much in Bois Sauvage: three convenience stores (none of which offered gas for sale), an elementary school, three Catholic churches, a park that consisted of a baseball field, a concrete basketball court, rusty slides, swings, monkey bars and park benches, and a couple of hole-in-the-wall nightclubs that their Uncle Paul frequented that served moonshine under the counter and specialized in playing dirty modern delta blues. (The twins' personal favorite was a song called "It's Cheaper to Keep Her.") They needed a car to get to all of the places they were putting in applications, because they were all at least two towns over in each direction along the coast, in Germaine or Ocean Point or Lausianne, beyond the reach of Bois Sauvage and St. Catherine. In the hot air of the room, Christophe had breathed out, "Thank God Cille got us a fucking car," then threw his arm over his head so that his armpit would cool and the sweat would dry along the elongated rigid expanse of his chest, his ribs, the hollow of his stomach and belly button. He'd started breathing hard within seconds: he was asleep.

Joshua was envious of Christophe's ability to fall asleep like that, instantly dead to the world, free from the weight of waking life, anywhere, anytime. Once he'd fallen asleep during the eye of a hurricane Andrew that hit the year they were eight, and he hadn't woken up until after the storm had passed. While he had slept, Joshua had stayed awake, transfixed, staring out the window at the hundred-mile-per-hour winds uprooting pecan trees from the field next to the house. Joshua stared at the ceiling, felt the fine puffs of heat from the sluggish fan, and wondered about the days to come. He didn't really want to work at any of those places, yet he didn't know where he did want to work. Would every night of the rest of his life be like this one: dreading the morning, the endless monotony of the repetition of days, of work that he hated, spiraling off into old age? He'd sighed and wiped a slick hand across his chest. He didn't know, but he was tired, and the dread of these new thoughts seemed as heavy and oppressive as the heat. He had lain staring at the circling fan until he glanced at the alarm clock and saw it read three, and had blinked, all the while listening to his brother's breath stutter into snoring in the next bed. He only realized he'd fallen asleep when he opened his eyes and saw Ma-mee standing over him. He heard the cock crowing from the chicken coop in the backyard, and felt Ma-mee's touching his scalp as she muttered, "Wake up."

Joshua leaned closer into the form, marked the boxes indicating he hadn't been convicted of a felony, provided three references (Uncle Paul, Ma-mee, and his auto mechanic teacher from Vo-tech) and signed his signature. He looked over at Christophe's paper and found it wrecked. Christophe's sprawling, furious scribble spilled across the page in wide arcs, and his words tumbled down the margin of the application at the end of each line. Joshua smiled. Christophe never could color entirely within a line. Christophe pocketed the pen and looked up and grimaced at his brother. His fingertips were stained with ink. Joshua followed Christophe to the counter where they both slid the applications as a pair to the assistant manager, some kid with thick-lensed glasses and a large nose and broad, bony black shoulders that had graduated from St. Catherine's High School a year before them. He palmed them and nodded at the twins. Christophe rolled his eyes. Joshua knew he had absolutely no patience for people he considered "lames."

"We got to work at the same time because we got to share a ride. That's why we put down the same hours for availability."

The boy bit his lower lip and nodded. He bent to slide the completed applications in a small bin beside the cash register before speaking in a deep, gravelly voice. It surprised Joshua: he sounded like a croaking frog, like a ditch frog that called loudest after a summer storm, bloated with rain.

"I understand. I don't know if we going to be hiring anytime soon. Most of the people we just hired on full time been working here since before graduation."

Joshua turned to the door and saw Christophe pursing his lips as he followed. Joshua walked to the car and leaned his forearms against it. The sun had not yet seeped in enough to make the metal burn; for that he was grateful. He kicked the door. He was anxious, and this was the first place they had visited.

Christophe narrowed his eyes as he walked to the driver's side door of the car and fumbled in his pocket for the keys. Here it was seven in the morning and he already felt like a smoke: he was nervous. He felt like he'd fumbled and dropped his usual charm and sense of humor as soon as he stepped into the building. The metal bar of the door handle was cool in his grip: his fingers faltered on it and slipped away as he heard a high pierced whistle. At the side of the building, a dark, slim figure lounged against the brick wall, pulled hard on a cigarette, and waved. Christophe recognized him: Charles, who'd graduated with their class on Friday, was taking a break at the side of the dumpsters. He'd twisted his visor to the side and flipped it upside down so that his afro swelled out of the top like a small balloon. Christophe walked over to him, and Charles handed him the cigarette. Christophe took a quick puff and passed it back to Charles, holding the smoke in his lungs until he could feel the nicotine lap at his chest like a small wave and settle like foam over his skin. Joshua ambled over slowly, crouched on his haunches at their side, and shook his head no at the proffered smoke.

"Y'all come up here looking for a job, huh?"

Christophe nodded.

"Man, they ain't hiring for shit. They upped me to full time. We been having people come by here all day. They don't want to hire no more staff—they working the shit out of us." The tip of the cigarette sparkled red.

"We got all day to go." Christophe held out his hand. "It's probably the same at all the fast food places. Might have some luck at the dock 'cause Dunny stepdaddy said they was hiring. They don't accept applications until Wednesday, though."

The heat of the day was slithering across the half-empty parking lot with the ascending sun, and the smell of the warming asphalt filled Christophe's nose along with the smoke. Joshua watched a blue station wagon and an old beaten-up red pickup truck swerve past them into the drive-through lane. Christophe passed the cigarette back to Charles and nodded at the cars.

"Breakfast crowd. It ain't really going to let up until after lunch." Charles' nose widened as he smiled and laughed so that the smoke drifted out over his teeth grayish white. He had an overbite. "By that time, I done probably smoked at least two blunts." He tossed the cigarette to the sidewalk and crushed it beneath the toe of his sneaker. "Otherwise I'd kill somebody."

Joshua shook his head and pressed his forehead into his forearms, which were crossed over his knees.

"I hear you on that one," Christophe said.

At Charles' side, the door opened. The gangly assistant manager poked his head out, then a shoulder. He blinked at the three boys standing and crouching silently in the shade of the wall. He looked down at the ground and spoke.

"Charles?"

Charles crossed one leg over the other and made a point not to look at the boy when he replied.

"What, Larry?"

"We need you to finish break. Breakfast crowd coming in." He mumbled his last bit before the door clicked shut. "It's getting busy."

Charles rubbed his knuckles into his eyes. Next to him on the sidewalk, Christophe heard Charles whisper beneath his breath, "Tired of this shit."

"You know that if I had a blunt already rolled up I'd smoke with you. But I ain't got nothing today," Christophe said.

"It's alright. I'm going to roll up one when I take a bathroom break in about an hour." He swung the door open. "If y'all really want to work here, y'all should call and ask to speak to Gary in about a week. He the manager that do all the hiring. Something might open up. See y'all later."

From inside the restaurant, Christophe heard the boy with the frog's voice intoning orders in an endless procession. Charles flipped his hat over, jammed it down on his head so that his afro parted and fell in wilted tufts like dehydrated vegetation. The door closed and Joshua raised his head.

"That's what we got to look forward to," he said.

"If we get hired here and Kermit the Frog's our boss, I just might have to hit him," Christophe said.

"Yeah, so we can get fired…cause you know I'm going to have to jump in and save your no-fighting ass," Joshua laughed.

Christophe pulled Joshua to his feet, and Joshua walked to the car while Christophe began patting his pockets for the keys again. Joshua was staring at the pavement. Christophe spoke to the taut skin at the back of his brother's head, his meaty, sloping shoulders.

"We'll find something."

"I know."

The air was already difficult to breathe. The sun had boiled it dense so that it smelled strongly of salt and tar, and had burned the water of the gulf a dirty brownish blue. Unlocking the door and looking over the car and past his brother, Christophe studied the beach. He could see the barrier islands floating on the horizon of the water, appearing like bristling shadows of elongated reeds as they siphoned the current and blocked the clean blue-green wash of the Gulf of Mexico, blocked the water that swept up from the Caribbean, and impacted the beach that he saw with silt, with mud, with runty, dirty waves. He was calm; he was ready. As Joshua slumped and played with the stereo, Christophe turned the ignition. He hated those islands.

They visited four more places that morning: Burger King, Dairy Queen, Circle K, and Sonic. Burger King smelled like McDonald's. The orange of the décor made the interior of the restaurant darker than McDonald's. The boys didn't know anyone who worked there. After they left Burger King, they rode around and ate Whoppers, shoving the napkins they hadn't used in the glove compartment. Joshua said with a smirk, "Well, I guess the car is really ours now." They submitted applications at Sonic and Dairy Queen. They filled half the tank at Circle K, and completed their forms on the dashboard of the car, hunched over, itching wetly against the crushed cloth of the seats. Christophe had signed his name with a flourish, tossed the pen on the seat between them, and insisted that it was too hot to ride around in the car with no air conditioning on the job search. They'd gone home then, hiding from the hottest part of the afternoon in the living room with Ma-mee, catching the tail end of her daytime soaps and watching *Jeopardy*. They'd asked her to wake them up early the next morning and gone to bed after watching reruns of *The Cosby Show* at nine because Ma-mee loved Clair Huxtable. The twins had fallen asleep without talking.

The next morning, they'd driven to Chevron first. Piggly Wiggly and Wal-Mart and K-Mart were next on the list. The managers were all clones of each other: a short, plump feather-haired white woman for the grocery stores, and a shrunken curly-haired white man for the gas stations. They spent the morning waiting in lines, writing against walls. Christophe wondered why all the places they put in applications smelled like antiseptic. Under the gas smells and the new cheap clothes smells and the smells of plastic wrapping and the greasy, stale food, the weeks-old hot dogs, there was always the smell of Lysol, of ammonia, of some sort of stringent cleaner. Sometime after noon, Christophe called off the job search for the day after the second time Joshua fell asleep in the passenger seat, and Christophe saw the sweat beading and running down Joshua's face as if he'd been doused with water. He'd sweat like that since they were kids. Christophe had opened a napkin at a stoplight and laid it over Joshua's face like a caul and then took the next right and drove them home. When he'd awoken Joshua and told him to go inside, Joshua hadn't moved, but instead grunted at his brother and spent the afternoon asleep in the car.

Now they were in the parking lot of the dockyard. The main office, set in a little cluster of boxy, tin buildings, only accepted applications from noon to three. It was eleven. Joshua slouched in the passenger seat, his face resting on his fist, his other hand cupping a lukewarm Coke. They hadn't heard from any of the other places where they'd applied: they were waiting until after the weekend to follow up. The toast and scrambled eggs he'd eaten for breakfast had seemingly evaporated from his belly. He'd been nursing the Coke since they'd made it from Bois Sauvage into Germaine and stopped at a corner store before posting up in the parking lot. He took another sip and was so hungry he could feel the Coke trickle down past the center of his breastbone. The hunger dulled his nervousness: he found he was hesitantly hopeful. Finally, here was a place where they had more of a chance to get a position, a place where, if they kept at it for a while, they could make pretty good money—at least more than they could make working at Wal-Mart or McDonald's or Circle K. He didn't like it, but he could do it, and he could do it without some kid with horsy shoulders and a weasely neck monitoring his every move. He switched the radio on and when he heard the midday blues program, he turned it off.

Christophe was rolling a blunt. He'd spread a napkin across his lap. On his left knee, he'd placed the weed, rolled up in a small corner of a Ziploc bag. On his right knee, he balanced the cigarillo: a strawberry Swisher Sweet. He sliced the cigar down the middle with his pointer fingernail: he kept his fingernails long for a reason. The strawberry smell of the cigar's skin sifted through the car. Christophe opened the plastic bag and began to break it down in smaller pieces that would fit in the wrapper, and to cull the buds from the stems. He sprinkled the leaves evenly down the center of the skin. He licked the Swisher, and then folded the edges together, sealing it. The weed was strong; the smell of it had been thick and musky, and the buds had been damp and hard to break down. It would be good to smoke.

He lit the blunt by inhaling sharply on the end of it while he fired up the other end with his most recent lighter, which was a dull purple color. Joshua was surprised Christophe hadn't lost it yet: he'd had it for a few weeks now. He'd bought it the day after graduation. The day was overcast; the clouds clustered in a dense blanket in the sky, low and light gray, for as far as Joshua could see, out over the gulf and into the distance. It made the docks seem even more forlorn. The men moved slowly in their blue and black overalls, their T-shirts rolled up over their biceps to show their pining muscles as they bent and lifted and threw sack after sack of what looked like feed onto platforms that the forklift operator loaded onto a crane. They were unloading a trucker's trailer, and transferring the cargo to the hold of the ship sitting in the harbor. Joshua winced at the seeming endless line of workers, the endless quantity of pallets and bags. It was more than tedium: it was hard, backbreaking work. But he knew they could take care of Ma-mee with this money, fix up the house a bit, fix some leaks in the roof; they wouldn't have to decide between planting buckets and buying shoes. They could finally save and spend and earn and have something of their own, something that hadn't been given to them by their mother.

"I feel like we fixing to go play a game or something," Christophe said. He inhaled again, pulling the sweet, sticky smoke into his lungs. Joshua noticed he wasn't fidgeting anymore: the weed was calming him. He began to speak, and Joshua listened. Christophe could see it in his head: he'd pass this car to Joshua and buy his own car. A Cutlass. He'd paint it navy blue with a silver pearl, and put it on some dubs, some twenty-inch six-stars. He'd put a system in it. He would take the corners slow by the church and the convenience station and into the driveway so he wouldn't dent the dubs, and he'd play Pastor Troy so loud his trunk would rattle. Dunny would be jealous. He waved the blunt vaguely toward Joshua, his eyes half lidded, concentrating on relaying the vision of him riding up to the house, parking the car, of he and Joshua and Uncle Paul redoing the porch on the house, replacing the small sagging one with a larger, deluxe version that had room for a swing, and plants, and two ceiling fans. Ma-mee would like that.

Joshua didn't smoke too often; he hoped the blunt would stop his legs from shaking. He knew Christophe had some Febreze spray stashed underneath the seat, so they could mask the smell. As for the eventual job piss tests, he was sure they could sneak in one of their little cousins' urine when the time came for those interviews. Dunny had done it when he'd gone to interview for his job at the local Wal-Mart, and he'd passed. He'd taped a small plastic vial of it to the inside of his thigh: he said the worst part was ripping the tape off. Joshua puffed and held the smoke in his lungs before letting it out and breathing through his nose so that the smoke seemed to flow like water over a stone over his upper lip and into his nostrils. He loved that trick. Christophe could never manage it. Christophe grinned. Joshua took another quick puff, and then handed the blunt back to his brother.

"How long you think we'll have to work here before we can start doing big shit? Like fixing the porch? Before we get some benefits?" Christophe choked out around the smoke he was holding in his chest.

"Probably around six months. I think that's how long they usually make you wait."

Joshua felt his sternum tingle and leaned his head somnolently on the backseat. The back of his skull felt weighted by something leaden: in his mind, he pictured a ton anchor like the one he imagined anchored the ships in the dock dragging at the back of his brain. "This some good green."

"Dunny sold it to me. It was the last of that good batch he got from Big Lean. Had to bug him to do that. He didn't want to sell it because he wanted to smoke it all. Made me promise to save some so we could smoke with him. Maybe tonight to celebrate putting all these applications in."

"How long you think it's going to be before people start calling us back?" asked Joshua.

"Uncle Paul said by the end of next week. Dunny said two. He say Wal-Mart always needing people—we know the boat need people—so even if the grocery stores or Burger King'n'em don't call us back, at least we know we have two pretty good chances, right? Uncle Paul say to wait to go down to the shipyard where they build the barges…say we probably got better chances here and the other places first, cause most people they hire down there know a trade like welding or something." Christophe passed the blunt.

Joshua hit it twice, and stared out the window. His tongue felt rough, serrated: his taste buds slid against the roof of his palate as sharp and crusty as barnacles. His mouth was dry with the taste of the weed. It was the one thing he didn't like about smoking—weedmouth. He wanted more to drink than that Coke; he wanted more than the trickle in the bottom of the can. Then he remembered where they were, and why they were here, and why he'd have to swallow more spit. He attempted to work some up in the back of his throat. It had the texture of cobwebs.

"We need to start working soon. I got the feeling from Ma-mee that Cille's done with sending us money," Joshua said. His tongue seemed twice its normal size. "When you was in the shower, Ma-mee said something like Cille figure we grown and she must not feel responsible for us no more." Joshua didn't add that Ma-mee had snorted when she said it, that there had been an unspoken "as if she was ever responsible for you" tacked on the end that had floated in the air between them and landed in front of Joshua in his half–eaten plate of eggs.

Christophe sucked at the blunt and then ground it out in the ashtray.

Christophe patted his pockets and muttered. "Where the hell is my Clear Eyes?" He found it, and tipped his head back, easing it into the corner of his lids. "Shit, I could've told you that." He threw the small opaque plastic bottle into Joshua's lap. "Even though she said it, you had to know it anyway."

Joshua didn't answer. He was glad he didn't smoke that often: while he felt buoyed by water, streams of feeling licking his limbs, for Christophe, who had smoked longer and more than he had, smoking a blunt was almost like smoking a cigarette. Joshua applied the Visine and dropped it on the seat between them, and if possible, sank further down into the upholstery. He didn't want to think about Cille like that, think that she could just pass them off like a job she'd completed. Even though she hadn't come to their graduation, she had given them the car: surely she'd still be in their lives some sort of way. The skin of his throat pulled as he leaned his head on the door and glanced at the time on the dashboard. It was 11:45. Christophe pulled out the bottle of Febreze from under his seat and began spraying himself and Joshua with it. Joshua closed his eyes and let him spray; he turned into the door, baring his back to his brother so that he sprayed that as well. Joshua settled back and closed his eyes. He felt as if he was floating, and by concentrating on the sensation, he was able to let Cille slip from his mind. There was a river of static behind his eyeballs. He sighed, and felt her visage and her voice peeling and falling away from his brain like a loose flower petal.

Christophe led the way across the pier to the office as Joshua followed. He danced across the concrete, weaving through the working men, who were faceless in the sun's glare. Under the hot, salty wind, Joshua smelled Febreze. He blew out his breath and smelled weed. In the office, the floor was lined with faded dirty white and gray tile, and fluorescent lights shone in long, bright rows from the ceiling and cast everything in glassy yellow. As he stepped up behind Christophe at the counter and flanked his brother, Joshua thought about holding his breath. Christophe was leaning into the counter. The clerk wore wide, red plastic-rimmed glasses that covered half her face, and lipstick that matched her frames. Her short hair had been hairsprayed into a gray-blonde mane. Joshua saw that the lipstick had bled into the tiny creases at the corner of her mouth; her pale face seemed to be leaching away the color from her lips. Joshua knew she could smell the weed on Christophe, who had one elbow on the counter in a nonchalant assertion.

"May I help you." It was not a question; it was a statement. Her mouth cracked and Joshua thought he saw a flash of teeth. It almost seemed dirty.

"We came to fill out applications. Two, please."

Christophe smiled at Joshua, seemingly pleased with himself for the confidence in the declaration. Joshua let out a breath and immediately regretted it. The woman slid two blurry sheets of white paper across the counter. Christophe grabbed an application and pulled it across the table towards him as the woman dropped two pencils on the counter and pointed them to a row of chairs across the room against the wall. Christophe smiled at the woman and walked away. Joshua slid the paper across the cold countertop. The woman was watching him. He smiled at her through his haze, grabbed the pen, turned away, and exhaled. He was moving too slowly: every step took hours. Sweat ran from his hairline, and he shivered; he felt cold. When he sat on the chair next to his brother, he realized he had almost forgotten what he was here for.

Christophe was writing purposefully, quickly; his usually messy scrawl scrawled across the paper in tightly wound lines. Christophe looked up from his work and elbowed Joshua: Christophe jabbed the pencil toward his brother and made a motion Joshua assumed Christophe thought mimicked writing. To Joshua, it looked like his brother was carving something in the air; he held the pencil like a knife. Joshua began writing. The weed was churning him up inside; it was twisting him like a wet rag, wringing sweat from him. He filled out the answers he'd memorized. He plucked them formed whole from his head, and placed them slowly and succinctly on the paper. Christophe lounged next to him with his paper in his hand, and Joshua saw that he was kneading the corner between his thumb and forefinger as he leaned back in his seat and grinned to himself.

Joshua stared at his paper, determined that it was done, and grabbed his brother's from his hand and rose quickly. They walked back to the counter side by side. The woman was at her desk, staring at a black and green computer screen. She didn't move from her seat. Joshua placed the applications on the table as he blinked against the fuzziness in his eyes: his eyeballs seemed to have grown hair. Christophe set the pencil down beside him and called out, "Thank you" to the woman. The blonde head nodded at the screen. Christophe stopped in the blinding noise and sunlight of the dock and waited for his brother. Joshua was silent; he felt as if Christophe were pulling him along in a fine green fishing net through the throngs of men, the leaning machines, and the crates.

"I'm hungry," Christophe said at the car. "I wish we had a whole nother blunt," he mumbled as he backed the car out of the parking space.

Joshua waved his fingers in front of his brother's face; he was trying to draw patterns from the air. Christophe stared, and pressed the brakes. His eyelids fluttered open wide as Joshua grinned. Christophe laughed and slapped Joshua's hand away.

"Stop it," said Christophe as he put the car in drive.

Joshua turned on the radio. A blues singer's voice limped through the air between them. Christophe shrugged and said, "Leave it on." Joshua laid his head back against the headrest and stared at the gray blue water, at the shrimp boats buoyed like pelicans, their nets flared like wings. The car sailed across the barren, black sea of the parking lot away from the commotion of the pier. Christophe pointed with one finger toward the windshield, toward the west: homeward.

3

DURING THE NEXT FOUR WEEKS, MA-MEE ORBITED THE PHONE LIKE a moon. It was a rotary dial plastic blue phone; what she could see of it was a vague blur the pale color of boy's baby clothes. The boys went off to play basketball or lounged in their room listening to the stereo and reading old, faded issues of *Sports Illustrated* and *Low Rider* magazine or cut the grass or dozed on the couch or on the carpet before the box fan. Ma-mee sat in the easy chair next to the side table with the telephone on it and listened to the TV with the volume on low. The twins called places to follow up, and every manager or employee told them that they would call them back. Ma-mee took to picking up the receiver surreptitiously throughout the day, listening for the dial tone to assure herself that the damn thing was still working, that it hadn't short-circuited or malfunctioned during the night.

Joshua slipped money into Ma-mee's purse when they went shopping with Uncle Paul for groceries, and splurged on forties of King Cobra at $1.50 a bottle once a weekend. He tried not to spend much, but the money still disappeared from the small stash he kept hidden in a shoebox in the top of their closet. Cille called once when the twins weren't home and talked to Ma-mee for only a minute because there were customers in the store. Cille had told Ma-mee to tell the twins she said hello, and that she was planning on taking a trip down to Mississippi to see them toward the end of the summer when she got a little vacation time. Joshua had hated to admit that something in his chest eased when he heard Ma-mee tell him that. Something had opened behind his ribs and he'd felt wistful, sitting at the kitchen table with the light bulb burning, the radio playing old R&B, Luther Vandross crooning from the windowsill of the open window, greens on the table and the sun setting outside. He hadn't said anything in return, had kept the surge of emotion in his chest quiet, but Christophe had grunted and shrugged out, "That's cool," before shoveling another forkful of seasoned, steaming greens and rice from his plate into his mouth.

Bills were due. He knew Aunt Rita collected all the bills and paid them with money from Ma-mee's Social Security and disability checks and Cille's Western Union money orders that she deposited in Ma-mee's account every month. Without Cille's help, they would come up short this month, or barely scrape by. He figured that Uncle Paul or Aunt Rita would give them more money if they needed it—but something in him balked at the idea. He watched Ma-mee hover over the phone and check it when she thought he wasn't looking, and every day that it didn't ring with a call about a job, worry tightened his head like a vise. He knew Christophe had more money than he did saved up in his own secret stash (on the floor under his bottom dresser drawer), but he also knew that while he grew quiet and tight with dread and frustration over their unemployment, Christophe reacted by getting angry, by refusing to limit his spending. It was almost as if he believed that if he spent like he had money, if he acted like he didn't have to worry about money, then he'd have it: a job would inevitably make itself available. He refused to live like he was poor.

When he and Christophe lay in bed at night and Joshua attempted to talk about putting in applications at businesses that were four or five towns away, a forty-five minute or hour commute, he'd reply, "That's too far away from Ma-mee. We can't be that far away. What if something happen?" Joshua did notice that he stopped taking the car out riding as much, that he called Dunny more often to pick him up: gas cost money. Christophe went out to visit girls more, played ball at the park, and instead of paying to go inside, hung out in the parking lot at the one black nightclub in Germaine on Saturday nights. They revisited the places on their list, filled out more applications just in case the employees had lost the first ones. Joshua fidgeted around the house, washing clothes or sweeping or vacuuming or attempting to make red beans and rice and cornbread for dinner. While Joshua made the follow-up phone calls, Christophe harassed Uncle Paul and Eze, insisting that they needed to talk to somebody. None of it seemed to be working.

After four weeks of reality rolling over them like an opaque fog, Joshua sat on the front porch steps, his hair a wild brownish-red afro. He was picking it out for Laila, who'd agreed to braid it. Christophe had parked their car in the front yard alongside Dunny's: they were shirtless, leaning half-in Dunny's trunk, shifting his speakers around and adjusting the controls on the amplifier. Joshua had just washed his hair, but the water had already evaporated from it. It was tangled and dry and getting harder to comb through. A strong gust of wind cut through the leaves of the lone beech tree that grew in the front yard, and the leaves chattered over the call of the brush of the ubiquitous pines, the tinny rattle of bass from the trunk of Dunny's car. Were they taking speakers from Dunny's car and moving them to the Caprice? Inside, the phone rang. Ma-mee picked it up before the end of the first ring.

"Hello?"

Joshua peeled his T-shirt away from his stomach and closed his eyes, straining to hear Ma-mee's voice.

"What's up, Laila?" Dunny drawled.

"Hey Dunny. Hey Chris. Where your brother at?"

From inside the house, Joshua heard Ma-mee answer, "Yes."

"He over there on the porch steps, waiting for you. Why don't you do my hair after you do his?"

"You gonna have to pay me something for that. Five dollars at least." Laila laughed.

"Aaaw, that's messed up. Is he paying you?"

"Hey, if I'm going to be here for three hours doing hair, one of y'all got to pay me something. You asked second, so it's going to have to be you."

"You just think Joshua cute—playing favorites and shit." Joshua could tell Dunny was speaking around the tip of his black, could hear the clench of his lips as he spoke.

Laila giggled, and through the wind, Joshua felt the sun slashing across the skin of his legs, making them burn. Inside the house, Ma-mee asked, "You sure you don't have another DeLisle on that list?" He opened his eyes to see Laila leaning against Dunny's car, punching him in the bicep and smiling, and Christophe placing two ten-inch speakers and an amp in the trunk of the Caprice. There was a fine red dust in the air. Joshua followed Ma-mee's voice into the living room to see her breathe, "Alright then. Thank you." She hung up the phone and stared in his general direction. Her eyes were trained somewhere in the middle of his chest. Her housedress was a pale yellow, the color of the light shining through the pine needles and cones outside. He stopped just inside the door.

"Who was that?" Joshua asked.

She gripped her forearm so that her arms crossed her lap. She smiled, let it slide away, and looked across the living room in the direction of the porch and the front yard.

"Man from the Dockyard. Say he want you to come in Monday at ten for an interview." Ma-mee pulled at the neck of her dress.

"What about Chris?" The bass thumped through the door behind Joshua.

"They didn't say nothing about Chris." She looked away from the door toward the silent TV. "They just want you." She ran her hands over the lap of her thighs, and then let her palms fall open at her sides, facing upward, facing him. "Somebody else'll call for Chris. Or maybe they just want you to start first." She paused. "I don't know."

Behind him, Joshua heard the door open and close. Christophe's face was dark in the shadowed room, his eyebrows a taut line across his forehead.

"Who going to call for Chris?"

Ma-mee opened her mouth as if to reply, but said nothing. Joshua thought that her forehead was wrinkled and her lips drawn up in a way that made her look like she was about to cry. His arms felt heavy and long and apelike at his sides.

"Man from the docks just called." Here Joshua's voice thinned, and he had to expel the rest of it like a cough from his throat. "Said he wanted me to come in next Wednesday for a interview, but—he didn't say nothing about you."

"Oh."

The tips of Christophe's fingers were pinched and burning from cutting the wires, from twining them one about the other to gather the sound, to harness the music and amplify it in the speakers. Installing the equipment was like guessing at a combination lock, feeling for the correct number of turns and stops, for hidden numbers. He'd spent the last big chunk of his money on that. Underneath his dresser drawer, he had two twenties, a five, and five ones. Fifty dollars. He'd bought the speakers, CD player, and amp from Marquise through Dunny, who was selling his system because he was getting a new one. He'd thought it too good a deal to pass by. He felt duped, standing there, the sun beating at the windows of the shadowed room, all of it dark and quiet, the atmosphere of it seeming to wait on something. Stupid thing to say, oh. He turned toward the door, away from the dim-lit expectant silence of the room, from their searching eyes. He thought of an insect tearing itself from a web with the help of the wind.

"Okay then." Christophe pushed the screen door that opened to the porch. "I got work to do," he said. It slammed behind him. The floorboards of the porch, uneven and swollen in the heat, snagged his feet. Dunny was in the trunk again.

"Joshua in the house?" Laila asked.

Christophe loped past her. The brightness of the sun, the sky, the red dirt of the driveway, the flowering fuchsia and green of the azalea bushes was blinding after the inside of the house. He slammed into the side of the trunk of the Caprice and leaned over Dunny, his forearms braced on the warm metal. Why was it parked? It wasn't enough for him. He needed motion: he needed to move.

"Leave it."

"What the fuck you talking about leave it? We almost done, young'un."

"Man, I don't feel like working on it right now. We can work on it later. You got a cigar?"

Dunny stood straight, his white T-shirt brown across the stomach where he had been leaning on the car, his braids tight and clean over the curve of his skull. Christophe glanced at him and looked away. He realized his leg was kicking by itself at the tire, rousing red dust in clouds across his worn white Reeboks.

"Let's ride," Christophe said.

"What's wrong with you?"

The hurt and love and jealousy in Christophe's chest coalesced and turned to annoyance that bubbled from his throat.

"Shit, ain't nothing wrong with me." Christophe heard this come from him in a hiss. "I don't want to talk about it right now. Can we just go?"

Dunny closed the trunk. The metal sounded hard and loud, as harsh as the burning sun, when it clattered shut. Dunny pulled a black from behind his ear, a lighter from his pocket.

"You need a smoke." This trailed behind him as he ambled toward his car. Christophe beat him it, jumped through the window, and slid into the passenger seat, Dukes of Hazzard style. Sometimes the passenger door jammed and stuck when he tried to open it. He didn't feel like jiggling the handle for a good three minutes. Dunny leisurely pulled his own door shut.

"Don't be putting your feet on my seat when you jump in the car." Dunny lit the black and handed it to Christophe.

"Fuck you."

Dunny laughed, and the car growled to life. The stereo intoned. The music shook the air; it squeezed Christophe's throat. Christophe saw Laila, her shirt pulled tight against her chest, her hand on the front porch screen door, watching them leave. He pulled on the black, the tip of the filter hot and malleable between his lips, and felt a cool tingling coat the simmer in his chest and begin to eat away at it in small bites. He blew out the smoke, and inhaled deeply on the second toke. As they turned from the red dirt driveway to the rough gravel of the street, he draped his arm out the window and tapped the ash away. Three small brown children with overlarge heads and bony knees were in the ditch as they passed, picking blackberries and dropping them carefully in large white plastic ice cream buckets. Cece, Dizzy, and Little Man. They jumped when the bass dropped in quick succession like a trickle of pebbles turned to an avalanche. The smallest and skinniest one, his belly showing through the front of his red jumpsuit with the curve of a kickball, dropped his bucket. When Christophe passed, he could see gnats in small glinting bronze clouds around their heads, illuminating their bulbous skulls like halos. Christophe saluted them with his pointer finger, and leaned back into the seat as Dunny accelerated.

They rode until the sun set, until it slipped between the chattering branches of the trees and painted a broad sweep of the sky in the west pink and red, until the heat wasn't so oppressive in the car. When Christophe got out at a gas station in Germaine to grab another cigar, he could feel the heat rising from the concrete of the lot. The streetlight over the gas pumps had attracted great swarming gangs of large black flying insects that were intent on racing each other into the bulb and dying. They met their deaths with loud pops. Christophe bought the cigar and was glad to get back in the car, to ride away from the buzzing lights, the streetlamps, the lonely, dusty gas station and the red-faced forlorn attendant, to drive along the highway on the beach, to cruise along the coastline.

Solitary, sparse stands of pine trees dotted the sandy median as they rode along. The moon was full and white in the black, nearly starless sky. As they turned from the beach and rode through St. Catherine to the bayou and neared Bois Sauvage, Dunny seemed to tire of the music. He pushed a button, and the lights on the stereo went off: the music stopped. Dunny hadn't asked Christophe about his sudden change in mood, his need to run away. Once they'd left Bois Sauvage, he'd simply pulled a sack from his pocket, and told Christophe to look in the glove compartment for a cigar and roll up. The marsh grass was a pale, silvery green as it whipped by outside the window. Here, the night sounds of the insects chattering one to another like an angry congress were loudest. The pine trees were inky black and lined the horizon, and the water was a dark blue, the reflection of the moon shimmering like a white stone path on its surface. Christophe thought it beautiful. He squinted against the salty marsh wind and saw that Dunny was focused on the road, his eyes half-lidded. Christophe took a long pull of the last of the last blunt, and handed the roach to his cousin. He was glad he wouldn't have to explain himself.

In Bois Sauvage, Dunny rode down the middle of the pockmarked streets, steered away from the edges of the narrow, ancient roads where the asphalt crumbled into pebbles that mixed in with the red dirt, the thick summer grass, and slid down into the ditches. The oaks reached out with tangled arms to form a tunnel over the car. In the yards of the few houses they passed, people, small shadows, sat on their porches or their steps drinking beer from cans, fanning themselves with fly swatters, burning small cans of citronella, and eyeing the patches of piney woods suspiciously, muttering about the descending summer heat, mosquitoes, and West Nile, which they'd heard about on the news.

Christophe watched the tree line, smiling faintly when he realized he could tell where he was going in Bois Sauvage by the tops of the trees, that he recognized the big oak at the corner of Cuevas and Pelage, and that the dense stand of pines on his right indicated that they were in the middle of St. Salvador St.: he and Joshua had played chase under those trees when they were little. Dunny and Javon were always team captains, and they would always pick the same teams: the twins and Marquise, all small and squirrelly, for Dunny, and Big Henry, Bone, and Skeetah for Javon. The smaller team invariably beat the larger team. Christophe and Joshua would always skip past Marquise and Dunny to hide together deep in the woods while the other team was counting loudly on the street. Christophe was the fastest, so he led Joshua in a general direction, but Joshua always had the better eye for hiding spots: he would bury them underneath a hill of dry brown pine needles or in the heart of a full green bush with dark leaves the size of their fingernails or in the top of a small oak tree, silent and perching like crows.

The other team seldom caught them. Dunny would give up and walk out into the open, into the dim light of the forest and give himself away, mostly because he was hungry or tired or had to go to the bathroom. Marquise would follow him, tagging along for food. Joshua and Christophe would stay hidden for hours, giggling breathlessly as Javon or Big Henry crashed through the underbrush beneath them, calling their names loudly and threatening forfeit and talking shit. Their members would drift away, complaining: Big Henry insisting he had chores to do, Bone yelling he had dinner to eat, and Javon spitting that he had TV to watch. Christophe and Joshua would stay where they were until there were no other human sounds around them, sometimes until the sun was setting, and then they'd run out to the empty street, hopping in delirium, drunk with their cleverness, wrestling each other down the length of the road. Christophe let his eyes close and his head loll back onto the headrest, and felt the car stop.

Dunny had taken him to the basketball court. What he could see of the grass in the court lights was long and bunched in tufts, overgrown with weeds. The iron barrels they used as garbage cans were rusting along the rims. Nobody had bothered to line them with black garbage bags since the last time they'd been emptied. The small, warped stand of white wooden bleachers was empty, the swings silent, the small wooden play set the county recreation board had commissioned without playmates. Dunny switched off the ignition, opened his car door, and said, "Get that ball from under the backseat." Christophe willed his arms and torso to move, grabbed the ball and threw it at Dunny, who ran to the court with it and made a sloppy, easy lay up. He dribbled the ball, half-walking and skipping back and forth on the concrete, shooting jumpers. Christophe watched Dunny on the court. When had he become the one who followed one step behind, the one who eyed and followed the other's back, the one who was led?

Now, he would have to find his way alone. He lurched toward the court that shone like a snow globe: the pale gray concrete spray painted with blue gang signs, the halo of the fluorescent lights that cast the scene in a glass sphere, and all those damn bugs circling and falling like black snow. He shuffled through the grass at a slow run and the long, blooming strands bit into his knees, etched fine stinging lines into the skin of his shins. By the time he reached the court, the high was pulsing through his head, his arms, and his legs with the beating call of the night insects: in and out, up and down, over and under and through. Dunny threw the ball at him, and he fumbled to catch it, his hands clumsy. He dribbled the ball through his leg; it glanced against his calf.

"You sure you can handle that?" Dunny asked. He stood with his hands on his waist underneath the goal. Sweat glazed his face.

"Nigga, I know you ain't asking me if I can handle a damn ball. I'll show you some ball handling, fat boy."

Christophe dribbled the ball again, bouncing it with his fingertips. Something about his handling was off. It felt like he was dribbling on rocks; the ball was ricocheting everywhere.

"What the hell are you trying to do to the ball? Dribble it or flatten it?" Dunny loped toward Christophe and raised one arm in defense. His fingers grazed Christophe's chest.

"Why are you locking your knees? Damn, Dunny, you think I'm that easy?" Christophe bounced the ball through his legs again. It cleared his thigh this time, clean and easy. He caught it, wobbled, and smiled. "Just needed to warm up, that's all."

"You been hitting the bottle in the car? You got a thirty-two ounce hid under the passenger seat?"

"I ain't drank shit and I'm about to school your ass."

"Chris, I was dunking on niggas when you was still pissing the bed."

"I ain't never pissed in the bed, bitch."

Christophe faked to his right, then jerked to his left, leaned back, and bought his legs together. He crouched and shot a fade away. He felt the ball roll from his wrist, across his palm, up the spine of his middle finger and away toward the basket. The release was good, but the shot flew wide. It hit the corner of the backboard, bounced off the edge of the rim, and arced back toward the court. Dunny snatched the rebound. Christophe grimaced.

Dunny hugged the ball to his chest, breathing hard. Christophe eyed his mouth, the pouch of fat and skin quivering under his neck. Dunny'd been good in high school: he'd had a flawless jumper, and he was the go-to man for defense on the inside. Christophe had gone to every one of his home games. Dunny had teased him mercilessly, grilled him, when he'd begun to play seriously in seventh grade. Dunny had sweated with Christophe on the court, had been an indomitable brick wall, and had yelled at him for hours. He was small, so according to Dunny, he should've been quicker, handled the ball better, and had a nastier jumper. He'd made Christophe so mad he'd wanted to cry, several times, but instead of crying, Christophe had flared his nostrils, rasped through the pain in his chest, and kept playing. He'd skirted and darted and struck at Dunny like a small, irascible dog. He'd gotten better.

Christophe remembered that Joshua had mimicked Dunny, had wrestled with his cousin chest to chest under the goal. He had learned to be the big man on the inside to Christophe's squirrelly point guard. By the twins' senior year, they were unstoppable. They spoke in a secret language on the court, communicated with their shoulders, their eyes, smirks and smiles. Christophe could tell whether Joshua wanted him to pass the ball to him into the inside for an easy lay-up by the set of his mouth. It was effortless, invigorating. They never smoked after a game: there was no reason to; they were already high.

Now Christophe looked at his cousin and felt something like hands behind his sternum constricting. Dunny had softened and spread like a watercolor since he'd graduated five years ago. Beer and weed had blunted his edges. The old Dunny would've shook him, spun, made the shot, and taunted him. This Dunny clutched the ball to his middle as if he were injured, as if the ball was staunching a flow of blood from his stomach. Even the blink of his eyes was slurred. Christophe lunged at his cousin and swatted the ball with the flat of his palm so hard it echoed through his fingers with the stinging burn of slapped water. The ball slipped away from Dunny, and his hands met in prayer before his chest. Christophe began to dribble back and forth between his legs. He meant it to be hard and sure. He wanted the impact of the ball on the court to sound like gunshots, for the ball to slice its way through the air into his hand, but it didn't. It meandered; it strayed. There was a line of tension pulled taut in his shoulders, and no matter how carefully he followed the old lessons of Dunny's phantom, he could not loosen it.

"You're palming the ball."

"Shut up, Dunny."

"You're supposed to finger it," Dunny said.

Christophe lurched to his right and snapped the ball, faking at Dunny with it. Dunny cringed. Christophe felt something in his knee stab at him with a quick, piercing pain.

"Who said I needed lessons from you?" Christophe crouched and shot. The ball rang the rim like a bell and fell away. Dunny caught it.

"Your sloppy playing did, that's who." Dunny grinned and shoved one large, meaty shoulder into Christophe's chest. He shot a fade away. It grazed the rim and escaped the capsule of light surrounding the court.

"You lost it….now go get it."

"It's your ball, Chris."

"No it ain't, Dunny. If I go get this mothafucka, you're not getting it back. I'm going to make you eat it."

Dunny breathed wetly. He shuffled into the darkness and reappeared with the ball. The night and the insects and the foliage flickered in and out of being like a fractured film. Christophe knew he'd smoked too much.

"I think you forgot who your Daddy was."

Dunny shoved Christophe hard with his shoulder as he dribbled. Christophe stole the ball and pulled away to shoot. He felt the skin of his face, his ears, and his neck burn hot. He narrowed his eye at Dunny's flaccid throat, his profuse sweating, his labored breathing, and spat his reply.

"I don't have a daddy!"

The ball sailed through the air and dropped neatly into the basket, caressing the line of the net as it fell. Christophe snorted, blew his breath from his chest in one quick huff and barely resisted adding a curt, "Bitch," to his declaration. His anger buoyed him, burned him clean and left his mind and body unfettered by the high. He was a simple working equation of mind and muscle blessed with a clean shot. For a second, he felt right. He let Dunny get the rebound.

"So, what was wrong with you today?" Dunny's dribbling echoed in Christophe's ears like a ponderous heartbeat.

"I don't want to talk about it." Christophe dug his fingers into his hipbones.

"It's about a job, ain't it? Joshua got called back for something and you didn't. You had to know there was a chance that would happen."

"Whatever." Christophe watched the ball shoot from Dunny's grip, meet the asphalt, and rush back to his grip once, twice. Dunny's fingertips seemed to suction the ball back, to kiss it. Dunny'd been right about that at least: his ball handling skills were almost perfect.

"Let it go, Chris."

"What you know about it, Dunny? You got a job. You got a hustle. You got a mama and a step-daddy to help you out."

Dunny stopped dribbling. He gripped the ball casually in one hand and rested it in the cradle of his hip.

"And you should know, asshole, that you got support too." Dunny rolled the ball against his belly, and then stopped. "You got your brother, you got Ma-mee, you got all our aunts and uncles, and most important, you got me."

Christophe swiped a bug away from his ear with his hand; it stung his palm. He eyed his cousin's puffy face, his half-lidded eyes.

"What the fuck that's supposed to mean?"

"You actually think I'm going to let you starve out here?"

Christophe watched Dunny's stillness and knew it for what it was: a gathering of energy and anger. He was pissed. Christophe had watched him fight several people, knock them to their hands and knees, force them to eat dirt with long, sure punches that had the force of machinery in them. Dunny'd fought often in his teenage years over money, perceived slights, subtle insults. His was a deceptive calm. Christophe stared blankly through his anger, his unsettled bewilderment, and watched Dunny's mouth move.

"You really think I'm going to let your dumb, ungrateful ass struggle out here when I can put you on to my hustle? When I can front you a quarter pound of weed and have you out here doubling your money?" Dunny stepped closer to Christophe. His eyes were slits, fringed dashes in the set canvas of his face. Dunny barely opened his mouth. The whites of his eyes and the pearl of his teeth were invisible in the dark. "What kind of a cousin do you think I am?"

Dunny wouldn't hit him. The only time he'd ever hit him was when they wrestled, and then they were always playing. Suddenly Christophe remembered the muscle beneath the meat: fat people were really strong. He guessed it was because they had more to move around. Christophe waved about in his hazy brain for an answer; he hadn't considered this. He'd always been somewhat single-minded. He'd grown up picturing his life in his head, plotting it as he went along: he'd made the basketball team in ninth grade, lost his virginity in tenth grade, led the team to all conference his junior year, successfully juggled several girls at one time throughout his high school career and never had any of them fight one another or discover his manipulations, and he'd finally graduated. There was a pattern, an order to his life. He dreamed things, worked for them, and they happened. He'd assumed this would continue after he graduated, that there existed steps to his life: a job at the dockyard or the shipyard where he could learn a trade, pay raises, stacking money, refurbishing Ma-mee's house, a girlfriend, a kid, and possibly, a wife one day. The idea of a legitimate job had existed as an absolute in his head. It was the fulcrum upon which the bar of his dreams balanced.

Christophe had dismissed dealing because he saw where it led: a brief, brilliant blaze of glory where most drug dealers bought cars, the bar at the club, women, paid bills for their mamas, and if they were really lucky, houses. That lasted around two years. Then the inevitable occurred. The coast was too small for anyone to remain anonymous for long. The county police hounded the local dealers, who depended on bigger dealers in Houston, Atlanta, and New Orleans for their cocaine. The cops saw the local dealers at the park, in the neighborhood, making runs for dope, put two and two together, and that was it. The dealers fell, then. They were running, hiding, haunted. They scraped together large sums of money and tried to put them away to support their families and their girlfriends and their kids and instead found themselves using the money to post bail, because the police picked most boys up three times a year, if not more. For most drug dealers, jail and hustling became a job and going home became a vacation. One or two weeks out, and they were back in again for violating probation for smoking a little weed, like Fresh.

He'd forgotten how several drug dealers Dunny's age looked. When Christophe saw their faces on their brief respite from jail, half the time he didn't recognize them, and the rest of the time, he was always amazed at how old they appeared. Those were the lucky ones. Others became addicts themselves, or died. He thought of Cookie from St. Catherine, who earned his nickname because as a dealer he had moved big weight, and never had less than a few cookies on him at a time. He had earned his name twice. Now, as a junkie, he begged dealers, his former comrades, for crumbs. He stood on the same corner in St. Catherine, everyday in the same worn blue jeans and denim shirt, which he called his suit, and stared at the cars that passed, never waving, in the evenings. An image of Sandman as he'd last seen him, drunk, his eyes blanched wide from his high, almost falling from the pickup truck. Christophe waved his hand.

Dunny was small-time: Dunny had done the smart thing. He held a steady job and only dabbled in selling weed—no crack or coke, and especially no meth or X to the white people living further out and upcountry.

"I ain't never really wanted to do that, Dunny."

"What you mean you ain't never wanted to do that?" Dunny ducked his head to catch Christophe's gaze.

"I wanted to get a job…work up…make some good money."

"Where did you think you was going to work, Chris? Doing what?"

"I don't know…the pier or the shipyard or something…."

"Nigga, it ain't never that easy. Everybody and they mama want a job at the pier and the shipyard. Everybody want a job down there can't get one."

"I could work somewhere else."

"Wal-Mart? Do you know what niggas start out making at Wal-Mart? Six-fifty an hour, Chris. Six dollars and fifty fucking cents. Gas is almost two dollars a gallon. Even working forty hour weeks and without rent to pay, how far you think that's going to get you?"

"Uncle Paul and Eze did it." Christophe looked away from his cousin, studied the sandy asphalt court. He shook his head no. He didn't know what he was saying no to, but he did it anyway.

"It ain't saying you can't do it. I'm just saying it's hard."

The fluorescent lights blinked. Once, twice. Christophe knew from experience what would happen next. The lights flashed bright and died. Their incessant neon buzzing sizzled away. The ringing chorus of the night bugs displaced it, smoothed it over, and submerged it as if it had never been. A droning filled Christophe's head, and the park was suffused with a calm, stately darkness. There were no streetlights in the country. Dunny's face disappeared. His white shirt glowed blue, and Christophe was suddenly aware of the stars, sparkling full to bursting in the sky above his head.

"I got to try," Christophe said.

Dunny's voiced snaked its way into his ear, wound its way around him with possibility.

"Well, think about it, Chris. If you decide that this is something you want to do, let me know. I can front you a QP. You can pay me back after you get on your feet."

Dunny's voice dropped. "If you buy more from me with your profit, and then sell all that, you'll double your money. Easy."

Christophe rubbed his hair, laced his fingers together, and locked them behind his neck before dropping them.

"I don't know, Dunny."

"Just think about it. You don't have to do anything you don't want to do in the end. You could find a way to make it. A broke way, but a way." Dunny's voice in the dark was suddenly soft, clean of anger and tinged with a wistfulness that surprised Christophe. "You could be lucky."

Dunny brushed past Christophe and walked with a tired gait to the car. The faint white glow of Dunny's shirt was like a beacon. Christophe felt his way along the hood. His fingers traced the grill as he rounded his side and climbed in, careful to hold his body upright with his arms braced so that he eased his torso into the seat; his sneakers brushed it.

"I hate when you do that."

Dunny lit a black and put the car in reverse. In the sudden flare of light from the lighter, Christophe saw Dunny's fatigue again: his eyelids looked swollen, and his mouth around the pale plastic tip of the cigarillo was slack. Christophe could hear the tires spew dirt and pebbles from the dirt parking space into the street. Dunny gunned the engine. The motor roared and they shot forward, passing through the weak, pale light of the wide-set yellow streetlamps some people had erected in their yards along the road. Christophe broke the textured, cricket-laden, tree-rustled silence with a timid request.

"Man, take me to your house."

Dunny nodded in reply and accelerated, passing the turn to Ma-mee's house. The weed had hit Christophe with a lethargic fist. He didn't want to face Joshua yet, and he knew his brother would be awake, lying with his eyes wide open in the darkness, staring at the ceiling, poised to talk, to conjecture, to confess.

Dunny led them in to the back door of the trailer. Christophe followed Dunny to the living room, where Dunny turned and offered him a short handshake. Christophe knew he would fall asleep on the sofa within minutes, but being away from his twin and Ma-mee, away from the familiar walls of his bedroom, would wake early in the morning with the first tentative infusion of sunlight into the living room, and would probably walk home. Christophe sat down, slumped sideways as his cousin disappeared to his room, and stared absentmindedly at the blinking red light of the VCR. It was the only moving thing in the room. He cradled his face with his palm and fell asleep.

Christophe snapped awake suddenly and could not remember the sound that woke him, but knew that some noise had. He pushed himself up and ground the heels of his palms into his eyes so that he could see the small digital clock on the VCR. It read 3:46. Christophe's skin slid back and forth and stretched pleasantly and eased the itch: his eyes burned. The bathroom light shone out into the hallway. The rest of the house lapsed into darkness. He looked toward his cousin's room, eyed his aunt's: nothing stirred. Christophe tiptoed toward the back door. On his way past the refrigerator, he saw a small note: Joshua called. He twisted the lock on the knob, stepped out onto the back deck, tried to ease the squeaking of the hinges by pushing the door shut in centimeters, and closed the door behind him.

From the wood next to the house, Dunny's dog barked loud, warning, staccato barks. Christophe felt buffeted by the incessant cry of the cicadas in the trees around him. He followed the road in the dark by feeling his way with his feet: one foot in the grass, another on the asphalt. Small animals rustled in the thick grass and blackberry briars that choked the ditch. It was hot enough for snakes. The landscape was drowned in black ink: he tried to peer into the darkness, to catch irregular sounds. He'd forgotten to pick up a stick. Few people kept their dogs on leashes or had fences, and every time he broke into the light after passing a stand of woods and saw a small sunken house or a rusting trailer, he'd tense up and listen for barks and growling, for sudden rushes of angry animal and fur. He could not find a stick in the dark.

Perhaps tomorrow someone would call. He'd go to the shipyard anyway and drop off an application during Joshua's interview. He repeated this to himself over and over, as he walked along. Fireflies burst into light and left neon-green trails behind them as they flitted along in the dense, dark air. They were like the ideas in his head, flaring and failing. Could he sell? Did he want to? How could he do that out of Ma-mee's house?

What the hell would he say to Joshua? A quick anger, a violent flash of hurt burned in his throat, and then dissipated. He glanced briefly up at the sky and saw that it was scudded with clouds. He was too tired to be angry. He'd deal with the sore jealousy he felt toward his brother, the sticky love, and the sense of shame and protective responsibility he felt when he thought of Ma-mee, tomorrow. He wanted her to be proud of him, not stumble across his weed one day while she was putting clean socks in his underwear drawer. He didn't know if he could face her if it came to that.

Something large rustled in the ditch to his right. He surprised himself by hopping to the left. Fear showered in sparks through his chest. In the dark, he stopped abruptly, his hands flexing into tight fists, his palms seeming suddenly empty. The fear surprised him. It was the kind of fear he hadn't felt since he'd been younger, since he'd stayed out playing in the woods with his brother after the sun set, after the street lights came on, and the black tree limbs suddenly seemed like fingers and he'd panicked at the irrational, instinctual feeling that something was closing in on him. After that first time in the woods, he'd sometimes get the same feeling when he was walking home, or when he was taking a shower by himself and his eyes were closed and he was washing his hair. Vaguely, a part of him associated the advent of this feeling with his own conscious comprehension of the power of the dark, of what it could hold and hide: possums, armadillos, snakes, spiders, dogs, and men.

Christophe hadn't felt this panic in years. The urge to run on and on down the asphalt and not stop running until he reached his house made it impossible for him to think. The thought was like a siren, a light circling and flashing over and over again in his head. He listened for the rustle again and heard nothing. He struggled to walk, but he broke into a trot anyway, and ran until he reached the next circle of light emitted from a small, wooden porch on a sagging house. He searched the lip of the yard and found a small stick that was only as long as his forearm and light. The sides of it were marked with small, velvety spots of fungus. It was hollow. Christophe gripped it hard and made himself stand still in the small bud of light that shone on the street. He made himself remain until he remembered where he was and what he was doing. He was eighteen and he was walking home in the dark and his house was only about a half a mile down and he'd lived here all his life and there was nothing in those woods that could hurt him—nothing. He just needed to breathe and calm down. He stood there until the fear ebbed. Then he set out into the darkness, dove into it like it was water.

Christophe walked quickly. The fear kept surging back for him. Someone was on the verge of grabbing him. His shoulders itched. He swung the stick back and forth with his hand as he walked. He surprised himself with a high-pitched laugh. What the hell was he going to do with this stick? He was clutching the thing like a machete. He shook his head, tried to batten the fear down in his chest, and waved the stick like a wand. He flicked his wrist as if to throw it, but he didn't. His fingers wouldn't let it go. He thought to laugh again, but he didn't. He quickened his pace. Vale's house. The woods. Uncle Paul's house. The woods. The field where Johnny kept his old, broke down horse. It grazed, snorting softly, and pulled up bunches of grass. Christophe was surprised that he could hear the grass rip. The woods. Ma-mee's house. He leapt over the ditch and ran to the porch. By the time he reached the screen door, he was sprinting. He threw the stick down next to the steps and pulled open the door and rushed inside. The fear had slammed into him, had choked him the most at the moment his hand closed over the door handle. He locked the door shut behind him and hopped across the kitchen floor and through the living room on his toes. He tried not to hit the worst of the boards that creaked.

Their room door was open. He eased into the room, breathing hard. He shucked his pants and squinted into the darkness. His brother was asleep: his back was turned to Christophe's bed, his face to the wall. Christophe heard him breathing deeply and slowly. The alarm clock read 4:10. He cracked open a drawer and pulled out a pair of basketball shorts and put them on. He lay down in his bed on his back and stared at the ceiling as he pulled the sheet up to his chest. Only when the flat sheet slid coolly over his shins did the fear fully dissipate in his chest. It dissolved so quickly that he felt foolish lying there in his bed. Still he could not help himself from staring at the room, from laying on his side so that he faced the door. The light from the bathroom shone in the hallway and draped the doorway with a little weak half-moon. He blinked at it, half expecting a shadow to move across it and snuff it out, and fell asleep.

4

MA-MEE WOKE AROUND FIVE MINUTES BEFORE SHE FELT THE FIRST heated touch of sunlight on her bed. When Lucien had built the house, she had insisted he put their room on the side of the house facing east, alongside the kitchen. Back then, he had bought the land from the county government for a little bit of nothing. He'd saved up working carpentry and yard jobs for vacationing white families who owned beach homes, mansions really, on the shore. It was what Paul did now. Lucien had been a hard worker: he was frugal, so he'd saved from the time he was twelve. After he'd married Ma-mee, then known as Lillian, at eighteen, he'd bought eight acres of property up the road from his father in Bois Sauvage. It was enough to build a house on, to raise a couple of small feed and food crops for the family, and to keep a horse or two. His brothers and his father had helped him lay the foundation, raise the frame, piece by piece in slow, painful spurts: Ma-mee remembered eating beans and portioning out biscuits for months to save money as they bought the house board by board. She remembered craving green things, craving watermelons swollen red with water, and after the house was completed, she was almost pleased enough with the produce to not resent the hours of work: of weeding and watering, her back a shield against the sun.

When the house was done, it was small and had an uneven look to it, as if all those boards had been nailed together crooked, as if they resisted fitting together cleanly. In those days, Ma-mee had hated waking up early in the morning to a day of hard work, of housekeeping and planting and childrearing, but somehow it made it easier to do so when the sun crept its way across the bed early in the morning, and she could rise to look out the window through the thin white cotton curtains to see beams of it lacing their way through the rows of corn.

Ma-mee lay in the bed waiting for the rising heat to take form in the room and grab her by the leg. The ticking clock, the sound of the scrabbling chickens in the dilapidated coop in a corner of the yard, and the listing hum of insects saturated the room. The sound was like another body in the bed with her. She didn't seem to need sleep these days. When she woke, she was instantly awake and alert. She couldn't go to sleep before eleven and always woke up minutes before the rising sun entered the room. She'd taken such pleasure in sleeping when she was young that her inability to sleep tired her in an abstract way. It marked her as old, along with the diabetes, the partial blindness, the changes in the community around her. When she was younger, when Lucien had been alive and her children had been growing up, some of her uncles and brothers had been angry, unreasonable chronic drunks. She knew some of her kids smoked weed. But the crackheads and drugs that seemed to steal the sense from people, these were new. It made her feel weary and worn to sit on the porch and squint out at the small dark spots she could see passing back and forth on the street, a few lonely, solitary crackheads searching for dealers, cousins or neighbors' children that walked the road and looked to her like flies crawling across a screen.

She did not like the slow ache of all her movements. It bothered her that she often dreamt in a language that no one around her spoke any longer, that she woke still thinking in creole French, to a wide, lonely bed, an emptying house. Her boys could not understand this. She was afraid of the lethargic feeling that washed over her sometime that reminded her of floating in water. She'd feel it while sitting in the chair in front of the TV staring at the blobs of color and light as she listened to one of the boys describing a show for her, and it made her want to close her eyes, to blink slowly, and just stop moving. Later, when she'd lie in bed at night with her rosary in her hand before she went to sleep and fingered the plastic beads, the litany of our fathers and hail mary's, she'd absently think that it was death approaching. She thought of gathering Spanish moss with her mother as a young child to stuff their mattresses with and pausing to look up at the sky when she was in a patch of sunlight to realize that the sun was not blinking on and off, but rather, clouds were moving quickly through the sky. They were passing between her and the sun and impeding the light. This is what these fits of lethargy and utter exhaustion felt like to her: a shadow passing over her, a scuttling cloud obscuring her from the sun of life.

It was tentative, the first touch. It was no more than a tap, really, there on the left side of her calf. It stung a little through the sheet. The day would be hot like all the rest. She lay there for a minute, felt the touch spread, felt the stinging bear down on her leg, and pushed herself up and out of the bed. It was time to get up. Paul had bought a couple of pounds of shrimp to the house the night before. She wanted to clean and cook them before the worst heat of the day, before they began to turn to meal and stink like warm flesh and sea salt. She pulled on a gown, and didn't bother with socks or slippers. She'd rather go barefoot.

Even though she had memorized the contours of the house long ago through habit, it still comforted her to feel her way through the rooms with her feet, to know that the facets of the house existed as absolutes even though it all looked to her as if she had her eyes open underwater. When she noticed the blurriness the first time, that's what she had thought, that there was excess water in her eye: tears, maybe. Things like that happened to older people. When she awoke the next morning, it was still there: a watery film. She denied it, afraid. She prayed and waited until she woke up one morning and realized the edges had been washed out of everything. She was drowned. Ma-mee walked to the kitchen in a sliding shuffle: carpet, wood of the hallway, scratchy carpet of the living room, the uneven tile of the kitchen.

Ma-mee heard it: a body rising, someone awake, one of the boys moving around in their room. She placed the plastic bag of shrimp in the sink, plugged the drain, and turned on the water so the ice could melt, so the shrimp could defrost. Which boy was it? The sounds were light and quick. They were moving fast, and they were trying to be quiet. A drawer slid shut a little too hard, and she heard a clipped tread. Christophe. So he would be the one up and running then. She sat down at the table just in time for him to come tiptoeing into the kitchen and stop short.

"Good morning."

"Morning, Ma-mee."

"You sleep alright?"

"Yes, ma'am." His voice sounded like he'd swallowed a mouthful of gravel.

"Sounds like you done had better."

Christophe shifted: he was leaning as if he was about to go. He was thinking of an excuse. She ran her fingertips across the wood of the tabletop and thought of his thick curly hair. She wanted him next to her, and she would not allow him to run. He took a step.

"Paul bought some shrimp by last night. Around ten pounds or so."

"Oh yeah?" He hadn't spoken so softly since he was a little boy.

"Yes, sir. More than I can peel by myself. They in the sink defrosting." She passed her hand across the wood again, and gave him her best sweet, flirting smile. "I'm glad you woke up so early. I was hoping you could help me with them."

She heard him brush his hands down the front of his white shirt. She knew that if she could see details, it would be wrinkled. Clean, but wrinkled.

"I got to take a shower."

"Alright."

"Yes, ma'am."

Christophe was looking at her, studying her. He whispered, "Yes, ma'am." He walked slowly from the room. Seconds later, she heard the shower running. She hummed to herself as Otis Redding's harsh, surging voice wound its way through her head. The cock announced itself from below the kitchen window, excited by the sounds of movement from the kitchen. She loved Otis Redding. She tried not to influence the boys with her affinity for sad love songs, with the melancholy in her that responded to them, but after Cille had gone to Atlanta and she'd been left alone in the house with the boys, she'd played his album over and over on a little portable record player she'd given Cille as a birthday present when she was a teenager: Cille had left the house without it. The Otis record was one of a few Cille had left: Otis, Harold Melvin and the Bluenotes, Earth, Wind & Fire, some boy that looked like a girl on an album cover that called himself Prince. She never listened to that one. But the others, the others she liked.

She kept the record player in her room now on a dresser in a corner. She rarely played it.

The small cassette radio player in the kitchen window had taken its place in the kitchen. The boys kept that radio tuned to an oldies R&B station, and that suited her. She liked to listen to it while she cooked or cleaned in the kitchen. Sometimes they would play some of the songs she liked, some Al Green or some Sam Cooke. Some song where the man sounded like he'd been crying in the recording booth when he made the song, like his fingers had been itching with the phantom feel of some woman on them when he'd hit the high notes in the recording studio. It was always a woman. She knew that there was something new that played music now, CD players that played hard shiny discs that looked like small records, but she was too old for those: her eyesight prevented her from reading the digital display on the stereo in the boys room, so she figured it was a waste to fool with it. She felt the shrimp through the plastic bag, felt the small bodies give under the pressure of her fingers. They were ready. The shower shut off in the bathroom, and she pulled the plug. The water gurgled down the drain like a throat: a noisy swallowing.

When Christophe walked into the kitchen in a T-shirt and shorts, barefoot, Ma-mee had spread newspaper over the table and piled the shrimp in the middle of it. An empty gallon plastic ice-cream bucket sat in the middle of the table next to the shrimp. She was waiting on him. He sat and passed his hand over his face. She thought he must be tired. She was surprised he wasn't wearing shoes. She expected him to come to the table in them so he could be prepared to run out the door if his brother woke soon—after kissing her hastily on the cheek and tossing some hurried excuse over his shoulder, of course. Christophe was the type of child to run from something for only so long, but she knew he was no coward. He would face it. She reached for a shrimp, for the grayish-silvery pile before her, the quivering mass of glistening sea-bodies, and peeled. The shell came away easily in her fingers; it was hard like plastic in some segments and gummy in others. Christophe grabbed a shrimp and followed suit. Ma-mee let the room settle, let the morning sounds gather around them. Christophe peeled the shrimp slowly and carefully: that was his way around her, and it was the exact opposite of his usual demeanor. She knew it for what it was: love. The shrimp smelled faintly like tears beneath her fingers as she beheaded them, broke open their backs, and made them shed their skins. She hummed a bit of Harold Melvin and under the table, swung one foot back and forth. He surprised her by saying something first. She smiled: she hadn't thought the silence that uncomfortable.

"I got that on tape, Ma-mee, if you want to hear it." He coughed into the back of his hand. "Uncle Paul gave it to me a long time ago." The paper crinkled as he used it to wipe. "I could bring it in here and put it in the tape deck so you could play it sometime. I know they don't play everything you want to hear on the radio."

She decided to spare him the risk it took for him to go back into the room he shared with his brother to dig around in the closet and wake him. She was surprised he'd even offered to get the tape, or for that matter, that he'd even mentioned he owned it. "Naw, that's alright. For some reason I done had all these songs running through my head this morning. I don't know what it is. But I don't want to hear nothing." She took in a deep breath. "I like it quiet in the morning."

"I ain't really been up this early before—so I wouldn't know."

Ma-mee heard that he was smiling. She laughed in reply.

"Like I don't know," she said. "When your grandfather was alive and we was younger, I used to hate getting up in the morning. And he loved it. Woke up right after the sun rose. He had to work, you know; the carpentry and the yard work and the little bit of corn field we raised for the animals, so he had to get up early. And Lord knows I had enough work so I couldn't have slept all day if I wanted to. I made myself get into the habit of waking up before him, even if it was only for twenty minutes just so I could come up here and sit down for a second before I started on breakfast. Just sit and listen. Soak up the quiet. I was snappy as a snapping turtle when I couldn't get it. And once I got started, I wouldn't let go neither."

Ma-mee saw a stretch of white in the dusky tan of his face. A smile.

"I ain't no morning person, neither. Too lazy, I guess." He snorted.

She shook her head no, and her hair brushed along her shoulder with the fine touch of insects.

"You ain't lazy, Christophe. You work good as anybody. You take after Lucien with the yard work. You better than Paul at landscaping."

He was picking at one particular shrimp. The shell must have stuck to the flesh. She knew he was trying not to yank away the meat with the shell. He was trying to be careful, to conserve food. She had expected him to say something, to reply to her in some way, but he didn't. He pried at the sharp tail fin with his fingernails. Ma-mee could feel her hands moving, could feel the naked shrimp falling away from her fingers into her own neat pile that was twice the size of Christophe's, but it seemed as if it was happening without her, as if the wet, lukewarm bodies were sliding through another woman's fingers. She realized she was squinting as if she could see him. He was stubborn. It wasn't something an outsider would expect from Christophe, the quick, hotheaded, trigger-tempered one—but they never conformed, those two. They harbored their secrets and held onto them: Christophe with his occasional slow, smoldering anger, and Joshua with his own occasional quick, glancing, irrational recklessness. Yes, they conformed to character, but these two traded skin like any set of twins.

Ma-mee remembered Christophe glowering when Cille left: he had holed himself up in the boys' room and sulked, moving listlessly from bed to bed, sitting with his back to corners. Once she found him curled up in the closet in a fetal position, asleep. He refused to talk about Cille, refused to even say her name when Ma-mee tried to explain why she'd left them. While Christophe wrestled long and slow with his own grief, Joshua expressed his pain in erratic flares of emotion: he ran around the house in circles, sobbing. After hours passed and she could not coax or threaten him inside, she gave up and let him run, thinking that he would exhaust himself. Over and over, around and around the house, the only word she could understand of his garbled litany was "Mama." After half the day had passed, he quieted. She stepped off the front porch and walked around the side of the house to find him sitting upright on his knees in the grass, his legs beneath him, his hands folded demurely in his lap, his head listing to one side as he nodded off to sleep, his mouth a perfect O.

"Just because Joshua got called back for a job and you didn't don't mean nothing, Chris." Ma-mee watched his hands still their tugging on the shrimp, watched him let the shrimp roll into the palm of his hand, watched it disappear in the blur of his fist. "Christophe, I wouldn't lie to you. I never lied to you," she said.

He opened his palm and grabbed at the tail: she saw a bit of gray come off easily. He had warmed it with the palm of his hand; he had coaxed it with the heat of his skin. He was resourceful. She reached across the table and cupped his now empty hand with her own, ran her fingers over the hard, serrated skin of his knuckles. He had fought with them numerous times, and scraped them on river rocks and tree bark and asphalt. He would find something for himself.

"This just means you have a little bit more time to look. This way you'll find something that suits you real good," she said.

Christophe circled her hand with his. His calluses felt as hard and tough as an oyster shell.

"I know, Ma-mee." His voice dwindled to a whisper. "I'll find something to do."

The shrimp were beginning to stink like a stagnant, landlocked, shallow beach pool. Reluctantly, she removed her hand from the tent of his own, and grabbed another shrimp.

"The heat coming," she said.

She realized she was squinting at him as if she could sharpen him with her stare so she could read his face. The pile of shrimp between them shrank. The sun slid across the window of the room and sent planks of light across the floor, and Ma-mee closed her eyes as she picked and peeled, picked and peeled, as the light crept under the table and submerged her feet. It moved upward and lent a halo of light to Christophe's head: a phosphorescent glow. Christophe peeled, working away at the pile, and felt the heat brush the back of his calves. The shrimp ripened and seemed to melt into the paper, to blur the words gray.

As the sun rose in the sky, Joshua slept in the twins' room. He wrapped himself in a sheet, fought it as sweat wet his face and dampened the cotton fabric, and dreamt vivid, colorful dreams. He smelled the sea salt of those small ripening bodies protesting the loss of their water to the dry air and dreamt that he was on the pier pulling at woven sacks pregnant with frozen chicken that, regardless of how hard he pulled, would not move.

Joshua's walk down St. Alphonse Street was a crawl. It was ten and the heat and humidity of the air pulled at him like a net: it reminded him of his dreams, of the salt and sea. He wondered if shrimp felt like this, if they struggled against the thick fingers of the current created by the encroaching net in hope of escaping, of moving forward. When he'd awoken that morning, his brother was gone. The crooked, taut sheet was the only indicator that his brother had been there. Christophe had made the bed sloppily. When he walked into the kitchen feeling as if his eyelids were glued together and rubbing his face against the light, Ma-mee had been wiping down the table. The air smelled of seafood. She answered his question about Christophe's whereabouts, told him that he had been there, but had woken up early in the morning and left. When he asked her if Christophe had said anything to her about the call and the previous day, she'd paused midswipe, and then shook her head no. Joshua had sat on the sofa and watched *The Price of Right* with her, gulped down a bowl of cold cereal, and left after shrugging into a discolored tank and a pair of baggy jean shorts. He decided to go walking in search of Christophe, who he guessed was probably somewhere with Dunny.

By the time he was a house and a stand of woods away from Ma-mee's house, he'd peeled off his shirt and slung it over his shoulder where it hung drenched and limp as a dishrag. Insects seethed in the woods and called loudly to one another; they seemed to cheer the heat. The asphalt shimmered like a handheld fan down the length of the road, and his feet dragged along the pebbles embedded in the asphalt. The sun glinted sharply as a knife off the wet gold of his arm. The heat made him want to stop, to be still, to sit and breathe. He paused under a patch of shivering shade thrown by the reach of a pine tree. The sunlight glittered around him at the edges of the bristles' fluttering shadow The dark reminded him of being submerged to his neck in the river in water so tepid, when compared with the loaded tropical day, it verged on being cool. He wondered if that was where his brother was. He wanted to feel weightless and buoyed.

Five feet away from Joshua, a snake blacker than the asphalt lay sunning itself. It writhed lazily, flicking its tail as it soaked up the baking heat of the concrete. When he was younger, he had been terrified of snakes, but now, he wasn't. Either it didn't notice him, or the temperature of the day had made it loathe to move. It seemed to be made of the same stuff as the asphalt: its skin like the polished grain of the pitted, ancient street. The snake eased its way to the side of the road. He thought about the stories Ma-mee told them, about how they were so hungry when they were children. She told them her brothers had caught snakes by their tails on hot summer days like this, had ran with them to the closest tree and bashed their small, oblong skulls against the trunks, of how they had bought them home and skinned and deboned them, of how they had eaten them in a gravy stew with rice. Ma-mee said that often they found whole mice in their stomachs. Joshua imagined that the meat would be flaky and chewy, and taste faintly like brown leaves and dirt. The snake raised its head and flicked its tongue as if it could taste Joshua's sweat, his exhaustion, the steady hunger clenched in his stomach. He had heard that some animals could smell these things, could smell fear.

Joshua walked around the snake; he gave it a wide berth. It seemed to nod at him, and he frowned at it until he was out of the shade. The sun seemed to beat the sense out of him. Its burn echoed the revolving, sucking burn in his stomach. He was glad he'd gotten the job. It would be good to be able to buy food for the house and not have to ration soda, to abstain from eating too much shrimp because he was trying to save some for Ma-mee, for his brother, for later; it would be good to not have to eat oatmeal in the morning. He was so damned tired of eating oatmeal and sugar, of parsing out the teaspoon of condensed milk on top.

He hated condensed milk. It would be good to have a little money in his pocket so he could go out to eat sometime, pick up a basket of fried catfish and hush puppies for dinner for the family. Take a girl somewhere, maybe. He closed his eyes and stumbled, sure he could almost smell the food. Ma-mee maintained that she had kept them fed and fat when they were little: she was proud of the fact, and she would brag about it to her friends, to her daughters, that the twins had never wanted for food. Joshua remembered otherwise. He remembered eating handfuls of corn flakes and watery powdered milk, of eating tuna for weeks at a time, of dreaming of pizza as an eight year old. He remembered being perpetually hungry, regardless of how much he ate. Even now Joshua associated his infrequent brushes with satiety with bliss: the full weight of good food in the stomach, a mouth wet with juice, and the sated, languorous feeling that massaged his chest and back when he had eaten well. Down the street, someone was standing in Laila's driveway, and he could hear music blasting from a truck parked in Uncle Paul's yard. He doubted it was true, but perhaps Christophe was at Uncle Paul's house, or perhaps Uncle Paul had seen him. Regardless, the shade in Uncle Paul's yard was too good to pass up. He jumped across the ditch and jogged to the truck.

It was Uncle Paul's Ford. He was under the hood with a wrench in his hand. Rust laced its way along the seams of the gray truck, and Joshua had no idea how Uncle Paul had kept the thing running for this long. It was his work truck, and he was forever alternately cussing it and cajoling it. At the least, Uncle Paul would have some water in his refrigerator: if he didn't know anything about Christophe, Joshua could get a drink and head back down the street to Ma-mee's house to lie on the relative cool of the living room floor and wait for dusk to look. Joshua leaned against the truck and Uncle Paul jackknifed in surprise and almost banged his head on the hood.

"What you doing sneaking up on folks, boy?"

"Looking for Chris. You seen him?"

"Naw, I ain't seen him." Uncle Paul set the wrench on the edge of the grill and rested his forearms against the iron grate. "I'm surprised you out here looking for him in this heat."

"I'm alright. I think I'm going to head back after I leave here."

"How ya'll like them shrimp I brought by? I figured since I was down there at the docks checking on some fish for Rita, I might as well grab some shrimp for Ma-mee. They was some good-sized shrimp, too, for only three dollars a pound. She fry them up this morning?"

"Yeah..."

"I bought me a couple of pounds, too. I might bring 'em to Mama's tonight. Not like I got somebody to cook them up for me over here anyway."

"Stop trying to be a player and then maybe you could keep a girlfriend."

Uncle Paul was at least a head shorter, and when he took off his mesh cap to wipe his forearm across his forehead, Joshua saw that he was prematurely balding.

"Can't help what's in the blood, son. No, you sure can't help it." Uncle Paul replaced his cap and kicked something at his feet, something that was shoved underneath the hood of the car, and Joshua heard a dull clunk. "Have a beer."

Joshua normally didn't drink in the daytime. It was sort of an unspoken rule he played by: smoking, yes, he'd smoke a blunt or two while there was daylight, but he didn't like to drink. It made him think of drunks. It made him think of Rollo, who rode up and down the main street in St. Catherine and lurked around the Vietnamese corner store buying 97-cent King Cobras all day, whose eyes were perpetually watery and bloodshot, and who always had the sickly sweet smell of alcohol sweat on him, even in the winter. It made him think of his father in those yards, of him leaning against trucks like these with those goddamn blue blocker shades on, drinking beer after beer, laughing and smiling at jokes Joshua and Christophe couldn't hear as they walked past. Joshua shrugged his shoulders and hesitated. He was so hot, though. He could imagine the cool, salty fizz of it on his tongue. Fuck it. He would have just one, and then he would walk home. He pulled out a Michelob longneck, unscrewed the top, and took a deep swallow.

"I hid them because I know if niggas saw them they'd come asking for some. Hold it low, boy. I don't want to be supplying the whole neighborhood."

"Ain't nobody out in this heat, Uncle Paul, except you and me." Joshua tilted the bottle back again. He was so hungry he already felt a little dizzy buzz behind his temples.

"That's what you think, Joshua. Look like we ain't the only ones out here, and look like I ain't the only pimp in the family." Uncle Paul nodded towards the street and started laughing.

"What the hell you talking about?"

"Ain't that Laila?"

Joshua squinted out past the yard and saw a brilliant white shirt and short red shorts, a pair of thick tan thighs and slender, swinging arms, and coal black, curly hair. Yes, Laila. He was surprised at the way the beer caught in the back of his throat at seeing her. He swallowed. He hadn't seen her since he let her braid his hair after Christophe left: he'd been in a stupor, and hadn't complained when she led him to the couch and plucked the comb from his head and began braiding. She was so fine he couldn't take his eyes off her legs, from the taper of her waist, but the sudden thump in his chest when he realized it was her walking up in the yard surprised him. He looked past her breasts and stopped at the crooked, flashing grin on her face, and wanted to stay there. There was feeling. Sometimes, when she smiled at him like that at school or in the street, so shy and brave all at once, it reminded him of Cille. He shifted on his feet and let the bottle rest between his chest and the truck; it clinked once, twice against the grill. He didn't want her to think he was like some old drunk with nothing better to do with his time than drink. He tried to look casual as a small wind stirred listlessly in the branches of the pecan tree overhead and disturbed the shade, rippling it momentarily so that the light stabbed his vision.

"Hey, Paul."

"What's a little sweet thing like you doing out here in this heat? You going to melt."

Laila rolled her eyes and stared at Joshua.

"I heard it all before, Uncle Paul."

Paul broke out into a loud bray of laughter.

"Hey, Joshua."

"What's up, Laila?"

Joshua nervously swung the bottle back and forth. Laila leaned against the door of the truck and propped one forearm on the side mirror. Her move made one breast rise higher than the other. Her hair brushed against the contours of her cheeks with the wispy languor of cattails, and Joshua found himself glad that there was another small coughing breeze for a reason that had nothing to do with the heat. He tried to still his hands. "I thought that was you down the road."

"I was looking at a snake. Big black one. I guess it was a king snake."

"Where was it at?"

"Right in front of Uncle Paul's yard."

"You should've told me," Uncle Paul interjected.

"I didn't even see it." Laila rested her head on her forearm, and watched Joshua steadily. "I hate snakes."

"I used to, but I wasn't scared of that one," Joshua said.

"It's good to have snakes around. They eat up all the rodents. Keep the mice in check." Uncle Paul seemed determined to break into the conversation.

Joshua stuck one finger in the mouth of the bottle. He was thirsty again. Maybe he'd just have to take one more sip, regardless of Laila. She seemed so innocent. He knew she drank once in a while, but the beer in his hand suddenly seemed as loaded with potential menace as that snake in the street, and he wanted to drop it. He wondered if he could cough and drop it at the same time, if he could cover up the soft thud of the bottle hitting the dirt. The breeze blew again, a bit more forceful this time, and he could smell her: sweat and salt and underneath it all, cocoa butter.

"I heard you got called back to the pier," Uncle Paul said.

Uncle Paul probably thought he was doing Joshua a favor by mentioning his future job in front of a girl, but his declaration made the beer smack Joshua with a biting nausea. It made him think of Christophe. Joshua grimaced and let the warm glass slip from his sweaty fingers and drop to the ground without a care for the sound or the sudden lukewarm spill he felt coat his leg. He had drunk all but a sip of it. Where was his brother? Laila had heard the bottle; she stared at Joshua and the black, greased machinery glistening underneath the hood.

"Yeah," Joshua said.

That back that was his own yet was something else, that back that he knew better than his own had walked away from him and become an alien thing: it made him feel like he was perpetually on the verge of crying.

"They make pretty good money down there." Uncle Paul winked at him and turned up his beer.

"I guess so." Joshua felt an obstinate quiet, bidding Uncle Paul to shut up. Laila wiped her bangs away from her forehead: she was sweating tendrils of sweat down her forehead like fine lines of cursive at her temple. He wanted to touch her, to wipe all the sweat away.

"It'll be good to be working. I know how you boys is: you like to spend money, go places, do things."

"What you talking about 'you boys'?" Joshua kicked and hit the bottle by accident and was ashamed: it ricocheted under the truck and clanged as the glass hit the metal underbelly of the machine. Joshua pushed himself away from the metal grill and slung his T-shirt over his shoulder. "I got called back. Chris didn't. I gotta go."

"Alright, nephew."

Uncle Paul's farewell was lost in the swish of the grass against Joshua's legs. It itched when it slid, almost sensuously, against the slick layer of the beer on his skin. He was walking fast; he was leaning forward, cutting against the sun with his head down. He had to get away from Laila. They were all making him crazy.

"Joshua."

Laila was shuffling along next to him. He kept walking.

"What's up, Laila?" Joshua said it in a way that he knew would make her go away: he said it quickly, curtly, dismissively. He was already on the street: the shock of the asphalt through the bottom of his soles surprised him. He walked faster.

"I know I may look tall, but I'm not. My legs is around three times shorter than yours."

She was almost running to keep up with him. He didn't slow down. She was still there, trotting along next to him. As shitty as he felt inside, he couldn't bring himself to tell her to go home, to leave him alone. He sighed and slowed down.

When he banged through the door, he grunted to Ma-mee and walked straight to his room and sat on the floor. Laila stopped to talk to Ma-mee in the living room. He stared at Christophe's neat coverlet. The ceiling fan clicked and whirred above him like some irate bird. He felt himself growing sleepy, even though his stomach whirled with beer, with Laila and those slick tan legs in his living room. A sudden weight on the bed startled him.

"One of your braids came out in the back."

Her hands cupped the crown of his head and lifted, and he felt the warm familiar enclosure of her thighs on his shoulders. He let her hands guide his head so that his ear rested on her thigh. Her fingers teased a braid from his head, combed his hair out. As Laila braided his hair,

Joshua felt the muscles in his neck melt from strained cords to wide, lax threads. His head rested smoothly in the cup of her leg. He kicked absently at his brother's bed. Laila wasn't moving: she was done with the braid, but she was still and quiet beneath and behind him. He wanted to turn his head and mouth her thigh. The day was a prescient, dozing thing outside the window: the insects breathed a droning snore. Laila slumped against the wall behind him as patient and present as the bright outside. Joshua absently wondered if Laila had fallen asleep as he felt his own eyelids grow heavy. He wanted to rest his eyes.

Joshua had known her since he was little, had protected her, carried her over the deepest ditches, and made sure that when they played hide-and-go-seek, she was hidden in a good spot. Christophe and Dunny and the others would tease him about wanting to be her boyfriend. The first time he really noticed she'd grown up was one fall afternoon in his senior year. She'd had softball practice, and the boys had basketball practice. All of her teammates had left, and Joshua walked from the gym to get some water and saw her waiting for her mother to pick her up. He'd sat with her, ignoring Christophe and Dunny's teasing, their threats to leave him. Christophe and Dunny had peeled off their practice jerseys and sat in the car next to the bleachers, rolling and smoking blunts. Joshua had fanned himself with his practice basketball jersey and rolled his eyes at them and sat next to her, quiet, cracking a joke once every five minutes or so. He liked to see her smile. Her breath was a lullaby.

Outside the window, Christophe stopped. He'd had Dunny turn the radio low when he dropped him off. After he'd talked to Ma-mee earlier that morning, he'd called McDonald's, and asked to speak to the manager that Charles had told them about. Steve had answered the phone with a quick Southern accent.

"Hello?"

"Hello, my name is Christophe DeLisle and I dropped off an application about three weeks ago and then another one around a week ago and Charles—he works the day shift—told me to call back and ask to speak to you because you handle all the applications and..."

"Charles doesn't work here any more."

The manager had hung up then. Christophe had only pressed the button to hang up the phone and call Dunny to bring him to the shipyard, to Oreck for applications. He'd even stopped at one of the convenience stores in Bois Sauvage and told them he was interested in a job when he saw a handmade Help Wanted sign in the window. He wanted to apologize to Joshua. He wanted to get his opinion about Dunny's proposition. He needed Joshua's reasoning, his slow deliberation; Joshua would help him find his way. He'd walked around the house because he wanted to enter the back door and go straight to his room. He wanted a chance to gather himself. . He stood on his tiptoes at the window and peered inside, balancing himself by laying the flat of his palms against the worn board siding. The boards beneath his hands splintered like toothpicks, and a sliver stung him. In the room, he could see Joshua sitting on the floor with his head lolled back on the bed. It was resting on Laila's thigh. She was slumped over. Both of them breathed deeply and evenly: he guessed that they were asleep. Christophe frowned past the sudden feeling that he wanted to punch through the screen of the window and startle them awake. It didn't look like Joshua needed his apology, or his company. He pressed his hand hard into the house, hard enough to feel the splinter drive its way further into his skin, hard enough so that it felt like a blade instead of wood, and then pushed himself away and out into the day.

The sun would not leave them: even after it set, it left a residue of heat in the evening. Christophe, stone-drunk under the barebulb lights strung between the trees at Felicia's party later that night, thought the blanketing heat was a vestigial presence, something made even more present by its absence. The bulbs burned like dying stars on the wire draped over the arms of the old, twisted oaks in Felicia's parents' front yard. It was her eighteenth birthday party. She was flitting from one group of people to another, along the tables laden with barbecue and potato salad and hamburgers, flirting. She was one of the girls he'd fucked with in high school. He liked a few things about her: her brownish-blonde hair, her hips, her fierce sense of determination—she usually got what she wanted. She was silly, though. Talking to her was a chore. Now, the most he appreciated about her was the party: it was good to see everybody he hadn't seen since graduation, and to have a place to get drunk and high and not have to worry about the police.

Dunny passed him a blunt. Christophe expected to feel the burst, the sudden pleasurable explosion of THC in chest, but he felt nothing but relief at breathing again when he exhaled. He was numb. Evidently, he'd drunk and smoked himself sober. He spit into the grass. Dunny was laughing at Javon, who was attracting girls like mosquitoes in the passenger seat. Skinny Skeetah and short Marquise were passing a bottle of Crown back and forth in the backseat. Christophe hadn't said much of anything to any of them. After Christophe had left his house, he'd walked back to Dunny's and wandered from the sofa to the car until the sun set. He'd rolled up blunt after blunt on the way to the party. The smooth cigar paper on his tongue made him think of Joshua's face against Laila's leg. He'd only uttered something else beside yes or no when Dunny had stopped at the liquor store and asked him what he wanted to drink: Mad Dog. Dunny had rolled his eyes.

He came out the store fifteen minutes later and handed Javon a bottle of Remy and his change, tossed the bottle of Crown in the backseat at Marquise and Skeetah, and dropped a brown-wrapped bottle of Hennessy in Christophe's lap. Christophe had made to pass it back, ashamed through the haze of his high at his lack of money, at the $3.50 in change he'd given Dunny to buy the Mad Dog that surely must've been as leaden as a fishing sinker in Dunny's shorts pocket. Dunny wouldn't accept it. Christophe had decided that he would wash away the lump of pride in his throat. He'd popped the bottle and drained the neck in one gulp.

After five or so swallows, it had started tasting like sugar water, and Christophe relaxed as the drunkenness swept him up and buoyed him along. It felt good. He hated to think it, but it seemed like what he needed—until he drained the bottle so that only a lick of brown liquor was left at the bottom and they were parked in Felicia's yard in a cluster of cars and people, and he felt terribly sober. The darkness hadn't softened anything: the glint of gold teeth, the bright tint of jerseys, the hard, clean casts of car bodies, and the bottles emerging from the dirt as durable as seashells—they were all around him, all distinct and singular. He wanted it all to recede, but it wouldn't. The liquor and the weed had failed him. The only thing that would ease it all would be if he passed out, and he knew he had to wait for that to happen, so he stood at the front left tire of the car and held the Hennessey absently in his hand and leaned against the hood and hoped that he'd be unconscious in Dunny's backseat by the time Joshua showed up. He felt his eyelids flutter close, and then snap open. Oh yes, it was coming.

Joshua jumped over the ditch and landed in the yard and pulled his cap low to hide his face. He hadn't seen his brother all day, and he'd felt particularly naked and awkward and aroused when he woke up and found Laila there in his bed with a patient, kind look on her face. He'd told her he'd see her at the party; it was the most polite way he could ask her to leave, and it was still a lie. The only person he wanted to see was the only person that didn't want to see him, it seemed. He didn't bother calling Dunny to ask for a ride; he didn't want to hear Dunny lying to him on the phone at Christophe's behest, telling him for some reason or another that he didn't have room in his car. He'd walked over to Franco's house and gotten a ride with him. They'd parked down the street from Felicia's, close enough to see the lights and hear distinct voices. They'd smoked a blunt. Franco was ambling over toward a group of younger girls with his arms out, his new outfit crisp and starched to a cardboard stiffness, so Joshua loped his own way, looking for his brother.

Christophe raised his chin from where it had eased down to his chest and saw a shadow weaving its way across the lawn between the cars and he knew that walk because it was his own twin and goddamn it, he cussed to himself, he hadn't passed out in time. Joshua stood, his hands in his pockets, next to Christophe. Christophe realized he had missed him.

"Hey, Chris."

It seemed so unnecessary to Joshua that he had to greet his brother.

"Joshua."

Christophe upended the bottle and poured it in a weak stream down his throat. It stung a trickle down his esophagus. Christophe closed his eyes and was grateful for it while it lasted. When he opened them, his twin was still there.

"Fuck it."

"What you mean, fuck it? I didn't even say anything yet."

"You didn't have to...I already know what you want to talk about. And I just...I don't want to talk about it right now."

Joshua leaned nearer to his brother and sniffed.

"What all did you drink?"

Christophe shook his head, and saw the world blur and tilt. Okay, so he hadn't drunk himself sober. Just when that thought seemed consoling to him and guaranteed to help him get through the conversation he was trying to have with his brother, his stomach settled and the world lurched aright, and he felt dreadfully, seriously present.

"You avoiding me." Joshua said. He looked at his brother's profile. Christophe was staring off into the yard. He looked like he was on the verge of passing out.

"Nobody said I was avoiding you."

"You still doing it."

Christophe grabbed Joshua by the arm and half dragged him around the bumper of the car, away from the lights and the people.

"Chris."

The side of Joshua's thigh ached where Christophe's violent, clumsy pull had made him bump into the trunk of the car. He tripped out into the darkness after his brother. Christophe stopped at the edge of the woods, and Joshua stood next to him, close enough to brush against his arm for a second, to feel reassured. A frog croaked loudly and insistently somewhere in the underbrush. Christophe was silent, his hands hanging open palmed, his fingers wide as if he were searching for something he'd lost.

"Don't worry about it," Christophe said, surprisingly clear.

"I'm sorry, Christophe."

Christophe touched his lips with his fingers, and then licked them.

"I guess I must have dropped the bottle back there somewhere. There wasn't anything left of it anyway. And nothing more where it came from," he whispered.

"I said I was sorry, Chris." Joshua tried to draw Christophe back, but he knew his brother would only come back when he wanted to. Perhaps he was too drunk. Perhaps it wasn't the right time for this conversation. "I don't have to take the job. We could look for another one together."

"No. One is hard enough to get, specially a good one." Christophe moved closer to Joshua and looked at him intently.

"Are you sure?" Joshua asked.

Christophe's breath blew in hot, wet puffs over Joshua's cheeks. His nearness was almost confrontational. Even though he was so close, Joshua had to strain to hear what Christophe said.

"We can't always do things the same."

"We'll work it out—working different places. You just take the car and drop me off and then when you get off, you could come pick me up."

"No."

Christophe's eyes looked glazed and all pupil in the dim light from the party. Joshua heard some girl scream in laughter. Another car stereo system rumbled to life. Christophe blinked and pursed his mouth. He looked sick; he looked as if he wanted to spit.

"I don't mean it like that."

Joshua tried to grab Christophe's arm to steady him and instead brushed against his T-shirt, and he smelled the pungent aroma of weed waft from Christophe's clothing, and suddenly, he knew what Christophe was talking about.

"Christophe."

"What?"

"You're not talking about what I think you're talking about, are you?"

"What you think I'm talking about?"

"Selling."

"What if I am?"

"No."

"We been looking and calling for a month and I ain't got shit. I ain't got no more money left. Ain't nothing coming through. Dunny going to front me a quarter pound and help me get on my feet, and then I'll look again."

"You ain't got to do that."

"What I'm going to do? Sit around and beg these fucking folks for a job and eat off of you and Ma-mee? I can't do that." Christophe was gesturing widely, his hands out to his brother as if he were waiting for him to grab him and pull him toward him. Joshua felt the pain that he thought would be eased by this talk sharpen in his chest. "I gotta do something…and if that mean I got to make my money like this for a while, then that's what it mean."

"This wasn't part of the plan."

"Fuck the plan."

"Give it a couple weeks more."

"You ain't listening to me," Christophe said. "I ain't got shit."

Christophe grabbed his T-shirt and tugged it over his head. It slithered off and Christophe stood before his brother, his chest bare and wet and heaving. His movements were slurred. Christophe pushed his hands into his pockets and upended them, pulling the soft, cotton ears out.

"I have no money." Christophe backed away from his brother and cupped the back of his neck with both hands so that his elbows and chest spread and widened like wings. "But," he whispered, "I got options."

Christophe let his arms fall. Tomorrow, Christophe wouldn't remember any of this. Tomorrow, Joshua would get up and eat grits and eggs and Christophe would bring him to the interview and then they'd come home and help Ma-mee with dinner and eat and go to the park at St. Catherine's and play some ball until the bugs got too bad, and then they'd go home and sleep. Tomorrow, Christophe would bring him to the dock and on the way back, they'd find other places to look for a job and Christophe'd get called back for an interview and start working somewhere and he'd forget all of this, let it recede from him like the vomit did now, as he bent over and let a milky stream of alcohol pour from him and puddle on the red clay and sandy earth. Joshua stood with his hand firmly planted in the center of his brother's back and felt Christophe's muscles protest the liquor, and said the only two words he thought would make it so.

"It's alright."

5

JOSHUA'S INTERVIEW HAD BEEN EARLY. WHEN THEY RETURNED FROM the interview, Christophe, reeking of vomit and sweating alcohol, had tripped past the azaleas in the front yard and murmured an embarrassed "Good morning" to Ma-mee before rushing inside to fall into his bed. Joshua had sat next to her, waited for the house to fall silent, before he told her that they had given him the job, and that he would start on Friday. The next day, Christophe woke before Joshua and from what Rita told her later over the phone, spent most of his evening at her house, playing videogames and waiting for Dunny and Eze to come home, when he bothered Eze about his contacts at the shipyard. Thursday night, he appeared out of the darkness, showered, and fell asleep early with Joshua. She woke both of them at dawn on Friday, and then Christophe did not come home after dropping Joshua off on his first day of work. Ma-mee assumed he was filling out more applications. She had stretched the phone as near to the porch as she could, turned the ringer to loud, and sat in her favorite chair, waiting. The twins circled each other.

Ma-mee kneaded the wood of the armrests: the chair was old. It was the last thing Lucien had made for her. He'd made it while he fixed the chicken coop in the backyard. Paul had wanted to fix the coop himself, to save his father the trouble of tottering around with an unruly hammer and errant nails, but Lucien had refused his help. He was a stubborn sixty at the time; he still dyed his hair black, and walked and swung his arms like a young man. It was only when he had to concentrate his muscles on

details, on pinpointing a nail or threading a needle, that his body betrayed
him, that his aim veered or he started shaking. Ma-mee was fifty that
year. Cille had been pregnant with the twins, then, and still living with
them. It had taken Lucien two weeks to repair a reef of boards that would
have taken him a day when he was younger. She'd watched him from the
window in the morning while she was sorting collards or snapping green
beans: his progress was like watching the sky to gauge the movement of
the clouds. For days it seemed he'd wander around the coop and nothing
would change, and then suddenly, she'd notice a small change where one
hadn't been before. At dinner, he'd say he was simply taking his time: he
didn't want to do a sloppy job.

A week after he was done with the coop, she'd walked out on the
porch one still morning to hear him banging on something under the
hood of the pickup truck, and to see an elegant, simple chair with hand-
carved flourishes that looked like clam shells at the ends of the armrests
on the porch. When he came inside to wash his hands at the kitchen sink,
she'd walked over to him with clumps of cornbread dough in the sieves
of her fingers to kiss him. She remembered that he'd stood still then, like
a shy boy, and bent his head slightly to her so she could reach the fine,
damp skin of his cheek with her lips. She remembered the way his skin
had given, softer and more yielding than it had ever been in his youth.

Ma-mee let the memory slide from her shoulder like a slipping sheet.
It felt like waking: to her age, to Lucien's death, to the day and the absent
twins. The cicadas roused themselves in the trees outside. The day was
shaping into a bright, pulsing bulb. She slumped a little in her chair.
She thought of making cornbread for dinner: sweet, as Lucien had liked
it. She let her eyes close, felt the heat diffuse through her, and surprised
herself by wanting nothing more than to sleep.

His smell roused her. The scent of beer sweating through the pores of
someone wafted to her, strong on the wind; they were close. She squinted
out into the yard and saw someone standing just beyond the screen. It
was a man; she could tell by the width of his shoulders and waist. The way
he stood reminded her of a community dog: lean, starved, the bend of his
torso that made him look as if he were perpetually looking for something.
She didn't recognize the silhouette through the dull gray screen that was

detaching itself from the porch, peeling away from the wood to gape open and allow flies into the house.

"Who you?" She spoke loudly enough for her voice to carry past him. This was Bois Sauvage. There were no strangers, everyone knew everyone. She didn't like not being able to recognize him.

"You don't remember me, Miss Lillian?"

"No, I don't." The scent of him wafted over to her and she exhaled sharply: he smelled of fermented, overripe alcohol, cigarette smoke, and sour sweat.

"It's me, Miss Lillian. Samuel."

Surprise surged in her chest, and she blinked to mask it. Ma-mee heard him cough and gather phlegm. Against the glare of the day, he bent over and spit.

"How you doing, Miss Lillian."

"Fine. You been…?"

"Getting my life in order. I was over in Birmingham at a center. I had got into them drugs sort of bad. But now I'm better."

Ma-mee saw him raise his arms and hold them above his head. He was making himself comfortable. He had to notice that she hadn't invited him on the porch. He'd been a handsome, charming boy when he was a teenager, but even then there was something about him, about the way he moved, that was untrustworthy. She'd listened to him and Cille argue about his drinking, about his flirting with other girls, and she knew he didn't see Cille. Ma-mee saw him drunk at the Easter ballgame a couple of times; he was a moody, unpredictable drunk. She remembered him grabbing Cille's arms once, when he was ready to leave the ballgame and she wasn't; he had yanked her towards his car. Ma-mee had passed Cille in the hallway, fresh from the shower, her girl slender and wet, wrapped in a towel like a child, and seen that he had left bruises on Cille's arm—four, dark and perfect as watermelon seeds. She had told her daughter he wasn't any good, but her child was stubborn. After Ma-mee found out Cille was pregnant, she'd resigned herself to the idea of Samuel: there was nothing she could do.

"What you come back here for?" The question sounded sharply in the air, like a slap.

"Miss Lillian."

For a second, the way Samuel slid side to side on his feet reminded her of him as a teenager. She saw his face as it had been: wide, generous smile, brown black eyes, a weak jaw, and a sandy-brown, curly Afro. Something about the way he stood reminded her of the twins. She felt a twinge of sympathy for him then in her stomach, like a small insect turning and burrowing in the earth.

"How's the boys? They eighteen now, huh?"

"They just graduated." Ma-mee remembered Samuel's last official visit with the twins; it was their sixth birthday. He'd bought them matching pairs of shoes. They were blue high tops and had small puffy decal stickers of robots on the sides. The twins had worn them religiously for several weeks until the decals had fallen off. Samuel stayed for an hour or so, gave them their presents, refused cake, and then left. He'd twitched the entire time and looked out the window frequently. Ma-mee had wanted to catch him in the hallway on one of his trips to the bathroom, and away from the boys, to shove him against the wall and wrap her hands around his throat and squeeze and feel his damp neck give.

Lucien had only died two years before, and she knew she was a little crazy, that loss had made her a stranger to herself. Her grief at Lucien's passing had burned through her; it had left her black and fallow as a stretch of forest burned by lighting—a landscape of cinder and truncated, spindly, pines whose bodies were twisted black as their tops were still waving and dull green. A year after Lucien had died, Cille left, and the only thing that kept her sane were the twins; how precious their round, large, curly-haired heads, their gap-toothed mouths, their constant questions had been to her. Ma-mee could not understand how Samuel could not love that. They had been bewildered in the beginning, and she'd had to make excuses for Samuel, but then they'd gotten older, and they'd learned how not to miss him. They'd stopped asking about him. They'd spent their time running around the neighborhood in packs with Dunny and the other boys, shooting BB guns and riding their bikes and playing basketball. She was glad she hadn't had to lie anymore. "Joshua got a job down at the pier. Christophe's looking."

"Oh. Well, alright." Samuel pushed away from the shaded cool thrown by the eaves and retreated to the glare of the sun. The light seemed to diminish him so that his outline was smaller than the effluent, leafy azaleas, so that he was all spindly arms and legs; a naked bush. "Can you just tell them that I'm home now and that I'll be around?"

"Sure." It had never made a difference whether he was around or not. After that sixth birthday, Ma-mee knew he had still been around the neighborhood. Paul would see Samuel around, tell her about it, always begin his sentences with, "I saw that sonofabitch...." Ma-mee knew jailhouse fervor when she heard it. She barely resisted snorting, and instead picked up a piece of flattened, thick, layered newspaper from a small card table near her chair and began fanning herself.

"Thank you, Ms. Lillian." There was nothing more she wanted to say to him. "See you later."

"Goodbye, Samuel." The light ate at him, pared him away in pieces as he walked away, until he disappeared when he hit the road. Ma-mee fanned herself faster, noticed, and then stopped. She wouldn't tell the boys; part of her felt that telling them would be giving something to Samuel. She smelled wisteria and crepe myrtle, and she tried to relax, to shake the encounter away with the heavy musk of the flowers. He had made her feel dirty. Even if he had just completed some kind of rehabilitation program, he still had that jumpiness about him, that anxious, unsettled air. She thought of her niece Iolanthe, who came over every week or so to borrow sugar or cornmeal, and Blackjack, one of her cousin's children, who would sometimes wander over in the day and offer to cut her grass for five dollars, and other drug addicts around Sandman's age in the neighborhood who were addicted to drinking and all kinds of dope. They all acted the same; all moved as if they were perpetually waiting for something astounding to happen: a tornado, a flood, an earthquake.

So, she wouldn't tell the twins. It was quiet; there were no boards creaking, no breathing sounds, no doors creaking open or closed. She raised her face to the air, knowing that she probably looked like an animal, like the stray dogs in the neighborhood did when they caught the scent of a rabbit that had strayed into a yard from the wood. Would she rather have Samuel approach them in the street and casually mention to them that he had come by and talked to her? She didn't want to lie to them like that; protect them, yes, but leave them to be surprised, no. She had heard them talking about him. She had noticed how they hated to say his name. She would mention it to them and not make a big deal of it. She'd prepare them. Ma-mee ran through a list of ingredients in her head; she would make cornbread. She would set it on the board above the sink and let it cool so it would be sweet and light, and she would defrost the red beans she'd frozen. The evening would be quiet, and outside in the dark, even the insects would be sated. Ma-mee would ask Christophe to play those tapes on the radio during dinner. The ribbon of Al Green's voice would tie the evening. Perhaps she could tell them a couple of funny stories about Lucien; perhaps she could make them laugh. Then she would say it.

The seagulls meandered in threesomes through the air over the dock. They paused to alight on the concrete railings bordering the water, and pecked inquisitively at the asphalt, at sodden lumps of paper and flapping wads of napkins and hamburger wrappers. The sun was so bright it blanched the surface of the water crystal. The glare hurt the eyes as it shimmered and rebuffed the sun. When the birds flew out away from the dock over the water, they disappeared. Even so, Joshua heard them calling in rough, scratchy voices to one another as they skimmed over the salty, distended waves.

Joshua knew that there were some places in Alabama where the water was blue, where it was clear enough to see the sandy bottom, but here in Mississippi, it was so gray. He was grateful for the sun in that way; it threw a glamor over the water and made it appear to be something else. Joshua picked up another twenty-pound sack of chicken, loaded it on a pallet, and grimaced as he wiped away a splatter of pasty bird shit from his forearm. He'd stuck to Leo's back, squinted against the violent shine of the man's orange overalls, and stooped so he could hear Leo over the clanging of the ships' bells, the waves, the gulls, the grind and churn of the cranes and lifts and men as Leo trained him. He'd been loading sacks for close to an hour. He smelled of sea salt and sweat salt and musk. He bent to pick up another sack when he felt a hand grip his elbow; he hadn't heard anyone call his name. Leo stood at his side.

"You can go take a break, now. I'll have you load a few more pallets when you done, and then you can leave for the day. We don't want to tire you out too much—we want you to come back tomorrow." Leo smiled;

one of his front teeth was chipped. Leo must have seen Joshua looking, because he gestured to his mouth with his gloved hand and said, "Got this in a dirt bike accident when I was sixteen. Glad this was the only thing I broke."

Joshua ducked his head, a gesture he knew probably seemed like a bow to Leo, and walked to the office building to retrieve his lunch from his narrow gray locker. The air was so cold and dry in the building that it shocked him; he started shaking and had trouble fitting the thin key shaped like a heart into the lock. There was a small cafeteria with long wooden tables and metal chairs in the building, but he didn't feel like eating there. He was hungry, but he knew he wouldn't be able to eat inside; he could see himself sitting on a hard chair by himself in a corner of the room, his shoulders rounded as if to block out the room, the men quietly joking and shoving spoons into their mouths. He walked outside and turned from the building and followed the seawall away from the boats and men and the work and climbed up and perched on the edge of the wall facing the sea. All of it was an unpleasant rumbling to the left of him.

Joshua heard the seagulls screaming above him, and he watched them land a few feet away from him. They dropped gracefully from the air to palm the hot, tarry asphalt. He pulled his sandwich from the bag and was surprised to see that it was flat. He hadn't had anything else in his locker; he had no idea what could have smashed it like that. The locker had been cold, but even so the jelly had melted and slid out of the sandwich to smear against the plastic bag; the peanut butter bubbled away from the sides of the doughy, mashed bread. The sandwich had been small and meager that morning, but it was all he had time to fix, and now, smashed as it was, it seemed even smaller and more meager, and his stomach was a sucking black hole. He hadn't made more because he hadn't wanted to eat the last of the bread.

His shirt was losing the coolness it had taken on while he was in the building. The heat was squeezing him again, squeezing him as it had when he was lifting and throwing those sacks. His hands had felt like they were going to spontaneously combust inside those thick, padded suede gloves. He had wanted to punch Leo in the face while he was coaching him, punch himself in the face for taking this stupid, hard job, had wanted to strip off his pants and the heavy, cumbersome boots, and walk home. Collapsing of heat stroke while dodging traffic, hitching a ride, anything had to be better than this: anything but facing Ma-mee and Christophe and feeling like he had failed. He licked jelly from his finger. He would endure it.

"You know we got a cafeteria, don't you?" Leo had snuck up on him again. Joshua shifted on the seawall, away from the glassy sheen of the water, to answer.

"Yeah, I know. It's too cold in there for me." How in the hell did he sneak up on people when he was such a big man? "What you think so far?"

"It's alright." Joshua swallowed and glanced back toward the water.

"It gets better once you get used to it."

"Yeah?" Out on the horizon, the islands were dark, thin fringes. They reminded Joshua of eyelashes.

"Yeah. The first day is always the hardest. Your muscles got to get used to the work. Pretty soon, you won't even think about it."

"Oh." A seagull flapped its wings next to Joshua's head and landed on the seawall. Joshua shooed it away with the sandwich. The bird didn't seem to mind. It squawked, nodded its head several times as if it were stabbing the air with its beak, and hopped toward him again. Leo yelled "Hey!" and waved at the bird. It fluttered backwards and away, startled. Leo yelled again, and it took to the air.

"Flying rats." Leo spat. "Well." Leo was looking at Joshua as if he was waiting for him to say something. Joshua didn't want to talk—he wanted to leave. "Let me know if you need anything."

"Alright." Joshua shoved the last bite into the hollow of his cheek, and chewed. Leo walked away across the parking lot. Joshua watched him go and eyed the birds hopping about on the asphalt. He wondered if the pavement burned their feet. They danced closer to him. He folded up the paper bag: he could re-use it. One of the birds, perhaps the one that had just landed on the seawall next to him, swooped down a foot away from him and shrieked. Joshua didn't wave it away. He squinted at the bird and its followers. He was bracing himself against the heat: his neck tense, his shoulders stiff. That was the wrong way to go about it. He forced himself to loosen his chest and inhale the air, to invite it to him. It was bearable then. As he walked through the cluster of birds, they hopped behind him a small way from the wall, like a posse. They stopped and called to him when they realized he had nothing to offer them. He looked back to see them fluttering away toward the garbage cans; they floated haphazardly along in tandem with the blowing napkins. He wiped his face with the hem of his shirt. He didn't agree with Leo; they weren't filthy, and they weren't flying rats—they were just scrabbling and hungry, like everything else.

Christophe woke to a furtive scratching sound, the sound of a fingernail against wood, and then a soft tapping. He opened his eyes and remembered it all: the drinking, the smoking, the admission, the blackout, the blurry, drunken drive he'd taken the morning after dropping Joshua off at work, the weekend he'd spent running from his brother like a darting deer, this morning's silent, long drive. He'd sat in the parking lot of the Oreck vacuum company until the time had come to drop off applications only to be told that they weren't accepting any because there were no open positions. Back at the house, he'd snuck into the back door while Ma-mee on the porch. It was late in the day, and here he was in the bed with no job and no prospects and his brother was gone. He slid the pillow, cool on the underside, over his face and pulled it to the side so he could see out one eye. Laila stood in the doorway, ready to knock again.

"Hey, Chris." She said softly.

"Hey, Laila." Christophe managed to grind this out through his parched, closed throat. He blinked at her with his one open eye, shut it, and pulled the pillow back over his head. She was bright and clean and pretty and wearing short shorts, as always.

"I came over to do your hair."

"What?" Christophe spoke into the pillow and instantly regretted it. His mouth stank.

"Joshua didn't tell you?" Laila stuck her fists into her shorts. "He asked me to come over today and do your hair."

"Oh." Christophe wanted to cover his face with the pillow again and go back to sleep, to tell Laila and her legs to go away, but who knew when she would be able to braid his hair again. Only she could do it well; he imagined it was because she braided his twin's hair regularly: her fingers familiar and fond of his brother's hair. He shouldn't be jealous, but he thought about Joshua again, and knew one of the reasons she liked him so much was because of his light eyes, his easier to braid hair. His hair had to be neater; prospective employers would think him lazy and unreliable if he wore his hair wild and curly. "Alright." He sat up. "It's going to be a minute, Laila."

"It's alright. I'll be in the living room with Ma-mee."

Out of the shower, Christophe threw on whatever he pulled out of the drawer first, grabbed some moisturizer and a comb, and walked to the living room.

Laila was sitting on one of the sofas. Ma-mee sat across from her in her easy chair. They were watching *The Price is Right* on TV. People were cheering in a messy, colorful blur. He shuffled over to Ma-mee and kissed her and barely caught himself from tumbling in to her chair. She gripped his arm and smiled. She wasn't squinting; something about the smile seemed off. Christophe thought to say sorry, but as he opened his mouth, she squeezed him again and let him go. He was still clumsy with sleep. He sat between Laila's knees.

"Did you bring rubber bands?" Laila's question surprised him. No, he had forgotten the rubber bands in the room. Her kneecaps were marked with thready scars.

"No."

"It's alright. I brought some." Christophe felt her shift to pull them out of her pocket. The scars drew closer before moving away. "They're brown. Joshua likes them brown…so I figured you did too." She hesitated. "Is that okay?"

"Yeah." Christophe wondered about Joshua then, wondered if he was sweating out his own braids at the pier.

Christophe felt the fine tail of the comb like a finger on his scalp. It divided his head into sections; it traced rivers of forgetting on his skin. It felt good. He started to doze, and then Laila's hands jerked him awake. She was shaping the first braid. It hurt like hell. She yanked each section of the braid tight; it was like a lighter burned along his scalp. He was tempted to pull away from the pain, but he knew that if he wanted the braids to look glossy and to last, he couldn't. He was vain about his hair, but most boys his age that sported long hair were; it was a point of pride to sport the most unique, the tightest braids, and when his hair was done, it was like wearing a new outfit; he felt rich, almost. From Ma-mee's chair, he heard a soft snore.

"Hey."

"Huh?"

"Can you do me a favor?"

"Yeah."

"Would you mind grabbing me a piece of bread out of that loaf of bread on the table?"

"Um, yeah. You sure you don't want nothing else with it?"

"Naw." Christophe slumped into the sofa.

"Okay." Christophe leaned forward and Laila threw her leg over him and stood. She walked to the table on her toes with her arms out to the side and her palms flat as if she were walking across a balance beam. He found himself watching her ass, her shorts pulling tight and smooth with every mincing step she took. She had such thick hips. Christophe closed his eyes and only opened them again when he felt Laila softly nudge his shoulder, and he smelled the doughy bread. He took it from her and shoved a piece into his mouth. Laila sat behind him. At least she was nice; he guessed that if Joshua had to be messing with somebody, at least it was someone who would be considerate enough not to wake Ma-mee from her nap, and who would do his hair for free.

"I saw your daddy today."

The bread turned dry as sawdust in Christophe's mouth. He looked at the ragged piece of bread in his hand, and he could not take another bite.

"Who you talking about?" It came out sharply. It cut through the drowsing of the crickets filtering in through the windows. He would not have thought he had it in him, to be that loud and that mean.

"I'm talking about Sandman." She was whispering and he was sorry that he had yelled at her. Her hands were still. Shit, she'd only done one braid. God, he was an asshole.

"I'm sorry. I didn't mean to yell at you."

"Mmmm-hmmm." She shifted, and he leaned away to give her room to settle herself, to move her delicately traced knees away from him. When he leaned back, she resumed braiding.

"You sure it was him?" Christophe began to knead the bread into a ball with his hand.

"Yeah, I'm sure."

"How you so sure?" There it was again, the rancor. She stopped braiding again. Except for her hands on his scalp, he would not have known that she was behind him.

"I remember him from a few years back. He look the same, Christophe. He a little shorter than I remember, but he still the same man."

"What you mean?"

"I saw him out on the corner of Anne and Lapine." What little spit there was in Christophe's mouth had the gritty, pasty consistency of cement. He vaguely wondered if he spit right there on the carpet whether it would be thick and gray, whether it would harden into a stone before his eyes in the time it would take Laila to complete another braid.

"Over by the church?"

"Yeah." She hesitated. "He was leaning into Javon's car."

"He was buying?"

"That's what it looked like to me." Her voice had sunk so low he could hardly hear her. The crickets offered a chorus of affirmation.

Christophe raised his hand and waved it in the air as if he was shooing away a mosquito. He let it fall limply in his lap and sank further into the carpet. The enthusiastic shouting of the miniscule crowd on the TV sounded loudly in his ears and overlapped Ma-mee's soft, easy snore. So, Sandman was done with rehab and he had come back, and according to Laila, he was doing the same old shit. He waived his hand again, and Laila grabbed a handful of his hair. Her knees squeezed his shoulders like football pads. He wondered if Ma-mee had heard anything yet. She liked him about as much as he and Joshua did. Christophe put his head down; Laila sighed behind him as she pulled his head up.

He hated it all. He hated the idea of running into the ones that sold, Javon and Bone, and of having casual conversation with them and seeing that momentary glance, that sliver of pity in their eyes when they looked at him. The crowd on the TV was clapping and it sounded like water rushing over stones. The drug would hollow Sandman out again. He would start out sneakily and then he would not care anymore, and he would be out there, really out there. Christophe leaned on his elbow hard, welcoming the arcing pain as he shoved the bone into the floor. Christophe wondered whether he would come asking for money. Ma-mee snorted in her sleep and it was loud; he didn't slump back into the sofa until he heard her exhale in a long, soft whoosh. She blew her breath out in a way that reminded him of when she blew on his scrapes when he was younger, when her breath eased the pain when he'd fallen from his bike and the skin had peeled itself away from the bud of the wound to leave a bright, red burning flower.

He didn't want to see Sandman. Laila yanked at his hair, struggling to free a knot, and then pressed his scalp gently, tender and terrible at once. He was anxious for her to finish, so he could be away from her awful beauty, so he could go upcountry, away from the heart of Bois Sauvage where he imagined his father lurking. Involuntarily, he ground his jaw and bit into his tongue and tasted a salty bitterness. He was sure he was bleeding.

6

THE SKIN ON CHRISTOPHE'S HEAD WAS PULLED SO TIGHTLY HE felt like he was having trouble blinking. He walked with his head down, holding it like a newly coiffed offering; it felt as if it had been scrubbed raw, cleansed for sacrifice. He had waited until Laila was done with his hair, waited until she had tied it close to his scalp in a vortex of swirling, precise braids, and then he had sat there, thinking of Sandman. Perhaps Laila felt awkward waiting for him to acknowledge her, but Christophe hadn't cared: he ignored her. He wondered if Sandman was lurking somewhere outside under the pines or in the sunshine. He laid half-propped against the sofa on the floor and stared at the ceiling, at the way the water was eating away at the white plaster and had etched expansive brown sketches of faces. Laila left. Ma-mee had awoken with the slow creak of the screen door as it closed and had asked after her. Christophe kissed Ma-mee, reminded her to call him at Dunny's house when Joshua called, and left. He thought about driving, debated whether he should walk back in the house and grab the keys once he was outside and the crepe myrtle was nodding drowsily over his head, but then decided to walk; he had no money for anything and Joshua wouldn't be paid for another two weeks.

The heat made Christophe feel like a mule dragging a plow through thick, red chalky clay like the kind he had seen on basketball trips to the Mississippi Delta. The people had been uniformly dark there; Christophe had heard his assistant coach say that there was no mixed community there, and that things had been more savage in the flat, red country.

Christophe had stood on the court for his first game in the delta and had looked out at the wash of faces and noticed that whites sat in one section while blacks sat in the other. He had ordered a Sprite at the concession stand after the game and a woman, brunette with thin red lips and a gold crucifix on a thin gold chain around her neck, had not looked him in the eyes when she took his order, and had placed his change neatly on the counter out of reach of his outstretched hand. After playing to a tie, the St. Catherine's boy's varsity team lost in overtime. The trees, the hills, and the crops rolled past outside the bus window. When they arrived home at the end of the trip, the team had discovered red dust from the roads had sifted through the open windows of the bus to drift down on them, coated their uniforms, and turned them pink.

Christophe watched the gravel as he walked. If he caught a glimpse of Sandman, he didn't know what he would do. The houses were silent: the yards were empty. Everyone was at work. A couple of black stray dogs trotted up to him and sniffed at his pants legs. Their tongues hung like red wet exclamation marks from their mouths. They followed him along for a couple houses and then wandered off to sit in the shade. Christophe wished for that simplicity, wished that he could sit in the shade as a scavenging mutt resting his jaw on his paws, breathe little clouds in the dusty grass, and sleep.

When Christophe reached Dunny's yard, the first thing he noticed was that the spaces where Aunt Rita and Eze usually parked were bare and worn, like empty nests worn into the earth by sleeping animals. Dunny's car was parked in the shade of a large, leafy pine tree. Dunny had told Christophe that Eze had been bitching about cutting the tree down for five years or so, saying that it would fall on the trailer in a hurricane, and that it could attract lightning to the house in a thunderstorm and fry everything, but Aunt Rita had told him that it would stay, and Christophe was glad he would be alone in the house with Dunny.

Christophe looked up at the sky to see where the sun was; it was around two. Dunny worked half-day at the plant two Fridays a month, and Christophe hoped that he wasn't asleep. He knocked once, then harder, and heard a muffled "I'm coming." Christophe slipped into the cool, air-conditioned innards of the house. He blinked his eyes, saw only a textured, velvety darkness. He blinked and realized Dunny stood before him in his boxers, his belly lapping over the edge of his shorts like a fat tongue. He smelled like sleep and dried sweat. Dunny locked the door behind Christophe.

"Why didn't you call before you came over?" Dunny said.

"Why, so you could cuss me out as soon as I got here for waking you up?"

"You still woke me up." Dunny led Christophe back toward his room. Family pictures cluttered the walls. Aunt Rita had pared her furniture when Dunny became a teenager: she said there was little need for decoration when she was living in a house full of men. A skinny sofa, a worn loveseat, and two deep, velour-covered chairs lined the wall, all facing a large entertainment center. The coffee table, the end tables adorned with vases of fake flowers, the china cabinet of crystal glasses Christophe remembered examining in his youth while wondering if Cille had one like it in Atlanta: all these were gone. The path to Dunny's room was a straight one: the line in the carpet looked worn as a forest trail. Once he was in his room, Dunny sat on the full bed that took up most of the tiny room, and lounged against the wall.

"At least this way, I only woke you up once, nigga."

"Even once is too much. You know what time I had to get up this morning and go to work? Six."

"At least you only had to work half a day."

"Yeah, whatever. You should've called—I would've picked you up." Dunny was grinning.

"Yeah, right nigga. First, you would've cussed me out for calling you, and then you would've told my ass to walk."

"That's about right." Dunny laughed Christophe sat on the edge of a chair draped with clothes "Why the fuck is it always so cold up in here?"

"You know I'm about to sleep for another two hours, right? Ain't nothing going on right now anyway. Why you didn't wait until the sun set to come over here?"

"I ain't want to change my mind."

Dunny scooted to the edge of the bed. He leaned forward, and Christophe could smell the sleep on his breath. "You saying what I think you saying?"

"Yeah."

"Well, alright then."

Dunny pulled on a T-shirt that was a muddy yellow at the armpits before crouching in front of his chest of drawers and pulling out the bottom drawer. As Dunny mumbled to himself and rustled unseen packages, Christophe noticed how the fat at Dunny's sides bulged from the bottom of the T-shirt; it looked like he had gained weight since the beginning of the summer. Christophe imagined it was uncomfortable for him, kneeling there on the floor, crouched like a little kid playing marbles or jacks. Dunny stopped his mumbling, reinserted the drawer, and tossed a dark green baggie toward him. Christophe fumbled to catch it. His fingers were cold.

"That's a quarter pound. You should make $400 from that. When you done sold it all, I'll give you another one for $200. That's what I'll ask for them—so basically it's like I'm giving you this one for free."

"Alright."

"And make sure you hide it where Ma-mee can't find it. I done heard stories from Mama about her stumbling over Aunt Cille's weed stash or finding bottles of Uncle Paul's moonshine. The last thing you want is for her to find a quarter pound of weed in your drawers."

"I'm not stupid, nigga. I know how to hide shit."

"Make a smoking sack when you first get it...that way you don't smoke too much and you don't lose too much profit. Oh shit, I almost forgot." Dunny pulled the drawer out again, and Christophe heard more plastic rustling. The QP filled a Ziploc sandwich bag: it was bigger than Christophe thought. He had no idea how he was going to sneak it home. "Here some sandwich bags." Dunny tossed a half-empty box at him. Christophe let them fall to the floor. "You don't want to steal Ma-mee's because she'll get suspicious."

"I was planning on stealing yours." It was a weak joke.

"Ha, ha, nigga. And this," Dunny threw a small black cloth bag at him, "is a scale. You'll need it. This way if niggas want to complain and say you gave them too little, you can show them the scale and shut them up. You don't want to get a reputation for peeling niggas. That's the way you lose clientele." Dunny loosened the drawstring and pulled the scale from the inside. He inserted his finger into a small keychain ring at the top of the scale, and then rummaged under the mattress with his other hand and pulled out a small clear baggie of weed. "My smoking sack," he grinned. He clipped the sack onto the other end of the scale and Christophe watched the needle on the small scale slide to five grams. "It's a dub sack. Twenty dollars. A dime sack is 2.5 grams. Half of a dime sack is a blunt. If you can help it, don't sell blunts. It's hard to make money on blunts because you got so much loose change in your pocket and you end up spending it."

"What is this, Pine Selling 101?" Christophe couldn't understand where the jokes were coming from. Something about it felt manic, panicked, and he had a flashback to his run home after his basketball game with Dunny, of pine trees shuffling into a fence around him while the cicadas sounded like an alarm and something breathed and followed at his back. He opened his mouth and a high, giggly laugh came out; he hadn't heard that laugh since his voice changed. For some reason, this was even funnier, and he doubled over the sack he was holding in his hands and crushed it to his chest, and it cushioned him like one of Ma-mee's old needle-pinned sewing pillows. The smell of it was strong; it was good stuff. When he sat up, Dunny was staring at him. His hand was still in the air, and the smoking sack dangled like a Christmas tree ornament from the branch of his finger.

Dunny unhooked the sack and balled it into his fist. He cupped it in the hollow of his hand like a raw egg: careful of the delicate shell, and sat down.

"You sure you want to do this?"

Christophe held the QP so that it sat on his flat palms like an offering on a plate. Part of him wanted Dunny to take it. He looked at his cousin, and then down at the bag. Or not.

"I got to." The weed was dense and packed with buds. Dunny scooted forward.

"Maybe you ain't cut out for this. You got to know how to stay calm, how to get everything you can out of this and make the shit worth it. You think you can do that, Chris?"

"Yeah, Dunny."

"You sure? Really though."

Christophe looked at the baggie and noticed there were small, opaque pockmarks where the stems had pushed against the baggie. Christophe smoothed them over with his hand as if he could wipe them away. The plastic stretched clear and then dimpled again.

"I'm sure. I'll do it til I get on my feet and find something else."

Dunny dropped the bagged scale on top of the QP of weed. The black bag punctuated the baggie like the pupil of a dull green eye. It was staring at Christophe.

"Alright, cuz. I'm going to hold you to that," said Dunny.

"You do that."

They talked for a while longer; Dunny lounging in his bed while Christophe squirmed on the chair, the sack and the scale balanced smoothly in his hands. Christophe was still talking when he noticed Dunny had fallen asleep with his mouth open. Christophe walked to the living room. He carried the sack and scale away from him, handled it the way he would handle something poisonous and biting, handled it like a snake. Ma-mee hadn't called yet, but he knew that Aunt Rita and Eze should be getting home sometime soon. The last thing he wanted was for them to walk in to him sleeping on the sofa with a quarter pound of weed in his lap, so he stuffed it down the front of his shorts. They were baggy enough so that the weed nested in the bulge of his crotch. He was careful not to lean over into the sofa or to lean back; the skin of his head was still tight, his braids were still fresh, and he didn't want to ruin them.

He tried to watch TV but instead dozed fitfully, jarred awake every few minutes or so by his body tilting forward or sliding backward, when he'd jerk upright to preserve his head. His lurching nap on the sofa made him feel like a boat sliding into a slip, wary of the sea and the dock. When he woke thirty minutes later, Dunny was still asleep, so Christophe walked home. The baggie irritated him. It chafed at his side like a burr grown to monstrous proportions: a prickly sticker bent on making the carrier spread its seed. He murmured hello to Ma-mee, and in his room, he closed the door, locked it, and sat on his bed. He pulled the bag and scale out, stood, and grabbed a chair from the foot of his bed and slid it over to his closet, where he climbed up and reached to the back of his shelf and pulled out a shoebox. He opened it and saw the familiar letters and pictures, scribbled on in pink and purple ink, embroidered with small drawings of people and lower case I's with hearts for dots. They were all the letters and pictures he'd received from girls over the years. Felicia's name shone like a neon sign. He scooped the paper to one side, deposited the bags, and covered them over with letters. He shoved the box to the back of the closet and propped an old pair of his basketball shoes on the top of it to disguise the smell, and stepped away and down off the chair. He sat on the edge of the bed with his head down, staring at the floor and his hands until Joshua called for a ride home from work.

Joshua didn't expect the silence after he fell into the car, shining with sweat and stinking. His T-shirt gathered under his arms and rolled into the fold in the middle of his stomach. He thought of pulling it clear, of fighting it into some semblance of smoothness, but he didn't have the strength to wrestle with it as his brother started the car and pulled out of the parking lot. Instead, he sank back into the cloth cushion, laid his head on the headrest, and fell asleep.

Joshua expected jibes when he awoke; he had been jarred awake by his own snoring, and as he opened his eyes to blink at the pines and the slumbering, reclining oaks shading the car on its way to Bois Sauvage, he noticed drool running in a slimy line down his chin and wiped it away. He expected a laugh, but received nothing. Joshua looked over at his twin to see his face filmy with sweat, his mouth set in a falling line. The radio was silent. Joshua saw that Christophe's hair had been braided into neat, looping rows; the hairstyle mirrored his own and curled along his brother's head like a handful of glass beads. Joshua recognized that style; it was Laila's.

"Did Laila come by and do your hair? I asked her to yesterday."

"Yeah."

"Oh." Joshua rubbed his eyes; the sweat seeped into them and burned them shut again. Christophe cleared his throat to speak. It sounded as if his brother was about to vomit.

"He back."

Joshua stared at his brother dumbly. He was too tired to think. Who was back?

"Him."

The answer unfolded in Joshua's head as neatly as an elementary pupil's letter: easy along the edges and crisp until it lay revealed before him, a little creased but otherwise clear, and written in a bold, clumsy hand.

"Him."

So that was why his brother was so quiet. Joshua turned and threw his arm over his seat.

"Who told you?" Joshua asked.

"Laila."

"She saw him?"

"Yeah."

"Where?"

"In Bois Sauvage. On side of the church."

One of Joshua's earliest memories was of him and Christophe in the yard with their grandfather, and of his grandfather coaching them to drive a sow and her two piglets back into the sty. The pigs had been fat and short and obstinate, and stank of sour corn. His small, chubby hands had slid away from their muddied skin uselessly, and Pa-Pa had laughed at the two of them. Joshua thought that had to have been easier than this conversation.

"Doing what?"

"You know what he was doing."

Christophe, who never drove with both hands on the wheel, had one at seven and one at two. Joshua pulled his shirt over his head; it rasped against his skin wetly. It was like skinning a squirrel, and his naked back felt good as the wind buffeted him through the window.

"She was sure?"

"He was leaning into Javon's car."

The sweat chilled him and as the wind flashed across his skin. Christophe hit a bad, marsh-eaten patch of road, and a dull throbbing bloomed in the small of Joshua's back. Christophe was frowning and ignoring him. Joshua had heard stories about boys who never really knew their fathers who met them when they got older and didn't recognize them. The twins had been at least thirteen or fourteen the last time they saw Sandman: what would he look like now?

When Joshua followed Christophe into the house, the living room was dark and empty; Ma-mee was in her room. He could hear her humming and shuffling, faintly. In the bathroom, he turned the cold tap on until he couldn't turn it anymore.

Under the spray of the water, a loop of Sandman twelve years younger on one of the last occasions he had spent time with them kept playing in his head: Sandman, in a dirty T-shirt and navy pants with a spindly fishing pole in one hand, handing him and his twin two overlarge, taped fishing poles with string tied to the end with ragged, dirty bits of orange feathers and sinkers attached. He had taken them fishing out at one of the boat launches on the bayou. Joshua had dropped his stick, and the water had closed around it like a fist, had sucked at the small leaden sinker, and it had sunk.

Christophe had offered to let him take turns holding his own stick but Joshua had refused and spent the rest of the time seated on the edge of the launch, a shadow of his twin, and watched Sandman. He stared at Sandman's mouth, which never seemed to close, and counted the teeth he could see and his moles. Sandman had not noticed until it was time for them to leave that Joshua did not have his fishing pole, and then he scolded him because he said the sinkers cost money. He had seemed big, absent, and mean. Joshua walked into his room, wanting to recall that day to his brother so he could grasp the situation, could think it out, so they could remember again who Sandman had been and who they were now, and found his twin gone, and the room empty. The curtains at the windowsill fluttered a weak hello.

Christophe needed to move his stash from the house, so he left before his brother finished showering. Ma-mee was shaking out the pillows of her bed, and when he left she was beating one of the cushions from her chair in her room against her dresser, and muttering something about dust. After shoving both bags in his underwear, Christophe went around the back of the house to the shed; his grandfather had used it as a barn and later, as a workplace for his carpentry, and when they were young men, his uncles had kept their car there after his grandfather had gotten rid of the cow and his horses. Ma-mee and the twins never used it for anything; the tin roof sagged, and random car parts, feeding chutes, and stalls crumbled into one another in a stuffy, sweltering maze. Christophe faltered at the door; the barn seemed to gather heat inside, to pull it lovingly into its mouth.

Christophe crouched to the right of the opening, clutching at the bags. His fingers hurt. He picked his way past a hulking car engine and an empty oil barrel drum laced with cobwebs and rust, and cleared a space on the sawdust and dirt floor. He took out the weed and set it on his lap and began to measure it out carefully. Christophe peered at the silver scale in the dim light of the barn and counted under his breath, culling the stems, filling and weighing and adjusting the bags; too little here, and too much there. He pulled sandwich bag after sandwich bag from his pockets like a magician; he had forgotten to take them out after Dunny gave them to him. Sweat ran down his forehead and pooled in the creases of his eyelids; when he blinked, they rolled in fat teardrops away from his eyes and down his cheeks, and stung. He bagged it all, and the sacks lay on the earth in front of him in a small semicircle. He squinted at them. In the dark, they looked like small spiders' egg sacks. He put three dimebags and one dubsack into his pocket. He bagged the rest together in one sandwich bag along with the scale, stashed it in an old Community coffee can, scanned the yard, and ran out the door.

7

CHRISTOPHE HEARD DUNNY BEFORE HE SAW HIM CRUISING TOWARD the park. Dunny drove to the basketball court, dodging Skeetah and Marquise who were walking their pit bulls, and parked his car in the dirt parking lot. Javon, Bone, and Remy had parked their cars under the shade of the pine trees at the edge of the park: Christophe watched them pass paper bags he knew held thirty-two ounces of beer back and forth across the gleaming hard tops of their cars in the distance. Crackheads circled them warily, like mosquitoes. Dunny walked over to them and spoke. Christophe slumped, almost curled in half over the picnic table bench. He watched Dunny approach, and did not move when his cousin sat next to him. He had not been able to approach the boys: he had not known how.

"Sold anything?"

"Naw."

Dunny pulled at him then, away from the empty court and bench hard as a tomb, back across the park to the dirt lot to his car and the other boys. Christophe followed to Javon's car where the boys stood in a cluster. Skeetah and Marquise had jogged from the street to the park, and they stood by the bumper of Javon's car with their dogs. Skeetah's was a bitch, stocky and so white that it hurt Christophe's eyes to look at her. Marquise knelt behind his black dog and smoothed its haunches, whispering into its clipped ears, which he had pierced with silver bars. The dog turned and licked his face. Javon, tall and lanky, leaned against his car, a '65 Impala he'd had painted a variety of blues and black; it reminded Christophe of a waning sunset when the sky faded from a deeper blue to darker. Javon laughed at Marquise's dog as Dunny walked closer. Javon was a couple years older than Dunny; Dunny had followed him through elementary, through junior high, and on to high school. When Christophe saw him on his first day of first grade on the bus, he'd been shocked at Javon's pale skin, the freckles like splattered grease across his face, and his coarse, fiery red hair. Christophe could not understand how someone who looked black could have such white coloring. His eyes were most unsettling: his iris blended into his pupil so that it was all black, fathomless. He had stared at Christophe that first day on the bus and Christophe had turned back around in his seat and scooted closer to Joshua. Later, as Christophe grew up and played with Javon and the other older boys in Bois Sauvage, he stopped noticing Javon's color; now it mostly occurred to him only when he looked in Javon's eyes.

Javon was funny, always laughing or joking about something, the center of attention. He had a strange, predatory temper, though. Once, in a varsity basketball game, Christophe saw Javon take offense at a whispered comment by a white boy; Christophe had heard Javon tell Dunny later that the boy had called him a "red-haired wigger." Christophe and Joshua had been on the junior varsity team, but during varsity games, the coach would let them sit on the bench with the varsity players, fetch water, and learn plays by osmosis. Christophe had been close enough to see the white boy lean into Javon, smack him with his chest. Javon had dropped the ball and rushed the boy, punched him in the jaw and then fell with him to the floor, where he straddled him and started choking him. It took both referees to pull him off the boy. Later, they found Javon had cracked the boy's jaw. Javon had used his intelligence, his charm, and his legendary temper to work his way up from a petty dealer to a supplier; he was the main carrier of cocaine in Bois Sauvage.

"I don't know why he went and did that—piercing his ears like that and putting them bells in there. Ain't shit but a waste of money. What if another dog rip them out in a fight? And look at him licking all over Marquise. Damn dog look gay." Javon laughed. Next to him, Bone passed Remy a black and mild cigar. Remy put the cigar in his mouth and inhaled as he pulled his long, bleached dreadlocks away and tied them into a knot at the back of his neck. The smoke curled around his face like a veil.

"Guess he thought it was cute."

Bone coughed a laugh of smoke. Christophe twitched a nervous smile.

"Y'all better stop talking about my dog." Marquise stood. He was as short and small as his dog was large and wide, and skinnier than Skeetah, which Christophe thought was hardly possible. Marquise loved fighting dogs. He worked at Wal-Mart as a stock boy and had saved up to get his canines capped in gold. He grinned wide and they showed. "He love dark meat."

"I guess he won't be coming over here and fucking with me, then." Javon laughed again, and the gold fronts across his upper teeth gleamed. Marquise pulled at his dog's leash and began to call commands to the dog. It began to do tricks; it jumped as high as Marquise's collarbone and spun like a top in the air.

"Christophe the boy with that fire now. If anybody come to you for dimes and dubs, he got it," Dunny whispered.

"You putting him on?" Javon asked.

"Gotta take care of my cousin."

"For sure."

Christophe felt those black eyes on him, and he stared studiously at the dog and fingered the bags in his pockets. "I heard the other one got a job down at the pier. Joshua. They make good money down there."

"Yeah." Dunny replied.

Christophe glanced at Javon, at the sunlight glancing off his face: his stubble glittered.

"I ain't seen him around much."

"He started working today."

"Seen they daddy, though."

Christophe tried to look disinterested. It was as if someone had dusted Javon's cheeks with chili powder.

"Sandman?"

"Yeah."

"So...?"

"Yeah, just so he know." Javon turned to the group. "Y'all niggas want to play a game? It's cool, I understand if y'all don't. I'd be scared if I had to play against me, too."

"All you do is talk shit. Ain't nobody scared of you, Mutumbo," Marquise said.

"Alright, Minute Bowl."

The other boys laughed. Christophe spit and scraped his shoe and spread it into a silvery smear. It looked like a long, glittery, serpentine fish.

"I got a ball in my car," said Dunny.

"Let's go," Javon said.

The boys set off across the grassy field to the court. Christophe waited at Dunny's car while Dunny rooted in the trunk for the ball, which he tucked under his arm like a football. He motioned to Christophe with his head and they followed in Javon, Marquise, Remy, Skeetah, and Bone's wake.

"I heard...."

"I know he's back."

"Javon say...."

"Doing the same old shit."

Christophe punched the back of the ball so it flew from Dunny's grasp. It sailed into the golden afternoon air and landed in the weedy grass. Christophe scooped up the ball and dribbled it so hard that it actually bounced back into his hand. He sprinted toward the court and slid onto the concrete. He dribbled through his legs once, spun like a tornado, leapt, and dunked the ball with a loud clang. The rim rang like a tuning fork, and quivered.

Joshua woke and was disoriented, and only the sound of Ma-mee laughing and the absence of the rooster crowing confirmed that the sun was setting instead of rising. Ma-mee's voice rang from the living room; at first he thought she was talking to someone, that some older man was in the house, but then he shook his head and realized it was the TV. He rose and brushed his teeth again, and slipped on some old basketball shorts. He hadn't seen Christophe since the car ride home, but the evening was cooler than the previous one had been, and he could guess where his brother was. He set out walking towards the court. Light dabbled through the trees, fading and dull; the touch of it on his skin through the leaves was a weak, half-hearted thing, but still it stung, and made him realize that he was sunburned from his first day of work. He heard voices at the basketball court.

It looked as if Christophe was winning. Joshua stopped at the aging, wood-curled bleachers and sat down. They were empty. Remy sat on the other side of the court on one of the stone benches, a blunt in his mouth. Christophe was tearing across the court, using all the advantage of his smaller build, his short, wiry muscles, his athleticism, to punish the other boys. His voice rang out as he threw a perfect jumper. It flew in a short, quick arc, faster and more clipped than his usual shot, and rebounded off the backboard and through the net.

"Nineteen."

They were playing to twenty-one. Joshua wanted to speak to his brother in their own language.

"I got next."

Joshua saw Dunny nod, so he rose and took off his T-shirt. His muscles groaned in his arms. He ignored them. Christophe scored his last three points while Joshua stretched his back and walked off the ache in his thighs. His brother's winning shots were violent; they ripped through the air with more speed and power than usual. Christophe called endgame and stood there with his hands on his waist and his head down, breathing hard through his nose and his mouth; sweat rolled down his forehead and flew from his lips to hit the ground like spittle. The other boys ran to the water spigot the church had installed at the edge of the bleachers and drank. Joshua walked toward his brother as the others wandered back to the court slowly.

"Three on three. Me, Joshua, and Dunny against Marquise, Javon, and Bone. We play to twenty-one," said Christophe.

"Take the ball out, nigga." Dunny threw the ball at Christophe and Christophe caught it with the tips of his fingers.

"Alright." Christophe stepped off the court into the grass and eyed the boys. Marquise jumped and waved his hands in front of him, looking like an overexcited, anxious squirrel. Bone hit Joshua hard with his shoulder. Joshua glanced over to see Dunny almost wrestling with Javon to get in position. Christophe slapped the ball with one hand and raised it over his head and Joshua looked at his brother. Christophe was staring at him, really seeing him for the first time since the phone call, it seemed, and Joshua felt his stomach lurch. They were talking again. Christophe bought the ball cleanly across his chest, looked to Dunny, and then let the ball fly to Joshua. Bone stumbled; Joshua knew he had forgotten such a big boy could move so quickly. Joshua went in for a lay-up and scored. Bone grabbed the rebound and passed it to Christophe and mumbled, "Your ball."

For the next thirty minutes, the twins talked to each other for the first time in days, even if they only opened their mouths to grunt, to bare their teeth, and to emit forceful breaths like expletives when they suddenly stopped to shoot, to spin, to score. Joshua played with a small, tremulous smile on his face. He set the picks for Christophe. Christophe fired nasty, quick passes to him under the basket. This was their conversation. Christophe's frown grew more severe as he played; it cut into his face, pulled the edges of his mouth down. He played well. Christophe spoke to Joshua in three pointers. Joshua answered with soft nods: brisk lay-ups on the inside.

Christophe lobbed the ball at Joshua, who stepped to his right, shook Bone, and scored. No one spoke. Joshua knew that he and his brother were speaking over each other in the wordless speech of twins, that they were talking so quickly their play was becoming blurry and indistinct, slippery and unknowable: it was a foreign language. Javon pulled his shirt over his head and threw it into the grass. He was good; he was almost as fast as Christophe, and Dunny seemed too slow to guard him. He was scoring most of the other team's points. Marquise stole the ball from Christophe and made a hasty, high lay-up that verged on a dunk. He hung from the rim slinky as a dangling bead. Still, Christophe led them, grim and determined, and as Dunny yelled out the score, Joshua realized they were leading by three: 19–16. The last two points were harder to make; Dunny pulled something in his knee when he came down from making a shot, so they had to wait for him to stretch it out. When Dunny walked back on the court, he was even slower, but this just seemed to make Christophe better. The ball ricocheted between the twins like a pinball. Christophe faked a lay-up and passed the ball to Joshua, who scored. Christophe took the ball out and passed it to Joshua, who passed it back to his brother, hard, and Christophe sank a fade-away. He called, "Game."

Joshua bent over, and he inhaled and it sounded like he was sobbing: the breath dragging through his throat. Christophe was standing under the goal, his head down, so all that Joshua could see was the intricate line of his braids, his dark, slick neck. At the spigot, the others drank and walked away in a joking clump back through the brothers, across the court to Remy on his stone bench. Joshua heard Javon over the others.

"Shit, after that workout that little nigga gave us, I need to smoke."

Remy sent out a sputter of blue smoke in the air and coughed, "Good game." Joshua joined his brother at the spigot. Christophe turned the handle so it emitted a warm, sulfurous stream. He slurped at the water. He was more winded and tired than Joshua thought. Christophe's back undulated with his drinking. He dunked his head beneath the flow and stood, and the water ran down his forehead and face in a deluge. Joshua wanted to wipe it away; it bothered him, it reminded him of the veil of blood on the big Jesus statue hanging from the cross in the St. Salvador Catholic church that had always scared him when they were younger and attended mass with Ma-mee. Joshua knelt to drink as his brother had; Christophe sank down the fence. Joshua made himself stop drinking even though he wanted to continue, and lowered himself into the grass next to Christophe and looked over his head. Weed smoke wafted to him from across the court.

"So, you seen him today?"

"Naw. I only came down here about an hour ago and ran into Dunny."

"What you think you going to do when you see him?" Joshua was tentatively pleased that the conversation was continuing beyond the court. Even though he was angry about his brother leaving him in the car, the way he made him feel responsible for the phone call he didn't get, it was good to be sitting in the grass next to his brother. Christophe sighed.

"He ain't never been nothing to us, and he ain't never going to be nothing to us." Christophe said. "Don't matter what he say. I'll ignore him just like he been ignoring us all these years—say the least I gotta say, I guess."

"You'll probably see him before I do."

"I know."

The water was running downhill from where Christophe sat and was pooling around Joshua's shoes in the grass. "About last night…"

The crickets were waking in the woods rimming the park, seeking each other out. Joshua did not know how to continue, so he paused.

"What about last night?" Christophe began ripping up small bunches of grass and throwing them in the puddle. He watched his hands.

"About what you said…or what you didn't…I mean, what you meant." Joshua trailed off. "What you said you was going to do."

Christophe crossed his arms over his legs and looked off into the distance. "I done started already."

Joshua pushed his fingers into the earth. He tried to think of something to say, but his mind was a blank. The question, "What do I say?" echoed through his skull.

"It's just weed, Joshua. Not crack." Christophe said. "I'm not selling crack, Joshua." Christophe whispered this.

"You going to keep looking." Joshua said it like a statement, but both he and his brother knew it was a question.

"Yeah." Christophe gripped his calves. "I shouldn't've done that; now I'm going to be itching."

"I can keep a eye out down at the dock." Joshua said. He didn't want to rub his job in his brother's face, but there was always the chance that something else would open up. According to Leo, people got into accidents all the time. Anything was possible. He watched Christophe nod slowly and rest his chin on his forearms.

"I'll find something," he muttered.

On the bench across the court, Remy passed the blunt to Dunny. Marquise was scissoring his arms back and forth in the air as if he was weaving on an invisible loom; he was telling them a story, maniacally. Javon and Bone rubbed shoulders and laughed. Above Joshua's head, something buzzed and popped, and he looked up to see the court lights had switched on. The wind pushed at Joshua. Christophe had buried his face in his knees; he was curled into a damp ball. Joshua wanted to brush away the conversation like a gnat.

"So, what's up for tonight?"

"Ain't shit as far as I know." Christophe's voice was muffled. "You know how we do, though." A grasshopper sounded loudly behind Joshua, seemingly from underneath him, and Christophe raised his head in slow alarm.

"We'll find something," Joshua said quietly.

Christophe blinked, and Joshua bared his teeth.

Skeetah was standing in front of Christophe, and he was asking him for something. Dunny had handed Christophe a beer around fifteen minutes ago. Christophe had been thirsty and the beer had been cold and biting; he had downed it in gulps. Now, the beer was lapping at him with many tongues and he was sitting in the passenger seat of Dunny's car and his twin was sitting on the hood of the car looking at him through the front windshield and Skeetah was before him asking for a dime sack with a handful of crumpled bills held out in his hand. Yes, they had found something to get into. Christophe set the can on the ground and kicked it so hard it skidded away and rolled along like a bowling ball pin. The cicadas were all in heat, all screaming it seemed, all buzzing along with the beer through his veins.

"You got it, right? A dime sack. Dunny told me to come to you."

Cigarette lighters and interior lights and lightning bugs lit the dark; they were on one of the many dead-end roads in Bois Sauvage. This one, like many of the others, had no streetlights, and wasn't ringed by houses or yards, but by pines and undergrowth and was unpaved. Christophe swore he could see the Milky Way.

"Yeah, I have it."

Christophe looked at his brother. Joshua was trying not to stare at him. He could tell by the way Joshua sat slumped over the hood of the car, by the way he was half turned, as if he was on the verge of sliding off and walking around the door to his brother. Christophe glanced at Skeetah and away again to his Joshua, and had the sure feeling that when he looked at his brother, his brother would look away. Skeetah wanted his dope.

"Well, here; here it is." Skeetah held out a handful of bills to Christophe. Even in the weak light coming from the ceiling bulb in the

Cutlass, Christophe could see they were torn at the edges and fuzzy with wear; worn from hoarding. Christophe put both hands in his pockets, one lined with lint, and the other bulging with a green egg. He worked his finger around the tie in the bag and pulled out one of the dime sacks; the weed felt like a nest in his palm. He pulled it out and held it in front of him inches away from Skeetah's hand.

"Alright, then." Skeetah grabbed the sack and gave Christophe his money. "Thanks, cuz." Where his hand touched Christophe's, Christophe felt pads of thickened skin calloused from the constant rubbing of leather dog leashes. The dollars were sturdier than they looked; they were hot from Skeetah's pocket and coarse and durable and real in his hand and he realized this was the first money he'd received in over a month. He took the money The bulge of the weed and the bills, crumpled into a ball as they were, scratched at him through the thin film of his pockets. He crossed his arms and rocked back in the seat and laughed.

Joshua woke the next morning before his brother; his stomach was hurting. He had watched Skeetah round the car, slip a cigarillo out of his pocket, juggle a dimesack in his other hand, and bend over the hood. Joshua had gripped the beer can in his hand and over the give of the crackling metal, he had glanced over and saw his brother laughing with his head thrown back and his eyes shut in the car. His face seemed frozen in a grimace, and if Joshua hadn't heard the laugh, he would have thought his brother was in pain. Joshua's beer was salty and warm as blood. He and Christophe had stumbled into the house ringed by the rustling slithering call of cicadas. They supported each other mutely, drunk. Christophe's grip on Joshua's shoulder had hurt him. The way he'd laughed after he'd sold the sack, like it was easy and good, hurt him.

They had kicked off their shoes, peeled off their T-shirts and shorts, and fallen into bed. In the morning light, Joshua saw that Christophe had kicked his sheet to the floor in the middle of the night. Joshua wanted to go back to sleep, but he had to pee. He picked the sheet up from the floor and laid it on the bed next to his brother, his face turned away from Joshua and into the pillow. Joshua gathered dirty clothes from the floor. In the bathroom, the hamper was overflowing. He could not hear Ma-mee in the house. He sorted the clothes, making three mountains of them, and when he was done, he dumped the whites into the washing machine on the back porch off the kitchen. Everything smelled of sweat and alcohol. On the front of the magnet-freckled refrigerator, a note greeted him in round, fat handwriting that he recognized as Aunt Rita's: *Took Ma-mee to the grocery store with me this morning. Will be back later this afternoon. Love—Aunt Rita.* Joshua began to go through the pockets of the darker clothes, picking out bits of forgotten items like ticks. He would check to see if Ma-mee needed him to make more cornbread for the leftover red beans; he'd eaten half the pan the day before. Joshua pulled a wadded piece of paper from some of Christophe's shorts; it was an old, water-smeared receipt with an illegible name and a phone number scrawled across the back. Joshua set it beside him on the sofa. He would probably need to make more rice, too. Uncle Paul always ate all the rice. He reached into another pair of pants and pulled out a small wad of bills; they were Christophe's pants from the night before. From the other pocket, Joshua pulled out a sandwich bag; it was a dub sack. Joshua wondered what would happen if he didn't cover this time, didn't shove the money and weed under Christophe's pillow, when the phone rang.

"Hello?"

"Joshua." The woman cleared her throat.

"Yeah?" He squeezed the sack.

"It's Cille." His recognition of her voice slammed into place in his chest. How long had it been since he had talked to her?

"Hey, Cille."

"Is Ma-mee there?"

"Naw, she not here right now. She went with Aunt Rita to the grocery store."

"Do you know when she'll be back?"

"I was 'sleep when she left this morning." The phone was slippery.

"Well…I'm sorry I couldn't make it to your graduation. I couldn't get the time off." Cille's voice was different from Aunt Rita's. Deeper. He didn't know how to respond to her apology, so he gave her the answer he thought she wanted.

"It's alright."

"No, it's not alright. I'm sorry."

"Okay." He felt like she was waiting for him to say more. What else could he say? He accidentally kicked the pile of shirts and pants. Her clothes always smelled of perfume. He remembered that.

"So, what have y'all been up to?" What did she care? Did she care?

"I got a job down at the pier."

"So, the car coming in handy, huh?"

"Yeah." He should be more grateful. "Thank you."

"You're welcome. How you like your job?"

"It's alright. It's work."

"It's always work, no matter what kind of job you do."

"I didn't mean it that way." He breathed hard into the receiver. "I'm just happy I got a job."

"Well, me too. What about Christophe?"

"He ain't got one yet." Joshua clenched the baggie of weed and cash. "He working on it, though."

"Yeah, I'm sure he is. So, that mean y'all doing alright as far as money go, right?"

"Yeah." His answer was automatic. He would never ask for it. They had never asked for it.

"Well, that's good." He heard her pull the phone away from her mouth to murmur to someone else. He wondered where she was; whether she was at her apartment or on her cell phone out at the store or in her car. It was a quiet whisper, and it seemed intimate. "So, I was calling to talk to Ma-mee to tell her that I was thinking about coming down to visit in a month or so. We got a three-day weekend coming up, and I thought it would be nice to come down and see y'all."

"Okay." She sighed into the phone; it sounded like a hurricane in his ear. He pulled the phone away and barely heard her voice when he pressed the phone back.

"They got a blues festival that weekend, too, in New Orleans, and I thought...."

"Oh." He almost wished he hadn't pressed it back so quickly.

"So, just let her know when she come home, okay? Tell her I'll call her in about a week."

"No problem." She made a small noise in her throat; she wanted to get off the phone. "Alright, then," Joshua said.

"Well, take care of yourself and I'll call back in about a week, okay? Maybe I'll be able to talk to Christophe then."

"Alright." He would hang up the phone first. He didn't want to be to slow, to hear her line click dead while he was still waiting for her to say something else. He would hang up as soon as she said goodbye. He waited. She was quiet.

"Did anybody take pictures?" It took him a moment to figure out what she was talking about.

"Yeah. Aunt Rita took a lot of them."

"Good." Her tone was higher. He realized his grip on the phone was a little painful, so he relaxed his fingers. "Bye, Joshua. I'll talk to you soon." Click. He was too late. He eased the phone onto the cradle. From the wall in the kitchen, he heard the clock then; the minute hand was tapping its way around the face. A dark blue T-shirt slid down the slope of the pile at his feet, a loose rope of wind wound its way through the screen and against his leg, and a fly, fat and noisy, buzzed its way around his head like a small airplane. Joshua let the fly land on his arm, and wondered why he could not hear the ticking all the time; why did it jump out at him during the oddest moments? He watched the fly wipe its face and shuffle forward; he glared at it, willing it to be still. He wanted everything to stop. The fly shook its wings and took flight from the damp, pitted, pale-brown surface of his arm with a hiss. Joshua picked up the pile and a pair of basketball shorts slid from his fingers and puddled on the floor. He heard the fly buzzing sonorously as it circled the room. It probably shitted on me, he thought.

8

MA-MEE HADN'T BEEN ABLE TO START THE COLLARD GREENS. THE most she'd accomplished was washing them in the sink, where she felt the dirt of the garden at the back of the house give underneath her fingers like the silt of a riverbank and wash down the drain. Joshua had done the laundry while she was grocery shopping with Rita, and when she walked in the door, the house smelled of comet and fabric softener; he had cleaned the kitchen, too. She found a bushel of greens in the sink. Joshua had picked them. He said the heat was wilting them. The twins had jumped up from the floor to run outside and get the groceries from Rita's trunk and when Joshua brushed her on his way to the counter with a bag, her chest hurt. She did not want to tell them about Samuel. The twins snorted laughter at the TV, and she could not bring herself to take out the pot, to cut the seasoning, to begin cooking. She sat down next to Joshua on the sofa. Lying on the floor, Christophe rolled over to face her.

"I got something to tell y'all." She had made a mistake in not sitting in her chair. A fly was buzzing a slow funeral dirge around the living room. It would die soon. She hesitated.

"We already know," Christophe said.

"You do?"

"Yes, ma'am. Laila told me and I told Joshua. It's okay. He had to come back sometime."

"Who told you?" asked Joshua.

"He came by the house." Christophe sat up. Joshua scooted closer to her. She laid her hand over his and began making small circles on the back. It was the way she'd rubbed his back as a baby. She made herself stop. "It's alright. He came by and asked after y'all. He wasn't bothering me none."

"He didn't ask you for no money, did he?" Christophe was on his knees. The fly had stopped buzzing. Perhaps it had died.

"No. I just don't want y'all to be surprised."

"I should've been here." Christophe breathed.

"You can't be here all the time, Chris."

"Maybe I should say something to him. Make it so he won't come back over here and bother you." He paused. "He on that stuff again. I heard."

"Naw." Joshua was almost off the sofa. Ma-mee's hand fell to her side. "Just stay around. He know Uncle Paul be coming home for lunch." Joshua swallowed, then said it. "He wouldn't steal from his own blood."

"Ain't no blood. He a junkie, Jay. You know how that go."

Ma-mee made a shushing noise. "Don't let him bother y'all none. He just a sad man." She closed her eyes and saw his younger face; that lovely face so like her boys' own, but sneaky, shifty, as if it lacked the integrity of bones underneath. "Just a sad, lost man."

"So you don't want me to say nothing to him, Ma-mee?" said Christophe.

"I'm sure." She patted Joshua's arm and sat in her own chair. She let her hands hang over the armrests. "Felt like I done walked some miles."

"Cille coming." Joshua said this. He looked folded into the sofa.

"You talked to her?"

"She called the house while you was gone. Say she coming down in around a month—at the end of July or around the beginning of August, I guess. Some music festival or something happening then, too. Or, something like that." Joshua's voice dwindled to a slow, piecemeal halt. Christophe was rocking back on his heels. He must have not known.

"Well, that's good. Been a while. It'll be good to see her." The twins were looking at her. The joints of her fingers and her wrist were suffused with pain, and she grabbed her wrist and tried to squeeze it out. She wanted them laying on the floor and lounging on the sofa together. She would cook them a big meal, make them lazy and easy with food. Pain arced through her kneecap. She would make them forget.

She rose and walked slowly, limping to favor her tight knee, and palmed Christophe's head. "These greens ain't going to cook theyselves." She touched his face. "I could use some help though." He rose, and his cheek slid down and away; the bone was sharp beneath his skin. Joshua rose and she palmed his cheek as well, felt the bone heavy and dense beneath the soft fat of his face. They cooked.

Christophe began waking up before his brother. He'd never been an early riser, but now he found himself suddenly, painfully awake every morning at 5:30, when he'd feel something like a cramp in his stomach. Each day, he heard Ma-mee easing her way down the hall to the bathroom, and he'd realize that the ache in his stomach was his bladder, and he couldn't go back to sleep because he had to pee. Then Christophe would do something he hadn't done since he was little. He'd rise and walk carefully out of the room, stepping lightly to ease his bladder, and creep out the back door. The morning would be gray, the air lukewarm, and the grass at his feet always. He'd force it out, quickly; he was ashamed that he was peeing off the back steps like some five-year old who couldn't hold it. They used to do it all the time when they were little, when Cille or Ma-mee or Aunt Rita or Uncle Paul or someone else in the family was in the bathroom, hogging it. Back inside, he'd turn off the alarm clock and lie back in his bed and listen to Joshua snore and Ma-mee slide shuffle back to her room to wait for 5:45, when he would rouse his brother. Ma-mee would make them a quick breakfast, and then he'd bring Joshua to work. By the end of Joshua's second week of work, it was routine.

Christophe never went directly back to the house after he dropped Joshua off. He'd ride back along the beach and nervously eye the fresh-cleaned glass of the storefronts for Help Wanted signs, for bits of neon orange and black that said NOW HIRING. Some he would pass over when the store looked especially dingy or dirty. He'd peer at gas stations and fast food restaurants. Sometimes, he would pull into the parking lot of the place and circle it. He'd park and leave the engine running and eye the door, always to see some dim shadow moving about on the other side of the glass. They all seemed to be waiting for him. He'd think of the sandwich bag of weed at home, of the old pre-paid cell phone Dunny had given him, of the money to be made. He'd think, I'll wait until I finish selling what I got. Might as well get the money—it's there. Then I'll come back for real. He would think of Ma-mee at the house, waiting on him, of Joshua at the dock making honest money. He would run into one of the convenience stores with a sign out on the front, grab an orange juice, snatch an application, and then drive to Bois Sauvage through the bayou and past his home and up deep into the country where the small, tin-roofed shotgun houses were spare, where they squatted in the woods and overgrown fields like nocturnal animals, like wary possums or armadillos; solitary, seeking shelter in the wood, perpetually surprised by the passers-by. Few black people lived up here. He had no problem avoiding Felicia's house. He liked the way the houses disappeared and the road snaked underneath the cover of the trees and laid itself out like a vein along the body of the country. He would ride through the morning until the sun was bright and heavy above him.

Sometimes, he'd stop to put some gas in the tank at the old, shrunken convenience stores hidden in the country. The gas was always ten cents cheaper in these places, and some redneck with a beard was always behind the wooden counter, and when he passed over his money, whatever ceiling fan was blowing in the place would inevitably ruffle the plastic beer ad banners and the tacked up confederate emblems like prayer flags. He rode until he began to know his way better. He'd ride until he couldn't ignore the small red light and the constant chatter of pages through the pre-paid cell phone at his hip. He'd reluctantly turn and go back. He rode without music as he eyed the sky to see hawks always somewhere above him. He'd park the car along the ditch at the front of the yard and walk over to the park and sit at one of the wooden picnic tables hidden beneath the short, shivering oaks. They knew where to find him.

They'd amble over at regular intervals, it seemed; alone or in pairs. Once about every hour or half-hour or so, he'd see them off in the distance. They seemed to materialize from the heat-drenched air like sudden rain. He'd watch them amble slowly across the dusty red baseball field or pick their way through the pine trees and oak that cloistered the perimeter of the basketball court. He ate potato chips and drank Gatorade while he waited. He folded his arms over the top of the table and laid his head down and stripped off his shirt. He stretched over the top of the table on his back and watched the light etch the veins of the dark green leaves into beautiful relief. He dozed to the pulsing, drowsy cry of the crickets in the long-stemmed grass and the trees around him. He waited for them to come: other drug dealers, or high school students playing hooky, or people on their lunch breaks from driving trucks hauling rocks and sand, or attendants working at convenience stations the next town over, all people he'd grown up with and always known. When they came to him, he'd shake their hands. They would joke with him, and he'd smile. He'd give them what they wanted and they'd lay the bill close to him on the table, where it would flutter and jump with the wind, where it would pulse and twitch like a living thing. One pocket was for dime sacks, the other for dubs; he'd put the money in the pocket with the dime sacks because there was more room. Feeling sick, excited, and ashamed because he was excited, he'd eye the road for dark blue cop cars. Whenever he saw any, which was once every week or so, he'd dart to the ditch and hide in the underbrush, watch them cruise past through the cover of weeds and bushes until they went away, until the vegetation would make him itch and rashes bloom across his legs.

On the police-free days, his clientele would leave him and he would be alone again, staring at the grain of the wood of the table or up through the leaves of the trees, and he would think about what he was doing. He'd realize that he was placing it in their hands, now, that he was hardly thinking about it when he handed it over. He realized that this was something he did, now, like helping Ma-mee with dinner or playing basketball or driving Joshua to work. He sat on that bench in a procession of days, each one longer and hotter than the last, and told himself that this was not what he was. He'd sell until a little after three and then walk home to Ma-mee, the dark cool of the house, and they would wait for Joshua to call. She would ask him if he'd had any luck finding a job. Remembering those signs, his morning dalliance with the asphalt of restaurant and store and hotel parking lots, he would tell her yes, he had looked for a job. He'd think to himself; it wasn't a lie—he had looked. His weed was beginning to smell like the barn; like rust and earth and oil. After he picked up his brother, after it was dark, after they'd eaten dinner and Ma-mee had fallen asleep, after she'd been quiet in her bed for at least an hour, he'd make sacks. With his brother asleep on the sofa in front of the TV, most times with the phone cradled loosely in his hand from talking to Laila, Christophe would ease out of the house and go to the barn with a flashlight. He'd shine his light on the spastic bats fluttering through the open eaves, the warm, burrowing rodents secreting themselves in the narrow crevices of machines, and like a small, hairy animal himself, he would squeeze between the oil drums, squat sweating in the dark, and do his business. Now he kept his weed in the shed, locked in a small iron toolbox he found, behind the empty coffee cans on a shelf. When he returned to the house, he would wake his brother and bring him to bed. Christophe wondered if Joshua was doing it, waiting up for him on purpose, or if he was simply too exhausted to move and so fell asleep. He read judgment in the way Joshua slept wide legged and square kneed on the couch. Still he woke him to walk to bed and sleep.

Christophe had arrived early at the dock. He'd gotten tired of sitting around at the park. He told Joshua that the clouds had come in fast, that when he saw them rolling in while he was lying on his back on the picnic table bench, they looked like pictures he had seen of mountains. They had rolled across the sky and bulldozed away the blue. While Joshua rubbed his face dry on his shirt sleeve, he strained to hear his brother over the staccato drumming of the rain on the roof and the hood of the car. It slashed sideways against the windows.

When they were seven, they had found an old gray abandoned house deep in a coven of oaks behind the church and had spent an afternoon throwing rocks at the warped planks and yelling to scare away ghosts. Neither the twins nor Skeetah had ventured inside the house, whose roof had sagged under beards of Spanish moss. The rain sounded like the white pebbles had when they had smattered against the wooden face of the house. Through a clear spot, Joshua saw that the rain was coming down so hard the world seemed to have disappeared: it had washed the docks, the concrete parking lot, the men he knew were running to their cars through the downpour, away. He and Christophe had only run away from that house that day when Christophe decided that he had had enough of throwing rocks, since no one was brave enough to run inside, and the sunlight in the woods was fading. He had grabbed Joshua's hand in a slippery grip, and pulled him away and they had run forever, it seemed, with Skeetah at their back yelling at them to slow down, until they finally crawled out of the woods just as the sun was setting in a red and orange blanket in the sky.

Christophe and Joshua had jumped the ditch dividing the woods from the street as one, and only when their feet had landed on the asphalt did Christophe let go of Joshua's hand. Joshua looked at his brother now wiping the glass furiously, muttering and cussing about the broken defrost in the car, and wished for it to never stop raining, for the rain to become a biblical flood so that it would not only wash him through space, but through time, away and back to that day in the beginning of his world. Christophe made to start the car, and Joshua stopped him.

"Naw. Let's just wait it out. It's too heavy right now to see."

"Alright." Christophe cranked the car. Joshua reached over and turned the thermostat knob to cool. The vents expelled air that smelled musty and old; it smelled like weed. Joshua let his bare arm adhere wetly to the windowsill.

"It smell like wet dog in here." Joshua sniffed and lowered his arm. "Oh. That's me." He leaned his head against the window. When he got in the car, he had noticed that Christophe had the radio off. Both of them liked the sound of the rain.

"I want to give you some money. Put it with what you going to give to Ma-mee. Tell her you worked overtime or something," Christophe said, glaring out the front window.

"Today?" Joshua pinched his forearm to stay awake.

"Every time you get paid, I'll just give you a hundred. Tell her they paying you more than you thought they was."

"What if she know I'm lying?" Joshua looked out the passenger window.

"Just tell her you work through lunch and when I don't pick you up on time, they pay you overtime."

She would never know that she was receiving money from both of them. She would not want to take the money even from him. She would fuss and say that they got along on her Social Security and Medicaid just fine. He would slip it into her purse.

"Here." Christophe dug in his pocket and took out a wad of bills folded in half. The bills looked worried over, faded. Joshua didn't want to give them to her.

"Where's the wallet Cille gave you?" Cille had sent them matching leather wallets on their fifteenth birthdays. The twins had carried them everywhere even though sometimes the only thing in them were pictures of Ma-mee and Cille and Aunt Rita and their own wallet-sized individual basketball team photos: Joshua had worn the wallet until it curved in the middle and the leather that rubbed against pocket of his jeans was dull and textured as suede. He still wore it.

"It fell apart."

Joshua did not let Christophe know that he knew that Christophe had saved it; Christophe had stashed the wallet like some drooping and wilted prom flower in one of his love-note shoeboxes in the top and back of the closet. Christophe counted three twenties, four fives, and twenty ones. He handed the larger bills to Joshua with one hand and apologetically gave the ones to his brother with his other hand and shrugged, "For change." Joshua grabbed both handfuls and sandwiched them together before shoving them into his wallet.

"Alright then." Joshua slid the wallet into his back pocket. It felt as if he was sitting on a thick, dirty balled-up sock.

"I smelled it." Christophe said. "Ma-mee always say we got that blood in us, the kind that know things, that Bois Sauvage blood. I know she can tell the weather, but I swear, before them clouds came and before I even knew they was on the way, I smelled it in the air. It was like a metal kind of smell." Joshua nodded, and his head slid back and forth against the glass. He knew it left a greasy smudge. "Shit, soon as I jumped up from the bench after I saw them clouds, it started coming down hard. I just stood there for a minute, though. It felt good." Joshua nodded again. He had been slow walking across the parking lot to the car.

The twins sat like that for the thirty minutes it took for the rain to ease up. Joshua closed his eyes repeatedly and tried to sleep; he couldn't. He was surprised that he couldn't. He watched Christophe blearily; he realized that Christophe had taken out his braids and pulled his hair back into a frizzy, short, ponytail. Joshua hadn't realized his brother's hair was that long; Christophe's hair had always grown a little faster than Joshua's own. It had been a couple of days since he had talked to Laila; he'd have to call her and see if she could braid their hair again. He knew his own hair stank like cold wax, and that when Laila combed the braids out, it would come out in ropy knots. He knew he wouldn't care, and he wouldn't complain, as long as he could feel the press of her thighs against his shoulders.

After the rain fell away in fits, after it eased up and the worst of it withdrew out over the gulf like a woman gathering her coat and leaving a room, Christophe drove them home. The swish and sway of the windshield wipers echoed through the car. Joshua thought to ask his brother for a blunt, because he wanted the smoke to massage the residue of muscle ache from his arms and legs, but he didn't. If Christophe didn't have something rolled when he picked Joshua up, then he didn't want to smoke. Christophe only handed Joshua a blunt to light and smoke twice since he had been selling. Both times, he set it on the dashboard when Joshua got into the car; Christophe placed it there as if he didn't wanted to hand it to his brother. Joshua half-shut his eyes and listened to the rain fling itself at the car.

At the house, Christophe opened the screen door to the porch and let if fall without holding it open for his brother. Joshua sighed and licked his lips as he mounted the steps and sucked at the water and salt he found there. When he followed his brother into the gray, humid living room, Christophe had stopped. Laila was sitting on the sofa. Ma-mee wasn't in her chair.

"Where's Ma-mee at?" Christophe's voice was slightly hoarse; he sounded as if he hadn't spoken in days. Joshua figured that his brother didn't talk much while he was sitting down at the park waiting for customers. Joshua thought about him often while he was lifting and throwing bags of chickens and crates of bananas. In his mind, Christophe wasn't sprawling across the bench with his charismatic dark limbs, but instead was round-shouldered and stooped, and his eyes were always studying the road as he waited for clientele and the blue flash of the police. In his head, he saw

Christophe's face through a metal screen, and his worry angered him. Sometimes, jealously, he pictured Javon or Marquise with him, and he wondered if Laila ever walked down to the court, and if she talked to him. "And why you ain't got the TV on?"

"Miss Rita came and picked her up. She said they was going shopping." Laila crossed her arms, and then buried her hands into the crevices of the couch cushions. She looked nervous. "I just, uh, I told her I would wait on y'all. Wasn't nothing good on TV," she whispered. Christophe turned back to look at his brother.

"I got stuff to do." Christophe turned away and receded down the hall. Joshua sat on the sofa at the other end from Laila, and placed his cap carefully on the armrest. He smoothed it with his wet, dirty hand, and then began to quickly unlace his boots. Ma-mee would kill him if he got mud on the carpet. He'd forgotten. Shit.

"So, how was work today?"

"It was alright."

"You usually get off earlier than this, right?"

"Yeah, but the rain...." Joshua pulled off both of his boots and laid them on their sides. He hesitated, and then picked them up and set them outside the front door on the porch. When he sat back down, Laila seemed closer to him on the sofa. From the back room, he heard nothing; it was as if his brother wasn't even there. He wished the rain would fall harder outside; the silence that pervaded the house was unnerving. "So." He was sure Laila was scooting closer to him. It was like watching a minute hand on a clock move; he could never see it, but he'd blink, and it would be in a different place. "You going to get a summer job?"

"Naw, I don't think so. Summer's almost halfway over, now. Fourth of July is like, next week." She was staring at him like a bird.

"What you do all day then?" Niggas didn't look at each other when they talked; he'd noticed that. They looked straight ahead and away most of the time; unless you were about to fight or making a joke, you never looked at a man in his face.

"I baby-sit my little cousins. My auntie pays me fifty dollars a week." Yes, her knee was touching his, now. All he could feel was a pressure there as he studied her knee, tan and round, lightly touching his leg through the dirty press of his jeans.

"That's cool." The long, ripe line of her thigh was beside his. He felt a muscle cramp sullenly in his calf. He ignored it, and looked at her face. It was red.

"Joshua?"

"Hmm?" He could feel her breath on his face as she spoke to him. She smelled like lotion and licorice.

"Are you ever going to kiss me?" It was a whisper. She was staring at his lips and his eyes. She turned redder; she must've realized that she was nearly in his lap. She looked at the wall. A knock sounded from deep within the house; it sounded as if Christophe was breaking something. Joshua knew her skin would be soft, that it would give under his fingers like water so that he would not be able to tell whether it was really there. Her blush made him want to smile. She was determined, and shy, and stubborn, and he liked her for it. He knew he stank, but he didn't care. Joshua leaned forward and placed his hand next to her shoulder on the back of the sofa and kissed her. Her hand came up to the side of his face; her fingers on his cheek felt as light as an insect. She opened her mouth and her lips and tongue were warm; he shivered as slivers of water made their way from his hair down the back of his neck. He pulled away, hesitated, and then kissed the corner of her lips with his mouth closed, and sat back. She wiped her hair back away from her face and smiled. He felt awkward and stupid; what if Ma-mee or Christophe had walked in?

"I need to go take a shower."

"Alright." She ducked her head and swallowed, and he wondered if she was still tasting his mouth on her tongue again, if she was remembering it like the flavor of ice cream or juice. He knew he would not be able to forget her taste now that he had it for the first time; he wanted to kiss her again, to coax her onto his lap and run his hands down the warm curve of her back and turn her face to his with his mouth, but he wouldn't, not in the living room, not with his brother knocking around the house. Dunny had always joked about them sharing girls, but it had never been that way between them.

Joshua showered quickly. By the time he got out, Ma-mee was walking down the hall and Laila wasn't in the living room anymore. He readjusted the knot holding the towel at his waist.

"Laila told me to tell you she had to go home. She had something to do. She said she was going to call you tonight." Ma-mee paused. "She sweet on you, huh?"

Her gown was pink and bright and new.

"Got a new gown, huh?"

"Joshua," Ma-mee pinched his arm. Joshua covered it with his hand and cowered. She laughed and pinched him again.

"Ow. I'm sensitive." He laughed.

"You like her?"

He didn't know what to say.

"She like you. Be nice to her." She rose on her toes and he leaned down into her. She pinched him again. "Men shouldn't have eyelashes like that."

Ma-mee turned and touched the wall once and twice with her hand as she walked through the living room and into the kitchen. He heard her get a pot from one of the cabinets, and a second later, turn on the faucet. In their room, Christophe had fallen asleep in the middle of counting his money, and was stretched out with his arms thrown over his head as if he had been surprised, his mouth open, the bills ragged and bunched underneath him. Sometimes he still slept as he did when they were younger: wild, fighting with the walls and wrestling with the sheet. Joshua pulled the pillow so that it rested squarely under his brother's head; Christophe's snoring abruptly stopped. Joshua hurried to find clean, dry clothes and pulled them on quickly: he would slip the money into her purse while she was in the kitchen.

Joshua did not sleep well for the rest of the week. His dreams alternated between nightmares about his brother and hazy glimpses of Laila. By the end of his third week of work, Joshua felt as if he'd never done anything else besides work at the dock; the summer rains had begun, and his life was straining against bags and throwing heavy boxes and rain and salt stinging his eyes and the sun parting the clouds like a knife and burning down upon him and steaming the men's skin and the endless concrete. Everything smelled of metal and stank. Ma-mee packed small lunches of tuna fish and potato salad and apples for him, and he ate his lunches alone, on the pier, or when it rained especially bad, at a corner table in the cafeteria with some other black men around his own age from Germaine; he laughed at their jokes and their conversation sometimes, but was often silent. He woke up each morning drained, and the brutal monotony of work at the pier stunned him. Something about it felt insulting and wrong. He was jealous and would often not speak to his brother on the way to work, disgusted by the fact that Christophe would spend his day chilling at the park. His paychecks made him feel a little better, but still he was glad when the weekend came. He fell asleep early on Friday night, and woke with Christophe near noon. It had rained earlier that morning, but when they woke the sky was barely studded with clouds, a deep, rich blue. The twins dressed and walked to the court, and Joshua waved at people sitting on their porches or cutting grass with rusty push lawnmowers. Christophe punctuated his waves with dribbling their basketball. Otherwise their walk was quiet, their mutual animosity a veil between them.

It seemed that nearly everyone they knew was at the basketball court. A crew of boys from St. Catherine were running a game with some boys from the neighborhood; as they approached the court, Joshua saw Skeetah fly into the air and swat the other team's ball away from the goal and out of bounds. Marquise retrieved the ball and threw it back into play. Joshua and Christophe walked toward the small bleachers, and were surprised to find them laden with clumps of people: Joshua saw Laila sitting with Felicia on the bottom bleacher. He'd talked to her briefly the night before he'd fallen asleep, had known that she was going to be there, but had not given that as a reason to his brother when he asked him if he wanted to go. He had not talked to his brother about his desire to take her to the movies, to eat at some nice restaurant, to play at the miniature golf place, or the fact that he had asked her to go out with him and she had said yes. Perhaps they could double date with Christophe and Felicia.

Some kids were running along the middle bleacher and jumping off the end, yelling as they hit the ground. Javon sat with Bone on the top bleacher. They were passing a blunt back and forth. Christophe yelled in the general direction of the court, "We got next!" and Joshua caught Laila's eye and smiled a close-mouthed smile at her and settled next to his brother on the bench. Javon nudged Christophe's shoulder with the hand holding the blunt: Christophe shook his head as he glanced at Felicia and muttered, "No thanks." Joshua followed his brother's lead and refused the blunt even though the smell was sweet. Joshua tried not to inhale sharply; he didn't want to look like some sort of junkie, sitting on the bleachers sniffing the air hard for a whiff of blunt. The little kids, Cece, Dizzy, and Little Man clambered back up and stopped in front of Christophe. They were glaring at him and Joshua. The little girl was older than the other two; she stood with her hands on her hips and she cocked her head to the side and glared at them. Her hair cloaked her shoulders in fuzzy braids and she was so light skinned that the skin across her nose and cheeks had burned. She opened her mouth, and Joshua saw she was missing her two front teeth. She was probably around six. Joshua coughed and laughed. The two boys behind her looked around two years younger than her; they wore short, tight T-shirts that hugged their potbellies and they stood together close as twins. One was light and one was dark; the dark one stuck out his tongue at Joshua.

"You sat in the middle of our game," the little girl said.

"We needed a place to sit. Y'all go play somewhere else fore I whip one of y'all," Christophe said.

"You ain't whipping me!" the girl retorted.

The lighter little boy, Little Man, raised his left hand and flipped the bird at Christophe. Joshua couldn't help himself; he started to laugh hard. Christophe's eyes turned to small, dark crescents and he choked out a laugh.

"Y'all better get y'all badasses out of here and go play somewhere. Get!" Christophe yelled.

Little Man had both hands in the air now, both middle fingers extended, and was taking turns jabbing them in the air towards Christophe. His dark clone, Dizzy, followed suit. Cece turned around and back to Christophe; her braids swung out and the plastic barrettes at their ends clicked softly as they shuttered against her face.

"Don't let me have to tell y'all's mamas. I know who they is…!" Christophe told her.

She glared at him and then grabbed each of the boys by the arm and yanked.

"Come on!" They screamed and ran after her; they tripped down the bench and Joshua watched them run across the park towards the swings. The girl never let go of their hands. When the trio was halfway across the park, Little Man turned and when Joshua squinted, he could see he was flipping them off again with his free hand as he was running. Laila was shaking her head and laughing while Felicia doubled over as she held her stomach; behind them, Javon snorted.

"Bad little fuckers."

Joshua watched the trio leap belly first onto the row of swings; they stretched their arms out and kicked with their legs and swung high in the air. Joshua had played that game; he knew they were pretending to fly. He gazed past them to the row of cars parked at the side of the ditch and saw Javon's car, and Bone's, and Marquise's, and a couple of others he couldn't make out. They weren't all empty; he saw shadows, and heard the bass from more than one stereo system. He watched the three swinging, saw the girl slow her swing and tumble headfirst from the rubber into the dirt. A figure skirted one of the cars and began walking across the field past the swings towards the court.

The little boys tried to follow her lead but instead squirmed from the seats and landed on their feet. Shrieking, they followed Cece at a run as she led them to the wooden slide. She sandwiched herself behind the two boys at the apex of the slide. They gripped each other between their legs, lined up in a row, and she pushed them down in a train. Joshua had played that game, too. The figure was nearing them; Joshua saw that it was a man, an older man. The man had pants on in the heat, and he had long, curly hair that he had topped with a navy blue baseball cap. Joshua looked at the way he walked and nudged Christophe with his elbow and nodded at the figure as he approached them and surfaced like a swimmer into sharp relief. The man was walking around the court. He was searching the faces of the people playing, and now he was pulling off his cap and peering underneath the trees to pick out the figures on the benches. For the first time in years, Joshua and Christophe saw their father.

Joshua's face was hot. He wanted to look away from the man, to watch the trio of kids, to watch the game on the court, but he couldn't. Sandman wasn't even looking at them; he was looking past them to

Javon. Joshua doubted that he even recognized them. Sandman slapped his cap against his thigh and walked underneath the trees to the side of the bleachers to Javon. Joshua glanced past Christophe at Sandman and saw that Christophe was staring straight ahead, and Joshua could see the muscle of his jaw jumping like a darting minnow under his skin. He heard Sandman whisper, "I got something for you, Javon." Javon jumped from the bleachers and shuffled away further under the trees towards the ditch with Sandman.

"We got next!" Christophe bit out. Laila was not turning to Joshua and smiling anymore. She bounced her feet and shrugged when Felicia leaned in to ask her if she was alright. Joshua swatted a mosquito.

"Somebody need to start a fire," Joshua said. Christophe was staring at him solemnly. Joshua shook his head no. Christophe sniffed and looked back toward the court.

"Y'all niggas heard me?" Christophe yelled.

Skeetah passed the ball to Big Henry and yelled, "Yeah nigga, we heard you." His voice quavered; he was breathing hard through his mouth. Javon clambered back on the bench. Joshua let his knee slide and stick wetly to his brother's, and then jerked it away. Sandman had put his cap back on so that all Joshua could see of him were his strong nose and his mouth. He was standing off to the side of the bleachers. He was looking at the twins.

"Good day for some ball." He said this as if he were speaking to the air. Javon grunted and pulled on the blunt. Joshua stared at Sandman. Christophe concentrated on the flurry of movement on the court. "Sure is a good day for some ball." Joshua saw something in Christophe's face break; the minnow flashed and disappeared.

"Don't you have somewhere to go?"

Sandman walked over to stand in front of them. The navy blue shirt he wore hung like a wet rag on his frame. His knuckles were bony and distended, as large as grapes.

"I was just trying to make conversation." Sandman was staring at them like a wary dog; Joshua could imagine a stiff, quivering tail on him. Joshua snaked his arm behind his brother's and squeezed Christophe's elbow hard. Christophe let out his breath as if he had been holding it. Joshua spoke intently and quietly.

"We don't want no conversation." Looking at Sandman's face was almost like looking at Christophe's. He had given them his full lips, his prominent nose, the reddish cast to their skin. Something about it was wrong, though; his features seemed confused. It was as if some child had taken pieces of a puzzle and forced them together so that they fit in the wrong way. Sandman opened his mouth wide in disbelief, and Joshua saw that his teeth were yellow and seemed smashed together in his mouth; gray lined them at the seams. He closed his mouth and it made a wet, hollow sound.

"I just wanted to talk to my sons." Joshua stared at his wide mouth and squeezed Christophe's arm harder. Christophe shook his elbow from Joshua's grasp and pulled the ball into his stomach as if it hurt. His fingers were blanched yellow against the orange rubber. He lurched forward and stared intently at Sandman, and when he spoke, his voice was strained.

"You ain't got no sons here. Ma-mee our mama and our daddy. Leave...us...alone." He bit the rest of it out. Christophe rocked back and looked away across the baseball diamond to the pines glistening there.

"Joshua...."

"You don't even know which one you're talking to." Christophe spoke without looking back at him, and his voice was small as if he spoke from a great distance. Sandman was staring down at his feet, so Joshua stared at the crown of his head, his thin, bony shoulders, his wet-rag shirt, his dirty jeans, and his black and blue tennis shoes. The pain in Joshua's chest and at the back of his throat was a panicked flapping.

"You don't know us." Joshua spoke softly. "Leave us alone."

Christophe heard his brother's quiet statement and through the suffocating anger, he felt that he could breathe. For a minute he had thought he would drown in it. He let out a slow, shaky breath and was surprised; he was so angry it hurt, he was so angry he felt like he was going to cry.

"Go 'head, Sandman," Joshua said.

Christophe let out another breath he did not know he had been holding. It was all so stupid. All of it. He felt like he was dreaming. He glanced at Sandman and saw him raise a hand as if he was going to say something, then Sandman clenched his hand into a fist and let it fall. He wiped his knuckles along the front of his jeans.

"I got business to take care of," he said, staring pointedly at the girls, and then walked away from the bleachers. Christophe could not help but turn to watch him. He jerked past the court and past the swings and past the car until he ambled out along the street, walking as if his joints were strung together with string, his gate as jarring as a puppet's. Christophe let the ball drop to the bleachers. It bounced and stopped in the valley between his feet. Next to him, Joshua sighed. Christophe felt something nudge his shoulder and turned to see Javon passing him the blunt.

"Here you go."

Christophe took a hit before passing it to Joshua. Christophe closed his eyes and held the smoke in his lungs until he could not hold his breathe anymore, until his diaphragm began to shake and convulse in the effort to force his mouth open. He wished he could go swimming. He wished the game would end so he could play. He let the breath whoosh from him, and blinked to find Joshua balancing the ball in one hand and pulling him to his feet with the other towards the vacant court to play. His feet hit the ground, and he could hardly tell he was running.

9

THEY DID NOT TALK ABOUT IT UNTIL THE DAY BEFORE THE FOURTH of July, three days later; Joshua had been dismissed early from work, and they were at the fireworks tent next to the interstate perusing the all-in-one pre-wrapped kits. They had been debating whether to get a bunch of individual bottle rockets and roman candles and rocket bombs; Joshua thought they'd save money if they picked and chose what they wanted, and Christophe wanted one of the kits because it contained a special super-bomb. In the picture pasted to the front, the bomb looked as if it burst into a rose: a glittering, deep blue rose. Christophe had never seen anything like that, and part of him wanted to buy it because he just wanted to see if it was possible. He wanted to know if someone could make something explode into such a beautiful shape, or if the small, inky drawing on the advertisement was a sham. At the end of their small argument over fireworks, he told Joshua this, and Joshua bent over the case silently and squinted at the base of the bomb. He was trying to read the small print.

"I wasn't going to hit him."

Joshua nodded. "I know."

"I thought I could, but once I saw him…."

"Yeah."

"I know he ain't nothing—but it was like looking at you. His face."

Joshua had lost the tiny print. He skimmed it like a crossword puzzle for a word, and found the small script. Christophe squatted next to him and leaned in to peer at the writing. His shoulders brushed his brother's.

Joshua sniffed. They had gone with Paul to a farm further up in the country to pick out a goat to barbecue for the fourth. The goat had small, intelligent black eyes, white and black spotted fur, and four marbled horns. Christophe had been freaked out by it; he had said it looked like the devil and Uncle Paul had laughed. They had watched the man slaughter it; he had done it the old way and bought a sharp knife quickly across the bottom of the throat, thrusting upward. Joshua thought he could have done it a better way, because he saw the goat toss his head and jerk after the blood started to cascade from his neck to splatter the muddy ground. Its mouth had moved soundlessly as if it was trying to breathe and it had kicked as if it was wiping at a tuft of grass in the earth with its foot, and then it had stilled. Christophe had asked the man why he hadn't shot the thing in the head. The man, who was thin and red-skinned at the neck and forearms and had a head full of thick, bushy white hair, had laughed. He said something about fried brains. Christophe said he was going to throw up. Joshua could smell the musty odor of goat hair and he remembered the rich, heavy, offal scent of the blood, now. Uncle Paul was at his house; he was smoking and basting the goat. He would tend it all night. The print was too small to read.

"I think we should get it."

Christophe needed to get a QP from Dunny, and he needed to dump Joshua. The fourth would be a good day for making money—everybody wanted to get high on a holiday. Christophe told Joshua he needed to see Dunny after they left the fireworks stand, and asked Joshua if he wanted him to drop him off at the house or at Laila's or by Uncle Paul's. He paused a long time. Joshua spoke against the fist on his cheek and asserted that he was alright, he wanted to ride. Christophe resigned himself to Joshua's company. They watched the headlights cut through the darkness before them and Joshua began to search through the CD for a song he wanted to hear. For the first time in a long time, the thought of waking up the next morning to the summer didn't depress him. When he was younger, Christmas had been his favorite holiday, but as he'd gotten older, he'd developed a new appreciation for the fourth. Everything about the day was an indulgence: the new outfit he'd treated himself to, the barbecue, crawfish, and shrimp, the largesse of his extended family, the liquor, the weed, the fireworks, the girls in short skirts and halter tops. On that day, the heat was more than bearable; it was welcome. As Christophe turned into Dunny's driveway and switched off the lights and the car, he prayed it would not rain the next day.

For all the bluster of the air conditioner in the trailer, the living room was hot. Aunt Rita was sitting at the table slicing boiled eggs into slivers. On the stove, a large pot of potatoes was boiling. Christophe smelled cheese; he bet macaroni and cheese was in the oven. Aunt Rita was sweating lightly around her hairline, and as Christophe bent to kiss her, he saw it beading in little droplets on her nose. When his cheek came away from hers, he felt the cool touch of moisture on it. She laughed at him and wiped his face. Joshua walked in behind him.

"My favorite nephews."

"We your only nephews," Joshua grumbled as he hugged her. She poked him in the stomach with the wooden handle of her knife.

"Same difference." Aunt Rita sniffed and brushed her hand underneath her nose and waved them away from her. "Y'all smell like animal. Joshua, you got that money you said you was putting in on the food?"

Aunt Rita glanced at Christophe, and Joshua studied his feet as he pulled his wallet from his back pocket. Joshua hadn't told Christophe that they were contributing money to the family pot. Joshua placed the bills on the table one by one, and he did not look at Christophe as he did so. Aunt Rita's earrings, red, white, and blue plastic flags, shook as she turned to Christophe. "Dunny in the back. He probably trying on outfits like a girl. He bought around three today." She covered her mouth and sneezed.

"Bless you. We went with Uncle Paul to pick out the goat this morning." Christophe wanted to surreptitiously lower his face to smell his shirt. He balled his fists in his pockets. Everything was dirty about him: his body, his money. In the dim house, even Joshua's shirt seemed brighter than his.

"Thank you. Go ahead, now. Y'all making the kitchen stink like hot animal."

"You making potato salad and macaroni and cheese?" Christophe called out. "Yeah."

"Where Uncle Eze at?" Christophe heard Joshua ask this behind him.

"I don't know. I think he went down the way by Ozene's house."

"Oh."

Christophe waited for Joshua to catch up with him and punched him hard in the arm, joking to release the worm of spite, and ran to Dunny's door. Why hadn't he told him? He yanked it open without knocking. Dunny was on his knees on the floor in front of his dresser, and the bottom drawer sat next to him. Dunny's back was to the twins and two large QP bags of weed lay at his feet. Christophe saw him throw a small sandwich bag into the empty maw of the drawer. It had been white. Dunny turned to face them and Joshua reminded Christophe that he needed to step into the room with a loud, "That's how you want to play, huh?" and a stiff punch to his back. Christophe tripped through the door and caught himself on the bed, and Joshua slammed it shut behind him. Christophe felt Joshua's arm grabbing him around the waist and lifting him up to bodyslam him on the mattress. Christophe's spine and back stiffened; he wasn't laughing. Joshua must've felt this, because he let him go. Dunny threw one of the QPs back into the slot, and then picked up the other one and held it out toward Christophe.

"Here you go." Dunny was still wet from his shower. Christophe didn't move, so Dunny threw the bag on the bed. It landed between Christophe and Joshua, and Dunny began pulling on his clothes. He pulled his shorts over his boxers so quickly that the fabric at the back ballooned over the waist of his pants like the skin of a frog's croaking throat. He stubbed his toe on the misplaced drawer. He knelt down and began shoving the drawer into the slot; the rail was misaligned so he banged it with the heel of his hand. It stuck.

"You should pull it back out. You keep banging on it, it's going to jam." Joshua lay back in Dunny's bed and fanned himself with the front of his shirt. Christophe sat dully, still.

"What you threw up in there?" Christophe asked.

Dunny stopped his shoving. The drawer shifted and squeaked in relief. Dunny pulled a pair of socks from his top drawer and pulled one on; he took his time smoothing the cotton fabric up and over his heel and ankle.

His hair was freshly braided. Christophe knew perhaps that he should let it go, that he should imagine that he imagined it, but he couldn't.

"You hitting the pack?" Christophe asked.

"Fuck no, I'm not hitting the pack!" Dunny glared.

"So you selling," Joshua jackknifed up in the bed, "and now Dunny snorting powder?"

"You got me fucked up!" Dunny frowned at Joshua and waved toward Christophe. "I don't know what he saw."

"Stop lying, nigga. Either you holding or you selling. Which one?" Christophe said.

"You didn't see shit." Dunny snatched the lotion from the top of his dresser and pumped the head of the bottle.

"You lying to me like I'm one of these niggas out here that ain't family. I ain't crazy, nigga. I know what I saw." Christophe said. He stood.

"What the hell?" Joshua said.

"Come on, Joshua. This motherfucker lying."

"I'm lying now?" Dunny threw his towel across the room. It landed on the bed in a sodden heap. Joshua stood. Christophe turned from the door and walked over to point his finger in Dunny's face.

"Fuck yeah. You put me on, you take care of me, and then you act like you don't know me when I ask you a simple ass question. Fuck you, Dunny. If you ain't going to be real with me, why should I fuck with you? Why not fuck with any of these shady niggas out here? Blood, remember?" Christophe hit Joshua with his shoulder as he passed him. "Let's go, Joshua."

"Damn, Chris. Calm down." Dunny sat on the chair next to his dresser. He crossed his arms and rubbed his foot over the carpet as if it itched. Christophe turned back to the room and walked past Joshua again, who watched both of them, his mouth puckered.

"It's like being a little kid. Sometimes you just lie cuz it's the easiest thing to do." Dunny said as he rolled his eyes at them. "It's not like I'm proud of the shit." He knelt and began pulling at the drawer. Between small grunts that sounded like he was hurting himself, he huffed. "Y'all niggas sit the fuck down." He wrenched the drawer free. Christophe flinched at the noise. Dunny reached into the bottom of the dresser and fumbled; Christophe heard plastic bags sliding and rustling against each other. Dunny had never told Christophe to get the weed for himself even though he knew Christophe knew where the stash was. Christophe had thought Dunny simply had control issues. Could he be snorting? It didn't look like he'd lost any weight. Dunny threw a small plastic bag to the bed between the brothers. It barely made a sound as it landed next to the QP. It lay on its side on the bed next to the large, green QP like a small, dirty yellow moon. Joshua picked it up. Christophe's jaw eased. It wasn't powder. He saw four bits of opaque crack in the corner of the bag; they looked like teeth.

"I told you I wasn't snorting powder." Dunny joked weakly as he sat. Christophe stared at him dryly, and Dunny grimaced.

"So you ain't smoking it." Joshua threw the bag back to Dunny across the room. Dunny snatched it from the air with one hand, and it disappeared in his fat, large fist.

"Funny, Joshua."

"When you start selling that?" Christophe's voice sliced neatly through the dry banter. He suddenly felt claustrophobic. Discarded clothes lined the floor like wood shavings in a cage. Dunny folded his arms again.

"I told you I been thinking about leaving the game. I was just trying to stack some more paper...I mean, I know this house mine when my mama go, but damn, I'm grown and Eze here and I know they just want to be alone sometime." Dunny opened his arms to them and the bag of crack glinted in his hand like a ring. "They got a piece of land, a couple of acres, an acre over that way." Dunny pointed to his left. "My mama hooked it up so I was paying the property taxes on it. It's going to be mine if the owner don't come up with the taxes this year. I just need enough to put a down payment on my own trailer...my mama said she'd co-sign for it." He threw the bag in the mouth of the dresser with a small tap. "I wasn't making the money fast enough. Javon put me on for a little bit." He felt for the drawer's grooves; the muted muscles in his shoulders jumped as he patiently adjusted it by centimeters, feeling out the mouth. The drawer slid smoothly into the metal tracks this time. "Think about it. I know y'all won't leave Ma-mee, and y'all shouldn't, but we could have our own spot. To chill. To get fucked up. All our own. Y'all know what's mine is y'all's."

"Dunny, you know what's going to happen." Christophe let the sentence dissolve in the air between them like smoke.

"Nigga, I'm the one that put you on. Big Cuz. Of course I know what might happen. But that ain't going to happen. These assholes ain't catching me with shit. That's why I keep it in the bag. If I get pulled over, I'm going to swallow that shit." He frowned. "Sides, I only been doing this for about a month and a half. I started about when you did. I give this shit another month, tops, and then I'm done. By then I'll have enough saved up to make up the rest of the money for the down payment and then that's it. I'm done."

"With everything?" Joshua asked. Christophe thought he sounded hopeful.

"Shit, you can't expect me to stop cold turkey." Dunny laughed and the sound of it dropped like stones from his mouth. He rubbed at his sole before he pulled the other sock over his naked foot. "Really though, I'm giving it up. Weed, too, by the end of the summer." He hesitated. "I'm in the game until my nigga's out." Dunny looked at Christophe meaningfully as he picked up his shoe. "I make enough money so that I don't need this shit. Want, yeah—need, no. I mean, I might still get a couple of QPs to smoke every once in a while, and sell a couple of dimesacks out my smoking sack, but fuck all this moving QPs. I'm tired of riding around shitting on myself whenever I see a cop car in St. Catherine's. Shit, I can't get no pussy if I'm always ducking and dodging the police whenever shit getting good."

Joshua surprised Christophe with a high-pitched laugh. "You can't get no pussy noway." Christophe looked down at his pockets. Dunny had given him a deadline. The weight of Dunny's words bore down on the curve of his skull, the angled slope of his shoulders, to rest in the dry, veiny skin of his dark hands. It rested in them like something palpable, something material: like the heavy, sawdust-filled medicine ball they'd thrown to each other in basketball practice.

"Y'all want to go by Javon's house?" asked Dunny.

"What for?" Joshua said. Christophe pocketed the QP and flexed his hand over the bag; it crunched and gave in his fist.

"I ain't got time to go out to Germaine tonight and wait around on Lean. I need another QP, and Javon got some." Dunny pocketed a roll of cash bound with a rubber band.

"Man," Joshua hesitated, "I told Laila I would stop by and see her tonight before I went home."

"Shit, we can pick her up, too." Dunny shrugged. "We just going by Javon house. He always got a gang of niggas over there anyway."

"You drive," Christophe said.

"Fine." Dunny led the way out of the door. Christophe barely resisted the urge to crush the bag of weed in his pocket, to flatten it into a pancake, a disc that he could sling across the room like a Frisbee. He wondered if it would fly far, and if the drawer on Dunny's dresser was open, if he could sail it into the hiding spot from the bed. After Christophe watched Joshua walk out the door, he rose and felt his way along the wall until his hand hit the light-switch. The room went dark, and Christophe pulled the door shut behind him.

Joshua stood on his toes before Laila's window and reached up and knocked. The side of the house her room was on was shadowed, and the woods leaned in so close that he felt the touch of underbrush at his back. A leaf caressed his ear. The light clicked on in the room, and he prepared to duck as he saw the curtain flutter: Laila's face shone at the window and she smiled at him. She disappeared. Dunny had parked on the curve. Joshua waited for her at the ditch. Surreptitiously, he lowered his head to sniff at his shirt, to gauge his funk. Yeah, he stunk like goat and musk. She had called often after the kiss. He had waited until Christophe left the house and called her back because he wanted to see her again, wanted to pull her into his lap and feel her weight, soft and sure, wanted to feel her mouth opening, wet and warm beneath his, wanted to cup the back of her head and pull her to him by her soft, curly hair. He didn't want to do any of this in front of Christophe, muted and solitary as he was these days. It was why he hadn't mentioned the money; he hadn't wanted to shame him. Joshua watched her run to him across the lawn on her toes. She ran like a girl, her legs kicking out to the side, and it made him want to pick her up when she stopped before him.

"Hey."

"Hey."

"You want to come with us by Javon house? Or you going to get in trouble?"

"Naw, my mama don't care. Y'all ain't going to be over there all night, is y'all?"

"Naw." He wanted to touch her. Joshua crawled in the backseat. Laila followed him. Joshua glanced at Christophe as they pulled away from the ditch. Christophe was slouched down in the seat so far Joshua could only see his hair, blowsy as a jellyfish in a current. He was ignoring them. Dunny tossed a cigar and a small sack to Joshua over the backseat, and Joshua began to cut at the cigar with his fingernail over an empty shoebox top he picked up off the floor. Laila had scooted over so her leg was against his own. The moon was high in the sky: it lit her thigh. He could barely see her face as the stereo boomed and dropped the rhythm, but he could feel her, dense and small next to him. Joshua realized he was leaning into her, pulled by her gravity, so he hunched over the platter of weed on his lap and tried to concentrate. He could smell honeysuckle coming in through the window, and he immediately associated it with her, as if she were blooming.

He handed her a flashlight he'd picked up from the floor that Dunny kept in his car for just this occasion and told her to hold it as he opened the baggie. The light jiggled and danced in her hand, and for a moment he forgot Dunny and Christophe in the front seat. It seemed that it was only the two of them in the dark, together. He swept the thought away from him with the seeds he brushed from the tray out of the window. This was a sentiment he had only felt for his brother. Laila switched off the flashlight.

By the time they pulled into the oyster shell driveway at Javon's house, Joshua had lit the blunt and passed it to Dunny, who had passed it back to him. Laila had taken two hitching hits and expelled the smoke in jagged coughs. Christophe had refused it. The driveway was clogged with cars, and light from what Joshua supposed was the TV threw bright, electric shocks of colors through the filmy curtains along the living room's front windows. The night was sticky and loud. The two houses Joshua could see from Javon's yard were silent, their windows dark and closed like lidded eyes. They sat in the car until Joshua and Dunny finished the blunt. Joshua rubbed his hand along the top of Laila's hair as they exited the car and followed his cousin and his brother into the house, and they all walked up the steeply sloped driveway lined with oyster shells. As he picked his way around the cars, the shells crunched and shifted under his feet and threw him off balance. Laila's hair had been fine and smooth as running water. He grabbed her hand when they got to the carport, and lifted her arm and ducked his head so that her hand rested on his own fuzzy braids. Dunny knocked perfunctorily and entered the door. Christophe followed him. Joshua and Laila paused on the steps.

"You going to braid me and Chris's hair tonight?" Joshua let her go and straightened, and her palm trailed down the side of his face to his shoulder. She pressed into his collarbone briefly.

"Yeah." She smoothed the sheaf of her ponytail behind her head. "If Javon got some rubber bands and grease." Half of Laila's face was lit by the room, the other side was shadowed and washed black by the night. She was smiling tentatively: her lips were pursed as if she were waiting for a kiss. He closed the door and kissed her lightly and quickly. Joshua pushed her on the small of her back and made her enter the door before him just so he could touch her. The room was bright, and it was filled with people. Felicia was sitting on the sofa, leaning over the armrest and laughing at the TV set on top of a bigger, broken wooden TV that looked like it was manufactured during the seventies: a comedian in a leather suit was limping across the stage.

Dunny had hit a possum once, and when they stopped in the middle of the road and shined the headlights on it, it had looked like that as it died. Felicia laughed harder; her smile was so different from Laila's—her teeth were brighter, sharper, less kind. Big Henry and Remy sat on the faux-velvet upholstered sofa with her. They had forties in paper bags in their laps. They drank at the same time, and Joshua watched the beer bubble and he was thirsty. He pushed the thirst away: he was already fucked up. Joshua sat on the floor in an open space as Laila disappeared to the back of the house where the bedrooms were. By the time he recognized the comedian was Eddie Murphy and began to chuckle, Laila was straddling his shoulders and taking down his braids with a comb in her hand. The carpet was grimy; everyone still had their shoes on. Flaps of plastic hung from the couch like forgotten clothes on a clothesline. The edges were sharp. Joshua saw movement and heard voices, loud and belligerent, in the kitchen where Christophe and Dunny had gone, and then he sank back into the sofa, into Laila's legs and her probing, steady hands, and he let the high usher him away from his steady worry about the both of them.

In the kitchen, Christophe leaned against the wall just inside the doorway. Marquise and Skeetah were kneeling on the floor; Skeetah had his hands to his mouth like he was blowing in a conch shell. He whipped his hand back and opened his fist. Dice clattered along the cracked and peeling tile floor and stopped just short of a pile of dirty green money at Javon and Bone's feet. The boys had pushed the kitchen table and chairs to a corner to clear the floor for craps. A bare light bulb burned in the low ceiling. Marquise was giving a running commentary while he slapped Skeetah on the back.

"Ah, shit, Skeetah. Craps, nigga. You can't roll dice for shit. You sorry. You should just go ahead and hand your money to me because the way you playing you just giving it away. Really though."

"Shut up, Marquise."

Christophe realized Franco was standing on the wall next to him, looking as if he was already wearing his fourth of July outfit: he wore a velour short set, the baby blue of it was as deep as the summer sky after a hard rain. His mother worked as a nurse and his father worked at the power plant, so he was always clean, had always been pretty and well-dressed ever since they were kids. He always had the newest shoes, the best baseball caps, the flyest fits. The line-up of Franco's hair that was so sharp it looked as if it had been cut with a razor, and Christophe looked away as Dunny crossed the room to shake Javon's hand. He remembered his own days of being fresh, of being clean, of smelling good—he sniffed the goat on his shirt and wanted to laugh at himself, but the urge died in the glare of the yellow fluorescent lights over the sink. He had ignored Felicia when he walked in the door; it was his way of imagining she couldn't see him like this. Bone rolled the dice.

"Seven." Bone called out, and knelt to scoop the dice. He gathered the pile of money from the floor and shoved it in his pocket. Skeetah stood. A hole the size of a quarter stretched at the neck of his navy T-shirt, and Christophe could see smudges of dirt smeared across his chest against the dark cloth.

"What you picked up the money for?" Skeetah asked.

"I won," Bone said.

"You ain't even going to roll again and give me a chance to win my money back?"

"Naw." Bone grinned and pulled on the black and mild cigar in his mouth.

"That's fucked up, Bone." Marquise pointed at Bone. "You know tomorrow the fourth and you know we just up in here playing for fun and you going to take the man money, anyway?"

Skeetah held his white palms out toward Bone; Christophe marveled at the fact that while the rest of Skeetah was so dark, his palms were pale and chalky. Calluses from his pit bull's leash sprouted across his palms like a constellation. "Man, c'mon, Bone. At least give me a chance to win my money back."

Bone stepped towards Skeetah. He had a rag tied low over his head so that it sheathed his scalp; Christophe knew he was trying to pack his waves down for the next day. Bone narrowed his eyes: they reminded Christophe of a snake's.

"Naw, nigga." Bone had a small grin on his face as he said this, but by the set of his eyes and the way he advanced slowly toward Skeetah until his tall bulk towered over him, Christophe knew he wasn't playing. "This what you two little niggas don't understand. I won the game. I take the money. Game over."

Dunny was shaking his head as he leaned on the counter next to Javon. He shrugged and whispered into Javon's ear.

"That is sort of fucked up, Bone," Franco said.

"You shut up, Franco. Ain't nobody asked you."

Marquise half-sat against the wall and looked away back toward the living room. Skeetah stared at Bone's chest with his eyes half-lidded as if he were sleepy, his arms on his waist. He was dangerously still. Christophe could tell Skeetah wanted to hit Bone, and suddenly, he hated Bone's clean-cut goatee, his expensive cologne, the gold loop gleaming in his ear. Christophe stepped in the middle of the two.

"Why you got to be such a asshole, Bone?" He heard rather than saw Dunny move from the counter. "That's some bullshit and you know it.

You got a whole pocket full of money and you can't let that nigga have a chance to get his money back?" Christophe stabbed his finger up toward Bone's eye and saw him flinch as he spit the words out. "You just being a bitch, that's all. Can't never let no other nigga get ahead."

"You better get your finger out my face," Bone bit out, but Christophe didn't care if he was the key that had turned in the lock to open the door to a confrontation. Joshua's face flashed in his brain, and he wanted it, suddenly.

"I ain't got to do shit. What you going to do if I don't?"

"I'm going to whip your ass."

Bone brought his hands up to shove Christophe and start the fight when Christophe saw a freckled arm whip out like a striking animal and push Bone backwards, and suddenly Javon was standing before him. Christophe had forgotten he was in Javon's house, that he was jabbing his finger into Javon's best friend's face, and that Javon had broken a white boy's jaw. He could not understand why he was not afraid. He wondered if Javon's face would turn another color if he hit him hard in the nose, if the cartilage and the bone would break under his knuckles, and if the blood would bloom red like a rose across his face.

"Chris. Chill out, nigga." Javon said, and Christophe saw that the pores of his face were large and defined and blended in with the freckles. "Ain't no need for all that." Christophe saw Javon's black eyes moving back and forth, saw that he was trying to gauge the play of emotions that confused even Christophe. Javon was looking at him. For some reason, this made Christophe rock back on his heels. He felt solid, tall. He nodded at Javon and stepped back and Dunny let him go. Javon turned to Bone.

"Pull the money out. Stop acting like you afraid to play," Javon said.

"I ain't afraid of shit."

Javon stepped so close to Bone his nose almost touched Bone's own.

"Well then play," Javon said.

Javon stood like a statue before Bone. Bone's nostrils flared. Javon let his head list to the side, and then he stepped past Bone to lean against the counter and pick up his pencil-thin cigar from where he had left it. He inhaled and let the smoke trail from his mouth so he could re-inhale it in through his nose; the yellow smoke ran out of him and into him, and it was the same color as his face. Bone threw the bills from his pocket to the floor where they scraped along the battered tile like crumbling brown leaves.

"I'm just going to win it back anyway," he grumbled. Bone dropped the dice to the floor. "I'm going to ride to the store and get some more blacks. Anybody want to ride?" No one answered him.

Christophe heard the door open and shut. He leaned around the corner to check on his brother, to see why his twin hadn't rushed into the kitchen when he heard them yelling, to find Joshua asleep on the floor between Laila's legs. She was pulling and threading his hair into an intricate weave of braids. The others were laughing at the television. A shelf in the corner twinkled with dust-cloaked porcelain figures: Christophe saw that they were small porcelain clowns invoking multiple poses of hilarity. A few lay cracked or tumbled on their sides; they looked as if they had fallen stricken in a field of ash. Laila looked up from her work to catch him studying her and murmured, "He fell asleep." Long, snakelike bangs had pulled free of her ponytail: the hair fell over her eyes. She was small and light next to Felicia, and as her hair waved before her eyes, he wondered if her hair would be as thick and slick as Felicia's in his hands. Laila looked pointedly at Christophe and raised her eyebrows at him, "You next."

Christophe suppressed the urge he had to walk over to his brother, to wake him, to pull him up and away from Laila and back two months into their world. His brother trusted her; his eyes were half open in sleep, and he lay against her as if he were wounded. Christophe returned to the kitchen to find Javon standing before him with a blunt in his hand, and Dunny shaking the dice so quickly his fist began to blur like a hummingbird's wings. Dunny was watching him. The smoke wafted in an amorous tendril up Christophe's nose: he was so tired of that smell, of the harsh, biting burn of it. He hesitated in the act of shaking his head no, of refusing the blunt, and sniffed again. There was something sweet about the smell, something unfamiliar and dense; something that crystallized like sugar in his nose. Javon smiled at him and dangled the blunt closer to Christophe's face.

"California. Some of my cousins brought it down."

Christophe grabbed the blunt. Still smiling, Javon leaned on the wall next to Christophe. Dunny swept the dice from the floor and yelled out "point," and then threw them back out. They rapped over the floor. Christophe held the smoke in his lungs and heard the dice like a knocking hand on a door: he inhaled again and a door opened inside him. He passed the blunt to Javon. Shaking his hand, Dunny pistoned his arm back and forth like he was trying to start an errant, rusted-over lawn mower. Christophe laughed, and Javon passed him the blunt.

Laila startled Christophe: she gripped his arm, and told him that she had been saying his name for a few moments but he must have not heard her. He followed her to the sofa; Joshua's hair was done, and he had scooted over to make room for Christophe and had fallen back asleep. Laila pulled the elastic band out of Christophe's hair and his head lolled back and he peered at her. She was as pretty as Felicia; her nose was smaller, but her lips weren't as big. His eyes felt veiled by cotton. He was floating. She giggled and said, "You high," and began braiding his hair. Someone got off the sofa and passed in front of the television like an eclipse of the moon. Christophe was not surprised when a red-dotted hand descended in front of his face.

"I rolled another one," Javon intoned. Christophe giggled. The fact that he could not feel Laila's hands yanking his hair was even funnier, since he knew from the way his eyes were jerking that she was doing so. Eddie Murphy guffawed: his laughter sounded like the bray of a donkey. Inhaling the smoke from the blunt was like breathing: as his chest shuddered he wondered if he had ever been able to take a breath without it burning, and if so, why? Something sounded like a shirt ripping, and Christophe saw that Joshua's mouth had opened wider and he was snoring. Christophe was so high his eyelids felt swollen shut.

Dunny interrupted Joshua's snoring by shoving him awake and telling him it was time to go. Skeetah and Marquise had wandered into the living room and were sitting on the floor, drinking beer, and everyone else was staring dully at the television, empty bottles in hand. Once in a while, Javon would make a joke and interrupt Eddie's act, and everyone would laugh. Christophe guffawed and rocked back and forth. Joshua frowned, and wearily rose. Christophe noticed belatedly that Felicia had left while he'd been getting braided up, and that his hand had been cupping Laila's foot. Laila wiped her hands on her shorts to clean them of hair grease, blushing. Christophe gave Javon a long handshake, and Javon insisted that he and Joshua stop by the next day: Javon had one hundred pounds of boiled, spicy shrimp and he was barbecuing, and he didn't want to have any left over on July the fifth. Christophe said he felt like eating it all now, and Javon had snorted and said he wouldn't pick them up until the next day.

Dunny drove to Laila's house first. Christophe watched Joshua walk her up to her front door. He thought Joshua wasn't going to kiss her because they stood in the light from the front porch and talked for so long. They seemed skittish around each other; while Joshua stood straight and solid as a bull, Laila leaned forward and away from him as gracefully as an egret. When they kissed, Christophe looked away. He could not remember the last time he had smoked so much; he knew it was before he began selling. Dunny pulled into his own driveway and parked; Christophe's eyes opened a bit more when the car stopped and without prodding, he got out of the car and walked to the Caprice and sat in the passenger seat. As Joshua pulled away, Christophe yelled out the window, slurring, that they'd see Dunny the next day at the picnic at Ma-mee's house. A fox darted out of the underbrush at the edge of a ditch and then disappeared again. Christophe looked at the tunnel of light preceding the car back to his brother and knew that when Joshua had awoken to see him holding himself and laughing soundlessly with his teeth bared, Joshua had believed his brother was in pain.

When Joshua drank his first beer on the morning of the fourth, he was sitting on the picnic bench that he and Dunny and Christophe had just unloaded off the back of Uncle Paul's truck. Three picnic tables formed a half-square in the fresh cut lawn around the iron drum grill. It was ten o'clock: the air reminded Joshua of melting butter. He watched Uncle Paul spread a red, white, and blue tablecloth over the last picnic table, and then mumbling something about the goat not being finished, he drove off. Joshua heard Aunt Rita and Uncle Eze arguing about who was bringing cold drinks for the kids, and he followed Christophe and Dunny into the house. Christophe seemed quieter this morning; he woke and dressed slowly, and when Uncle Paul offered him a beer after they'd plopped the last table down, he'd refused one. After Joshua and Christophe dressed, they walked out into the yard, the colors of their outfits blinding and crisp. The twins sat at a table with Dunny and Ma-mee and Aunt Rita, while Uncle Paul drove into the dirt driveway and slammed the door with a beer-slurred whoop and proclaimed that the goat was ready. Julian, Maxwell, and David sat at the other tables with their girlfriends and wives and children, handing out plates and measuring out portions, complaining about each other's grilling skills, and accusing each other of filching shots of moonshine from Paul's bottle. Joshua lugged one of the roasting pans of goat to the table, and after Christophe ladled some of the meat onto Ma-mee's plate, they began to eat. Joshua opened three bottles of beer. Each bottle sprayed small, icy geysers of mist as Joshua opened them to the heat. He passed one to Dunny on his left, and one past Ma-mee to Christophe on the right even though neither had asked him for one, and he took his first sip. He watched Ma-mee scoop a huge, barbecue-slathered bite of goat into her mouth, close her eyes, and chew.

They ate until they had to shove their pants down over the extended globes of their bellies. They ate, drank beer, brushed away flies, wiped sweat from their slick, cologne-scented faces with napkins, and then ate again. Christophe sucked ribs and shrugged away the platter of goat. Joshua could not stop himself from scooping more goat on his plate: Paul had cooked it so long that the meat seemed to melt like hot, syrupy candy in his mouth. Joshua remembered goat as a stringy dark meat, but the red spicy mass before him was nothing like he recalled. Joshua opened beer after beer and passed them: as the sun slid from its zenith to lick the tops of the pines, the beer and the heat made the day golden and easy for them all. Christophe seemed more his old self, quick to humor. After he kidded Dunny about him sneaking one of Aunt Rita's wine coolers, Christophe said that he wanted to go to Javon's house.

"Javon say he got a whole cooler-full of shrimp at his house: a hundred pounds. I'ma go get some for you." Christophe told Ma-mee.

"Y'all going to be back to pop the fireworks? I don't want them kids to be blowing up the big ones by theyself. They'll put somebody's eye out," Ma-mee said. Her hair was slicked back and shone like a silver cap: her profile was soft and falling.

"Yeah." Christophe nodded as he rose. "We going to pop the big ones when we get back." Christophe grabbed a bag of bottle rockets and lighters and pumps that rested by his feet and pulled out a handful and shoved them into his cavernous shorts pockets. "We going to pop these on the way."

"Hold on." Dunny rubbed his stomach and put one hand on the table. "Why don't we wait?"

"By the time we get there, all the shrimp going to be gone."

Dunny tossed his plate into the garbage can. "I feel like going to sleep." He rose and wove between the tables and islands of chairs and walked to the street. Joshua trailed Christophe as they skipped heavily across the lawn to catch up with Dunny. They hopped over the ditch and landed on the street in a swarm of gnats. As they walked, the gnats drifted along with them like a cloud of golden dust roused by the sonorous, beer-suffused sway of their bodies through the sunset. Joshua wished he'd grabbed another beer. Giggling children hid in the ditches and shot bottle rockets in front and behind them as they walked past; the sparks shot through the air like manic, fizzing fireflies. Dogs leapt in and out of the ditches and woods and barked. The yards they passed were packed with cars and lawn chairs and tables and people; the air suffused with charcoal and barbecue and sulfur. A caravan of go-carts swooped past them; pre-teen boys wearing wave caps and basketball jerseys drove with one hand while shooting roman candles into the ditches with their other. Joshua felt as if they were walking with a demented, royal escort.

"One of y'all badasses shoot me and I'm a set y'all on fire." Dunny yelled at the kids in the ditches.

Joshua wondered if the little girl with the clacking braids and the dark and light little boys were in the ditches right now, wiping blood from their legs where the blackberry vines had scratched them and giggling. He imagined them there in the mellowing dark, whispering. A bottle rocket shot past inches away from Dunny's belly, and Joshua heard rustling and laughing from the undergrowth.

"Y'all keep on. I got a bomb at the house!" Dunny shouted. The bushes were still. Joshua waved his cousin on, and bottle rockets whizzed past where they had been standing.

"They just playing."

"They going to make me go to war."

"Against some eight year olds?"

"Shut up."

"You need another beer." Christophe broke into the conversation, and as Bobby Blue Bland crooned from a truck stereo, so loud and funky Joshua could almost smell the sweat and the cigarette smoke and see the faded pool tables and the big hair eighties pin-up girls on the Kool cigarette posters at the local hole in the wall blues club, The Oaks. Christophe lit the bottle rocket and watched the fuse burn down to the paper, where it flared.

Christophe threw the rocket above his head into the air at the last moment, and the rocket hissed and shot into the darkening sky. It flew in a graceful arc and exploded in a burst of golden, showering sparks. Christophe handed Dunny an incense pump and a sheaf of red and blue bottle rockets, and he passed them to Joshua, who began to throw them into the air. Dunny ambled between them: for all his talk about shooting at the kids in the ditches, Dunny didn't like to throw firecrackers. When the twins were eight and he was eleven, he had been teaching them how to throw bottle rockets in a game of war with Skeetah and Big Henry and Marquise, and the bottle rocket he threw in the air had shot Big Henry in the eye instead of harmlessly glancing off his pants or singeing his skin or even burning a hole in his T-shirt. Big Henry's eye had been blistered shut for days after the fourth, and now Dunny would only throw bottle rockets when he was very, very drunk, which would usually result in him throwing a bottle rocket into a moving car or into a yard full of sated partiers. Christophe tried to keep them away from him, but Joshua guessed he was too drunk or reckless to care who he'd passed them to. By the time they reached Javon's yard, the sun had set. Joshua threw a bottle rocket back into the street and heard a loud, staticky explosion undercut by the squeal of go-cart wheels.

"Sorry!" He yelled. He heard laughter, and the go-cart sped away.

Javon had set out several white plastic lawn chairs in the balding yard; the grass grew tough and stringy, and had given way in several places to red, sandy earth. The yard was a field of people in crisp jean shorts and white shirts and short dresses lounging and smoking and eating and laughing with paper plates and plastic platters of boiled shrimp on their laps. A hundred gallon cooler of shrimp sat open next to Javon. He flipped burgers and prodded hotdogs as coals hissed. Bone sat in a seat next to the cooler, alternately wiping at his face with a paper towel and shooing away flies circling the cooler of shrimp. Dunny shook hands with Bone and

Javon, while Joshua grabbed a dark blue plastic platter. Javon set down his spatula and gripped Christophe's hand and spoke to him.

"I been betting everybody that I'll give them a hundred dollars if they can sit here and finish off the cooler, but it's only halfway empty."

"Couldn't nobody eat all that." Bone swigged his beer.

"I hope you got some plastic bags. Ma-mee love shrimp," Christophe said.

"They somewhere in there." Javon turned back to the burgers. "Want a hamburger, Dunny?"

"I'm so full. I done ate so much goat I feel like a goat. Mean as shit."

"You got some beer?" Joshua scooped shrimp onto his platter with his hands. He had torn his skin on the thin area just below his thumb fingernail; the shrimp were so spicy that the juice burned. The orange and cream rubbery bodies were a little warmer than the air. Bone handed him a beer. The bite of the beer inflamed the spice of the shrimp in his mouth, and he loved it.

"I told them to use two bags of shrimp boil with these…it cost extra, but they good," Javon said.

"Tell me about it." Bone burped and covered his mouth with his hand, too late.

In the house, Christophe looked out the window over the kitchen sink and saw Sandman with a rake in his hands: he was raking pine needles in Javon's backyard. Christophe stood and watched him stab at the ground with the rake until he paused and picked up a beer half buried in the grass and drank. He closed his eyes; they popped open and he peered into the can. After shaking it, he set it down and reached into his pocket, fingering his pipe before drawing it halfway out. Sandman's lips were moving. He talked to himself as he walked toward the door. The doorknob squeaked. Christophe turned hurriedly to the cabinets and began pulling them out and slamming them shut. The door opened and closed behind Sandman, and Christophe stopped in mid-pull and gripped the cabinet. What had he been looking for? Behind him, Sandman opened the refrigerator door, and Christophe heard the crack of a beer top opening.

"It's hot out there," Sandman said. He reeked of beer.

"What?" Christophe asked Sandman without turning.

"Just making conversation."

Christophe heard Sandman sliding along the counter toward him.

He could not take his eyes off the drawer.

"I thought I told you that I didn't have no words for you." Christophe's hand was shaking.

"I ain't asking you for nothing." Christophe smelled Sandman, ripe with cut grass and rank, next to him. "I mean, I'm just trying to make a living—just like you," Sandman said.

"Why don't you go back where you came from?" Christophe asked.

"This my place just as much as it's yourn, boy." Sandman slurred his derision. "Would be nice to see your mama, though. I bet she still look as good as she used to."

"Fuck you!" Christophe's arm bunched and contracted and the drawer was flying from the counter and swinging freely in his hand, and the contents: empty, ink-stained envelopes and pens and bottle openers and spoons, were flying through the air. They pelted Sandman's legs and dropped, or missed him and slid across the floor. Felicia walked into the kitchen and stopped short of the mess on the floor.

"What's wrong?"

"Where the sandwich bags at?" Christophe yelled.

"In here," she said, and opened a cabinet over the sink. Christophe grabbed a handful of spoons and pens and dumped them into the drawer and handed it to her as she passed him the box of bags. Sandman had backed away to the refrigerator again: he looked especially small and dirty next to the cream front of the refrigerator door. Felicia was wearing something tight and red: she glittered in the small room like a ruby, shaming Sandman's grimy clothing and face and the hungry beating of Christophe's heart. He ran.

Christophe walked up to the group and stood with a gallon size plastic Ziploc bag in his hand. Bone asked "You want a beer?" His buzz, gone: his brother, drunk as his father and keeping things from him; and Felicia, hard and cold as a jewel as she resumed her seat, not even looking at him.

Javon handed Christophe a beer. When Christophe took it from him, Javon's fingers were as cold as the beer bottle. Christophe peeled away the gold Michelob paper, dipped into the shrimp cooler, and dumped a spattering of shrimp onto his plate. He began to peel the shells away from the bodies and eat, and let the beer grow warm, untouched. At the nearest house, beyond a stand of woods, partiers were shooting firework cannons into the air. They shrieked into the navy sky and exploded in shapes: a red flower, a yellow sun. Javon was breaking down a cluster of purple-green weed for a blunt. Christophe pulled the tail away from the meat. He wondered if Sandman was still raking back there in the elongating shadows, and he imagined himself sneaking around the house, hitting him hard enough with a beer bottle to make him collapse. If Javon offered, Christophe planned to smoke. Another firework hurtled through the air, and Christophe watched it ascend and dropped the shrimp from his fingers when he saw it burst into a brilliant, sparkling blue flower. He watched the flower flare and fade like rain down the pane of a window. Another flower bloomed in the sky.

"Did you see that?" Christophe turned to Joshua to see him sucking the last foamy residue from a bottle of beer, his head tilted back. He was smiling around the bottle. Christophe wanted his attention. He kicked him.

"What!" The bottle shaded Joshua's mouth so that all Christophe could see of his brother in the dark was his eyes, which were curved like machete blades at the corners. Joshua wiped at his shoe with his free hand. "I know you ain't scuffed my shit." Joshua lost his balance and the bottle moved with him as he slumped momentarily over. "I ain't got it to burn," he mumbled. Christophe could see his mouth now; he was serious, he wasn't grinning.

"The flower," Christophe said drunkenly, and looked up as another blue rose erupted there.

"Oh," said Joshua. "I missed it." Christophe looked down and knew his brother hadn't even bothered to look because he was doubled over trying to peer at his foot in the dark. None of the others were looking at the sky: it was as if only Christophe could see the miracle of those blue flowers in that yard.

10

JOSHUA WONDERED WHY CILLE HADN'T SCHEDULED HER VACATION A week and a half earlier so she could have spent the fourth with them, but he remembered her jazz festival, and he told himself that was why she hadn't come to see them on the holiday. At least she chose to fly in on a Wednesday evening: he had asked Leo to let him off a little early so he could ride to the New Orleans airport with Christophe to pick her up. When Leo told him the supervisor had assented on Tuesday afternoon, Joshua had only nodded. He was tired all the time, now. It colored his hours with another longing besides wanting to be with Ma-mee, with Laila, to understand his brother, and tangentially, his mother: a longing for rest, a longing for the cessation of movement and worry about movement in the guise of gyrating cranes and flying sacks and shifting crates and ascending lifts and sliding pallets and diving gulls. When he went back to work two days after the fourth, he'd remained alert enough to get his job done, and passed the hours by daydreaming of swimming at the river with Laila. He'd imagined her on his back while he stood in the amber, silvery water: her body soft against him, her arms around his shoulders.

They took the back way to New Orleans. They forsook the fastest route, deviating from the long, dreary, straight line of I-10 that ran from the pines of Mississippi across the gray flat expanse of Lake Pontchartrain into the low swamps of Louisiana to the bright steel and warped, garish color of New Orleans; instead, they took I-90. When Ma-mee was younger, it was the route she took to the city. They headed west, and the two-lane highway shrank to a two-lane road, and then they were cruising along the skirt of Lake Pontchartrain. Uncle Paul called it Duke country, and Joshua figured Uncle Paul probably got his presentiment from a sign outside one of the camps; even though David Duke had been defeated as governor for Louisiana years ago, some fishing camp proprietor had kept a huge homemade billboard on the edge of his camp facing the road that read "Duke" in big white letters on a background so dark blue it almost looked black.

The road wound before them through marsh grass and sparse pines, and fishing camps dotted the asphalt's sides at regular intervals in tiny, half-acre lots. The camps squatted on the edge of the bay at the water; beyond them, Joshua saw the water of the lake on his right, and the water of the Gulf of Mexico on his left. The fishing camps had names like Bayou Fishing and Sauvage Critters and Rebel Rendezvous, and even though Joshua had often ridden to New Orleans with his brother or with Dunny or Ma-mee or Paul to the airport or to Bourbon Street or to visit one of Ma-mee's brothers, he had never seen anyone, any living and walking human beings, white or black, in any of those fishing camps. If it weren't for the bright paint and the neatly shelled driveways and the cut grass, he would've sworn that no one worked or lived there, that the place existed as a mirage, as an idea, as a foreboding relic to black people to remind them that outside their own communities, there existed enmity and history and dread hidden in the pines and the marsh that was based on the color of their skin.

In the summer of 1984, before Pontchartrain Beach Amusement Park closed, Ma-mee and Uncle Paul had taken them to visit the park. They'd just turned three, and all Joshua remembered of that day was the roaring battery of the colossal white Zephyr roller coaster that he was too afraid to ride, and the eerie emptiness of the fishing camps and the road leading to the park. With his arm out the window and the salty air whistling cleanly up his nostrils, Joshua remembered the way Ma-mee had held his hand while he watched Christophe walk off with Uncle Paul to ride the roller coaster. When Joshua had asked his brother what it was like after he'd gotten off, Christophe had only said that it was fast, and it jerked a lot. Christophe hadn't asked to ride again, and had instead been content to sit at one of the benches along the boardwalk next to his brother and eat the sandwiches that Ma-mee had packed for them. On their ride back to Mississippi, as Christophe nodded off next to him with his head resting on Joshua's shoulder, Joshua had sucked the remains of cotton candy from the seam of his fingernails, and watched Ma-mee dangle her hand out the window of the car and wave at the streaming night and rustling of marsh grasses.

Joshua understood why Ma-mee loved the drive: in the setting sun's light, the marsh grasses quivered and lashed violently in the wind, turning one way and another to catch the light and turn from green to gold to rose to wheat. The marsh greenery shuddered and bent into the caress of the air crossing from the gulf to the lake over the narrow inlet of sand and pine and grass; all of it shimmered and shone like Laila's face or Ma-mee's eyes or a broad, short, bow-legged pit in mid-leap through the air— something made beautiful for its own sake, something inviting adoration simply because it exists. Christophe turned the stereo down one notch so they could hear the music and the sounds from outside the car at the same time: the silky grass, the leaning and cracking pines, the insistent singing of the insects. Both Joshua and Christophe had showered and dressed to meet their mother in their new fourth of July outfits that Christophe had recently washed. After Christophe picked him up from work earlier that Wednesday afternoon, Joshua had starched both of their jean shorts into cardboard stiff lines; the creases in the legs were like box edges. They crossed a narrow bridge: Joshua was sure if he reached his arm out of the window of the car as Ma-mee had done that evening, he could touch the black rusted bars of the steel tunnel. The sun shone from the water in golden, glassy waves.

It was always a surprise when 90 emptied out into the city. Suddenly, they were in an old neighborhood east of New Orleans, and they followed the signs to meet up with I-10: once they were in the city, it was the only way they knew to get to the airport. The signs that led them to the interstate were small, green, and innocuous: they perched on skinny, nearly invisible iron poles and hid themselves in clusters of oak leaves and branches. The two hadn't really talked while they were getting ready, and now there was something perfunctory about the way Christophe drove.

He hadn't seemed excited when they left, and he'd tied a rag over his hair instead of oiling it for Cille. Joshua lay his head tentatively on the windowsill of the door and stared out at the projects. The red, faded two-story brick buildings squatted in obscure, unexpected places: they waited with patient tenacity in the sudden corners of the city. They sat perched at regular intervals in the maze of New Orleans streets; they spread over sandy, oak-studded lots and menaced the warped, salmon pink or turquoise blue old mansions that cringed away from them across the wide, grassy, oak lined avenues. The trolley cut like a razor blade on its tracks to separate the two. Everyone he saw in the streets seemed cut from the trunks of the ancient, bowing oaks. Joshua watched small dark children play inscrutable games on the sidewalks.

The balconies on the buildings looked as if they were going to sag and collapse into one another like cards. Women in stretched-out, oversized T-shirts and short skirts braided hair on their stoops. The boys who sat between the women's legs were shirtless or wore wide-necked, off-white T-shirts and wifebeaters. Those who were already braided or wore hats seemed always on the verge of crossing the streets at corners. They played dice games against pockmarked deli storefronts that sold beer, food, crawfish and shrimp poboys. They spoke to one another and gold shone when their mouths opened. Older, gray-haired women in long, shapeless skirts entered the dark mouths of the delis and surfaced with small brown paper bags. Men that reminded Joshua of Sandman walked along the sidewalks and crossed the streets heedless of the slow flow of traffic; they danced between the cars and stared wide-eyed at the windshields. Their hair stood in knotted, luxuriant half-afro-half-dreaded shocks.

The whole city seemed on the verge of collapsing, of coming apart and spewing into the streets to slide and submerge in the river. Joshua imagined it all gone: the levees, the sea of white aboveground tombs, the French Quarter, the flickering sparkle of the knot of shiny skyscrapers called downtown, and the huddling rows of high-windowed, wooden-sided houses warped soft by the salty, sulfurous air and the rain. Christophe stopped at an intersection, and Joshua looked out the window to see a knot of people clustered at a bus stop: they were mostly black. A boy who Joshua estimated was around his own age stood slumped into the glass side of the bus shelter. He wore a white bandana pulled so low over his forehead it rimmed his eyebrows. His skin contrasted so darkly with his bandana and his white T-shirt he seemed cut from a black and white photograph, and Joshua noticed the smooth skin of the boy's forearm was interrupted by a rough round scar of keloid skin. The mark shone shiny and round and blush colored, like pink lips half-open to a dark mouth. Joshua saw another scar on the boy's bicep; the scars were raised and angry and perfect and reminded Joshua of brandings he had seen on animals. Joshua knew what caused those scars: bullets. The boy sneered and raised the corner of his lip to show one perfect, gold-plated tooth. It looked like a dagger in his mouth. Joshua looked away. The light turned green, and they sped to Canal Street, the I-10 West on-ramp, and the airport. The highway rose and dipped and curved on a complex system of bridges the city had built over the city streets and houses below: Joshua closed his eyes against the nausea rousing itself in his stomach.

"You think you could slow down on them curves?" Joshua asked.

"Naw." The car accelerated. "She probably already there, and I don't want to hear her mouth." Christophe cleared his throat, and an airplane whined low overhead.

Through the waiving cattails and the short, new trees lining the approach to the airport, Joshua saw that Mayor Ray Nagin welcomed him to the Louis Armstrong New Orleans International Airport. Joshua's stomach clenched again. He looked at the clock. She would be waiting for them.

Christophe turned into the arrival lane and slowed to a crawl: this was the first time they'd ridden to the airport and picked up Cille without Uncle Paul or Ma-mee. They had no money to park in the garage. Joshua got out of the car and slammed the door shut. A pale cop in dark blue uniform nodded at him coolly.

"I'll go get her," Joshua said.

"I'll make the circle," Christophe replied as he turned the volume on the stereo higher and saluted the cop with his pointer finger: Joshua knew he was only doing it to annoy the officer. The trunk vibrated with beat. The cop's neck was glazed, and meaty. The policeman stepped to the edge of the sidewalk towards the car as Christophe drove off. He wanted to yell at Christophe about getting a ticket: he didn't have the money to pay for it.

The automatic doors to the airport entrance slid shut behind Joshua and a blast of cold air hit him in the face and the chest. Luggage carousels sat embedded at regular intervals along the corridor to his right and his left. Crowds of people surrounded the few carousels that moved; the people shuffled wearily, yawned with pasty mouths. Once in a while someone would dart forward and pull a taut, fat piece of luggage from the belt and drag it out of the way of the crowd. The family had gone to pick up Cille from the airport for the first time when Joshua was fifteen, and from that one trip, he knew that the carousels were usually slow, and that Cille's luggage always seemed to be last on the belt.

He passed a mother and a small girl sitting in the waiting area: the woman held the child in her lap and rested her chin on the girl's braided brown hair. The little girl wore shorts and her legs hung bare and slack next to her mother's long skirt. They were both dozing. Joshua looked for Cille and wondered if he would be able to recognize her immediately when he saw her. He pictured her as he last saw her: eating cornbread at the table, magenta lipstick that came off in smudged kisses on the golden top of the bread. He walked past the woman and the little girl again, and stood on the wall in the middle of the corridor. He felt as if he could not swallow, and every time he saw a short, pecan-colored woman with smooth skin and shoulder-length hair, he was startled. Joshua scanned the hallway and wished that he had a hat to pull over his face.

Cille stood on the outer rim of the baggage carousel nearest Joshua. She was wearing a tank top and long white pants, and she had a black carry-on bag slung over her shoulder. She was thicker than he remembered: the round plump circle of her upper arm was fleshier than when he had last seen her, and so was her face. Her hair had been curled into stiff ringlets; she must have fallen asleep on the plane because several curls in the back were smashed flat. She looked tired. In the profile of her body, her soft, falling chin, and the slight pouch at her stomach, Joshua saw Ma-mee. A man wearing a pink polo shirt and moccasins squeezed past her to elbow his way to the front of the crowd to pull a suitcase away from the pulley. Cille looked at him, her mouth slightly open, and rolled her eyes. Joshua was surprised at the sudden shock of electricity through his chest and up out of his throat that urged him away from the wall, that urged him to grab the man, to push him so that he lost his fat-fingered grip on his luggage and fell. Before he knew what he was doing, Joshua was walking toward her. Part of him would have liked to remain on the wall, unseen and watching her.

"Hey, Cille."

She turned to him and her hair moved like a dark cloud and obscured part of her face. Her eye shadow was smudged. Her face froze slack and soft, and then her eyes wrinkled and creased at the corners, and she was smiling, and she knew him.

"Joshua."

Cille held her arms out, bent at the elbow, to him. Joshua embraced her. He placed his fingers delicately on her back; he touched her with the pads of his fingertips as if he were balancing a basketball. Cille was patting his back lightly, repeatedly, as if she were burping an infant. He inhaled her. When he was younger, he remembered her wearing perfume that came in small, golden bottles that were shaped like shells, bottles that he could almost close in his childish fist. There were five of them. He wondered if she still had them. She smelled the same, she smelled to him like the day she left and they'd taken that picture that neither he nor Christophe wanted to take. He was so nervous. She drew back from him before he straightened and stood.

"You got another bag?"

Cille nodded, and Joshua saw a spray of fine lines at the corner of her eyes, light as chicken scratchings in sand, as she smiled another small, closemouthed smile.

"The gray one with all the flowers on it."

The man who had brushed past Cille was gone. Joshua wove through several people who stood still as pillars on the rim of the carousel with muttered, breathy "excuse mes," and before her suitcase disappeared behind the black plastic curtain leading beyond the wall to where the baggage handlers were throwing luggage, he pulled it from the line. The belt clanked and whined as it shuffled past, and behind its spinning protestations, he heard the baggage handlers crying to each other in broad, black New Orleans accents. The vowels sounded from their mouths long and sliding; he imagined their tongues to be pink shovels.

"Hey, now! Watch, there! You missing one, yeah!"

Joshua walked back to Cille. He was tempted to throw the suitcase over his shoulder like a case of chicken. He stopped abruptly in front of Cille. He wondered if she could smell his cologne. He wondered if she liked his outfit.

"Christophe waiting outside with the car," he mumbled. She nodded and hitched the carry-on further up on her shoulder. Her rings glittered gold. He expected her to walk ahead of him towards the door. "You want me to get that?" Cille shook her head, and her hair swung across her face again as she turned and began walking for the door.

"Let's go."

Joshua followed her. She walked listing to her side to balance the bag on her hip. He fell in line next to her and slipped his fingers under the strap on her shoulder and pulled it. He settled it on his own collarbone; he was unbalanced, but he didn't care. She had looked like she was limping.

"I got it," she said from behind him, her arms now weightless. Her hard-soled sandals clicked on the tile.

"It's alright," he offered.

Joshua walked through the heat lurking like a fog before the automatic sliding doors. The doors hissed open and he heard Cille stop next to him, and he looked down at her. Sweat was beading in a mustache over her top lip.

"It always seem hotter down here than in Atlanta," she said.

Joshua grunted. The Caprice's engine was loud and hoarse, and as Christophe pulled up to the curb, Joshua felt as if he was seeing the car for the first time. The gray-blue paint had an old, solid sheen to it. The trunk was silent, and Joshua looked back and saw that the cop was harassing a man in a black Lexus who was parked at the corner with his yellow hazard lights blinking. The man was arguing with his hands as a woman in heels made her way to him. All they needed were some new tires; rims, perhaps, around New Year's if he could save up enough money. Christophe bent quickly to unlock the trunk, and Joshua was careful to position her bags on the top and the sides of the speakers: he didn't want them to shift and pop anything. Christophe would kill him, and they couldn't afford new speakers. Christophe opened the front passenger seat door for her.

"Hey, Cille."

"Hey, Christophe." She held her arms out to him as she had to Joshua, and he moved in to hug her. Joshua saw he patted her on the back as she had patted him, and that Christophe was the first to move away.

"You sit in the front," Joshua said to her, as he opened the back door and climbed in the seat. He began rolling up the window. She hated riding with the windows down. Christophe and Cille slid in the car at the same time on opposite sides of the Caprice, and Cille rolled up her own window slowly. Christophe turned on the air conditioner and in the backseat, Joshua grimaced. He swore he could smell a hint of weed in the air blowing from the vents even though he had sprayed them with Febreze before they'd left; it smelled like stale hay. Christophe blew on a CD, wiped it on his shirt, peered at the back, and then slipped it into the CD player.

Horns sizzled and Al Green wailed. Normally, Christophe would turn up the volume until it sounded like Al was sitting in the backseat, until Joshua could almost imagine him as a young, wiry man, his teeth white and sharp in his dark face, looking as if he'd jumped from the album cover, sweating and screaming his song in their ears. Dunny would laugh at them when they listened to Al Green like that, but Christophe would tell him that Al Green could bump. Joshua would just close his eyes and listen to the music. It was like the jumping into the river for the first time after a long, cold winter, immersing himself in the warm embrace of the water after surfacing from the kind of winter where frost froze the grass to knife blades overnight and the pipes under the house burst if they didn't wrap them with blankets. Now, Al sounded timid.

"Thank God the air conditioner work in here. I felt like I was going to melt out there." Cille paused. "How y'all like the car? Eze sent me pictures."

"It's real nice. Thank you," Christophe said. He turned off the airport drive and onto the entrance ramp for I-10. Traffic was light; Christophe passed an old pickup truck with moldy lumber on the back going forty, and then a small black sports car sped past him so quickly he almost missed it. Cille laughed.

"Traffic in New Orleans still the same." The air conditioner was blowing hard and Joshua could feel the sweat drying on his skin until it felt grainy, as it had when he and Christophe were younger when they'd play in the ditches and in the red dirt roads and let clouds of dust settle over them. Joshua saw the Canal Street exit and wondered if Christophe would take it, if they would go back to Mississippi the way they came. He knew Cille hated taking 90; she thought the route was too long and too circuitous, and she said she didn't want to risk a flat out there in the middle of Klan country. Joshua hoped Christophe would take the exit anyway, would feign ignorance; Joshua could imagine the way the light would shatter across the windows in prisms as the sun set behind them. It would be a shame to ride with the windows closed. Joshua felt Christophe press on the brakes as the car slowed. Cille put her hand on the back of Christophe's headrest and spoke.

"I'm glad you decided to take I-10. I'm ready to get home."

Christophe accelerated and passed the exit. They were streaming past the suburbs of the city and entering a corridor of green low, swampy trees interrupted by strip malls and small cities of apartment complexes. They were made of brown brick and board and always had For Rent banners hanging from their sides: it was all ugly. Cille fell silent in the front seat, and he saw her head angle to the side, her shoulders slump: she was sleeping. He wanted to ask Christophe what he thought about her, whether he noticed anything different, but her lightly dozing presence stopped him. Christophe had been mostly quiet since the fourth, had answered most of his questions with silences. The trees waved soundlessly and cars cruised past them, and he could see her shoulder at the airport, see where the strap bit into her shoulder and left the flesh there red and tender like a hickey, when he pulled it from her. He and Christophe did not talk until he pulled into the yard in a steady rain, and Christophe asked Joshua if he wanted to wake her up. Christophe left the car to pull the suitcases from the trunk, and Joshua woke their mother.

Ma-mee had made red beans and rice. The day before, Christophe had come home directly from dropping Joshua off and had helped glean the small hard pale beans from the pot that were gray or dense as stones, to find those that could not be cooked. She could only tell so much by feeling them with her hands. She had asked Christophe if he'd had any luck with putting in applications, and after he'd told her no, he hadn't spoken as he helped. He'd left soon after they were done. She'd felt concurrently guilty and justified about her nagging while she'd ladled spices into the pot along with the beans: garlic, Vidalia onion, bell pepper, green onion, bay leaf, and thyme. When she heard the boys pull into the yard, the beans were bubbling and simmering spicy hot, the biscuits were right to the touch, giving like cotton under her hand, the skin on the chicken was crusted and cooling in a container on the table, and she was sitting in her chair before the television.

When Cille was a toddler, Ma-mee had left her in the yard with the boys and the scratching chickens to bring a load of clothes in from the clothesline, and when she walked out the back door, she found Cille squatting on the side of the house, grabbing fistfuls of tender green grass shoots with clumps of red clay adhering to them with her small hands and shoving it all in her mouth and chewing. Something about seeing her child like that had made Ma-mee want to laugh: the wide, long-fringed eyes, the direct stare, and the earnest chewing. Something else about it made her want to cry: the snotty nose, the dirt stained like vomit down the front of Cille's chest, her knotted curly hair. Ma-mee had brought Cille in the house, and attempted to feed her things that would make her lose her craving for grass and dirt. It wasn't until Ma-mee began feeding Cille biscuits every morning for breakfast—dense, floury, chalky biscuits—that she had stopped eating from the yard. Ma-mee automatically cooked them whenever Cille visited: perhaps her child no longer had a taste for them. The twins did. Weeks earlier, Christophe had even begun making biscuits for the family; he followed her recipe but still his biscuits were uneven, spongy soft but riddled with hard rocks of silty flour that startled the mouth. Ma-mee had changed the sheets on the bed in the extra bedroom even though no one had slept on them for over six months, and as she switched the television off, she could smell the lingering, close sweetness of the fabric softener. Underneath that was the aroma of wet wood; the rain had come suddenly, and after Ma-mee heard a slap of thunder, the quick drum of rain rolled over the roof. Below the knocking of the rain on the house like hundreds of hands, she heard a light step followed by heavier steps on the porch. The screen door creaked, and Cille was the first to walk into the living room.

"Mama?" Cille bent to hug Ma-mee and Ma-mee smelled her perfume, baby-oil, and something else: perhaps hairspray.

"Cille." She was rounder than she had been, softer. When Ma-mee hugged her, Cille's shoulder blade was a barely discernable hump beneath her skin; it was cloaked by fat and reminded Ma-mee of the smooth ripples fish made as they swam inches below the surface of the water.

"How you been?"

"Alright. And you? How was the flight?" Ma-mee led Cille into the kitchen. She grabbed a plate and began ladling rice in a bowl. She passed it to Cille and pointed toward the stove. "They got biscuits in the oven."

"I'm alright. A little tired. It was bumpy." Cille spooned beans over her rice. The boys traipsed silently to the extra room, their footsteps hitting unevenly on the thin carpet. "I was hoping you'd a made something?"

"I was trying to wait for y'all." Ma-mee passed Cille another bowl to fill for herself. "Boys, I got beans in here!" Ma-mee yelled. "Just some beans and a biscuit, please. I ain't that hungry."

Cille placed the full bowls on the table.

"Hot sauce?"

"Boys!" Ma-mee sat down. "Cille, they got a cold drink in the frigerator: Coke, I think." Before Cille could do so, Ma-mee rose from her seat and opened the old pine cabinets. She pulled out four glasses and balanced them against her chest as she walked back to the table. Cille popped the top on the two-liter and it hissed and gurgled. Ma-mee smelled the sugary, acrid smell of it. Cille poured. "How's your job going?"

Cille pushed Ma-mee's glass of water toward her and began to fill her own with Coke. She did not fill the boys' cups.

"Boys!"

"It's going alright, I guess. We just got a whole bunch of new products in so we had to remodel the floor and move the shelves around. Worked more nights, but that's more overtime for me, so I wasn't mad."

Ma-mee heard the boys shuffle in, and they busied themselves at the counter with their bowls; when Christophe placed the lid to the pot of beans on the counter, he set it down lightly so that she could barely hear it rattle, and when Joshua opened the oven, he eased it open soundlessly on its hinges. They sat down at the table. They were both taller than Cille; the blindness had washed away the defining characteristics that made Cille older, and if it wasn't for the way she held herself, stiff with her arms crossed before her and her wrists resting delicately on the table, Ma-mee could have imagined that Cille was the boys' shorter, younger, heavyset sister. Joshua slid a spoon across to Ma-mee so that it nudged at her fingers next to her plate.

"Since we all here, somebody should say grace."

"I will," Cille said.

"When you ready." Ma-mee nodded her head slightly, but kept her eyes on the twins.

"Thank you, Lord, for this food we are about to eat. Thank you for family and for a safe flight. Amen," Cille said. The twins weren't churchgoers; Ma-mee couldn't blame them for it. Since her blindness had set in, she had only been to church on holidays with Rita. She had made them go to church with her when they were younger, but since that visit to the doctor, they had fallen out of going. She didn't want to argue with them about it. Cille had become increasingly religious the longer she stayed in Atlanta. She had told Ma-mee she attended services at a Baptist church, which Ma-mee had felt an initial irrational negative reaction to: church to her meant Mass and white robes and purple satin sashes and gold communion cups and wine. Later, Ma-mee decided it didn't matter that Cille went to a Baptist church: at least she had someplace to go, a community, where people knew her. Ma-mee still worried about her, old as Cille was, in that city.

"Thank you, Cille."

"So, how's your job going, Joshua?"

"It's alright. Long hours, sort of boring."

"What about you, Christophe? You been looking, right?"

"Yeah, I been looking."

"You know you have to call them, right? They got to know you want it. I don't give nobody a job at my store unless they call and ask about they application."

Ma-mee's beans were spicier than she usually made them. She must have used too much Creole seasoning, too much cayenne. They must've been hot to Christophe as well: she heard him gulping down half of his dark drink. The twins' spoons clanked against the sides of their bowls.

"Y'all hungry, huh?" Ma-mee asked.

"I had a sandwich for lunch," Joshua said.

"You should eat more. Eating so fast ain't good for you."

"Anybody want another biscuit?" Christophe asked as he rose and went to the oven.

"No, thank you," Cille replied. "Christophe, you going to bring me to get my rental car tomorrow?"

"I thought you was using our car."

"That's too much trouble. Sides, I don't feel like getting up at dawn to go bring Joshua to work. I already made a reservation for a rental."

Christophe laid his spoon delicately in the crater of his bowl. It clinked lightly against the porcelain like the initial note of a wind chime.

"Yeah," Christophe said, short. Joshua yawned.

"Go ahead and go to bed," Ma-mee said.

"I'll do the dishes, Ma-mee." Christophe rose from his chair and cleared Ma-mee's place.

After all that cooking, she had not been hungry. The summer was nearing its zenith, and for once, the heat boiling against the windows bothered her. The fans had sluggishly stirred the heat thrown by the oven and the heat from outside the house. Ma-mee had felt as if she were sinking in a pot of simmering soup. For once, she wished for the end of the summer, for the short dark days, for the late dawns and early sunsets of winter. Joshua left Cille her plate, but picked up his own cup and plate and followed his brother to the sink. After the boys cleaned the kitchen, Joshua stood silently next to Cille, waiting a step behind her chair until she turned and saw him. Ma-mee noticed the straight dark bulk of him, the way he stood almost painfully at attention.

"You want me to get that for you?" Joshua asked Cille, reaching for her plate.

"No, thank you. I got it." Cille grabbed Joshua to stop him. She left her hand on him, and for a second Ma-mee thought he would fall over her onto the table: his silhouette looked unbalanced. Christophe kissed Ma-mee softly on the cheek, and she decided she wouldn't begin nagging him again about a job until Cille left, and that she was glad for the summer, glad for her full stomach, glad to have Christophe's lips on her skin.

"Goodnight," Christophe said.

Joshua pulled away from Cille.

"Night, Cille." Christophe threw this over his shoulder.

"Night, Christophe," Cille replied.

Joshua slid his hand over Ma-mee's shoulder: his hand felt rougher and heavier than it usually did.

"Night, Ma-mee." Joshua kissed her and drew away. "Night, Cille," he added, and then he was gone.

"I'm surprised they still wash the dishes."

Ma-mee watched Cille play with her bowl. She was tired, like the boys. She would follow them to bed.

"They good boys." Ma-mee stood. "I'm going to bed, too."

"You need some help?"

"Naw. Your bedroom ready."

Cille stood and lightly hugged Ma-mee; Ma-mee felt it as no more than a slight, extended flutter against her back. She hugged Cille solidly, and let her palms slide from the spine of Cille's back and out over her shoulder blades to her underarms. Yes, she had gained weight. Ma-mee's eyes stung and they blurred to an incoherent opacity, so she blinked and nodded at Cille and pulled away from her.

"Night, Mama."

"See you in the morning."

Ma-mee felt her way to her room. In the living room, the TV rumbled to life. Cille would stay up late, and Ma-mee knew if Cille didn't have to ride with Christophe to pick up her rental car, she would have found Cille asleep in front of the TV in the morning. Ma-mee pulled her housedress over her head, and noticed by the shadow mimicking her that she was undressing in front of the mirror, as was her old habit. She heard her child laugh at something in the living room, and the muted stumbling of one of her boys in the bathroom. As she leaned toward the switch on the wall, she wondered what Cille's face looked like now, if she was sprouting fine lines at the corner of her eyes that looked like bunches of spider lilies. Her father had gathered them at that age. She switched off the light.

11

CILLE WAS MAKING CHRISTOPHE NERVOUS. HE HAD DROPPED JOSHUA off in the heavy gray dawn and made his way back to the country to pick her up. The rental car was in Germaine, and Christophe only had time to brush his teeth and wash his underarms before he left the house. He thought longingly of the privacy of his park bench, the matted grass that the county officials had overlooked cutting, and the wind through the closest branches of the pines: the closest thing he could get to his own place. He was ready to be done with his family's errands and on with his work.

"Got any new prospects today?" Cille asked him. She sipped her gas station issue coffee.

"Couple places," he mumbled. He had seen a few new signs on his first trip to Germaine that morning, but he had not had time to stop and grab any applications and add them to the stash, thick as a nest of napkins, in the glove compartment. He watched the cup anxiously and hoped she didn't spill it. The first place she'd look for something to wipe with was the glove compartment.

"Mmm, hmmm." She breathed and nodded.

There would be no riding, no sleeping at the park today. Cille might see him. He would ride to Javon's house and park it around the back and sit there for the day: he knew Javon would be doing a little business, most likely from the living room and he knew he could still make the money he needed to make there. The plastic on Javon's sofa would be cool. Christophe couldn't think of anything else to say to her. She had showered and dressed and put on make-up, and she smelled clean and sweet. Christophe saw the Enterprise Rent-a-Car sign and hit his signal.

"What you doing today?" he asked.

"I'm going to see some friends. Might take Rita with me to do some shopping later." Cille patted him on the shoulder as he parked the car. The rentals gleamed like wet candy. The Caprice growled and suddenly it seemed too loud, too old.

"That's alright." She stopped him from turning off the car. Her perfume was strong, as heavy and layered as her pinkish-red lipstick.

"You sure?"

"I'm sure. Like I said, I made reservations. I'll see you at the house tonight."

"Alright then." She left the car. He watched her walk into the building with her head down against the sun, which lanced in bright waves through the muffling clouds, and he did not reach over to pull the door more firmly shut until she entered the tinted door of the building. The green sign quivered and rang as a gust of wind blew, and he wondered at how small she was, how petite she looked as she reached for the door, how she had to lean back with her weight to pull it open. She was soft, underneath. even though he didn't want to, he knew that. When he pulled into Javon's driveway, he muted the stereo and veered off the oyster shells and parked in the backyard beneath the sheltering branches of two oak trees, near to where he had first seen Sandman on the fourth. When Christophe knocked on the front door, hot paint cracked away beneath his knuckles and fell like confetti. A muffled voiced answered.

"Come in!"

Javon had pulled all the curtains shut, and he sat on the sofa with a forty sandwiched between his legs and a remote control in his hand. He was the brightest thing in the room, glowing a pale white in the gloom.

"What's up?" Javon asked.

Christophe wiped sweat from his palms on his jeans. He felt nervous.

"Uh—sorry about parking in your backyard. It's just, Cille's—well, my mama's here from Atlanta and I was wondering if I could come over here and chill for a while." Christophe gripped Javon's hard, bony, pale fingers in a handshake. He wasn't making any sense. "She think I be looking for a job, and I don't want her to see me down at the park, and everybody else at work, so I…"

"Sit down."

Christophe sank into the icy plastic cushions of the sofa.

"It's cold up in here."

"I can't stand to sweat." Javon changed the channel desultorily. "You can chill here long as you want. I understand you don't want your mama to know what you do." He switched the channel again. A woman in white sneakers flew through the air on a yellow vacuum in a commercial. "Far as my family know, I'm always about to get called back for a job or going on a interview." He fingered the remote control and a video popped onscreen: rappers wearing leather jackets mugged in front of cars that gleamed with the dull silver sheen of bullets, as wide-thighed women writhed in bikinis. Javon tossed the remote toward Christophe.

"You want to watch something?"

"I'm cool."

Christophe's eyes hurt: he let his head roll back and it hit the wall. A knock sounded, and he thought it was his head until he realized someone was tentatively tapping at the door. Javon set his beer on the floor, so hard foam rose to the top and spilled from the mouth of the bottle like lava. He ushered in a short, dark figure.

"Come on," he said, and the woman followed him into the kitchen.

Christophe knew her, but then, the entire hood knew her. Her name was Tilda, and she was around his mother's age. She lived in a square, sagging house with her mother, who everyone on the block called Mudda Ma'am. Tilda had struck an uneasy balance: she took care of Mudda Ma'am for most of the day, making sure she didn't wander outside and into the overgrown woods in a spell of senility. Every few hours, Christophe would see Tilda hurrying down the street towards Javon's: her hair pulled back into a tight bun, her shirt tucked into her pants, her hands in her pockets: Christophe knew she was fighting to appear nonchalant, unhurried, straightforward.

In his time selling from his park bench, Christophe had only seen Mudda Ma'am appear once: she wore a nightdress the color of wisteria and her gray hair was laid thick to her scalp. She walked with her head down and her hips pushed forward, curving in toward her soft, paunchy belly as if she were pregnant. She had tottered around the azaleas grown riotous, the grass grown in angry long bunches to the lip of the ditch: it had taken her twenty minutes. By then, Tilda was back, and she had ushered Mudda Ma'am back into the sad mouth of the house, away from the ditch where she had stood swinging her head blankly back and forth, up and down the tree-shrouded street.

Christophe tried to keep his eye on the new video that looked to have the same women as the last video, and he tried not to look at Tilda but could not help it. She moved jerkily into the kitchen and disappeared around the corner. The screen jumped into sharp focus, but then Christophe could hear her soft voice and Javon's low rough one over the scissoring, thudding music of the video.

"What you need?" Javon said.

"A dub."

Christophe willed himself to watch the women, gliding sleek and oiled like seals in and out of the fluorescent blue water of a pool, lying on their sides on white lawn chairs. The rapper wore a suit and fedora, and he held a cigar between his fingers as he gestured.

Tilda followed Javon from the kitchen, and Javon sank down into the sofa cushions next to Christophe. Tilda hesitated, then ducked her head at Christophe and skipped past the television.

"Sorry."

"It's alright, Tilda," Christophe shrugged.

Tilda smiled; her teeth were brighter than they would be out in the light of the day. Christophe knew the edges of the bottom and top front pairs were brown from the heat of the glass pipe. He had seen her picture in Cille's yearbook that she'd left behind when she'd gone to Atlanta. Tilda's smile had been wide and all white.

"Don't let all my air out, Tilda," Javon said.

The door shut with a whoosh and a muffled thump. Javon's phone rang. He took it into the kitchen. More glistening women jumped in and out of watery focus. Javon returned to the sofa and pulled a sandwich bag from his pocket. The bag was shredded and dirty. He tore one end of the greasy plastic and untied the knot, shook one small chip out of the cluster, and twisted it up in the shredded corner.

"Marquise fixing to come over here. Say he want a dub to sell and a dime sack. You got him?"

"Yeah." Christophe made his own small sack with one of a wad of sandwich bags he kept secreted in his pockets like plugs of chew. When he was done twisting the ten-dollar sack, he was surprised when Javon dropped the crack into his palm. He gripped it, and it dug into his flesh like a small pebble.

"What's this for?"

"For that."

A knock sounded at the door and Marquise opened it wide enough to slip in sideways. A rapper slid over the hood of a lime-green car and wove around streetlamps as he ran from the police.

"What's up, y'all. Good money today." Marquise didn't sit. "Thirty?"

"Yeah." Javon pulled at his beer. "Christophe got it."

Marquise pulled out thirty dollars, the bills faded and folded, and dropped them in Christophe's lap. Christophe offered the crack and the weed to Marquise palm up, feeling like his skin was shrinking away from them. Marquise plucked the bags from his hand. His fingernails were sharp and jagged.

"Alright, nigga." Marquise slid back out the door. Christophe felt a tongue of heat lick through the open door, and then dissipate in the chill air. He shifted and the money slid down the crevasse of his lap. He handed it to Javon.

"Keep it. I don't usually charge Marquise, so it's all yours."

Christophe thought about leaving, about dropping the extra ten to sit on the sofa in his place. What if an undercover came in and Javon handed to him to sell? Christophe would be guilty. But didn't Javon only sell to established clientele? Then Christophe thought of Cille somewhere out there in her bright, unfamiliar rental car.

"You sure?"

"Yeah, I'm sure. Sides, you helping me out." Javon rolled his eyes. "I done seen every one of these videos ten times. Want to play something?" He knelt before the television, and Christophe slipped the money into his pocket. He barely caught the controller Javon threw at him, and as he and Javon chose football teams and played, he lost. When the next knock echoed softly at the door, he was almost not surprised when Javon paused the game and dropped another soapy crumb in his lap. Christophe sold. When the door closed and he resumed the game, he played until his fingers hurt. He knew that Javon was giving him business by letting him hang out there, but he was also manipulating him into taking a risk; he was handling the crack—if something happened, he would take the charge. He did not realize it was time for him to leave until Bone pulled the door open and stepped inside, and Christophe saw the sun was skimming the tops of the pine trees. He had sold all of his weed for the day, and his money pocket was stuffed with bills.

Joshua was waiting for him in the parking lot.

"You want to drive?" Christophe asked him. Joshua paused in closing the passenger side door. Christophe shook his head when he saw the sweat dried to salt on his brother's face so that his skin looked lined with small, white crevasses. It made him look old. "Never mind, I got it," Christophe said.

"You did anything with Cille today?" Joshua asked.

"Naw. I brought her to get the car and then I sat by Javon's house."

"What she say she was going to do?"

"Visit some friends. Shop with Aunt Rita."

"So she supposed to be at the house tonight?"

"I guess so." Christophe hesitated. "Laila supposed to be coming over?"

"Naw. I told her not to come over til Saturday." Joshua grinned tiredly. "So, what'd you do all day?"

"Played some games." Christophe could not help it: he felt his voice tighten with the lie. He tried to follow it with a truth. "Sold all my weed today, though."

Joshua looked out the window, and when he spoke, it was into the wind.

"They got a opening at the dock. Somebody quit." He fingered the windowsill. "If you come in and drop off another application, you could say I was your reference. It might help."

Christophe nodded imperceptibly. He should be excited. Christophe saw a figure in the distance half-pedaling a bike. He was inching along next to the afternoon traffic. His arms were skinny and he wore pants in the heat, and he had a plastic grocery bag slung over the handlebars of the bike.

"I'll come in next week," Christophe said.

As Christophe neared the man, he saw the bag hung slack: a few bright aluminum cans shimmered through the opaque plastic. Something sank in his chest, and he felt sick.

"Look."

Sandman. Pedaling weakly along the concrete and wood boardwalk of the beach. He stopped and scanned the sand and grass at the side of the road, and then looked back against the stream of traffic. His hair was long and bushy.

"All the way out here in Germaine? On a fucking bike?" Joshua breathed this against the palm of his hand. "No."

Christophe watched the speedometer. As they neared Sandman, he tried to keep pace with the normal flow of traffic, but found himself speeding up. He didn't want Sandman to see them. How long had it taken him to ride his bike from Bois Sauvage to Germaine? Two hours? Three?

"We on the other side of the median, Chris."

They neared Sandman and passed him. They saw him stoop in the sand with his mouth open, and dig. When he pulled out a can, sand sprayed from the dirt-logged aluminum. Christophe jerked his head back around to the road, and put both hands on the wheel.

"Fuck," Christophe said.

Joshua wiped his face.

"Cille's probably home," Joshua said, and laid his head back.

Christophe pulled over into the right lane; other cars began to pass him. He did not care. When he looked back over at his brother, he saw that Joshua had closed his eyes with his mouth open to the wind.

At the house, Christophe awoke Joshua by giving his shoulder a shake, then exited the car with a slam. Joshua followed, his feet dragging in the long grass. They'd have to cut the yard this weekend. He walked up the porch stairs and through the screen door to find a cluster of hot-pink flowered plants lining the walls; they were smaller than azaleas, and their stems were knottier and woodier. Bougainvillea.

Christophe was already through the front door, already kissing Ma-mee on the cheek and falling into the couch before Joshua had even crossed the threshold. Cille was standing in the middle of the living room, smoothing a pale yellow pleated sundress over her legs. A tag hung from the strap at her shoulder.

"What do you think?" she said.

The yellow of the dress caught the sunlight diffusing through the windows. The color of the dress complimented her: it made her eyes seem lighter in the dark, her skin burnished tan. She knew it; she wore a lot of yellow. It was the color Joshua always saw her in when he thought about her in Atlanta.

"It's nice," he mumbled.

He wanted to walk straight to the bathroom and shower, but he felt he couldn't. He knew that she had probably been waiting on them to get their opinion. Waiting on him. She should know she is beautiful, he thought.

"We need to cut the grass on Saturday," Joshua said. Christophe was fidgeting, the hand he leaned on shook as he tapped his foot. Christophe nodded against his fist.

"Lawnmower need to be fixed." Christophe clasped his palms between his shaking knees. "Last time I cut it, the engine act like it didn't want to crank. I'ma go out to the shed and see what I can do."

"Christophe, they got mashed potatoes and corn and fried chicken on the stove." Ma-mee held out her arm to stop him as he passed by her on his way out the front door, but her hand only grazed his T-shirt.

"Alright. Need to see about that lawnmower, though."

"You have any luck today?" Ma-mee shot out.

Christophe stopped and Joshua heard the hinges squeal.

"Maybe," Christophe called softly.

The door snapped shut.

"He like cutting the grass that much?" Cille said. She smoothed the dress again and moved closer to Ma-mee. "What you said about the color, Mama?"

"I told you I liked it." Ma-mee reached out and grabbed at the skirt of the dress, rubbing it between her fingers. "Joshua, how was work?"

"Alright."

"Christophe told you what he be working on out in the shed? I asked Paul what it look like out there, but Paul say it look mostly the same, like Chris ain't really moved nothing." Ma-mee was kneading the weave of her easy chair, plucking at a few stray threads. Joshua was doing the same and then made himself stop. Cille was still standing in the middle of the room, looking at him.

"He ain't cleaning up or nothing—I mean, nothing to talk about." Joshua fumbled for the lie. "He be working on them saws and hedge-cutters and stuff. You know."

Ma-mee seemed so bent in the chair, so old. She looked at him and her eyes seemed more gray than blue, then, harder. She blinked and they watered. "Tell him to be careful in there." She breathed softly. "Got things that'll cut you in there."

"He get cut with something with rust on it, and then he have to go to the hospital for a tetanus shot. Lord knows what he could catch up in there. Y'all grown, though." Cille flicked the tag over her shoulder. "Messing around with all that junk out there. I'm surprised you ain't got Paul or Max or one of them to get rid of it since Daddy died."

"He left that for his sons and these boys here. I ain't got the right to take what's left to them." She shook her head and directed her comment to Joshua. "Go bring your brother some food, please?"

Joshua rose from the sofa and Cille grabbed him by the elbow and tugged him with her toward her room. She left him standing in the doorway.

"Yes, Ma-mee." Joshua called. Cille's bed was littered with clothes: bright silks in flower patterns lay strewn across the bed. She held up a red shirt against her shoulders and raised an eyebrow, and Joshua nodded. She smiled and laid it down in a different pile, and then picked up a sky blue dress and held it against her front. It made her look like a little girl. He nodded again.

"So when I'm going to be able to see this girlfriend of yours?"

Cille was leaning over the bed, folding shirt after shirt; Joshua watched her arms move, fat and smooth as a child's. She sat on the bed and peered at him. He didn't like the way she was looking at him: so expectantly, so speculatively. Ma-mee must have told her.

"Well, um, I told her to come by Saturday."

"Well that's good, since I'm going to be gone all tomorrow to the festival."

He wanted to tell her he knew, and that's why he had asked Laila to come over on Saturday, but he didn't want to interrupt her.

"Who's her mama and daddy?" she asked.

"Ozene and Lilly."

"Hmmm." She half-breathed and snorted, and then looked down at the carpet, where she traced circles with the toe of her sandal. "You like her a lot? Ma-mee says she comes by the house all the time. Say she a sweet girl."

"She is."

"Well, do you?"

"Yeah," he admitted.

It felt good to say it to someone, even if it couldn't be his brother. He thought of the way Christophe skirted him when he and Laila were on the sofa or in their room, the way he felt guilty watching his brother scuttling sideways like a crab, averting his eyes away from them until he was out of the room. Joshua saw Christophe walking out of the door, away from him and Laila, off the porch and out into the sunlight where the light ate his dark silhouette until he disappeared. Joshua would remember a biblical word then, forsaken, and he could not help pulling away from Laila, from regretting how he'd peppered Christophe with questions about jobs until he either shrank or blurted out "fuck." He was angry at Christophe's palpable loneliness, his withdrawal, and his own guilt.

"Is she cute?"

"She pretty."

The rasp of the words in his throat made him blush. He could hear the caress in them. He could see Laila's flushed face, her pink mouth, and then he focused on Cille.

"Well." Cille stood and he knew it was a dismissal. "Just make sure I meet her."

"Alright," Joshua said.

Cille pulled up a green silk shirt. He nodded and she laid it on the bed. He moved away from the door as she made to close it.

"You look better in yellow," he said.

Joshua did not think Cille heard it before she closed the door. He felt his breath against the wood. He could hear Ma-mee fiddling with the television. He walked in to see her turning the volume down and standing by the window that faced the garage; she grasped the curtains with her hands and palmed the glass before she moved back to the TV and turned it only high enough so that the voices whispered. Joshua fixed a paper plate of food and walked it out to the shed. Christophe sat before the lawnmower, his face almost smashed into the black steel of the engine, stabbing it with a flathead screwdriver. He shifted and Joshua saw a dark bulge, thick as a brick, shoved into the waistband of his pants. It stuck out beneath his thin white shirt. Christophe did not look up at him.

"Ma-mee told me to bring you some food. I'll set it right here."

Joshua set the plate on the top of a steel drum. Christophe jabbed the screwdriver, and Joshua heard the squeal of metal. Christophe closed his eyes so tightly his entire forehead wrinkled, and he sucked his lips in a grimace. He bent down so that Joshua saw only the crown of his head.

"I'll get it," Christophe said.

Joshua wanted to sit with him but Christophe was not looking up. His brother did not want him to stay. Joshua's skin was itching, and everything was hurting. He walked back into the house. After showering, he dragged himself to the sofa again, to Ma-mee. Laila called, and she sat patiently on the phone as he translated the moving images on the screen to Ma-mee. The sun set, and the night grew loud outside. Christophe switched a light on in the shed. On the screen, *Forrest Gump* was playing: he was running through the desert, his hair long and nappy, shadowed by a large group of people. When his love interest in the movie said Forrest's name, she reminded Joshua of Laila. Ma-mee hardly laughed at all, and when she did laugh, it was always at the wrong part. When sleep began to grab him with dark, delicious snatches, he got off the phone with Laila. The movie went off and Ma-mee kissed him and walked to her room. Cille was quiet. Joshua only woke when Christophe walked past him. Joshua followed him to the room and fell like a downed animal to the bed.

Christophe woke the next morning to the sun glazing the room a milky white. It was wrong. He looked at the alarm clock, jumped from the bed, and croaked, "Shit." Joshua's eyes opened wide with the movement, and he turned his head and saw the time on the clock and blinked hard, testing the vision, before he jumped up and began pulling on clothes from the floor. At the same time, they heard Ma-mee's bed rustling, heard the press and pull of the metal springs. They'd all overslept.

"What's the fucking chances?" Joshua said. Christophe shrugged and slapped the steering wheel. When he didn't speak, Joshua listed asleep, head butting the window and dozing. Once they arrived, Joshua stalked tiredly away from the car.

After Christophe drove off the lot, he didn't even bother trawling for Help Wanted signs. Christophe saw the asphalt, the salty sea rimming the straight road, and followed the line of cars. He watched for white and blue cop cars: they liked to sit in the piney median and wait for speeders. They would search him if they stopped him. He knew it. He took the quickest route to Bois Sauvage, and when he got there, he circumvented Ma-mee's house again, and drove to Javon's. He knocked at the front. His pocket was bulging with a green bag: he'd bought twice his usual supply to Javon's. He had pored over his stash the night before, removing the stems and seeds, breaking it down and bagging it, and had actually put in applications next week. Javon hollered at him to enter. It was as if Javon hadn't moved. Christophe could not be sure that Javon had changed clothes. The same videos were on the television, and later, they played the same video games. The same people came by: Marquise, Tilda, Bone, others. Christophe thought the slabs of crack could be the same that Javon passed to him to hand along. They felt the same in his hand: light, and hard as stone.

The weed in Christophe's pocket disappeared at a faster pace. He was almost happy until someone else knocked on the door and walked in without waiting for Javon's yell: Sandman shuffled toward the kitchen. Javon glanced at him, then stood and beckoned to Sandman. Christophe could not move his legs: they were crossed at the ankle, outstretched, immobile as two pine trees felled by a storm. He looked at them, their color turned dark from his days at the park, the same as his hands, the same as Sandman's face, and his ashy, scaly-skinned wrists, and he hated the color. Christophe stared mutely at the television, his eyebrows drawn, and refused to move; inside his chest, he quivered as if a driving rain was running through him, a storm pulled from deep in the gulf, a storm the same gray blue as the water.

"Could move out the way, young cat," Sandman mumbled.

"Could shut the fuck up and leave me the fuck alone, old man." Christophe spat. The words erupted from him. The quivering had moved from his insides, and he dropped the joystick and stood.

"Sandman! Don't let me have to slap the shit out of you again."

Javon snapped the remark like a wet towel from the kitchen. Sandman skirted Christophe and loped into the kitchen. Christophe sat down. He let the music play on the game, and Sandman appeared again at his left. His hat was pulled so low Christophe could only see the line of his jaw.

"Don't be coming up in my house starting no shit," Javon barked at Sandman as he opened the door. Sandman shrank further into his shirt, and slid out the door. When the next knock sounded at the door, Javon paused the game. He handed the crack to the person himself. The minutes passed by the dim VCR light and Christophe wondered if he would see Sandman again this afternoon after picking up Joshua. He wondered if Sandman had sold that paltry bag of sand-logged cans to pay for what he had just bought, or if he was hoarding the cans like a skinny gray squirrel hoards acorns. Christophe sold the last of his weed and his virtual football team went to the playoffs.

Tilda walked in and she and Javon disappeared around the corner, but instead of clustering in the kitchen, he heard them walk to the rooms at the back of the house. Christophe stared at the paused game. He went to the bathroom to pee and heard an arrhythmic bumping in the room next to the bathroom, and murmurs. He retreated to the living room but did not reach the door quickly enough to escape Tilda and Javon emerging from the hallway, musty with sex, and Tilda combing her red-peppered hair back into her bun with her fingers. Her hands were almost as plump and smooth as Cille's. Christophe left.

Christophe scanned the side of the highway as he drove to pick up Joshua, the beach and the sandy dunes, the pines and the pristine sidewalks and mansions on the other side. He did not see Sandman. He squinted past Joshua's nodding head and slack face as he dozed against the window and saw no skinny man on a bike. He forsook the shed and watched his brother sleep curled to the wall on his twin bed, and in the weak light coming in from the hallway, thought his brother looked more like his father now that he was skinnier. For the first time since they were both children, Joshua's face curved in at the cheeks. Christophe walked past Cille's empty room and wondered briefly where she was, who she was with at the festival, if she was safe. He pictured drunk men accosting her on Bourbon Street, saw her spinning and falling against neon lights; he shook the image away from him. She was a grown woman: shit, they were all grown, he thought.

Joshua woke to find the room as dark as it was when he'd fallen asleep the evening before, and momentarily he was confused: drowsiness, like a fine green fishing net, was tugging him back to sleep. He rose to peer out the window: gray drizzle, almost a mist, sifted through the air. He saw a dim white sun glowing palely in the sky, and he knew that it was morning. Laila would be coming by: he had grass to cut and bougainvilleas to plant. He heard voices on the porch. She was already there. Cille sat next to Ma-mee on the porch swing, and Laila sat in Ma-mee's chair that had the clams etched into it. Laila saw Joshua standing in the doorway. She smoothed her hair self-consciously, and his heart clenched nervously. Cille followed Laila's gaze. She wore yellow again, and she sported an entire row of gold hoop earrings in her ears; she'd curled her red-gold hair into a bun, and he thought she looked as young and pretty as any girl.

"Bout time you woke up, sleepyhead," Cille said.

"My boy was tired," said Ma-mee. "I figured he could use a good sleep."

"I couldn't sleep at all," said Cille, "with your brother out here cutting and digging soon as the sun rose."

"He ain't left nothing for you to do." Ma-mee said as she rubbed her forearms. Joshua could see gooseflesh ripple in a current along her skin like wind over a muddy puddle.

"You need a sweater or something, Ma-mee?" Joshua asked.

"I got this," Christophe yelled, his voice like iron spiking into the earth.

He was on his knees in the grass, and he was digging a hole: the dirt was black and veined with red clay. Joshua saw dark handprints across Christophe's shirt where he had wiped his palms. It looked as if a crowd had attacked his brother, pulled at him, and then let him go. The grass was already cut. Christophe had lined up the bougainvillea along the porch, and he was digging holes to plant them.

"What time is it?" asked Joshua.

"Ten," Cille said. She was crossing her legs and looking at Laila as she spoke. "Your brother was up cutting grass at six. By the time I got up he had trimmed the azaleas."

Joshua saw a pile of tree branches, twigs, and cut grass that Christophe had raked into a pile. It glistened with droplets of misty rain. Christophe stabbed at the earth with a small red trowel, ignoring them.

"Ma-mee wanted me to let you sleep, so I had a chance to talk to Miss Laila before you had a chance to warn her about me." Cille laughed and flipped her head. Her earrings shivered.

Laila sat with her palms folded together: her legs were shaking. Joshua sat in a chair next to her. He barely resisted the urge to pull her closer, to reach out his leg and slide it against hers.

"Hope you didn't scare her too much," Joshua said.

"Scare her? Of course I didn't scare her. She was telling me about her mama and daddy and the rest of her people. Found out I used to date her uncle in junior high school. He looks a little like her but he's taller and thinner. Handsome, too." Cille turned to face Ma-mee and touched her arm. "You remember Alonzo, Mama?"

"No, not really. You and Rita had so many little boys after y'all I had to beat them off. You more than Rita," Ma-mee said. "They got grits and sausage on the stove, Josh."

"I ain't hungry," Joshua said.

He brushed Laila's forearm: her head was down. The humidity had frizzed her curls and made them coil like vines away from her scalp: they fell forward and shielded her face. Still, he saw her staring intently at the patterns in the chair as she traced them with her finger.

"Then I realized her mama was on the homecoming court with me the year I got queen. She had her daddy walk her, right?" Cille said.

"No, ma'am. She had her uncle walk her because my granddaddy wasn't around," Laila replied.

"Well, I thought it was her daddy for sure."

"No, ma'am."

"You ain't got to call me 'ma'am,' Laila. Makes me feel old." Cille laughed, and Joshua marveled at how her gold and her white teeth and her hair seemed to sparkle, about how she seemed brighter than them all against the dreary canvas of the day.

"Yes, ma—I mean, Ms. Cille."

"I was just saying how Laila looks just like her mama. Same hair and everything, like her mama just spit her out."

The trowel echoed through the screen: Christophe dug and the earth came away in wet, slurping chunks. Joshua watched his pile of soil melt to a muddy pancake. Laila tucked her hair behind her ear and it snaked back across her face when her hand fell.

"I think she got nice hair," Joshua choked.

Christophe began sliding the spade to separate the plant from the pot; the steel scraped the plastic. It sounded like a saw, and the plant dropped and fell to the grass. Cille fingered her own fine, carefully arranged curls.

"I always wanted hair that was a little rougher. Had a little more body to it, more life. Some people are just lucky, I guess."

"Cille."

"What, Mama?"

Joshua could only see Laila's scalp, each tendril of her hair springing from her head as if to reach out and embrace the heavy air. The mist had turned into a light rain, each drop as fine as sand. If she had slumped any farther in her chair, she would curl into a ball. Joshua looked up at Cille and could not help the nervous fluttering that had turned to heat in his stomach: he wanted to slap her. He wanted to shield Laila from those blinding teeth, that gold.

"Come on, Laila. You look cold as Ma-mee."

Joshua pulled her up and past the swing. Ma-mee was staring in Christophe's direction, at the bougainvilleas alighting in the yard graceful as herons, blooming hot pink. Cille followed Joshua and Laila with a curious look. Her eyes were as bright and patient as a pit's. She was so beautiful it hurt Joshua to look at her. Instead, he kneaded Laila's small, hot hand in his own, and urged her back to his room faster. He rustled a T-shirt from his drawer and handed it to her.

"Put this on."

"I ain't cold."

Joshua shoved the shirt into her arm insistently. She tugged it over her head, and it fell to the middle of her thighs. He grabbed the sleeves and pulled, and she came to him and stood, small and hard against his chest. He hugged her.

"Don't pay no attention to her. I don't know why she being so mean."

Joshua let his hand fall along the curve of her spine down her back, and he stooped so that his face slid along hers, so that his lips stopped at her ear.

"I'm sorry."

He averted the thought of Cille, then. He shrugged away his brother and his bent, resentful shoulders, his lunging digging in the front yard, and let himself fall into Laila's open mouth. The insides of it were so soft, her body was small and sweating under the tent of his shirt. He would walk her home, away from Cille. He walked into the living room and heard arguing on the porch.

"I'm ashamed of you, Cille. Treating that child like that? I didn't raise you to be so rude."

"I been raised, Mama. I don't need no more raising. I ain't said nothing to that girl that ain't been said to her before."

"I won't have you talking like that to that girl in my house."

"I was leaving anyway," Cille said. Before Joshua could tug Laila forward so it wouldn't look as if they were eavesdropping, Cille entered the living room and brushed by him and Laila without looking at them. By the time Joshua and Laila walked to the porch, Cille was swooping past them again with her keys clattering like small chimes and her purse clutched in her hand, her face set so hard everything about her seemed smooth and impenetrable as rock. She walked away with her arms folded tightly into her sides as she gripped her purse, which made them appear less like arms and more like wings.

"Mama," Joshua called.

Cille stopped next to Christophe, and Christophe looked up at Joshua. Christophe was trailing a thin line of fire across the pile of wet foliage with a lighter set on high. The flame shot out and licked impotently at the wet plants. Cille waved her hand and spoke without facing them.

"I'm late for a show," she said. She walked to her car, slammed her door, and Joshua let Laila's hand fall and started after her.

"Let her go." Christophe blinked once and looked back down: Joshua saw bags that looked like purple bruises beneath his eyes.

"What do you know? You ain't in this." Joshua blurted. Cille started her car.

"Oh yeah, I forgot." Christophe stood and his voice rose with him. Joshua made as if to run to her car as she began to back out the driveway, ignoring Christophe. Christophe grabbed his arm. "I ain't the one she talks to. I ain't the one with the job and the girlfriend. What I say don't matter because I ain't shit to the house."

"You chose," Joshua bit out. He wrenched his brother's arm from his own, and stepped toward the retreating car. Cille peeled away. "Everyday, you choose."

"Fuck you," Christophe said.

"Boys!" Ma-mee yelled thinly.

Joshua pulled Laila, who had stepped beside him, away from Ma-mee standing with her hands flat against the screen of the porch door, away from his brother with the arched, fight-ready neck, the stillness of the harnessing swing, away from the house. When they reached the road, Joshua looked back and saw that Christophe had managed to light the pile: it smoked wetly in thick, white puffs, and drifted outward to obscure his brother.

Joshua didn't talk on the way to Laila's house, and once there, he did not want to let her walk inside, did not want to walk back to his own house, to his manic brother and Ma-mee finding her way in the rain-drizzled dark. He sat with Laila on her slimy, wet wooden steps, silent. He left her with the admonition that he'd be back and walked back to his house to find both his brother and Ma-mee gone: Ma-mee with Aunt Rita and his brother vanished, the earth showing in bald, wounded patches where Christophe had been. His brother had left the car, so Joshua took Laila to a poboy place in St. Catherine's to apologize. Joshua paid for the meal, and was defiantly glad to have a job. He sat across from her at a small, plastic table with a sticky checkered plastic tablecloth and watched the condiments from her shrimp poboy slide down the crevasses of her fingers, between her knuckles, to the wax paper. He vacillated between teasing her about her messiness and wanting to lick her fingers for her, to suck the vinegary ripeness of the pickle, the mayonnaise, the salt of the shrimp and the pepper. They sat in the nearly empty, cool, small-windowed restaurant until the clouds eased their pressure and gave into rain, and the sun re-emerged, dim and orange, on the horizon.

After they crossed the bayou to Bois Sauvage and entered the country, the tops of the trees turned black and swallowed the sun, and Joshua slowed the car. They were nearing The Oaks. The small, squat, thin-walled nightclub was set to the side of a baseball field: the proprietor specialized in blues and baseball games, and on Saturday nights, the dirt field that comprised the parking lot was usually packed with rusty pick-up trucks and late-model Mustangs. Joshua saw lights burning between the cars where small fires made of pine leaves and twigs had been set to smoking, to drive away the gnats, and he could hear the heavy thumping bass line of a blues song emanating from the club, even though it had no windows.

"Hold on a minute. My mama had wanted me to stop by here on our way back and grab her a plate." Laila grabbed his shoulder. Joshua turned into the parking lot, and eased the car to the edge of the field. "I'll be right back," Laila said.

"Here, get Ma-mee a plate, too. Catfish," Joshua added. He pulled out a twenty. He ignored the blood urge that flashed Christophe's and Cille's faces into his mind, too; he would not get them food. When he and Christophe were younger, Ma-mee would sometimes send them on their bikes to The Oaks on a Saturday with enough money in their pockets for a fish plate, which Christophe would carry back because he was the first to learn how to ride his bike without steering with his hands. Laila closed the door behind her, and the lock barely clicked. Joshua leaned over to shut the door fully and before the light dimmed, he saw a black and mild cigar on the floor, still in the plastic. He would smoke it, get a buzz, and it would help him sleep after he dropped Laila off, help him relax so he would not think about Cille in the other room or Christophe with his busy, busy hands. He searched for a lighter, but could not find one in the glove compartment, in his pockets, or underneath the seats. After cussing and dimming the light, he saw the glow of one of the fires in the dirt lot glimmering at him through the window. A woman laughed drunkenly in the dark, and another man shouted "brother-in-law" across the field. Small gnats pinched his skin with bites. Joshua wove in and out of the cars and stopped by the closest fire and waved the thick, heady smoke toward his face and his clothing to shoo the gnats away. He knelt to light the black.

"What the hell you follow me over here for? You trying to impress your drunk friends?" Cille spoke sharply, and Joshua looked up expecting to see her standing over him, her hands cupping her hips, narrowing her eyes at him, waiting for an answer. By the light of the fire, he saw her standing almost fifteen feet away from him in the dark, her back to him, the flames etching her back and her yellow silk dress in gold. Even in the dark, she shone. Joshua scooted away from the fire and waved the smoke from his eyes so he could watch her, immediately protective. The person she was talking to bobbed darkly a few feet away from her, and he shifted. His face blazed over her shoulder, the fire illuminating him. Sandman.

"You walk by me acting like you don't even know me," Sandman said. There was authority and force in his voice that Joshua hadn't heard since he was small.

"I don't," Cille said. In the shadows, Sandman was all lurching movement, while Cille was still. Suddenly, Joshua knew where Dunny got it from.

"Oh, you know me alright." Sandman's voice slid from taunting to hushed sincerity, deep and gentle. "You can't not know your babies' daddy."

"Samuel, what you want from me? That was finished a long time ago. You left me with them kids after my daddy died. You never cared."

"That ain't true. I was young and dumb...."

"Well, I wasn't. I dealt with it, and you didn't, Samuel." Her voice rose.

"Love don't just go away like that, Cille," Sandman said.

"It do."

The arch of the smoke turned, and he heard Sandman turn nasty in the haze.

"You couldn't live without me then."

"This ain't then." Cille stepped away from Sandman toward her car and through the curling smoke. Joshua saw his father drawn tight, one fist closing over the air where Cille had been.

"Cille!" Sandman shouted at her back as she slammed her car door shut. Under the sound of the bass thumping in the club and the nighttime insects, Cille's car prowled away from the fire and the weak lights under the eaves of The Oaks.

Sandman lurched upright, took one tottering step, and stood staring off into the night after Cille. Joshua looked down at his feet and wondered if he looked like that, always staring, always waiting for her to return. The smoke scratched his throat, the black faded to unlit in his hands as he felt his way to his car to wait for Laila. He kissed her in the car in front of her house. At home, someone was watching television: Joshua peeked through the window and saw a flash of a young Pam Grier pointing a gun towards the audience, quivering furiously. Joshua snuck through the back door. He placed the fish plate on his dresser and sat in bed, drunk with smoke. Christophe slept with his back to the room. The television stopped, and he heard a light tread: Cille. Her room door closed, and still he waited until he could hear nothing but the meeting of the bugs outside before he tiptoed to the kitchen, dumped the plate into the refrigerator, and fell smoke-tinged and dizzy into bed.

When Joshua woke in the morning, he was surprised to find that the sun had barely risen, and Christophe was still asleep. On his walk to the kitchen to pour himself a glass of water, he heard Cille and Ma-mee, already awake. He paused in the hall.

"I saw they daddy last night. I came back early from the city and stopped at The Oaks and he was out front with some of his old buddies—looked like shit. He used to be so—but I guess that was the problem, though. People that fine and know it, and then get things so easy, with his mama and his daddy babying him, never come to good anyway."

"He came by here. Christophe hate him." Ma-mee lowered her voice, and Joshua could smell biscuits. "You can't come in here treating them boys like that, Cille. One minute on and the next gone when they not who you want them to be."

"I still say Joshua could do better."

"You upset Christophe, too. I know he need a kick in the ass: busy for no good reason, still ain't got a job yet. But you can't be hard on him all the time, Cille. You got to show him something."

"I know them boys." Cille said. Her voice was tight.

"You got to give them more, Cille. Same way I gave you."

"You raised them, I know." Joshua heard Ma-mee stutter to stroke the argument, and Cille spoke over her again. "But they still got more of me in they blood, and I know my blood." Cille's chair scraped back. "I'll be back later. I got an extra week in my schedule." She paused. "Regional office called and told me they having some electrical problems with the store, so they going to shut it down for a few days." Ma-mee coughed. "I figured I'd stay if that's okay with you."

"Yes, Cille." Cille's footsteps sounded and she was gone. In the kitchen, he heard Ma-mee's stillness spread and make thick the room.

12

BEFORE MA-MEE WOKE ON MONDAY, BEFORE DAWN, CHRISTOPHE crept out to the shed to make up his sacks for the day. He had greeted Cille's announcement at their stilted Sunday dinner that she would stay for an extra few days with nothing but a silent surmise that he would go to Javon's. He remembered the mornings when they were still in school: Dunny's car leaden with smoke, the sun searing the sky a bright yellow, the marsh grass snapping in the wind. In those days, it always seemed as if it were spring, and everything was a new, tough green. Then, he had known things. Now, he parsed weed into sacks and the heat in the shack hovered and billowed with the rising sun, and he watched his hands clenching and pinching and pulling and tying, and he did not know anything. He did not know who he was. He rolled up a blunt there in the shed, plucking a cigarillo from the stash he kept for distributing to his loyal customers, and he succumbed to his weakness for a morning smoke. He did not want to go to Javon's house again, did not want to see him or hand out nuggets of crack, but he knew he would. After only four or five days of selling, he had made so much he could slip all of the help-money into Ma-mee's purse himself.

Christophe drove his brother to work that morning with his left hand at the apex of the wheel. He fondled the blunt in his pocket until he couldn't restrain himself any longer. At the next red light, he pulled the blunt out and lit it.

"What are you doing?" Joshua said.

"What does it look like I'm doing?"

"You never smoke in the morning. You don't never smoke at all no more."

Christophe pulled deeply on the blunt and let the smoke out in little puffs from his nose. Already the driving was easier. Christophe tried to blow the smoke in his brother's direction, maliciously. It was the first jollity he'd felt toward his brother since their fight on Sunday. He parked the car.

"They accepting applications today. Same time," Joshua said.

Christophe didn't bother to nod, and Joshua slammed the door. Joshua slogged his way through the ascending heat from the sun glittering out over the gulf. Christophe drove in slow arcs through Germaine while he considered skipping the application hour. He knew his eyes were red, but he turned around at the edge of Germaine and drove back toward the dock. He watched the men moving about, jerking against the weight of the salt and heat, and smoked another blunt. He fell asleep, then woke hungry and disoriented in time to see Joshua at the car door, who slid into the passenger seat and unwrapped his sandwich without speaking and began to chew. His hair was fraying from the weave of his braids, and he let his hands fall heavily to his lap after taking a bite. He was tired.

Christophe left the car before Joshua finished eating. The same woman was sitting at the desk. This time, her hair was redder than he remembered, and she did not smell so strongly of perfume. Men with salt dried to powder on their faces ambled about the hallways of the building, and Christophe sat in the waiting area and filled out his application on a copy of *A Hunter's Guide*: there were no clipboards available, the woman told him. He shrugged at her, smiled a closemouthed smile when he handed it back to her, and thought of the weed in the glove compartment as he walked to the car. Christophe rolled another blunt. Joshua sat with him until the hour was over, and then let his head fall back on the seat, and breathed out a long, loud sigh. He blinked hard, and directed his comment at no one.

"I can't wait to get paid."

He pulled at the latch of the door and was gone. Christophe drove back toward the country, parked in his usual spot behind Javon's house, and opened the door after knocking once. Javon ushered Tilda from the house.

"You missed some money this morning."

"I had some shit I had to do."

"Won't be nothing you can't make back tonight. If you want—I told them to come back by."

Christophe tossed a joystick up with his left hand and caught it with his right. He waited for the next knock on the door. He measured his words.

"Way I'm going, I'm going to sell all that Dunny done gave me soon. I go back too early, and he might wonder why."

"I got you."

Javon plucked the black cigar he'd been smoking from his mouth and appraised the twisted, desiccated tip. He threw it across the room in a perfect arc and it plopped like a drop of heavy rain in the garbage can. He pulled another from his pocket.

"Come back tonight, I'll have a QP for you. Whatever you pay Dunny for it."

Christophe sat on his hands. He wanted to roll another blunt. The weight kept them still.

"Why?"

Javon hesitated in lighting the black. Javon eyed him and opened his mouth, his gold front reflecting against all the pink like a candy wrapper.

"Because I feel like it."

Someone knocked at the door and two figures entered the living room: one he knew, but the other he didn't—and the other he didn't know was white. Blackjack, the junkie he knew, was so dark his skin looked like newly poured asphalt. He walked with his hands in his pant pockets, his arms lost in the loose folds of his T-shirt. His chest curved inward like a bowl. The white had a day's growth of beard on his face, all brown, his hair and his beard blending into each other. He was too clean. Christophe stood in the doorway of the kitchen.

"Who you bringing in my house, Blackjack?"

"He from upcountry," Blackjack said. He smiled and nodded at the man. "Called—"

"What makes you think I got what you or white boy want?" Javon said, his voice shrinking. Christophe stepped back further into the kitchen. "Get out of here."

"But Javon—"

Javon was so quick; one minute he was reclining on the sofa, the next he was upright, his open hand sounding like the snap of a leather belt against Blackjack's face. Blackjack stumbled into the white man, who fell backward into the wall and barely caught himself. He looked as if he were trying to sink into the woodwork. Javon's long nails had etched red, bleeding lines in the dark mask of Blackjack's face. "Get out my house," Javon said. "And Blackjack, don't come here no more."

"Just a bump, Javon," Blackjack said as he slid along the wall.

"I'm about to go get my mothafucking gun." Javon yelled. "Y'all trespassing."

Javon disappeared. Blackjack and the white man slammed the door and scuttled out into the yard. Christophe thought about leaving while Javon was rustling around in his room. Javon reappeared at his side in the dim hallway.

"You think he was the police?" Christophe asked.

"I don't know him, and I ain't taking no chances. They probably got Blackjack on something, so he trying to sell somebody else out." Javon was lax and limber where seconds before he had been taut. "I forgot I moved my gun—couldn't even find the gotdamn thing until they was already out the door."

Christophe wondered if they were watching the house, if they had noted his car here every day, if they had run the tag. Dunny had told him it was about chance in the beginning, about luck, about being smart and collected. Had he been stupid in coming here? Javon noticed him standing. He blushed, and it was as if the stain of the blush bled from his ears to pool in his face; it was like a wound inking water red.

"My house too far back in the woods for them to come running up in here and me not know about it," Javon said. Christophe was angry. He didn't want to sit, to nervously glance at the door every thirty minutes or so, waiting for a flurry of knocks and policemen with red faces and hard forearms to kick down the door.

"I don't feel like doing no business today. I'ma go."

"Alright then."

Christophe fingered the sacks in his pocket, thought about the money, Ma-mee, Cille, Joshua, the money. "I'll be back tomorrow." Javon sat and ignored him.

Christophe spent the rest of the day at the river, floating in the shallows, with a six-pack he'd bought at one of the up-country stores where they never checked for I.D. He let the beers bake in the sand in the sun, and then balanced them on his chest and sucked them down hot.

By the middle of the week, Christophe's morning smoke was anticipated. He half-heartedly waited for a call from the dock during dinner with Cille, Ma-mee, and Joshua. He concentrated hard on eating quickly and ignoring the sting of their newly born family dinner discussion. He left walking as soon as possible after he'd washed the dinner dishes. On Thursday, he hurried past Cille and Ma-mee talking in the living room on his way out the door while Joshua was in the shower.

"I'm going down the street, Ma-mee."

"You want me to tell your brother where you going?" Ma-mee asked.

Her voice stopped him in the doorway, and he brushed one foot back and across the warped doorjamb. She was waiting for him, Cille suddenly alert as a terrier at her side.

"I don't know where I'll end up."

Christophe released the door so that it tapped softly against the frame; he leapt from the steps. He felt badly about lying to her: he knew where he was going. He could not stand seeing her by the phone, waiting like the first time: he could not wait as he had the first time. He could not stand Cille's constant questions about where he had applied. The food-laden refrigerator shamed him; Joshua drank and ate the food their money bought and every time Christophe sat down to a meal, he felt like choking. Javon had taken to making Sandman leave out of the back door off the kitchen. Christophe knew that Javon was doing him a favor, one in turn for another, and that they were accomplices. He'd only been selling at Javon's house for a week and already he was worrying about the money bulging in green, rubber-banded balls in the toolbox in the shed. He hid it carefully from his brother. He decided to walk to Javon's house. He smoked and stripped off his shirt and thought of how the night made it feel as if he hadn't even taken it off. The haphazard streetlights were too bright: he wanted the insect-ridden dark all around him. He threw rocks at the bulbs as he passed them; they bounced off the wooden posts. The weed skewed his aim.

Christophe was surprised to see Dunny's car in Javon's driveway. He knocked and let himself in the house without waiting for Javon's voice, to find Dunny, Javon, Bone, and Marquise around the domino-littered kitchen table. Dunny was scribbling on the back of a shoebox top they were using as a score sheet.

"Lock the door," Javon called.

Christophe turned the lock behind him and pulled a chair from the hallway and sat with his back to the front door.

"What's up, cuz?" asked Dunny.

"Nothing."

"Why you ain't come get a QP from me? I know it's that time."

"Business been a little slow." Christophe tried not to glance at Javon, but he did. Javon was studying the dominos in his hand. He had not told Dunny, then. "I'll be to see you in a couple of days."

"How's having Aunt Cille back?"

"Temporary and fine."

Dunny laughed in response. Christophe had not spent any real time with Dunny since the fourth of July. He assumed his cousin was here because he had come to get powder from Javon, so he was not shocked when Javon pulled a packet of white powder from his pocket and placed it on the table. Dunny did not grab the pack, and Christophe wondered why Javon was letting the pack sit there, grimy and small, next to him at the table. Were they using it as a wager? Dunny wiped a shoebox top clean and handed it to Javon. The inside of the top was a smooth, dull black. Javon untied the plastic bag and dumped half the contents of the bag out on the inside of the top, and then pulled a razor from his pocket and began chopping at the clumpy powder. Christophe felt the pull of the door at his back, but his eyes were riveted on Javon, to his careful dividing of the cocaine into thin, delicate lines on the cardboard. He noticed the way everyone's faces at the table hadn't changed, as if they had been expecting this. Christophe had not known. Javon laid the razor down and bent to the table with the rolled-up dollar bill in his hand. He sniffed.

He pushed the top across the table to Bone. Dunny began washing the dominoes, swishing them back and forth with his large, thick hands. The air conditioning was cold on Christophe's neck: he felt as if someone was running a cube of ice back and forth across it. Bone passed the dollar and board to Marquise. Dunny was looking at his hands. Christophe watched Marquise straighten and make as if to shove the top across the table to Dunny. Dunny's hands stilled.

"You know I don't fuck with that shit."

"What about you, Chris?" Javon spoke, and his voice was raspy. Christophe looked at him and his eyes were wide and white. Javon smiled.

"You ever did it?"

"Naw."

"This some good shit. Clean." Javon's pupils seemed to spread like the gulping hole of a drain. "Here."

He held out the razor that he'd used to cut the cocaine. Christophe saw a faint sheen of powder on it; it dulled the blade.

"Taste," he said.

The weed had calmed Christophe: the jittery unease that he woke to every morning before dawn, that prevented him from sleeping, had receded with the smoke. Javon smiled at him wider and the black seemed to eclipse the white and he thought, *I've seen the movies, it will only numb my tongue a little*, and he took the razor in his hand and placed it like a communion wafer on his tongue. It was bitter. The razor slipped and his mouth was wetter than it had been and when he plucked it from his mouth, it was red.

"You cut yourself," Javon said.

Javon picked up his dominoes and began slapping them down on the table. He was talking very fast. Bone and Marquise were laughing and blinking quickly and Christophe thought perhaps he should rinse his mouth, perhaps there was too much blood. He was leaning over the sink spitting pink water onto the ceramic bowl when he saw Dunny behind him.

"You shouldn't have done that."

"There wasn't even hardly nothing on there."

"Your tongue numb, ain't it?"

"That's from the cut."

"Right, stupid."

"Look, nigga, don't act like you ain't done this shit before. For all I know, he probably do that shit to everybody."

Dunny slumped in the doorway.

"What the fuck is going on, cuz?" He braced himself on the frame. "Time for both of us to jump out of the game."

The bathroom smelled like stale, standing piss. The air-conditioned air from the living room failed to penetrate the back rooms. Christophe ignored Dunny.

"I feel sick," Christophe said.

"You do that shit again, and me and Joshua going to beat the shit out of you."

"Fuck you, Dunny." Christophe squeezed out of the bathroom. "I'm not the fucking crackhead in the family."

Christophe played dominoes with the others until the buzzing in his brain abated, and the dregs of the weed lapped at him and made him tired. Dunny sipped on a forty. By the time Javon won, it was drizzling outside. Christophe did not want to walk home in it, so he accepted Dunny's offer of a ride. He did not speak around his throbbing tongue. Back at Ma-mee's, he heard Dunny drive away after he turned off the kitchen light over the sink. The door to Cille's empty room was closed. Christophe fell asleep on the sofa with his shoes on.

Joshua woke to Christophe's empty pristine bed, and to the sound of the television. The sky was a dull gray. He walked to the living room, expecting Ma-mee, and found Christophe. He was crouched on the floor in front of the television, flipping through the channels manually by jabbing at the controls at the bottom of the screen.

"What time is it?"

"Got a storm out in the gulf. On the other side of Cuba. They say it's coming right for us." A storm pinwheeled across the TV in a neat arc through the blue of the ocean, blue as air, to land solidly in the gulf. The weatherman was yellow and wore a bad gray suit.

"You slept out here?"

"Should be here in two weeks or something." Christophe squinted as if he could feel the winds. He couldn't stop tapping the television stand.

He was wearing the same clothes he'd been wearing the day before. Joshua couldn't compete with the television, wouldn't beg an answer from his brother's back, so he walked past Cille's room to get ready for work. Her door was open, left slightly ajar, and she'd left her fan on. He cut it off. She hadn't come home the night before. Her perfume swirled and settled in the room.

In their room, Joshua pulled on his boots. He kissed Ma-mee and would have walked away quickly if she hadn't tugged at his arm. Her eyes were a dark blue in the rust-laced light.

"He smells like yesterday," Ma-mee said. Joshua looked down at her hand on his arm. He did not want to confirm that he knew his brother had hardly slept, that he was fidgeting, and that he hadn't taken a bath. Joshua chewed the soft pink inside of his mouth; he couldn't lie to Ma-mee. "I'm worried about him," she added.

Outside, the horn pealed loudly.

"He looking like his daddy," she said. Ma-mee's grip on Joshua's arm loosened, but still her fingers caressed him at his elbow. He bent to kiss her. Her skin was wrinkled and wet against his lips. It slid with his mouth. She smelled of vinegar.

"Take care of your brother."

He nodded and pulled away from her.

For once, Joshua did not fall asleep on the way to work, even though he wanted to. He had waited for Ma-mee to go to bed the night before, and then he had let Laila slide over him on the sofa, had let her sit heavy and soft as ripe fruit in his lap, and kissed her. She had run her fingers across the downy stubble of his face, over the soft hair of his sideburns, and he had wondered at the wetness of her mouth. He had imagined her insides, pink and breathing, the blood and bones and flesh that made her, and wanted to be inside her. Yet Christophe had not made it home, and Ma-mee slept the light sleep of the old in her room, and he knew he could not do it like that. He had kissed and touched her in the hot flickering dark and had driven her home at midnight. On his way back, the headlights had flashed over Sandman, stooped over the handlebars of his bike, pedaling his way slowly down the road: he had no hat on, and his neck was bare and burned red, even in the dark. His palm had flashed pale in the air, but Joshua had not slowed: he did not know if Sandman recognized the car. He supposed Sandman wanted a ride to the store, and once there, to borrow money. That is what crackheads did. Yet, still, his back was thin and narrow as Christophe's, and when the lights dissolved over his face and left him in the black, for a moment he thought he saw his brother.

He watched Christophe tap the steering wheel as he drove, jumping lightly in his seat, and wondered when his brother had become so manic. It had to be Javon. Why else was he twitching and gripping the steering wheel with both hands? He should say something. He could see the dockyard ahead of them on the horizon, stretching out like a finger along the smooth blue water.

"When you think we should start putting boards up?" The words were clumsy. Christophe turned to him, his forehead wrinkled, and turned down the stereo. Still, Joshua shouted as if the music were still playing. "It's the third one we done had this summer—ain't no reason for you to be so nervous."

"It ain't the storm," Christophe said.

"Well, then what is it?"

Christophe put the car in park and Joshua felt the frame jerk. Christophe pushed one hand against the dashboard, where his fingers slid wetly through the dust, creating winding trails like writing, and the other hand on the headrest of the passenger seat. He looked squarely at Joshua, his chin down. He opened his eyes wider, purposefully.

"It ain't nothing."

Joshua stared at his brother's mouth, and then out at the parking lot, the low seawall, the swooping seagulls dropping from the sky like rain. Christophe switched the gear into drive and pressed on the brake. He reached into his pocket with his right hand and pulled out a wad of bills.

"For Ma-mee."

"This early."

"I know. I got lucky these past two weeks."

As Joshua slipped the money into his pants, he eyed the clock and lost his patience.

"You fucking up," Joshua whispered.

Christophe slapped the steering wheel and turned on Joshua. "I'm making money, nigga! I make more in one week than you do in two. I'm trying, alright!"

"No, you ain't," Joshua said. He left the car with a slam.

Joshua could not stop thinking of Christophe under the leaden sky and the sun that he felt was melting his brother, evaporating bits and pieces of him to the clouds. He heard him again and again in his head, repeating: nothing, nothing, nothing. He saw Christophe turn, bracing himself to stillness on the wheel and the headrest, and saw his open mouth. He had seen a thin red line there, bisecting his brother's tongue, dividing it in two. Joshua balanced two boxes on his shoulders, felt his back strain. The line. At first he had thought he imagined it, but it did not disappear. It looked like a cut. He shifted the boxes to his hand and slid them down to the pallet. He slid his palms over the sides to smooth them, to correct the pile, and he felt the pallet lurch under his feet. A board must have broken.

How could Christophe cut his mouth that way? What food sliced the mouth in straight lines? Joshua forgot the seagulls hovering like vultures, the parking lot smelling of hot tar, the boxes and sacks growing in a column from his feet and saw Christophe's mouth but could not hear the words he spoke. Joshua's hands felt squeezed, smashed, and he lurched away from the boxes and fell to the pavement. Blood was on his hands and wrists. He bent over, and pressed his palms together and held them open like a book and saw that the skin had been slashed; it hung in petal-pink strips from the root of his pinkies to his wrists. A man standing next to him called out and he saw Leo running toward him. Leo pulled him into the office, and Joshua let himself be led.

"I was checking the box," Joshua said. His hands were stinging. A catfish had stabbed him with its dorsal fin once: it had throbbed like this. They had been swimming on the beach with little nets Uncle Paul had made for them. They had been eight then.

"One of them slats probably broke. They get rotted out by the salt water and the wind. Your hand got caught in the ties on the boxes. I done seen it cut before. Sharp as a razor."

Leo led him past piles of file cabinets, the receptionist, and a short row of computers to a small room, narrow as a closet, off the main office.

The blood ran down the seam of his fingers. Leo dabbed at his palms with alcohol pads, and then flattened a towel between his hands and sandwiched Joshua's big palms with his own. The pressure slowed the blood. When Leo peeled away the towel, Joshua saw that the cuts were roughly identical, and the meat beneath his skin was angry red.

"You might need stitches."

Leo drove him to the hospital in his own dark blue pickup truck. The cab had leather seats.

"It's new," Leo said.

Joshua elevated his hands to drain them and kept the towel pressed tight against the pain: he did not want to leak blood on Leo's seats. At the hospital, the doctor sewed twelve perfect black stitches diagonally across both of Joshua's palms. They were dark and tough as new tattoos. His hands throbbed and swelled. The doctor told him to take ibuprofen for pain, and wrapped his hands in gauze and tan wrappings that were light against his perpetually sunburned skin. Back at the dockyard, he called Ma-mee, even though he suspected that Christophe would not be there. He wasn't. When Ma-mee asked if anything was wrong, he denied it. He would tell her when he got home; he did not want her to worry. He thought of the park. He hated his brother for being there. He thought of calling Laila, and then Cille's cell. He thumbed through the phone book clumsily with the tips of his fingernails, until he found the number. Javon answered the phone. He sounded slow and high.

"Chris there?"

"Who this?"

"Joshua."

Suddenly Christophe was on the line, exhaling hard into the receiver. His voice was thick with weed.

"I need you to come pick me up."

Joshua heard a click, and then a dial tone. Instead of his usual thirty minutes, Christophe arrived at the edge of the dockyard in twenty. Joshua held his arms folded across his chest, and eased into his seat.

"What happened?"

"Cut my palms open on a tie on a box. Had to get some stitches."

"You alright?"

"It ain't that bad. They gave me a week off." Joshua heard clattering in the backseat, and looked around to find a sheaf of freshly scented plywood marked hurricane.

"Where you get that from?"

"Stole it."

Christophe stopped at a burger place, ordered for Joshua without asking what he wanted, and set the meal on the seat between them without speaking. Staring at his hands on the steering wheel, Joshua imagined his brother's palms, smaller than his own, pale and unmarked, and thought of the black scribbling on his own, of the added difference between them. He hated the immediacy of the wound: he wondered when he would be able to touch something again without the wrappings, feel warmth against his skin, and be rid of the throbbing pain. Joshua's soda was bitter, and the fries left a waxy coating in his mouth. At the house, he left his drink on the seat. Christophe picked it up, walked it into the house, and threw it away.

13

THE FISSURES ACROSS JOSHUA'S HANDS FELT LIKE FISH GILLS TO Ma-mee: the threads were tough, yet the thin slit of the wound was leaking a yellow fluid that made the flesh hot and soft. She had known something was wrong when Joshua had called. She had left Cille talking midsentence and immediately walked from the kitchen where she was chopping onions for butter beans and rice to the porch, when she heard their car: Joshua walked in before Christophe. He held his hands in the air. Even with her fuzzy eyes, Ma-mee could tell that the color of the flesh was wrong, that the curve of his fingers was too stiff, that something was over them, that something must have happened. Christophe walked in behind him with his arms drawn into his sides and his hands in his pockets.

Behind her, Cille hissed and reached around her to grab Joshua, to pull him to her, to ask what happened. Ma-mee had sat as Joshua told them what happened: the stacked boxes, the old crate, the rotting slats, the ripping pain. The blood. She asked him to unwrap his hands, to hold them out so she could touch them and reassure herself there were no broken bones, no fingers ripped from his hand at the root by the thick twine. Cille had laughed as if Ma-mee were foolish, and it was Christophe who bent over Joshua's hands to unwrap the bandages. He smelled as if he hadn't taken a bath. Joshua smelled of sea salt and sweaty, sun-baked skin. His palms were swollen, and she could see black etching where there should be a wash of pink and pale peach. The lifelines that bisected his palms like small ditches were replaced by gashes, the perfect punctuation of the stitches. Ma-mee pinched the knobby spines of his knuckles.

"Oh...Joshua." Ma-mee breathed. Cille brushed Ma-mee's shoulder in the huddle as she made to touch Joshua's open hands, and Ma-mee felt him startle. Cille paused, stone-heavy and still as she had been in the womb, skin to skin, and then moved away: Ma-mee felt cold air between them.

"They just cuts," Joshua said.

"Could've been worse," Cille said, and Ma-mee heard the concern evaporate from her voice like rain from a horse's hot flank. She backed away and sat across the room from them all on the sofa, watching. "Chris, why you just picking him up now?"

"I got to do some work in the shed. Find some boards for the windows. Storm coming." Christophe replied. His hands in his pockets, he was already shouldering his way towards the door. Ma-mee felt her family spinning away from her.

"No, you don't need to do nothing in the shed." Ma-mee piped. "Hurricane ain't even coming this way for sure."

He would tinker around in the shed, and then he would disappear. She would not know when he came home, and in the morning, he would be up and gone before she woke. Paul had told her he had heard Christophe was hanging around at Javon's house, and everyone knew what Javon did. She wanted him to be still, to be safe, to stop running from what was chasing him.

"I got work to do."

"Christophe!" Cille exclaimed. "I was talking to you."

Ma-mee bounded upright in her chair, felt her way to Christophe, surprised herself with how fast she moved. She gripped his arm. He could not move with her holding him.

"Stop it, Chris." His body was tight, turgid as a pine curving against a stormwind. She gripped harder. "Go take a shower. Help me take care of your brother." She felt him sag. "For me."

"Yes, Ma-mee." He nodded.

While Cille ignored them and wrapped thin leaves of her hair around rollers, Ma-mee worked in a tight, worried orbit around the kitchen: wiping the countertops, stirring the pot, kneading dough, washing dishes. She could not help herself. She dropped one of the pot lids to the floor and picked it up to hear Joshua mumbling into the telephone.

"I'll see you tomorrow, I promise. Love you too. Bye."

Ma-mee had not known that he was telling Laila he loved her, even though she felt she should have recognized the sentiment in the way he hovered over her, big and wide, his body bent to hers like a spoon. She had wanted to slap Cille for treating the girl the way she had. She had been ashamed of her daughter, of her sharp, self-assured, demanding beauty. Outside, the sun had finally set and it was dark, and Christophe sat next to his brother on the sofa. Crickets cried through the open window, and she heard a car go by on the street. The crepe myrtle outside the kitchen window rustled. Cille said she was tired and went to her room without eating. Christophe shoveled food into his mouth, and Joshua fumbled with his spoon, dropping it into the beans. Each time, his brother would pick up the utensil and wedge it between the wrapping on his fingers. Joshua laughed at it, shallowly, the first time, but then he was quiet. Ma-mee wanted to talk to them, to say something that would make her feel like she wasn't chewing and swallowing small pebbles, but she could not think of anything.

Joshua slept with his arms over his head, propped against the wall. The air tugged at him like warps of cotton against his skin. He felt exposed. He dreamed he was falling and jerked awake to the dark, quiet house: a rooster called in the distance. He walked into the kitchen to find that the clock on the microwave read 2:22. Light shone, etched along the cracks of the shed. He walked piecemeal from the house. The grass was turgid and wet with dew. When he reached the door, he knocked softly with his elbow. Christophe was kneeling amidst rust-laced steel drums, corroded engine parts, and steel toolboxes, surrounded by a nest of tiny, greenish brown bags of weed. He was counting them and dropping them into a larger bag. Joshua had not known that he was selling that much. He said what he had not expected to say.

"How you got that cut on your tongue?"

Christophe looked up, dazed, and let his arms fall slack to his sides. Joshua's hands felt as if they were going to burst from their wrappings.

"What you talking about?"

"You had a cut down the middle of your tongue. Look like it hurt."

"A razor."

"In your mouth?"

Christophe resumed shoving the baggies into the larger brown paper bag that was wet on the bottom. It was the kind of bag clerks slid forties into.

"I was fucking off at Javon's house. I just wanted to see if I could do it."

Christophe rolled up the bag and stood. He switched off the bare-bulb light affixed to a shelf and it was so dark that Joshua could not see his brother. He felt Christophe passing him. In the house, Christophe locked the doors, and Joshua turned to tiptoe to the bedroom and found him sitting on the sofa, staring at the television.

"I'm going to stay up and watch some TV."

Joshua saw the muscles in Christophe's jaw jump as he clenched his teeth. Christophe turned the television on and a televangelist in a powder blue suit strode across the screen, his hands raised to the air as if he were waiting for Mardi Gras beads to rain down on him from a parade float, a false providence. His eyes were shocked wide and as the camera zoomed in for a close-up, Joshua saw that they were as blue as his suit. His face broke as if he were about to cry. Christophe sat slumped into the sofa, barely blinking. Joshua could not move, stood standing and looking at Christophe, thinking of razors, of bags of white powder before they were cooked to crack, of Javon's supply. His slashed hands ached, and he left Christophe to fall asleep.

Christophe woke to morning cartoons at five. It felt as if someone had poured sand in his mouth while he slept. He was hungry. He cooked grits. He washed dishes. Soft white light diffused through the curtain and he looked at the phone, wondered briefly if someone would ever call him about a job, and if he really cared anymore. Javon would be expecting him today. He picked through the clothes in the dryer and tried not to wake Cille or Ma-mee or his brother, who he believed would want to come with him, boredom and bad feelings bedamned. He did not want Joshua to come with him. He did not know why he could not sleep, only that every time he felt himself falling like a feather, rocking on currents of drowsiness, he would see the baggies blossoming in rows around him, his pockets bottomless with them as if they were BB pellets, see the razor, see the powder on it and Javon's face, both white. When he woke, these were the first things he thought about. He did not want to eat unless he was starving, and he did not see the sense in taking a bath when he was living so grimly, when he was only waking and bathing and eating and getting dressed to go to Javon's and make money. Joshua's accident had scared him: what if his brother's hands had been crushed? What if he had to support the family?

Christophe thought he had time to spare, but Joshua woke at his normal time. He sat down at the kitchen table as Christophe pulled on his socks and stood.

"What we doing today?" Joshua asked. Christophe felt the fight flare and fall to ash in his chest.

Fuck it, he thought.

They left midmorning, after Cille had left the house without saying goodbye to any of them, and afterward they'd watched *Hollywood Squares* with Ma-mee: she'd snorted at the jokes the personalities told, but seemed too tired to laugh. They were silent on the short ride there. Out of habit, Christophe parked their car in Javon's backyard. He knocked once, a short, hard knock that was more of a punch, and walked into the house. Javon was sprawled on the couch with one leg hooked over the armrest, and he didn't bother sitting up when Christophe walked in the door. A black and mild cigar hung from the corner of his mouth, and he was wrestling with the videogame controller in his hand. He was playing Doom. Christophe sat on the sofa next to him, and saw Joshua hesitate in front of the closed door.

"Sit down," Christophe said.

Javon removed his foot from the arm of the sofa. Joshua folded his arms across each other and let his hands hang limply.

"Your hands alright?" Javon asked. "You could get paid for that shit, you know?"

Joshua shrugged noncommittally. Javon threw the controller in frustration, and Christophe saw his brother almost flinch: he could read it in the way his eyelashes flickered shut, the way his mouth twitched. He picked up the other controller from the floor.

"I bet you could whip Javon's ass in this one." Christophe looked past his brother to Javon. "He was always better than me."

"Everybody's better than you," Javon said.

"Shut the fuck up," Christophe said.

Javon beat Christophe in the game. Christophe let the controller fall to the floor when the first knock sounded at the door. He rose, let the knocker into the room, and Javon walked to the kitchen and left Christophe to shut the door. Christophe hesitated, and then waved Tilda into the kitchen. Everyone knew their places. Javon served Tilda, and she shuffled out the curve of the door with a shy waggle of her fingers.

Joshua had flinched. He tried to deny it, tried to reason with himself: he was only a few inches shorter than Javon, and after all his work on the pier, was probably as strong, yet he had flinched when Javon had thrown the controller with those pale, corded arms: they moved like snakes. He wanted to leave. If Laila weren't busy, he could pick her up and drive up in the country, down the hidden dirt road, narrow as a path, to the river. They would emerge from the tunnel of trees, thin as a snake hole, to the beach, the sun, the winding water. He closed his eyes and saw himself wading into the deep. Perhaps he could convince Christophe to come, convince his brother to swing from the rope in the top of the trees and fall to the deep, dark water. He opened his eyes to another knock on the door, to Christophe muttering and shrugging as he continued to paw at the controller, and to Javon walking past him, sinewy and lean. This was what Christophe did with his day: the crackheads came in a steady procession, Javon passed back and forth in front of the television like white static, Christophe pulled sacks of weed from his pockets like loose change.

Joshua's hands pulsed with the same pain as the headache slurring like a muddy, overfilled ditch at his temples. He was surprised to see Laila at the door, instead of Tilda again with another portion of Mudda Ma'am's Social Security check. Laila wore a ruffled white tank top and flip-flops, and the light from the open door blurred her edges.

"You letting out all my air," Javon said as he spit the black from his mouth.

"Sorry," she said, and scooted into the doorway.

She tried to squeeze between Joshua and Christophe on the sofa, but instead fell into Joshua's lap, awkwardly. He wished he could touch her with his hands, but he only grazed her shoulders with his fingertips.

"What you doing here?"

"I went over by your house and Ma-mee told me she thought y'all was here."

"What time is it?"

"It's starting to get dark."

Christophe moved from the sofa to the floor. Another crackhead rapped on the door, and Christophe pulled the knob.

"How's your hands?"

She pulled them toward her. They looked bulky and stiff as crawfish claws. She touched them and he could not feel it. He wrapped his arms around her as the crackhead passed over the television and eclipsed the glare of the game.

"Go home," he whispered.

"Why don't you come with me?" she whispered back, her lips touching his ear.

"Later, okay?"

Laila moved across his lap as Javon raised his voice in the kitchen. Joshua hooked her hand in one claw and pulled it up to his mouth; he kissed the smooth skin near her wrist. Her eyes were almost black in the gloom of the room; she leaned into him, and he knew she wanted to stay. Joshua glanced past the leaving crackhead. Christophe was watching them with his knees in his chest, openmouthed. An image of Christophe flashed in Joshua's mind: tracing his finger along plastic bags of Now and Laters back when they were kids going on bike-riding candy missions to the country store. Laila leaned in to kiss Joshua and he stopped her by speaking against her cheek.

"Go."

Laila closed the door so softly Joshua did not hear the latch click.

Christophe had been surprised when his brother had sent Laila away; he had expected her to stay, had sat on the floor in anticipation of it. He had hoped Joshua would leave with her; for once, he had wanted her to take his brother away. Christophe watched Joshua doze, watched him jerk awake and open his eyes and close them and his head fall again and again. It was dark. The volume on the television was low, but the crickets were so loud outside they buzzed louder than the game. He threw down the joystick. He was tired of playing. He kept dying. Perhaps it was time for them to go home.

A knocking sounded from the kitchen. No crackheads ever came through the kitchen; they knew it was safer to come through the front door because it was obscured by trees and a long row of bushes as tall as Javon. Besides, Javon hated for addicts to come through the kitchen door. It felt too personal.

"Who the fuck is that?" Javon said.

Christophe shrugged to no one and leaned around the living room wall and peered into the kitchen. Javon bent to part the curtains over the small window at the top of the door, and he swayed side to side, surveying the carport.

"Aw, fuck," he said, and switched the outdoor light on. The window lit like a television screen, and Javon opened the door and perched at the opening, leaving it ajar behind him.

"Sandman," Javon said. "What the fuck do you want?"

"I got that plywood you wanted for the windows." Sandman's voice was thin and reedy. It sounded like a whistle over Javon's shoulder. The sound of Sandman's voice kept Christophe leaning against the wood paneling. "You got a dime?"

"You don't get paid for work you ain't did yet, mothafucka. I told you I ain't fucking with you like that no more. I gave you a dub to clean my yard on the fourth, and you left it half done. I don't fuck with credit. Take that shit somewhere else."

Sandman looked skinnier than when Christophe had last seen him. His sternum had shrunk into his chest; his top was a shallow ditch. Joshua no longer resembled him in the least. He expected Sandman to duck his head, to leave, but he didn't. Sandman had lost his hat, and his hair was spiky and tufted as branches, his skin as weathered and knotted as pecan tree bark. He listed like a naked tree in winter.

"Come on, Javon, I know you got it."

"Leave the boards and get the fuck off my property." Javon was luminous in the light from the bare bulb outside the door. "Yeah, I got it and I told you I ain't giving it to you!" Javon said. He stepped out into the patchy, sand-eaten grass next to the door.

Sandman stopped and Javon bumped into him. Christophe could hear the bugs, big as his thumb, circling and weaving into the bulb, only to loop away singed to do it again.

"Who the fuck you think you is?" Sandman rasped.

Javon spit. Christophe stood in the doorway. Sandman's head topped Javon's shoulder, and his eyes glazed over Christophe.

Javon did not reply. He struck. His arm lashed out and he cupped Sandman's face hard; the noise was hollow and loud. The cuff sounded as if a watermelon had been dropped, split seedless and red in the dirt. Christophe surprised himself: a short, jabbing laugh pealed from his throat, high-pitched and giggly as his brother's. Sandman did not turn and crumple to the side as Christophe thought he would. Instead, he folded toward the earth, and then he leapt forward and grabbed Javon with his thorny arms around the waist. Christophe stepped through the door and stumbled over an empty forty bottle, which was clinking along the ground underfoot like a fallen Christmas tree ornament.

Sandman hit Javon in the face. Javon shoved him away and boxed Sandman's other cheek. Sandman growled and rushed him, and Javon stepped to the side; he was holding his cheek and laughing. Sandman flailed against Javon, his fists connecting with Javon's sides so lightly they sounded like small exhalations of air: *pfft, pfft, pfft*. Sandman darted to the right just as Javon reached out to box him again, and his fist lashed out, blurred, and cracked against the side of Javon's face. Christophe knew who had given him his own quick reflexes. Javon leaned back and away from Sandman and Christophe saw his eyes thin to slits and his mouth spread and his teeth show sharp.

Javon was not laughing any longer. He struck. Sandman reeled to the side and lurched to the ground. He ran toward Javon again, blindly swinging. Javon struck again, and Christophe noted the difference in the sounds: there was bone in this break, something hard about the hit. Sandman fell to the ground and Christophe heard glass shatter. Javon did not stop. He lumbered over Sandman and punched him deliberately with wide, artful blows; his arms swung as if he were clearing underbrush with a machete. Sandman kicked at Javon's legs and pulled himself along the ground. Javon was not stopping. He palmed a bottle in his hand and came down hard with it on Sandman's head. The glass shattered like a gunshot.

"Stop!" Christophe yelled.

Javon's shoulders were sharp and writhing as a pit's under Christophe's hands, and Christophe shoved him so that they menaced Sandman like a wave. In Christophe's head, there was a blank wall. The noise of the night insects ripped through it.

"You going to fucking kill him," Christophe said.

"You going to take up for this nigga?"

"You going to kill him and what's that going to do?"

"What, he your daddy now?"

"Fuck you!" Christophe yelled. His fingers bit into Javon's shoulders, and he pushed, just as he felt a solid body hit him from behind.

"What the fuck are you doing?" Joshua held him by the neck, squeezed the base of Christophe's skull, and Christophe struggled against him. "He's a old man, Chris." Christophe jerked away from Joshua as Joshua tried to fling him away. Anger buried itself in his chest.

"You don't know!" Christophe turned with the momentum of the push and punched Joshua. The face under his hand was his own as they struggled.

"Stop it!" Joshua sobbed, and Christophe landed a blow and felt Joshua land a blow but felt useless as if he were punching in a dream. Wet, teary, they wrestled face to face.

"Move!" Javon yelled.

Pain split Christophe's side. It drew a long, deep line over his torso, flaring from his hip to his stomach and he fell back. He looked down to find an oblong shard of glass protruding from the tent of his shirt. Sandman had stabbed him: he crouched to the side of Christophe, one hand receding from the glass knife. He wore a bloody crown, chunks of glass still in his hair from Javon's bottle. Sandman grabbed the glass and pulled, and with a wrench it slid from Christophe's gut. The blood had closed Sandman's eyes like a blindfold. He lunged again and suddenly Christophe was falling back and back until his rear hit the dirt. Joshua had pushed him out of the way. The insects fell silent under the beating rush of blood in his head and Joshua was sitting on top of Sandman, swinging and hitting him over and over. Christophe blinked and the world exploded into sound.

"I didn't mean it." Christophe heard Sandman mewl. "I didn't mean it."

Joshua's bandaged hands rose and fell and his back twisted from left to right and Christophe saw the bandages turn bloody; he saw Javon run at Joshua and wrestle him away from Sandman who lay limp in the dirt.

"Stop. Stop. Stop."

Christophe blinked again, but did not open his eyes. His front was so warm, even in the tepid, thick air. He could hear nothing but the beating again. A bottle rolled into his leg. He lay back in the dirt.

Joshua threw Javon away from him and picked up the red, wet spindle of arms and legs and head that was his brother and carried him to the car. When Javon grabbed his hand to stop him from cranking the ignition, Joshua felt the insane urge to bite him.

"You don't know what happened here," Javon barked.

"Fuck you!" Joshua spat at him. He cranked the engine and shoved Javon from the window with the other hand. Everything blurred and jumped back into focus. "I got my brother!"

The tires spit gravel. Joshua smelled burnt rubber. When he realized he could not see, he turned the headlights on. Behind him, Javon peeled out of the driveway in his own car. Pines flickered past Joshua and he saw a deer alighting a ditch in the darkness. He gunned the engine. Wind rushed through the window to choke him, and he drove over the bayou so quickly he did not see the black glitter of the water. Christophe curled small in the seat next to him. Joshua reached into his brother's pockets gingerly, plucked the few remaining bags of weed from his pockets and flung them out the window, one by one. The car swerved.

At the hospital, he parked the car on the sidewalk. He crawled across the seat and scooped his brother up as if he were a sack of chicken and carried him into the emergency room. He screamed. Short, fat people in soft green and blue scrubs ran at him and pulled at his arms. They yelled at him.

"Let him go!"

He ran with the stretcher down the low, gray hallway. They would not let him go in with his brother. He stood on the wall next to the doors that had swung shut behind his brother and wiped a red hand over his eyes. Blood bloomed like flowers across his shirt. He pulled the tattered wrapping from his hands and dropped it to the linoleum floor. The stitches oozed red. He was wet everywhere. He smelled the salt from snot and blood high up in his nostrils and thought he could be at the dock, in the car in the morning, riding along the sea with Christophe, all of it salty and blue, as if God's hand had passed over it, parting it, cleansing it, smoothing it flat. A nurse picked up his rags and escorted him to a room, made him sit on an examining table, and told him a doctor would see him soon. She left. He smashed his hands together between his knees and bent over them, mouthing his kneecaps. He knew that if anyone walked into the room, they would think he was praying.

14

JOSHUA LIED. THE DOCTOR ASKED HIM QUESTIONS AND HE LIED ABOUT it all. He said they were at the river, drinking, when it had happened. They were going for a midnight swim. They were planning to camp. It was a beer bottle. His brother had been running down the beach in the dark to jump in the water and had tripped over a half-buried log, and had cut himself on an empty bottle. No, no one else was there: just him and his brother. No, the doctor didn't need to call anyone else. They had no one else. Would Christophe be okay? Would he be alright? Was he still bleeding? Was he still breathing? Joshua wanted to ask his own questions, but didn't. The doctor touched a finger to Joshua's shoulder, and he looked up, shocked, away from the image in his mind of his dead, quiet brother.

"He lost a lot of blood," the doctor said, and Joshua nodded. "It's a good thing you got him here so fast." Joshua looked down at his blood, his father's blood, his brother's blood on his shirt. "He wouldn't have made it this far."

Joshua gazed at the doctor then: his bloodless face, his skin as pale as Javon's. He could see red, tiny veins like cursive around his nose and his eyes.

"His blood pressure is low, but we stitched him up. Whatever it was didn't hit any major arteries, but it nicked his liver. All we can do is watch and wait."

Ma-mee would be at home, feeling the uneven, dark wood of the house with her fingers, waiting. She would be up, sitting, listening for signs. Cille.

"My grandmother," he said.

Joshua called Aunt Rita first. Dunny picked up the phone. Joshua spoke in vague terms: accident, Christophe, hospital, Ma-mee. Dunny yelled away from the receiver and Joshua heard Aunt Rita in the background. He knew if he closed his eyes and pulled the receiver away from his ear a centimeter or so, he could mistake the siren of her concern for his mother's voice. He didn't. He called Ma-mee, and she picked up on the third ring. He told her slowly, told her they were coming to pick her up. He looked down at the blood on his chest and felt sick and asked her to bring him a shirt. She was quiet and calm, and he wondered if Cille was even home with her. He went back to the waiting room and sat in a chair, closed his eyes to the news on the TV screen, and opened them again and they were there.

When he rose to hug Ma-mee, she put her hand to his throat and stopped him. Before he could protest, she peeled his shirt away from him, up and over his head as if he were six. She handed his T-shirt to Cille, and Cille walked him to the men's bathroom with a pre-emptive, "Shut up, I'm your mama." Joshua washed the sink pink. In the waiting room, they sat in a nervous circle. When Cille began to ask Joshua questions, he lied. He told them the story he had told the doctor. When he got to the part about picking Christophe up from the ground and running with him to the car, he could hardly breathe, and the words caught in his mouth and he swallowed them back down and stopped speaking. After that, Cille did not ask him any more questions. Cille reached over to him and cupped his leg, but it was Ma-mee he leaned into, Ma-mee's neck he buried his face into; her skin was wet. She kneaded the back of his head and shushed him.

To Ma-mee's bleary eyes, when she walked into that waiting room on Rita's arm, Joshua had looked as he had the day he and his brother had been born, as red as he'd been when the doctor had taken him and Christophe from Cille by C-section. He was the brightest thing in the room, and he smelled of blood and salt. She could not help but pull the shirt from him and send him immediately to the bathroom: she needed to touch him first, and then she needed to see him with the blood washed from him. She'd brought the brightest, bluest T-shirt for him she could find. It was a shirt Cille had bought for him years ago for Christmas; Ma-mee was surprised he could still fit into it. When the doctor came for them and told them they could see Christophe, Joshua would not move. Cille led her to Christophe's room where she trailed her fingers across his face: the shadowed lump of his body looked so small under the sheets. She left Cille sitting next to Christophe's bed, and Joshua met her in the hallway outside of the room. He still smelled of salt. The white monotone of the hallways was blinding her.

"I tried to save him," he whispered to her.

"You did, Joshua."

"It don't feel like it, Ma-mee."

"I know."

They wandered through the hallways back to the waiting room. They sat and waited. Joshua roamed the circuit to Christophe's room and back again, over and over, until Ma-mee made Dunny fetch him, made him sit next to her so she could hold him in place. He would not run himself to sleep this time. Ma-mee held Joshua's wrapped hands in her own, wishing she could feel the skin through the bandages, wishing he were little again. She wanted him to be small, for his skull to fit in the curve of her hands; she wanted to be able to pull him into her lap and enclose him in the circumference of her arms. She wanted to be able to carry him to his bed and put him to sleep next to his brother.

Dunny had to drive the car home because Joshua refused to do so. Joshua watched Dunny from the porch as he cleaned the passenger seat with a brush and soap and water; he scrubbed away the blood until there was nothing left, then rolled up the windows and left the car to smolder in the sun. Joshua spent his days skirting the trees at the rim of the yard looking toward the road, looking for a silhouette that could have been Sandman's, remembering the feel of the flesh of his father's face melting beneath his fists. His hands hung useless and clumsy at his sides, and when he woke in the morning to his brother's empty bed and his hands, he could not believe what they had done. Cille drove them to the hospital in her rental car.

"My job expect me back on Monday," she said. Joshua had watched her from the hallway when they were first preparing to leave the hospital the night before; he went to fetch her because the sun had been rising, and Ma-mee had needed to go home and take her medicine. Cille had been sitting at the side of Christophe's bed, one hand on the sheet next to his head, staring at his face. She would not touch him.

"Yeah," Joshua replied, and he heard the *go home* in his voice, and he hoped Ma-mee did not hear it, but he knew she did. None of them spoke. At the hospital, while Cille was escorting Ma-mee to the bathroom, he crouched next to the bed and whispered in his brother's ear, telling him: wake up, come back, it was an accident. Rita came and went with food. Christophe slept through one day, then another, his blood pressure low, his chest rising and falling slowly. When he awoke a day later, Joshua was slumped by the window in a chair, staring at Cille, wondering when she would begin packing up her bags to go home; it was the end of the week. Ma-mee was at Christophe's bedside, stroking his scarred, serrated knuckles. Christophe opened his eyes and Joshua jerked upright in his chair. Christophe blinked, stared at the ceiling, and turned his head to look at Ma-mee and Cille, and then at Joshua. Ma-mee stopped rubbing his hand.

"Christophe?"

"Yes, Ma-mee," he croaked.

"You alright?"

"Yes, ma'am."

She covered her face with the same hand that had been stroking him, and breathed hard. Her mouth opened in a thin, pink line and she inhaled as if she was going to say something, but closed her mouth instead. She did not remove her hand from her eyes.

"What happened, Chris?" Cille asked as she stood behind Ma-mee, her hand on her shoulder.

Christophe's eyes shifted to catch Joshua's face. Joshua did not move. Christophe looked as if he swallowed to wet his throat, but when he spoke, his voice was still a hoarse, shallow croak.

"It was an accident."

Joshua exhaled. He felt as if he were buoyed on water, floating on his back in the river with his hands dug into the cold, white sand. For the first time in days, he felt weightless. Christophe croaked again.

"It was an accident."

Ma-mee dropped her hand. Joshua could see the glaze of tears in the bags under her eyes. She wiped them away.

"Don't let it happen again, not any of it." Ma-mee paused. "I think you trying to kill me."

Christophe's leg twitched. Joshua walked to the other side of the bed. His brother was grimacing.

"Can I have some water?"

Cille clumsily poured Christophe a small, plastic glass and helped him slide forward into a slight hunch to drink. She held the back of his head. She tilted the cup and succored Christophe like a baby. Water dribbled from the cup down his chin, and Cille wiped it away.

The doctor sent them home later that day with the admonition that Christophe should rest, after he sent a social worker to the room to process paperwork to have the hospital bills waived. Cille drove them home, and once there, she piecemeal packed every bit of colored lace and silk she'd festooned the room with, and loaded it all into her rental car. She did not ask for Joshua's help, and he did not offer it.

"I'm returning the rental to the airport in New Orleans." She listed in the middle of the living room and looked at all of them as she spoke, and yet Joshua thought she looked at none of them; they were a window. "Work." This sound erupted from her like a hiccup. Joshua thought she would say something else, but she didn't.

"It was good having you so long, Cille." Ma-mee was looking in the direction of Cille's voice, but her gaze was off, uncentered.

"Yes, Mama." Cille gripped her purse strap like a backpacker would. In the room's half light, her usually light eyes were glassy and black like the water of the bayou at night shattering cold light from houses along its surface. "Maybe the next visit we can work on getting the yard together, and everything will be quieter."

"You need help, Cille?" Christophe asked this from his makeshift bed on the couch. At first Joshua thought Christophe would correct himself for not calling her Mama, at least in parting, and he thought Cille would correct him, but she only twisted the strap around her finger until it turned the tip white, and neither corrected the other.

"Like you can move," Cille smiled a little, "and no, I don't."

"Goodbye." Joshua was staring at the soft skin of Ma-mee's chest, the way it fell like a curtain from the rod of her collarbone. How underneath was solid and hard as oyster shells, sure as the bottom of the bay. He just wanted Cille to leave.

"Goodbye." Cille didn't look at him either. "Y'all take care of each other."

"Be safe on that road, Cille," Ma-mee said, her voice falling to a wheezing whisper.

"I will, Mama." And with a shivering of gold and magenta and silky black, she shimmered like a mirage in the room, turned, and was gone.

That evening, Rita cooked for the family while Dunny sat on the floor next to Christophe's head and told him he deserved to hurt a little more for being such a dumbass—what the hell had he been drinking to stumble over a log at the river and cut himself wide open on a piece of glass? Christophe had turned his head into his pillow.

"Wouldn't you like to know?" Christophe said.

Laila joined them. Joshua led her back to the room and she told him that she had heard that Sandman was missing.

"What you mean?"

Joshua spoke this into her shoulder. He tasted sweat and smelled cocoa butter. He breathed in the roasting grass and dense pine from outside.

"Ain't nobody seen him. I was by Javon's yesterday and Marquise and Big Henry was talking about how they ain't seen him riding around or on his bike or nothing. They thought he might've went back to rehab or something. Javon say he ain't seen him either. Then Tilda jump in and say she thought she saw him back up in that old house in the woods that you say you and Christophe used to throw rocks at, but when she called him, he disappeared. You know how the country is. Everybody think they know but nobody do. Skeetah say he saw somebody with a cast look like Sandman over in St. Catherine."

He stroked her with the skin of his wrists, and she picked at the wrapping on his hands.

"You want to tell me what happened?" she asked him.

He kissed her shoulder, openmouthed. His breath was hot.

"Not yet," he breathed.

Christophe woke quickly when Joshua sat next to him; he peered at the clock and it cleared and he saw that it was five-thirty in the morning. Christophe pushed the sheet away from his torso: it was hot, even for the morning: it was hurricane-heralding weather. Joshua was rewrapping his hands.

"Ma-mee up yet?" Christophe asked.

"She still sleep." Joshua yanked at the yellowed, tangled gauze.

Joshua's head was so close to Christophe that he could see that his brother hadn't shaved; red-brown, wiry hair sprouted from the side of his face and under his chin.

"You told them I tripped and fell at the river?"

"Yeah."

"What'd you do with all the weed that was in my pockets?"

"Threw it out the car on our way to the hospital…it was only about three or four dub sacks, though."

"What about him?"

Joshua recounted the stories about Sandman Laila had told him.

"I figured he wasn't dead…but still. Javon…"

"All he was worried about was hisself."

Christophe kicked the sheet so that it shivered from his legs and bunched against the cushions. The floor fan hummed, and bits of dust set sail like dandelion seeds from its plastic frame to drift through the air. The skin around Joshua's stitches was a light, pale pink. Christophe thought of the way only Javon's head and hands had flushed red when he was toying with Sandman, of how the rest of him had seemed starkly white, of how he'd acted like he wanted to swing at Christophe, and how Sandman had disappeared. He would have never gone to Javon's on that first day if he had known: he should have driven to the bayou, to one of the hidden boat launches and sat all day, regardless of the money and the weed and the way Javon had seen him in that kitchen. Javon had looked at him once: he was no killer. Still, where was Sandman? Rehab, jail, a hospital, with his people in Germaine or St. Catherine? Joshua opened and closed his hands, slowly, testing the skin. He rubbed his fingertips over the matching scars.

"I didn't know I was going to hurt him that bad. I just did it." He prodded his cuts. "All I could think about was saving you."

"You think he knew it was me?"

"I don't know. I was just…hitting him. Like I couldn't hear nothing—I thought you was dying.."

"I couldn't hear nothing either." Christophe laid his hand flat across the bandage on his stomach.

"I think I almost killed him, Chris," Joshua whispered. "If he's even still alive."

Christophe looked closely at his brother, noticed the way the muscle shrank into the hollows of his collarbone, the way the skin under his eyes seemed permanently smudged black. His teeth glistened.

"You was trying to save me, not kill him. It's a difference," Christophe replied.

"Is there?" Joshua asked him, his voice barely registering.

"Yeah, it is."

"You didn't do nothing wrong. Javon ain't no killer. Sandman probably just decided to leave, go back to rehab. Or maybe he in jail. The cops could've come picked him up. You know he ain't never stayed no place long—at least, no place close to us."

Outside, a loud car rumbled by. Christophe grabbed his brother's wrist and held it, felt the blood beating beneath his fingertips, sat so still he heard his own blood pounding in his ears. Joshua's pulse matched his own. Christophe's arm began to ache, but he sat that way, holding his brother, and Joshua remained still. Christophe cleared his throat and broke the silence.

"Wasn't nothing here for him anyway."

"I'm sorry about hitting you. I didn't know."

Christophe closed his eyes, but did not remove his hand from his brother. He shrugged. His brother, their wounds, Ma-mee dimming like a bulb, his parents' places unknown and orbiting them like distant moons: it was enough.

"Me too. When the sun start going down, let's go fishing."

Joshua gave his brother his pain pills, and Christophe fell asleep. Joshua lay down on the floor, folded his arms into a pillow, and nodded off on the scratchy carpet. Minutes later, Ma-mee found them like that, and turned the fan higher. The bright sun tried to ease its way around the edges of the curtains, to suffuse the room with heat and insect chatter and the babble of pines, mimosas, pecan, and oak. Ma-mee shut the screen door against the drowsy gossip of the bees on the fuchsia flower clusters of the crepe myrtle, cleaned, and listened to her boys sleep.

Dunny drove them to the bayou. They'd decided to go to one of the smaller bridges, one that was only as long as two cars, to fish. There was no traffic. The sun perched on the tip of the marsh grasses in the distance, framed by egrets and still pine trees. The water was dark brown and deep and muddy and smelled of eggs, and the twins sat on the grass at the edge of the bayou and dangled their poles out over the water. The rusted steel rigging of a sunken fishing boat protruded from the feathered lap of the small bay in which they fished. Joshua balanced his pole with his fingertips as he clenched it between his knees; he had to ask Christophe to thread the bait onto the hook. Christophe wasn't even holding his own pole; Dunny had balanced it for him between two buckets. Dunny lounged in the sandy, stubby grass and smoked a black and mild cigar. Sweat ran across Christophe's belly and leaked into his wound and itched.

"People talking," said Dunny.

"About what?" said Joshua.

"About Sandman. Wondering where he at and why he disappeared," Dunny replied.

Joshua cranked in his reel and shook his pole.

"I went over by Javon's house the other day," Dunny continued. "He had some old fucked-up band aids hanging off his hand. Said he cut himself by accident last week."

The wind puffed disconsolately at Christophe's face and he let his head loll back on the hard, dirty plastic of the bait cooler.

"Bad luck everywhere," Christophe spoke to the pink striated sky.

Dunny sat up and hugged his knees and then rolled back. He eyed the twins.

"Y'all telling me y'all ain't have nothing to do with none of this?" Christophe reached for Dunny's black, but Dunny stopped him. "It's bad for you."

"Come on, Dunny."

"Y'all going to answer my question or what?" Dunny said.

Joshua yanked hard on his line, pulled it upward, and unclenched his knees. He reeled the line in with his fingertips. Christophe saw a hawk gliding on updrafts in the distance.

"No," Joshua said.

"I ain't stupid."

"Neither is we," Christophe breathed to the clouds.

The pain medicine made him feel that he was floating. He could see faint wisps of white moving with infinitesimal patience north. The winds were moving; the storm was coming. He watched Joshua reel his line in; a small, silver brown fish gasped and flopped at the end of the line. It twisted piteously and sprayed Joshua and Christophe with warm bayou water.

"Here." Dunny grabbed the line and enclosed the small fish in his hand. Christophe could not see it anymore. He heard it there, flapping wetly against Dunny's skin. Dunny began to pull the hook from the fish's mouth, and Christophe could see a faint line of blood on the metal.

"I don't know why y'all niggas wanted to go fishing anyway. Chris can hardly move, and if you get fish juice in your hand it'll probably rot off and die. Y'all some goddamn geniuses."

Dunny pulled the hook from the fish's mouth cleanly and let the fish fly. The sun caught it and turned it pure silver, and then it dropped to the water with a crystal plop. Joshua threaded a piece of raw meat on the hook and threw the line out again.

"I was drunk at the river," Christophe said.

"Yeah?" replied Dunny.

"Yeah."

"We got into a fight," said Joshua.

"Over what?"

"Over me getting a job," said Christophe.

"He acted like he didn't want to work," said Joshua.

"I was going to talk to you about that shit," said Dunny.

"Well, ain't no need now," said Christophe.

"Joshua let go with his temper, huh?" asked Dunny.

"We was drunk and that nigga would not shut up," said Christophe.

"I should've known to leave him alone, but he said some shit about Laila always being over at the house," Joshua said.

"I didn't really care about that shit. The way he kept rubbing his job in my face was what really pissed me off."

"I got drunk and didn't know when to stop."

"He would not shut up. So I told him he could kiss my ass and took off running toward the car and that log jumped up and next thing I knew I was bleeding."

"I thought he was playing for a minute, but when he didn't get up...."

"He must've carried me to the car. I don't remember nothing after that except waking up in the hospital feeling like I just got over the flu or something."

"Y'all niggas is wild," Dunny replied. "And I don't believe a word y'all just said." He passed the black to Christophe.

"Thank you." Christophe inhaled and passed it back.

"I heard they got openings down at the shipyard again—working on government contracts and shit," Dunny said, as he shook out his ash into the grass. A whistling bird flew off into the distance, trilling along until it disappeared into a line of moss covered Spanish oaks arching over the water. "I could take you down there on my half-day Friday."

"Who knows?" Christophe pulled up a bunch of grass and let it fall from his fingers. "I could get lucky, right?" Joshua reeled in yet another small, brownish fish. Dunny snatched the line away from him again.

"What the fuck is it with all these fucking small-ass mullets you pulling out the water, Joshua?" Dunny carefully pulled the thread of the hook away from the fish's mouth. It thrashed a little slower than the last one, with less effort. "What was this one trying to do, commit suicide?"

"With the water smelling like that, I wouldn't be surprised," Christophe said.

"We need some rain," Joshua spoke. Dunny wound his arm back like a baseball pitcher and threw the fish farther out into the water. The fish was so small, it created no waves when it disappeared with a throaty plop. "And it's coming."

"Why don't you go jump in?" Christophe asked Dunny. "It's hot enough."

"You crazy? You know they got alligators and snakes and shit in this water."

"I don't see none," said Joshua.

"That's cause both you and Christophe ain't all there."

"You think it do any good to throw them back?" Christophe asked.

"What you mean?" asked Joshua, his eyes dark.

"I mean, do you think either of them will survive?"

Dunny wiped his hands on his pants and began rooting in his pockets. Dunny pulled out a lighter and threw it on the ground next to him as he rummaged. The cattails quivered. The sky was turning purple in strokes, and the sun was setting the pines in the distance ablaze. Dunny twirled a found black between his fingers and lit it; he spoke around it with the corner of his mouth.

"Eze told me he done seen mullet that's seventeen pounds. Don't think just cause they little now, they ain't about shit. Them some little savages."

Joshua resettled his pole between his knees and slowly brushed sand from his wrappings. Christophe eyed the sun burning orange as molten metal on the horizon through slitted eyes. Somewhere along the shoreline, Christophe heard a heavier plop, as if a turtle or a baby alligator had catapulted itself into the cool, dark, still water. The Spanish moss in the oaks hung thick and limp as a woman's hair, and Christophe could imagine the mullet sliding into the obscure, mulch-ridden water. He could see them angled at forty-five degree angles, sucking mud and muck from the bottom, growing long and striped.

They would float along with the smooth, halting current that was slow and steady as a heartbeat. He could imagine them sliding along other slimy, striped fish and laying eggs that looked like black marbles as the sun set again and again over the bayou and hurricanes passed through, churning them to dance. He could imagine them running their large tongues over the insides of their mouths and feeling the scars where the hooks had bit them, remembering their sojourn into the water-thin air, and mouthing to their children the smell of the metal in the water, the danger of it. They would survive, battered and cunning. He imagined schools of mullet dying old and fat, engorged with marsh and water to bloated proportions until the river waters that fed into the brackish wetlands swept them along with the current. Out and out through the spread of the bay until their carcasses, still dense with the memory of the closed, rich bayou in the marrow of the bones, settled to the bottom of the Gulf of Mexico and turned to black silt on the ancient floor of the sea.

THE END

Acknowledgments

My agent, Jennifer Lyons, believed in me from the first line. She, along with Doug Seibold and everyone at Agate Publishing, gave me invaluable feedback and incredible opportunities. I never could have written this book and become the writer that I am without the University of Michigan, and the great writers that I worked with and met while I was there: Peter Ho Davies, Nicholas Delbanco, Laura Kasischke, Eileen Pollack, and the members of the cohorts above, in, and below mine. I would especially like to thank Elizabeth Ames, Natalie Bakopoulos, Joel Mowdy, and Raymond McDaniel. Thanks are also in order for those who nurtured my beginnings: Nancy Wrightsman, Kristin Townsend, the Crounse family, and Dr. Robert J. C. Young.

Many of my friends gave me fortitude along the way, especially Mark Dedeaux, Maurice Graham, Jillian Dedeaux, Clinton Starghill, Brenna Powell, Mariha Herrin, and Julie Hwang. Finally, I would like to thank my mother, Norine Dedeaux, for always providing, and my father, Jerry Ward, for always listening. I would also like to thank my sisters, Nerissa and Charine, for being and believing, my grandmother Dorothy for inspiring, my cousin Aldon for holding my hand, and all of the members of my extended family for giving me a place where I belong.